code
name :Nanny

code name : Nanny

CHRISTINA SKYE

A Dell Book

CODE NAME: NANNY
A Dell Book

Published by
Bantam Dell
A Division of Random House, Inc.
New York, New York

This novel is a work of fiction. Names, characters, places, and incidents
either are the product of the author's imagination or are used fictitiously.
Any resemblance to actual persons, living or dead, events, or locales
is entirely coincidental.

Dell is a registered trademark of Random House, Inc., and the colophon
is a trademark of Random House, Inc.

ISBN 0-7394-4372-0

Manufactured in the United States of America

To C. and C.
Thanks for all the happy trails. . . .

code name 'Nanny

prologue

The house was bare, white wall to white wall. Naked windows opened onto cold, rain-swept hills. Noises echoed, jarring in the empty space.

A young girl with brown hair walked through the silent rooms, her back ramrod straight. There was no reason to cry, Summer Mulcahey told herself. It was just a house now, not *their* house. The new family would be here any minute, backing up the drive in a shiny red station wagon packed with noise and children and dogs.

No, she wouldn't stay, not to watch strangers take over these rooms, trampling on her memories.

Shoulders rigid, Summer sat down on her battered suitcase, letting her mind touch the walls, searching through fifteen years of memories. She wanted the past carved into her mind, so she could always find it because the past would make her hard and strong.

She needed to be strong now.

There was a *thump* down the hall. Behind her the door swung open. "Aunt Sarah's down in the car." Her sister gestured impatiently, a brighter, rounder, more graceful version of Summer. "I want to go now."

"In a minute."

"You said you were ready." Jess's voice was strained. "You said you hated it here, Sum."

There was no fooling her twin, Summer thought ruefully. They had always read each other too well. "I do. But before I go, I want to remember the good parts." She took a deep breath. "Sneaking pancakes when Mom wasn't looking. Dad building our tree house." Her voice wavered. "You dancing in your red sneakers on that ugly picnic table that always rocked."

"I remember." Jess rubbed her cheeks sharply. "But they're gone now. Mom was . . . strange for a long time, if you ask me."

Both girls had suffered because of it, but neither mentioned that.

Summer's eyes stung, but no tears fell. "She couldn't forget Dad, Jess. She always called him her hero and said he would take care of her, no matter what." Summer glared out at the lawn sloping down to the river. "No man is *ever* going to take care of me. It's stupid to let anyone make you weak like that."

Jess hugged her arms to her chest. "How do you know? You're only fifteen."

"I just know." Summer leaned out the open window, the cold wind on her face. "Dad shouldn't have died, Jess. He wasn't even on duty. He was just going down the damned street for some damned milk."

Jess Mulcahey hated it when her twin cursed. Frowning, she crossed the bare floor and took her sister's hand. "I miss him, too. Sometimes I think I hear the front door open. I keep waiting for him to walk in, whistling Nat King Cole." Jess swallowed hard. " 'Unforgettable.' You know, the one he always sang to us at bedtime."

"I remember." *God help me, I'll always remember,* Summer thought. *But I'll be smart and I'll stay strong as the big trees along the river. No man is ever going to sweep me onto a white horse to make me feel safe.* Summer scowled at the room, repeating her silent vow. "Just remember, the world isn't safe, Jess. And no matter what they say, there aren't any more heroes."

"Maybe there are."

"Trust me, we wouldn't be here alone if I were wrong."

Silence fell. Down the lane the wind shook the poplars and the world seemed to condense, pressing down on Summer with iron fingers. The room was choked with the smell of loneliness.

First they had lost their father, then their mother. Now the two girls only had each other.

Jess broke the spell first, opening her neat blue coat and pulling out a fluffy white cat. Summer pressed the small, wriggling body to her cheek and felt as if she were waiting for something important to happen, some sign that it was over, finished, and they could finally leave.

But no sign came.

There should have been something more, Summer thought angrily. There should have been a chance for explanations and good-byes. Already her parents felt distant and unreal.

Jess pressed her lips together hard, trying not to cry. "Look, Zza-Zza's ready to leave, and Aunt Sarah is waiting. She says we're going to get our own room with pink curtains."

Summer didn't answer. The woman downstairs wasn't their aunt, just a family friend, and the arrangement was temporary, but Summer wasn't cruel enough to point that out to her grieving sister. Jess wasn't strong like Summer was, and she needed to be protected from some things.

"I want to go, Sum." Jess's lips quivered. "Everything's sad and awful here now."

Things wouldn't ever be the same, Summer thought. No amount of pink curtains could change that. Her childhood was over, and she had to be strong now. For Jess and for herself.

Maybe for her dad, too.

Summer took a last look out the window. An old-fashioned wooden swing hugged the grassy slope to the river beside a crooked picnic table. Once there had been long walks and days of laughter here. There had been water fights and double dare and wild laughter.

Gone now. Almost forgotten, in fact. Two shattering deaths in the last year had done that, leaving the bone-deep emptiness that gripped Summer now.

A man from the Navy had come to the house one night. He had sat in the living room, speaking quietly, with care and concern. At first the two girls thought there had to be a mistake. They were certain their adored father would be coming back any second, whistling one of his favorite Nat King Cole songs.

But he hadn't come back, and they hadn't seen his body even at the funeral. Jess had cried for three straight days, but Summer couldn't seem to shed a tear.

No more laughter.

No more Nat King Cole.

No more touch football by the river.

One week ago their mother had stopped her constant coughing and slipped away. The doctors had called it pneumonia and complications, but Summer thought it was too many memories and a heart that just stopped trying.

Summer wished she could cry, but she couldn't. Maybe her heart was frozen, and it had just stopped trying, too. If so, she was glad. That would make her strong, and she didn't want to feel things.

Her sister shifted impatiently from foot to foot. "It's too quiet here. It's creepy, Sum. Let's just go."

"I'm ready." Summer tried to smile, holding out the struggling cat. "You take Zza-Zza while I get our suitcases."

Jess stuck out her lower lip. "No way. I'm going to carry my own stuff. You don't have to help me all the time."

"I'll do it, Jess. I'm stronger. Besides, you're better with Zza-Zza." Jess had always been the soft one, the easy communicator. Summer was all spunk and grit, the one who held off the bullies after school and fought the monsters hiding under their bed at night.

Since their father died, there had been too many monsters to count, and their mother hadn't seemed to notice.

Summer glanced at the window seat where she and Jess had dreamed about pirate ships and desert islands. Now the window looked small, and there were no dreams left.

Down below the house the river raced on, carrying leaves and small branches that bobbed and twisted in the fast currents. Her mother had always warned them not to get too close or they'd get carried away.

Instead she'd been the one carried off.

Summer shoved away the memories. She wasn't going to get all stupid and blubbery. Things changed, and you had to change with them. Besides, Jess needed her.

"You're right," she said ruthlessly. "Let's go. There's nothing here, anyway. This room is dumb. So is this house."

A bird sailed low over the cold river where December trees guarded a slate-gray sky. More leaves floated past, brown and twisted, long since dead.

Summer grabbed both suitcases. When she walked outside, she didn't look back.

chapter 1

Summer wasn't frightened. Not exactly.

Anxious, maybe. Determined.

Okay, just a little frightened. Being around rich people always left her on edge, and these people were *very* rich.

She saw the house first, huge with gray stone walls and a broad wooden porch. An immaculate swath of grass sloped down to rugged boulders above a restless sea. As the taxi rounded the drive, Summer sat up straighter, feeling light-years away from the cement and sprawl of Philadelphia. She'd spent most of the last five years within fifteen miles of the Liberty Bell, but it was clear that Carmel was going to be a whole new planet.

The driver eyed her in the mirror. "Haven't seen you before."

Summer made a noncommittal sound, rolling down her window and nudging off one black high heel, which was pinching her toes badly.

"Got a nice family up there." The driver nodded up the cobblestone drive toward the big house. "Lookers, all of 'em. Even the little one, odd as she is."

Summer frowned at him. " 'Odd' how?"

"Guess you'll find out soon enough." His head swung around. "What are you, family, friend, or CNN bureau chief?"

"So you get a lot of reporters down here?"

"Buckets full all summer. Had that woman, Diane Sawyer, a few days back. Skinnier than she is on TV. Guess they all are." The driver's eyes narrowed. "Notice you didn't answer my question."

"That's right, I didn't." Summer looked away, mindful of the assignment that brought her here. Her carefully constructed story seemed almost real to her after the month of preparation she'd endured back in Philadelphia. The fact was, this was no vacation, and Summer was neither family nor friend. This was work with a capital W— FBI fieldwork.

She'd had tough assignments before, but never so close to big money and Washington power politics, and the situation left her edgy.

Do the job, she told herself sternly. *Forget about the nerves.*

The driver pulled to a halt near a wall of bougainvillaea flaming crimson against fieldstone walls. "Lotta people sniffing around lately. Brought up a bunch of Hol-ly-wood types last week." The man sniffed with disgust. "All Bel Air this and Ro-de-o Drive that." He stopped the taxi and twisted around to face Summer. "Outsiders. You can spot them a mile away."

Summer glanced at the meter and counted out the hefty fare, then added a fair tip. "Movie stars, you mean?"

"Those, too. Senator Winslow was here to meet them once or twice. Him, I'd recognize anywhere. A popular man with the ladies, and easy to see why, with that calm grin and the way he looks at you like he's really listening.

Probably all a big act. The way I see it, most politicians are rats looking for a hole." He took the money Summer held out. "You don't look like you're from Hol-ly-wood, though." As before, he tore the word into three disparaging syllables. "Don't sound much like one of those airheads from Washington, D.C., either. Too normal for a damned reporter." He studied her some more, putting some thought into it. "Odd thing is, I can't say *what* you look like."

Which is part of the reason I'm so good at my job, Summer thought. She opened her door and hefted her suitcase, which was full of navy suits and dark shoes just like the ones she was wearing. In her particular line of work, plain and inconspicuous were definite job assets.

She decided a little gossip wouldn't hurt her assignment. Bending close to the window, she nodded at the driver. "Sharp eyes."

"So what are you?"

Summer tucked her briefcase under her arm and smiled. "I'm the new nanny."

As she rolled her suitcase along the perfectly cut lawn, Summer scanned her base of operations for the next month. Her host, Cara O'Connor, wasn't on hand to greet her, but that had been expected since Cara was currently hard at work in San Francisco, where she was the city's youngest female assistant DA.

Summer quickly learned from a chatty housekeeper named Imelda that her two charges were upstairs finishing their homework over lemon bars and fruit drinks, awaiting her arrival. Praying she wouldn't be called to explain verb tenses or non-Euclidean geometry, Summer followed the housekeeper out to a Spanish-style guesthouse nearly hidden by towering oleander bushes. Imelda left so Summer could unpack and change before going to meet Cara O'Connor's two daughters.

Wiggling her feet, she kicked off her shoes and dropped her suitcase on the sofa, which was covered with fluffy pillows. Fresh roses filled the air with lush perfume. Summer trailed one finger along the wall of solid fieldstone that led to a six-foot fireplace.

Some digs. Not that she was going to get tied up in knots about it. No, she was going to treat the O'Connors like any other assignment.

Summer was about to start undressing when she heard a sound down the hall. Crossing the room quietly, she peered around a corner.

There was a naked man in her shower.

Six foot four inches of naked man, judging by the view she had from her location near the living room.

Summer took a sharp breath and forced herself to be calm. Granted, she had just staggered off two back-to-back flights and her eyes were burning with exhaustion, but that was definitely the outline of a male body behind the tall glass shower enclosure. She was pretty sure that ringing sound was water running, while that other sound, low and rumbling, was a dark male groan of satisfaction.

Her stomach clenched. Either there was a big mistake or this was another trick. She had suffered constant hazing on the job over the last months, from little things like papers taken off her desk to coffee spilled inside her locker. As the junior field officer, Summer had been prepared for a certain amount of hazing.

But this crossed the line.

She glared at the broad shoulders moving back and forth beneath a stream of hot water. No doubt this little surprise came courtesy of her fellow agents back in Philadelphia. With a few well-chosen questions, any one of them could have pinpointed her newest assignment.

Not all of them hated her, but most of them did, and words weren't going to change that. As Summer stood listening to the sound of the shower, something stabbed hard at the center of her chest. They wouldn't forget. They wanted payback, any way that would hurt her most.

Well, to hell with her pals back in Philadelphia and to hell with their crude tricks. Summer was staying right where she was. They weren't going to spook her.

Silently she checked the small desk near the sofa. A tan envelope lay on its side next to a painted Chinese vase. Across the middle of the envelope she saw her name written in small, elegant letters.

Her name. Her rooms. No mistakes there.

Exhausted and grimy from hours of travel, she stared at the cozy fruit basket on the lacquer dresser. The lush roses in crystal vases. No *way* was she leaving.

Summer set her briefcase down carefully on the thick rug. Her raincoat landed on a sleek leather ottoman nearby. Fighting her anger, she scanned the room again. There were no signs of someone living here—no dirty socks on the floor, no clean shirts hanging in the closet. The bed in the adjoining room was perfectly neat, with no dents in the pillows.

Beyond the living area, water continued to strike the glass walls of the shower. As Summer glared at her intruder, the towel hanging over the door slid free. Suddenly she had an unobstructed view of a narrow waist, sculpted thighs, and a world-class naked body.

A little voice whispered a warning.

Punchy with fury, she ignored it. Squaring her shoulders, she sat down in a velvet chair at the entrance to the bathroom, where she had a full view of the sunny shower enclosure.

He was singing an old Beatles song—low and very off-key—when the water hissed off.

The shower door slid open.

Definitely a world-class body. The man had the sculpted shoulders of an athlete in superb condition and abs to bounce a dime off. As he ran his hands over his face, drops of warm water clung to the dark hair on his chest, then slowly traveled lower.

An odd tingle shot through Summer's stomach. She hadn't planned to look, but she found herself looking anyway. There was no avoiding the fact that the man had *excellent* muscles.

Especially when he turned and saw her, his body locking hard.

"Don't tell me you're the maid." He had the hint of an accent, something smoky and rough that Summer couldn't trace.

"Guest," she countered flatly. "And unless you talk fast, you're spending the night as a guest of the local police, pal."

A smile played across his mouth. "Now you're terrifying me." The roughness was there again, but there wasn't a hint of anxiety in his cool smile or the slow way he scooped up his towel and tossed it over his shoulder, where it concealed nothing.

Obviously, modesty was a foreign concept to the man.

Summer prayed to six patron saints for the ability to stay cool under his unrelenting stare, but the prayers weren't working. Heat rose in her face and fingers of awareness nudged a dozen sensitive nerve centers. Probably the result of the industrial-strength Dramamine she'd taken on the plane, dulling her normal edge.

Or maybe it was the man's cocky smile as he draped the towel low around his waist.

She was an expert in the Weaver stance and shotgun recoil. She knew about bomb dogs, wire fraud, and chain of custody for criminal evidence. But no one at Quantico had taught her the proper procedure for a naked smart-ass when said naked smart-ass was standing in your shower whistling "Penny Lane."

"Get out," she said tightly. "Otherwise you're going to be kissing the floor, and trust me I won't make it nice."

His brow rose. "You know judo?"

"Aikido."

Suddenly his eyes were dark and focused. "You're the new nanny?"

"That's right. And you are?"

"Gabe Morgan—landscape and general contracting. The girls told me you weren't coming until later tonight. My shower's been acting up, so I thought I'd sneak over and clean up before you arrived."

As an apology, it stunk. As an explanation, it was passable—assuming that Summer believed him.

Which she didn't.

" 'The girls'?"

"The two O'Connor kids. Audra and Sophy. They told me when you were to arrive."

Summer smiled tightly. "As you can see, they were wrong."

"In that case, sorry for the intrusion. No reason for things to get off on the wrong foot because of it."

"I'd say it's a perfect reason."

He crossed his arms, and Summer worked hard not to stare at the fine display. There was a small scar near the top of his shoulder that curved down in a tight hook. From a gardening tool?

"The old nanny let the girls run wild. Clearly, you're going to be a lot stricter."

"I'm not getting paid to let them run wild, Mr. Morgan."

"Call me Gabe."

Why was he standing there holding a conversation in his towel, for heaven's sake? Why didn't the man just *go?* "I doubt I'll call you anything until you get some clothes on."

"Too bad." Once again the grin teased his lips. "Clothes can be damned overrated, ma'am."

"Not by me."

Gabe Morgan shook his head. "Things were just starting to get interesting, too." He gave a two-finger wave as he crossed the living room. "I'll talk to Audra and Sophy about this. I'm pretty sure it's their harebrained idea of a joke on the new nanny. Meanwhile, enjoy the shower, now that I got things all warmed up for you." He tightened his towel, opening the front door. "By the way, they're good kids, but you should tan their hides for this little stunt. It's a war out there, and the kids are winning, from what I hear."

"Thank you for the astute advice, Mr. Morgan. I assure you, I know how to do my job," Summer said stiffly.

"Glad to hear it. Let me know if you need any help."

Summer crossed her arms. "I won't." She'd studied enough books on the subject in the last three weeks to tackle anything that was thrown at her.

So she hoped.

The towel slid lower on his lean hips. Summer was pretty sure her mouth was hanging open. She might drool any second.

"Whatever you say. 'Night, Ms. Mulvaney."

She hadn't told him her name.

The door closed. Summer sank back in the velvet chair outside the shower, feeling steam brush her face like a warm caress. She tried to forget his body and his grin— and failed at both.

During her FBI career she'd had her share of aggravating assignments. Some of them had been high profile and some of them had put her squarely in the path of grievous bodily harm.

Something told her *this* one was going to take the cake.

Gabe Morgan felt like shit.

Leave it to Cara O'Connor's kids to set up something low-down and sneaky like this. Not that he minded being caught buck naked, but the new nanny had looked angry enough to char steak.

As soon as the door to his guesthouse had closed, Gabe tossed down his towel and prowled through his living room. The woman didn't even look like a nanny, for God's sake. Since Gabe had only met one other nanny in his life, he didn't have a lot to compare by, but he was pretty sure nannies were starched and prim, expert at holding hands, defusing temper tantrums, and hiding any real, honest thoughts.

Not Summer Mulvaney. Beneath that dark suit she looked strong and surprisingly well-conditioned. Besides that, there was her kick-ass attitude. The woman was cool and confident, with an intensity that had caught him by surprise. She didn't mince words and he was pretty sure she didn't take crap from anyone.

It was a trait Gabe Morgan had always admired, whether in men or women.

But something about Summer Mulvaney bothered him. She didn't come across as your average, garden-variety nanny or nurturer. Then again, maybe he was crazy. There was no denying that this job was starting to get to him.

Frowning, Gabe shoved away thoughts of the new nanny as he rustled through his bureau, tugged on clothes, and located three fresh surgical bandages. He'd tackle fifty sit-ups and twenty squats, then see if he could push himself any further.

After that, he'd wrap his knee and take a short break, then start all over again.

He was so used to seeing the scars on his body that they might as well have been invisible. Even the memories had begun to blur, their grim details fading into a gray-green blur of jungle sky and blue-green water.

Followed by screaming pain.

But Gabe Morgan was an expert at pain. If a day went by without it, he worried that he was losing his edge. If a week went by, he started to feel bored.

Which was probably why he was so good at his current job.

But as he looked outside, he found himself remembering the nanny's eyes when he'd turned in the shower. They were more gray than blue, more angry than afraid. Strange mix.

Strange woman.

He shook his head, irritated. Summer Mulvaney had great legs—or she would have without that bland blue skirt covering them down to the knees. Not that he would get a chance to see her legs or any other interesting parts of her body up close.

A damned shame.

But Gabe didn't have time to waste on irrelevant things like his emotions or the new hired help.

It was time to get back to work, he thought grimly.

chapter 2

"There she is." Laughter rippled over the yard, and a small figure raced over the grass. "I told you she was here. She's taking me to ballet class today."

Pull yourself together, Summer told herself. *How bad can two kids, math classes, and an illegal ferret be?*

But had the little girl said something about a ballet class?

Forcing a smile, Summer crossed the grassy slope, glad she had taken time to straighten her dark suit and smooth her hair, as two pairs of eyes devoured her. But where the younger girl stared with infectious enthusiasm, her older sister responded with defiance.

"You must be Sophy." Summer held out one hand as the slender nine-year-old stopped in a restless tangle of arms and legs. "I'm Summer Mulvaney." The false name was close to her own and sounded natural enough, reinforced by several weeks of careful rehearsing. "Your nanny told me all about you."

"Will she be in the hospital long?" Sophy O'Connor shifted from side to side, her pink sneakers covered with dust. "She's not going to—to die, is she?"

"People don't *die* from appendicitis, Sophy. I told you that already." Stiff and hostile, Sophy's sister watched

Summer, arms crossed over her stomach. "Stop acting so *completely* stupid."

"It's *not* stupid." Sophy's face clouded as she jammed her small fists into the pockets of her pink jumper. "You can die from a bee sting, and Mom said things can happen to people—things you never expect." She stared at her dusty feet. "I just want to know, Audra. From an adult, not you."

Innocent as it was, this barb cut deep. "I *am* an adult. Almost. I'll be fifteen next week." Audra made a flat, angry sound. "Why do I even bother? You're *such* a geek."

Summer decided the bickering had gone on long enough. She would have to interrogate them about their prank with her shower, but first, introductions were due.

She held out one hand, mustering a smile. "You must be Audra. Your old nanny told me all about you, too."

Dark, wary eyes glared back at her. "So?"

"She said you like to ride."

A shrug. "I used to, but not anymore. Riding is kid stuff."

Summer kept her smile in place. "So you don't ride now?"

Another shrug. "I've got more important things to do." Audra straightened the belt that hugged an impossibly small waist.

"Like what?" her sister asked curiously.

"God, Sophy. Don't be such a baby."

Sophy blew out an angry breath. To Summer's surprise, she tucked an arm through Summer's, dismissing her sister. "Are you ready? Ballet class starts in half an hour, and Patrick has a snack ready for us."

Patrick?

Right. Cara O'Connor's chef was thin, expressive, and a dead ringer for Colin Farrell, if she remembered correctly.

Sophy was staring at her expectantly. "Imelda told you about ballet class, didn't she?"

Sophy's ballet class at four.

Summer-school homework at five-thirty.

Dinner at six-fifteen.

Cara O'Connor's precise schedule was currently overseen by Imelda, the efficient housekeeper with clever eyes and a laugh that filled the whole house. "Imelda gave me directions for driving you to ballet class in town. On the way we'll drop your sister off at the aquarium so she can volunteer."

"It's public service, not volunteering." Audra stuck out her chin. "I need one hundred hours every year for my college résumé. Kaylin Howell had five hundred hours and she *still* didn't get into Stanford."

"You told me Kaylin Howell made all C's," Sophy said innocently. "You said even if she had ten thousand hours, it wouldn't help her."

"Shut up, Sophy."

"I doubt your mother would like you two to argue this way." Summer was completely out of her element, but she wasn't about to let her new charges know that. "And don't think you're off the hook about that little prank with Gabe Morgan, because you're not."

Sophy swallowed hard. "G-Gabe? Did he tell you—"

Audra cut her off sharply. "Whatever he told you, it was a lie."

Summer chose her next words carefully. "He told me that you had assured him I wouldn't be here until later tonight."

"So what? That's what we thought." Audra shrugged carelessly. "Imelda must have told us that. Or maybe it was someone else."

"But, Audra, Imelda didn't—"

Audra whirled around. "Shut *up*, Sophy."

Sophy's lip started to tremble. She bumped Audra hard with her hip. "No. And stop bossing me around."

"I'll boss you however I want, dork."

Fighting an urge to scream, Summer moved closer, separating the two girls. "Sophy, why don't you grab your ballet shoes? I hear that your teacher is strict, so you don't want to be late."

"But what about your clothes? It's mother-and-daughter day."

"I'm driving you."

Sophy stared back, wide-eyed. "But I need a partner for class, too. Didn't Mom tell you?"

Summer cleared her throat. "Not that I would be dancing." Awful images burned into her head. Mother-and-daughter day? God help her, she was going to put on tights and a tutu?

"There must be a mistake. I don't . . . dance." Summer could barely say the words. She hadn't danced, not in public or in private, for more years than she could count. Maybe never.

"But you have to. Everyone else will have a partner." Sophy's big eyes filled with tears. "Tiffany Hammersmith has her aunt *and* her mother coming."

Tough it out, Mulcahey, Summer thought grimly. "So are there some kind of shoes I have to wear?"

Sophy shook her head gravely. "Not just shoes. Leotard and tights and everything. Our teacher is *very* strict. You can't come to class in street clothes."

Pink leotards? Pink slippers?

Summer suppressed a gag reflex at this vision. But the job came first. If this was the job, she could handle it— even if it meant suppressing an urge to vomit.

"Fine." Summer forced a deathly smile. "Let's get to it."

"I'll show you where everything is. Mom said you could wear her clothes, except . . ." Sophy hesitated. "Except you're a lot taller than she is."

"They stretch, Sophy." Audra had seen Summer's uneasiness and focused in on it immediately. "They'll fit. Have you done a lot of dancing, Ms. Mulvaney?"

"Enough," Summer lied calmly.

"For your sake, I hope so. Sophy's teacher is really rotten with beginners. Especially when they're *adults*," she added nastily. She stared at Summer, then shrugged. "I have to go get Liberace."

The pet ferret, Summer recalled. "Why do you need to take him?"

"We always take Liberace. He stays in the car in his cage. And we take him for a walk when we get home," Sophy said patiently. "We park in a garage next to the school."

"I'll get his cage and help Sophy get ready," Audra said. "But first I need my bag from the potting shed." She pointed to a weathered cedar building at the far side of a free-form swimming pool. "Could you get it for me? Otherwise we'll be late, and then Sophy will get in trouble."

She seemed surprisingly concerned for her sister, Summer thought. Maybe Audra wasn't the grouch she'd first appeared to be. "What does the bag look like?"

"Red nylon with a big black zipper. It's got my nametag on the handle, so you can't miss it. I left it on the back wall near the potting soil."

Summer started to ask what Audra was doing with her bag out in the potting shed, but Sophy distracted her, tugging at her arm and pleading with her to hurry so her ballet teacher wouldn't rip her into tiny pieces in front of all her friends.

"You can get your ballet stuff from my mom's room," Sophy called out. "I'll get everything else ready."

With a mental eye roll, Summer sprinted across the lawn. She was pretty sure she'd rather face a felony homicide investigation than a class of smug, collagen-enhanced, size-four California mothers and their bossy daughters.

She was starting to have a whole new respect for nannies.

The potting shed was clean but tiny, its walls filled floor to ceiling with pots and soil mixes and pruning tools. As Summer stepped inside, dust motes spun in the sunlight, carried by a breeze from a single narrow window.

Up the hill she heard Imelda call to Sophy from the house.

Aware that the clock was ticking, she headed straight for the back wall, searching the cedar worktable. No nylon bag. No potting soil, either.

Frowning, Summer checked the floor, but there was no red bag wedged between the clay pots and the vermiculite mix. She heard Imelda's voice again as she rummaged behind the worktable. Where had Audra left the wretched bag?

Something blocked the sunlight.

She spun around, still in a crouch.

"Looking for something?"

He was a wall of shadow against the late afternoon sun, and he looked tough as gunmetal in faded jeans and a black tee shirt that hugged tanned, muscular arms.

Summer stood up awkwardly. "Audra's bag. She said that she left it out here near the potting soil. Red nylon with a black zipper."

"No potting soil here." Gabe moved past her, frowning. "I don't remember Audra bringing her bag inside. The girls know this shed is off-limits because I keep pesticides and some pretty deadly stuff in here."

Summer scanned the room again. "Audra said it was here." She frowned at Gabe. "If you've got poisons out here, why don't you keep the door locked?"

"Never had a problem before. The girls are old enough—and smart enough—to follow directions when their mother lays down the law." The gardener dug under a burlap bag and cursed when he pulled out a pair of old sneakers. "I wondered where these were hiding."

Summer tried to control her impatience. "Sophy has a ballet class in forty minutes, and I need to find that bag before we leave. Do you have any idea where it could be, Mr. Morgan?"

He rubbed his jaw. "I told you, I haven't seen it. Maybe Audra was confused. Or maybe she—"

The door banged hard behind them. Gravel skittered outside the window.

In one swift movement, Gabe grabbed the door handle and shoved, but nothing happened. "Probably the wind." He gave another push. "It gets pretty rough here near the coast."

"Let me try." Summer leaned around him and gave the door a shove.

Nothing moved.

She frowned at Gabe. "What's going on?"

"I think we just got nailed." He jerked the door handle impatiently. "Again."

chapter 3

ummer glared at the door. "Then help me *un*-nail things," she said tightly. "I've got to get Sophy to class on time. She's terrified of her ballet teacher."

Gabe put his shoulder to the door and rammed hard. The whole shed shook, wall to wall, but the door didn't budge. "No good. If I push again, this roof may come down on our heads." Striding around Summer, he searched the single window. His strong hands traced the sill, then worked slowly along the bottom frame, but that didn't budge, either.

"Locked. Looks like someone jammed a piece of wood to hold it that way, too." He pulled a gardening stool in front of the window and climbed up to examine the top of the frame. "This one has a screw added up here. I could break it free, but it might take a while."

"I don't want to leave the girls alone, so this has to be fast." Summer found another stool and climbed up beside him. "Why don't we break the window?"

Gabe shook his head. "Not with all those mullions."

A mullion was some kind of fish, wasn't it? Summer frowned, trying to make sense of what he'd said.

"These little pieces of wood can get pretty messy,"

Gabe muttered. "It could take an hour or two." Their hips bumped as he reached up to the fiberglass roof.

Summer ignored a sharp *ping* of awareness. Good God, the man was built. "No other windows." She looked up. "One small skylight."

"But I doubt either of us could fit through."

"There has to be some other way." Summer pulled out her cell phone and dialed tensely.

"Good thought. Imelda or Patrick can come out and check the door."

But no one picked up at the house. The line was busy—once, twice, six times. "Off the hook," Summer muttered.

"Either that or Audra is yakking with one of her friends. If those girls set this up, I'm going to burn their backsides myself," Gabe said grimly. "It's definitely a war out there, kids against the grown-ups. Too bad no one warned the grown-ups." Gabe studied Summer. "You sure you're a nanny? No offense, but you don't exactly look like the type."

"And what type is that, Mr. Morgan?"

"Gabe, damn it. And the type is small, fluttery. Lots of chatter and big hair. Black reading glasses on a gold neck chain. You know."

Summer tried the house again on her cell phone, then gave up in disgust. "What century are *you* living in? There are male and female nannies now, and they aren't white-haired ladies with knitting needles, either. For your information, being a nanny today requires high qualifications and serious educational credentials, along with security training."

"No need to bite my head off. I was just making a comment, not maligning the gravity of your profession."

"Weren't you?" Summer jammed her cell phone into her pocket and stared at the locked door in disgust.

"Speaking of professions, you're a landscaper. Why don't you call one of your ground crew to come open the door?"

"Only me working today." He ran a hand through his hair, making it stand up in unruly spikes. "The rest of my people are setting trees in a new home up north of Monterey."

"Just great." There were other people to call, but Summer refused to start day one of her new assignment with a rescue plea to 911. There had to be some other answer.

"I'm going up there." She studied the narrow ledge next to the skylight in the fiberglass roof. "I'll need a ladder."

"All I have is a four-footer." The gardener shook his head. "But it isn't safe. I'm not sure how much weight this roof will hold. I can guarantee that it won't hold me."

"There's no other choice. I'm supposed to be taking care of the girls."

Gabe pulled a ladder across the room and rested it against one wall, looking unconvinced. "Are you sure you want to do this, ma'am?"

"I'll be fine. Just make sure that this ladder doesn't tilt and dump me."

The roof was higher than it looked, Summer discovered. After climbing to the top rung, she had to stretch onto her toes to find a footing near the skylight. Carefully resting one elbow on the ledge, she prodded the heavy top panel.

"You need any help?"

"I've got it." With a dry creaking and a sprinkling of dead leaves, the skylight panel opened. Now Summer had to get outside without bringing the whole shed down on top of them. It was hot with the sun beating down and no breeze, so she stripped off her dark suit jacket, dropping it on the potting bench beneath her. Then she unbuttoned the top buttons of her shirt and rolled up her sleeves.

When she looked down, she swallowed hard. Gabe was pulling off his sweat-dotted tee shirt, revealing a tanned torso dusted with dark hair. Summer saw a scar she hadn't seen before, just at the center of his chest. "Landscape work must be dangerous."

"I don't follow you."

"Your chest and your shoulder." Summer pointed down. "Scars."

Gabe wiped his damp shirt across his face. "Any job can be dangerous. It depends on how you do it."

Summer felt the ladder move. "Hey, hold on, will you?"

Gabe moved closer, one hand on the ladder. The other closed around Summer's hip.

He saw her glare and shrugged. "Just making sure you're safe, Ms. Mulvaney. Give it a shot before we sweat to death in here."

Ignoring the hard fit of his fingers across her rear, Summer probed the ledge. When nothing felt shaky, she lifted herself up, balancing on one leg.

A big gull landed on the roof inches from her head, shrieking loudly, and Summer recoiled without thinking.

"Easy there." Gabe's fingers dug into her hips.

"Damned bloody bird." Summer waved a hand. "Shoo. Get away."

The big white mass didn't move.

"Get going already!"

After a little squawk, the bird flapped its long wings and sailed back into the air, headed toward the beach. "Crisis averted." Summer caught a breath and looked down.

Gabe was behind her, on the ladder now, his body pressed against her. Summer felt the damp brush of his chest on her arm and the flex of his thighs. She'd had some X-rated daydreams before, but this was better than any of them. "All clear. I'm going out."

"Be careful. Ms. O'Connor will murder me if anything happens to you."

Ignoring the beads of sweat skimming down his gorgeous abs, Summer swung around on the ladder and carefully braced one elbow in the skylight's ledge. When nothing shook or caved in, she slowly put her whole weight on the roof beam.

Nothing toppled, always a good sign.

"That's the way. Nice and easy."

When she pulled herself up and wedged her arms inside the skylight, Summer could see all the way to the house. No one was in sight. "I'm going," she said tensely.

"Go. I've got you."

Summer took a breath and wriggled through the ledge. The process was slow since she had mere inches to spare, and her breasts rubbed against the metal lip of the skylight with every movement.

"Take it slow," Gabe muttered.

Summer was aware of his warm breath somewhere near her stomach. Her shirt had pulled free and when she looked down Gabe's face was inches from her navel, his eyes hard as he looked up at her.

Something warm shot down through her body, but she refused to pay any attention. "I've got to turn sideways," she said hoarsely. "There's a metal ledge outside that I need to reach."

The strong fingers tightened at her waist. "Bon voyage."

Summer wriggled back and forth, wincing as her breasts caught, wedging her in the tight opening. "Damn."

"What's wrong? Did you see something?"

"No one's out there. It's—I'm caught."

"Your shirt? Take it off. I won't tell."

"Not my shirt." Summer grimaced in pain. "My—chest. This opening is a lot smaller than I thought."

"I see." Gabe cleared his throat. "In that case, it's your call. If you can't fit through, we'll just wait. Imelda's bound to wonder when you don't turn up for Sophy's class."

But Summer didn't take failure kindly. Life had taught her there was always a solution when you looked long and hard enough—and were willing to put up with a little pain.

"I'm trying again."

"Ready down here."

Grimly, Summer shoved her shoulder through the narrow opening and turned awkwardly. Her head and neck were through, and then her other shoulder angled up. Next came the hard part as her breasts scraped the metal lip of the panel. Gritting her teeth, she reached over her head, flattened every inch she could, then pulled up until she was halfway out on the roof.

"You okay up there?"

"I'm fine." Except for her shoulder, which was aching, and her breasts, which would probably have a few bruises tomorrow.

"Don't press it. I want to be sure that roof will hold you, so give it a few seconds before you go any higher."

Summer took a deep breath of the sea air racing across the lawn. The man was pretty smart—for a landscaper. And like it or not, there was something soothing about his low, calm instructions.

Not that she needed any instructions.

She felt the ladder move slightly and looked down. "What's wrong?"

"Not a thing." His face was cast in shadow below her. "I was just thinking."

"If you found a better way to get us out of here, Morgan, I might have to do something slow and painful to you."

His smile was a slash of white in the gloom. "I was just thinking about all the things a man could do to a woman from this position." Gabe's hands tightened suddenly. Her skirt was now riding low on her hips, and Summer realized just how close his mouth was when his breath touched her naked stomach where the bottom of her shirt had slid open.

"I don't know what you mean," she said breathlessly.

"Oh, I think you do." His breath moved over her skin, hot and moist like the steam from his shower, caressing the sensitive skin below her navel. "You've got a great stomach."

"Forget about my stomach," Summer said hoarsely.

"I'm trying, believe me. But it's not working."

Closing her eyes, Summer was assaulted by a hot vision of his strong shoulders and naked thighs as he'd emerged from her shower. Something fluttered deep in her stomach, just inches away from his clenched mouth.

The things a man could do to a woman from this position.

The thought was dangerous, erotic.

And Summer absolutely, positively refused to think about it. "Too bad, Mr. Morgan. Because I'll be interested in sex with you just about the time the Chinese give up tea for Gatorade."

The problem was, he hadn't had a woman in almost eight months, Gabe Morgan thought grimly. The second problem was that the woman was too damned close for sanity.

He was covered with sweat and he had a knot in his left thigh, but he couldn't let go of Summer Mulvaney's strong, slender body or she'd fall.

Hell, maybe he'd fall, too. And over the last year he'd had more than enough problems.

First he'd double-timed it out for a nasty mission in the Philippines. After that had come the offshore surveillance op in the middle of a godforsaken sea-lane near Borneo. During his second month at sea, a shipboard explosion had tossed him and three others into Pacific currents for two days before a Navy ship had scooped them up. Then had come a HALO accident, when a jump had gone bad. In the hospital, the doctors told him he held some kind of a record for broken bones, and Gabe believed it when he woke up in a big white bed with tubes in four places and his body burning like someone had rammed him through a giant garlic press.

Six months in rehab had brought him back to seventy percent of his fighting strength, and Gabe was battling for more every day. He only wished he could track down the idiot who'd designed the shipboard ignition wiring that had exploded. It would have been a pleasure to teach him the value of quality control the old-fashioned way.

With Gabe's fists shoved down his throat and any other available body parts.

He touched his knee by reflex and scowled. But he'd get by. That's what SEALs did.

His first order of business was to yank his mind out of the pleasant gutter where it was currently wallowing, thanks to the sight of Summer Mulvaney's flat, naked stomach inches away from his mouth.

Oh, the things a man could do against an amazing stomach like that.

Like making that stomach clench hard in sweaty, groaning sex that went on all night.

Sweat trickled down Gabe's brow. "It could happen. They've got McDonald's in Peking. Gatorade can't be far behind."

"Back off."

"Some of those things could be pretty damned memorable, honey."

"Like getting your nose broken by my knee?" Summer muttered. The words were rough, as if she were having trouble breathing.

Gabe knew the feeling. "That's one possibility. Of course, with the right woman, a broken nose would be worth it."

"Trust me, I'm not the right woman." Her voice was low and tight.

Just like her lace panties, only inches away from Gabe's face.

"And stop pulling down my skirt."

Gabe bit back a sigh of regret at what could have been a major spiritual experience and looked up toward the roof. *Mind out of the gutter, sailor.* "Don't blame the skirt on me. And do us both a favor, okay? Get up on the damned roof."

"With pleasure." Summer kicked one leg, smacking Gabe hard in the head. "Sorry. It's—pretty cramped up here, but I'm almost through." As she spoke, her ankle flashed down, striking his shoulder. The one that still gave him occasional painful moments.

Gabe bit down an oath, climbing higher on the ladder. Something about the woman was nagging at him. She seemed efficient, calm. Too calm?

"You okay? Sorry, I didn't mean to—"

Her naked stomach twisted, shoved into his face, and Gabe had a mind-blowing impression of rose-scented soap mixed with a faint edge of sweat. "Just get out on the damned roof," he said harshly.

Before I tear your clothes off and take you against the wall.

"I'm trying, but there's a piece of metal caught in my skirt. Give me a minute here."

Gabe closed his eyes as the rose-sweat scent hit him again. It was woman and sex, innocence and eroticism, and the combination went straight to his groin. He winced with the sudden straining at his zipper, and when he opened his eyes, there was a bead of sweat on her stomach. It took a monumental act of willpower not to lick it off with his tongue.

The straining at his jeans got tighter. "Let me have a look. I'll get you free." He had to do something fast.

Something besides pull off her skirt and see what she looked like naked beneath it.

"No, I'm almost done. Just one more tug and—" She made a little puffing sound and bucked hard against his hands, one leg digging into his chest.

"Take it easy or you'll kick us both over."

At least he could talk. For a minute there, with her stomach pressed against his face, Gabe had been sure he'd never talk again.

"You can stop holding me so tightly." Summer wriggled against his hands. "Morgan, are you there?"

"Still here. Just trying to hold you steady."

"Well, loosen up, because I'm going out to the roof."

Her body rose slowly, and Gabe shook his head when her skirt dipped a few more inches. Maybe this was some new kind of Navy torture. Maybe she was here to test his reflexes, willpower, and mission readiness.

If so, God help them both.

Her legs dangled, twisted sharply, then disappeared through the skylight.

Gabe breathed a sigh of relief and celebrated by reaching down to adjust his jeans a few inches lower.

Summer inched down the slanting fiberglass roof, her hands slippery with sweat. What if the roof caved in, trapping Gabe? What if she slipped and went flying?

She forced down the grim possibilities and worked her way to the edge. When one foot was anchored against a wooden eave, she slid down the rest of the way and sat very still, getting her breath.

She was covered with sweat, but relieved. "Gabe, I'm ready to jump."

"Nice work. Be careful."

"You bet." Summer swung her legs out and dropped into a big bush, landing with knees bent, staying loose and moving with the flow of the fall. She crawled out of the plant, brushing leaves and flowers off her head, then pushed to her feet, racing for the door.

A big piece of wood was shoved through the handles. No wonder Gabe couldn't make it budge. Angrily, she pulled the branch free and opened the door. "*This* is why we couldn't get out."

Gabe took the branch, frowning. "I'm definitely going to tan those girls' hides. Are you okay?"

"Just dirty. I misjudged my fall and landed in some kind of shrub."

Gabe pulled a red blossom from her hair. "Dirt looks good on you, Ms. Mulvaney."

Summer felt something flutter in her throat as he gently

turned the bright flower in his callused fingers. No way, she told herself.

There wasn't going to be anything physical between them today or any other day.

"I don't want Sophy to miss her class, but they're going to answer for this latest trick." Summer shook her head. "As soon as I'm in the car I'll call their mother and—"

Gabe's hand closed around her arm. "Stop."

"Stop what? Why should I—"

"Because I said so." His voice was low and harsh. "Just do it."

chapter 4

His fingers tightened.

Summer's instinctive protests died when she saw the muscle flash at his jaw. "Gabe, what's wrong?" she whispered.

"Don't move. Not a single muscle." He was motionless in the quiet room. Dust motes drifted through the filtered sunlight, in air heavy with the pungent smell of damp earth.

Summer swallowed as he pulled a leather glove out of his back pocket and slipped it on slowly. She forced her body to freeze, her eyes locked on his face, on the single bead of sweat slipping down his forehead.

His hand rose. In a blur of motion he swept the glove hard across her shoulder and then slapped the wall. When he opened his hand, he blew out a little breath. "Got it."

"Got what?" Summer's heart was hammering like a freeway pileup.

"The brown recluse spider that was crawling up your shoulder."

She closed her eyes, shuddering. "I *hate* spiders."

"This one won't bother you or anyone else." Carefully Gabe pulled off the leather glove and shook it on the grass. "Amazing how something so small can be so damned nasty. A friend of mine got bit a few years back, and it wasn't pleasant."

Summer did a quick search of her arms and legs. "It must have been on the roof. Or maybe in that shrub. Maybe there are more of them on me."

Gabe pulled her out into the light and ran a hand over her hair, then down her back and hips. Turning her around, he checked her face and neck, then inspected her skirt down to her legs. "You're good to go. No more nasties that I can see."

Summer smiled hesitantly. "Thanks for being so calm."

"You're pretty good in the trenches yourself." His eyes narrowed as he brushed dirt off Summer's nose. "Learned that in nanny school, did you?"

"We learned a lot of things in nanny school." Summer's throat felt tight, her pulse erratic. He was too big, too quiet, too *close*. "Just like I told you, it's a real profession now."

"So you said. Didn't you hear me tell you to stop moving?"

"I thought it was just an excuse to rile me."

"Never take anything for granted. When I say things, it's for a reason. Always."

The tension between them tightened. As she looked into his eyes, Summer felt the oddest sensation of falling.

A door slammed up at the house. "Ms. Mulvaney, there you are. Sophy, she is calling you many times." Imelda, the housekeeper, was staring across the lawn, one hand shading her eyes. "You will be late for her ballet class, I think."

Ballet class. Summer glanced at her watch and stifled a curse. "We'll just make it, if I run."

Gabe cleared his throat. "I doubt they teach you to wear your skirt like that in nanny school."

When Summer looked down, she saw her skirt was un-buttoned, riding low on her hips. The pale lace of her panties was clearly visible before she straightened the dark wool and jerked the top button closed. "One word and you're toast, Morgan."

"I've got a lot of words, honey. Somehow they just don't seem to apply in this case." He leaned back against the shed and waved at the house. "You'd better get moving. Be sure you ask Imelda if she saw anything, because I want my facts straight when I talk to Ms. O'Connor later." His smile faded. "This is one joke those two little hooligans aren't getting away with."

Tugging on his shirt and tool belt, he headed off toward the back fence.

Never take anything for granted.

Funny thing for a gardener to say, Summer thought as she sprinted toward the house. But Gabe was right. One or both of the girls were responsible for the locked door, and they needed to be severely reprimanded for their latest trick. Unfortunately, pinning them down now, with the clock ticking for Sophy's ballet class, would be hard.

"Sorry," she muttered as she raced up the steps past Imelda. "I got tied up in the potting shed."

"Sophy, she is waiting for you. The first room to the right at the top of the stairs," the housekeeper added.

Summer took the steps two at a time, tucking in her shirt as she went. Not that she was nervous about a silly dance class with a surly Russian ballet teacher. If things got too rough, she could always pull her service weapon and shoot out a few kneecaps.

But the pleasant fantasy faded when she reached Cara O'Connor's room. A pink leotard lay on the bed, flanked by pink tights and pink toe shoes. Both looked at least two sizes too small for Summer.

I can't believe I'm doing this.

The girls stopped arguing when they saw her. "We're going to be late," Sophy said shrilly.

"Not if we hurry." Summer swept a glance at Audra, who stared back coldly. "And after your class, we need to talk about what just happened in the potting shed."

She could have sworn Audra snickered, but Sophy stared back, wide-eyed. "What do you mean?"

"I mean that the door got locked. I had to climb out through the roof."

Sophy's eyes got bigger. "Really? Gabe tells us we're not allowed in the potting shed on account of there's pastry seeds in there."

"Pesticides, stupid." Audra squared her shoulders. "That's why we don't ever go near the potting shed."

"Except you left your bag there," Summer pointed out coldly. "Or so you said."

Audra shrugged.

"Want to tell me why?"

"I forget."

"We're going to be late," Sophy cut in anxiously. "Don't you want your clothes, Ms. Mulvaney?"

Summer began shoving the clothes on the bed into a sports bag. "What size shoes does your mother wear?"

"Eight," Audra said nastily. "Her dance costume is a size six."

Impossible, Summer thought. She finished putting away the clothes and frowned. "This ballet outfit has sleeves, doesn't it?"

Sophy nodded quickly.

"Fine. Are you two ready?"

There was a flushed look of excitement on the younger

girl's face. "I've been ready for hours. Liberace's already downstairs in his cage."

Summer remembered that they had to take the girls' pet ferret. "Be sure he doesn't get out of the cage, because I won't be stopping in traffic."

"I'll be careful." Sophy pulled out a pair of pink gloves and smoothed them on over her hands. "Can we go now?"

"Head 'em up, move 'em out," Summer muttered.

Audra glanced at her sister. "Race you to the car, Sophy. First one there gets to choose the music."

The two charged off in a chorus of taunts and laughter, and Summer shook her head. For a moment Audra had seemed almost human. Then again, maybe that had been sheer imagination. No matter what, the two girls were going to have to face the music tonight when their mother got home.

Dropping off Audra at the Monterey Bay Aquarium was Summer's first task. A burly guard let the teenager in through the staff entrance, then walked over to the car.

"You must be the new nanny. Ms. O'Connor told me you'd be starting today." He watched Audra stride inside. "Don't worry, we'll keep an eye out for her. Ms. O'Connor told me about the security arrangements."

Sophy stared at the guard. "What does that mean?"

"That your mom is an important lady," Summer said quietly. "Because she's so important, we all need to be very careful. No taking rides with anyone but close family, no wandering off. Things like that."

The guard walked back inside, but Sophy continued to frown. "I don't understand. Why do we have to be more careful now?"

Cara O'Connor's decision to keep the girls out of the loop about the threats was a bad idea, from what Summer had seen in family threat situations. Children were entitled to know about things that affected their lives, as long as they were told in simple, nonthreatening language. But Cara had been adamant: no mention of danger or details. Nothing that would frighten the girls.

Sophy stared out the open window, picking at her nail. "Tiffany Hammersmith gets to ride her bike to school. She even gets to ride to town alone on Saturdays. Mom says I'm too young to do that."

"She's right." Summer had ridden alone everywhere when she was Sophy's age, but the world had been a different place then, and her mother hadn't been trying high-profile criminal cases in a major urban center.

Sophy sank lower in her seat. "Sometimes the other girls call me a baby," she said quietly.

Summer swung around, shocked. "That's not true. They're just being nasty, honey."

Sophy picked at her pink knapsack. "It doesn't bother me anymore. At least—only a little. Besides, Tiffany Hammersmith is stupid. She wears thong underwear. I've seen them when we change for gym class."

Summer shook her head. "Thongs are highly overrated." Summer had tried them once—and only once—since intimate discomfort was not one of her life goals. "By the way, is something wrong with your hands?"

"No." Sophy avoided Summer's eyes as she smoothed her soft pink gloves and flexed her fingers carefully. "I just like to wear them. Sometimes my hands get cold."

Was that normal? Summer wondered. But she decided not to push Sophy for more details. "Watch out, Michael Jackson."

"Michael who?"

"Long story, and it's not important. We're here." After she parked in the shaded parking garage, Summer watched Sophy gather her things. "You really don't know anything about my getting locked in the potting shed?"

Sophy's face clouded. "I know Audra's been pretty mad. She really liked our old nanny and she said she was going to make our mom fire you. But she didn't tell me anything else."

Little girls with Hello Kitty bags and bright backpacks were streaming by, headed for a low building with floor-to-ceiling windows. In the doorway a woman in black leggings and a black sweater stood ramrod straight, nodding stiffly to each of the entering students.

Summer squared her shoulders. Now or never. "Let's do it."

Sophy's teacher stopped them at the door, and her eyes narrowed as she looked at Sophy's gloves. "Have you practiced your pliés this week, Sophy?"

"Yes, Madame. Twenty minutes every day. More on Saturday."

The woman studied Summer. "This is your new governess?"

Summer smiled and held out one hand, which the dance instructor touched in a perfunctory motion. "And you, Madame, have you much dance experience?"

"Not here on the West Coast," Summer lied calmly. "You probably have a different way of doing things, so I'd better watch at first."

"No watching. Sophy will require a partner." The woman's tone was cold and brisk. "Without a partner she may not participate. This was stated clearly when the summer began."

Summer put a hand on the girl's shoulder. "No problem. I can handle whatever is required."

"In that case, show your governess where to change,

Sophy. And I require that you both be prompt or you will be asked to leave."

Thirty small bodies stood nervously at attention before the long wooden bar. Summer ignored her embarrassment and the pain in her cramped toes, lining up with the other mothers and trying to understand the staccato orders that came in French and accented English.

"*Glissez,* Tiffany. Shoulders back, and head straight, if you please. *Do not giggle,* Fiona." As she patrolled the room, the ballet instructor tapped her charges with a wooden ruler, straightening an arm or correcting the bend of an elbow.

"And one and two. Like swans, if you please. Not like gorillas."

A giggle slipped out somewhere amid the line of pink leotards. With a sinking heart, Summer realized it had come from Sophy.

"It amuses you, Sophy O'Connor? *Bien,* you will come to the middle of the room and demonstrate your pliés for all of us. Perhaps that will amuse us, too. And you will remove your gloves first."

Sophy's face flushed fiery red as she peeled off the pink gloves and set them on the bar at the wall.

"Your partner will also join you, to count the beats."

Summer walked out onto the dance floor, resisting an urge to tug at her leotard. "Count when I nod," Sophy whispered. "One to ten."

Summer smiled at Sophy, offering moral support, but the girl's face was tense with concentration.

At Sophy's nod, Summer began her count, feeling a surge of pride as Cara's daughter moved into a series of perfectly graceful dips. At least they seemed perfect to

Summer, who had never been graceful or patient or popular as a girl—and still wasn't.

After the last move, Summer smiled broadly. "Great job."

But the instructor had different ideas. She pursed her thin lips, pointing at Sophy. "Clumsy lines. Crooked back. You will turn no heads with such flat feet, Sophy. From now on you will increase your daily practice time to one hour."

A titter ran through the other girls, but it was quickly suppressed by the instructor's cold glare. "Back in line, all of you. Third position. Partners will call out movements. *Vite, vite.*"

Summer felt a haze of sweat on her brow. At Quantico she had squatted in a tactical Nomex suit under the sweltering August sun. She'd run obstacle courses in frigid rain and fieldstripped her weapon in total darkness by feel alone.

But nothing beat ballet classes for sheer hell.

When the girls filed to the studio door thirty minutes later, the instructor singled Summer out. "You studied dance in the East, Ms. Mulvaney? How curious that I have never seen such feet positions before."

Summer smiled, volunteering nothing. The witch should be teaching sharks at the aquarium, not innocent girls.

She noticed that Sophy pulled her gloves on as soon as they left the room. "Are your hands still cold, Sophy?"

"A little."

"Have you told your doctor?"

A tight head shake.

Summer started to speak, but Sophy bowed her shoulders and plunged into the chaos of the big, open changing room, clutching her backpack. She looked slightly sick, Summer thought. Most of the other girls were staring and Summer heard a whispered "baby" as they walked to the front row of lockers. She had a sudden and entirely wonderful idea for retaliation.

Sitting down next to Sophy, she toed off her pink slippers. "When are you going to pick out your new dress?"

Big gray eyes blinked at her. "What new dress?"

"For the wedding. Rehearsal dinner, remember? Tom Cruise is coming and you don't want to wear just any old rag for Mr. Mission Impossible, do you?"

Sophy stared up at her, knapsack clutched to her chest. "Tom *Cruise?*"

"Sure." Summer bent down and picked up her street clothes, dropping her voice to a whisper. "Play along, and we'll *really* give them something to gossip about."

Sophy began to smile. "Oh, right. I forgot all about the rehearsal dinner. Do you think he likes pink?"

"Why don't we call and ask? Tom owes your mom a favor since she agreed to be a legal advisor for his next movie." Summer hid a smile. Heads were starting to turn, just as she'd hoped. "You know what he said to your mom?" She could feel the curiosity growing, hot and sharp, as she bent closer to Sophy. "Laugh. Really loud."

Sophy's clear voice rang out on cue.

"That's what your mom told me, word for word." Summer tossed Sophy her shoes. "How about we call him on the way home?"

Sophy blinked. "You mean, I could call Tom Cruise? Right now?"

"Absolutely." When Summer stood up, thirty sets of eyes lasered in her direction. "Ready to go?" she asked sweetly.

All motion stilled in the room.

"You bet," Sophy bubbled, shrugging on her knapsack. "I bet Tom likes pink best."

"Bet you a dollar he goes for red. Really hot red." Summer pulled out her cell phone and tapped it thoughtfully on her chin. "Why don't you call him and see? The number is already programmed. Just press three on the speed dial."

The silence around them was fierce as they walked through the room. This time no one whispered "baby" or anything else at Sophy.

Summer hoped Cara O'Connor wouldn't mind the white lie. At least Sophy was standing tall now, a grin engulfing her face.

Not bad for her first day on the job, Summer decided.

chapter 5

Assistant DA's Office
San Francisco

It was supposed to be the most wonderful week of her life. She was healthy, successful, engaged to a wonderful man—and about to choose her wedding dress.

But Cara O'Connor sat stiffly at her desk, tied up in a thousand little knots.

Her softly tailored suit was immaculate as she spoke on the phone, jotting shorthand notes on a yellow legal pad with the pen her daughter had given her last Mother's Day. "I don't believe any of this, Tony."

"Believe it. Chain of evidence was shot to hell. The nurse at the clinic bagged the blood sample, but he didn't take it to be refrigerated until after he handled a gunshot wound and had a smoke on the fourth-floor balcony."

Three weeks before, an eighteen-year-old Berkeley coed had been shot, assaulted, and left unconscious in a Chinatown alley. She'd managed to stagger to a small neighborhood clinic, where she was treated before police were called. Once she was lucid, she'd targeted her attacker as the honor-student president of a fraternity near her dorm. According to her account, they'd argued and he'd threatened her with the gun, then shot her and assaulted her.

The case should have been open-and-shut, but faulty

procedure in collection of physical evidence could hammer the strongest case full of holes.

Cara closed her eyes. "This guy gets a medal for stupid."

"Afraid it gets worse. Our friend thought he'd be helpful, so he cleaned the bullet they pulled out of the patient's chest and wrote her name on it."

Cara muttered a few choice phrases. A good defense lawyer could demand that the bullet be pulled as evidence, given this kind of mishandling. "What about her hands? Any signs of struggle? DNA evidence recovered?"

Her colleague sighed. "He washed her up with Betadyne. Cleaned her real good. Said her parents wouldn't want to see her like this."

"Don't tell me we've got *nothing*?"

"The forensic people are going through her clothes and the other evidence now. We may get lucky, but the nurse dumped everything in a pile, so there's a chance of cross contamination."

Cara braced herself. "Do I want to hear this?"

"Probably not. A couple of tourists came into the clinic with food poisoning right about then. They threw up all over the victim's clothes and shoes."

Sometimes fate spits in your face, Cara thought, and this was one of those times. "Make a note to see this nurse gets a crash course in preservation of physical evidence, okay? Threaten to yank his license, whatever, but see that he doesn't pull a stunt like this again."

"You got it."

"Now give me some good news, Tony. Tell me that we've got a deal in the Rothman case."

Marcus Rothman was a prominent gay painter who had recently learned that his longtime lover was walking out for a younger man. Rothman had planned a nice, civilized farewell meal—and then fed his lover his favorite sushi, nicely marinated in wasabi and Drano, resulting in a particularly unpleasant death.

"Rothman's counsel said they'll go for temporary insanity. He just saw the Drano and acted without thinking."

Cara gave a cold laugh.

"Yeah, I happen to agree, but Rothman has been undergoing therapy for long-standing abandonment and relationship issues. His therapist has volunteered to testify."

"Can we establish that Rothman bought the Drano *after* he found out he and his lover were quits?"

"Tried that. The Drano's been under his sink for years. Old bottle, date-stamped 1998."

Cara cursed silently. "Keep working it. See if he bragged to anyone. Try his doorman or cleaning lady." But she knew Rothman might slip away. Sometimes you took what you could get.

She flipped through a recent deposition from a defense lawyer. "I'm still waiting for that good news."

"Try this. Barnhard's people will go for voluntary manslaughter in the freeway road-rage incident."

"Hmm."

"Are you okay, Cara? You sound like you're off on a Jeep trek in Mongolia. Lots of mental static on the line."

"I'm fine, Tony." Cara looked at the framed photo on the small antique table to her left. Two girls held up flaming marshmallows on crooked sticks. Their faces were streaked with dust, their hair tangled, their smiles incendiary.

The photo was six months old. Sophy was an inch taller now, and Audra was more reserved and serious, but her daughters were still knockouts.

Cara knew that they were both under stress. Despite all

her reassurances, they were worrying about how the wedding would affect their future. Since the picture was taken, Sophy had lost a tooth, and Audra wanted to dye her hair blond. To top it off, the new nanny was coming tonight, and both girls were unhappy about that.

If only there had been some other way.

"Cara, you still there?"

"Right here." She forced her thoughts back to work. "Go on, Tony."

"Andrews is hanging tough. He figures our case is too thin."

The assistant DA closed her file with a snap. "Not anymore, it isn't. We just took testimony from the girlfriend in Vallejo. It seems our man Andrews bragged about the murder while he was drunk, then waved a wad of bills he'd received as payment. He even had a picture of the woman he was supposed to kill. His employer was very efficient."

"So now we've got them both. Nice work. Tell me why you don't sound happier."

"Just tired, I guess." Cara sipped her cold coffee and grimaced.

"Or distracted. I keep forgetting you're getting married in a week."

"Ten days, actually, but who's counting?" Cara stretched, wincing at the sharp pain in her shoulders.

"Who's *counting*? Me and half the population of San Francisco, that's who. You were in the style section of the *Chronicle* last week, and I hear you're mentioned in an evening TV spot on Sunday. Everyone wants to know what kind of dress you're wearing and what color flowers you'll have. Even my wife was pestering me for details this morning."

"It's not about me *or* the dress." The dress Cara still

hadn't picked out yet, she thought guiltily. "This is about Tate. He's very popular."

"Senator Winslow's not the *only* popular person, kid. Be careful or this wedding will turn into a three-ring circus. By the way, where are you two tying the big knot?"

"Sorry, Tony. I love you dearly, but that's a state secret. If I talk, I'm toast, senator's orders." She laughed softly. "We agreed the ceremony would be strictly family, but we're having a big reception in Carmel. You should have gotten an invitation weeks ago."

"Right here on my desk. I wouldn't miss it for the world. If I tried, my wife would divorce me." Her colleague hesitated. He had been protective of her ever since Cara had met him while working in the public defender's office. "Are you sure this is right for you? Tate Winslow is a stand-up guy who's been the best thing that's happened to California since the Beach Boys and liposuction. Even a blind person could see that you're crazy in love." His chair creaked. "But . . ."

"But what, Tony?"

"The man's got his eye on Pennsylvania Avenue. His press people can waffle all they want, but we both know he's going to run. Then your life will be public, Cara. Every part of it, for you and the girls. You'll be swallowed alive, badgered incessantly by press, campaign donors, media consultants, press, legal advisors, press. Oh, did I mention press?"

Cara laughed. "I get the picture, Tony. Don't think I haven't seen it myself. Every smile recorded, every word dissected. Every hour accounted for." She closed her eyes, suddenly very tired.

And very afraid. For her daughters, more than for herself.

"Damned right. Every detail in your past will be exhumed, inspected through high-powered microscopes. You two will become the next best thing to reality TV. They're going to want to know if Tate snores and what you wear to bed."

"No and no comment."

San Francisco's youngest female assistant DA sat back sharply, knocking a clay pot with dried bougainvillaeas to the floor. As Cara stared at her daughter's shattered gift, a first-grade Mother's Day project, she felt a stab of sadness. She'd have to collect the pieces and glue them back together before Audra saw them. But not now, when she was already late for a meeting.

"Thanks for the warning, Tony. Tate and I are prepared for whatever gets thrown at us. And right now I'm late for a meeting with the M.E., so send over those papers. I'll run through them tomorrow."

"Will do. You're a tough negotiator, Ms. O'Connor." Once again he hesitated. "I never meant that it was a bad idea, Cara. Just that you should be prepared for what comes next. The political process can be vicious, especially with what you've got on your plate from the Costello appeal."

"Costello won't walk, no matter how many appeals he files. We had a clean conviction right down the line. As for the appeal, I don't expect to be handed the easy assignments because I'm a woman."

"Hell, Costello scared the shit out of me. Gender's got nothing to do with it. Watch your step." He blew out a breath. "And I'm hanging up now before I make an ass of myself."

The line went dead, and Cara sat back slowly. Richard Costello, her last high-profile case, was a poster boy for equal-opportunity sadism. He'd trafficked in human cargo through four border states and Canada. An eternal pragmatist, Costello smuggled whatever commodity had the highest value at the moment. Cocaine in, luxury cars out, Toyota car parts out and people in. He had made millions off the vast blood trails that flowed between Mexico, Central America, and the United States, and he had bribed, intimidated, or murdered all who stood in his way. At his peak, dozens of DEA and INS agents filled his payroll.

According to rumor, a few of them still did.

A very bad man.

He had tried to bribe Cara half a dozen times during his trial. On the day of his sentencing, he had given her a new message: She would die and her skin would be hung up as a trophy in his house, payment for her involvement.

Cara was used to death threats, but lately the thought of what Costello might do to her children left her paralyzed with fear.

She tackled three more short calls, dictated a note to her assistant, and then sat back slowly. Sunlight glittered off the cars flooding Bryant Street. Even six floors up she could hear the angry scream of horns and braking tires.

And she was late for her meeting. Why did she feel as if she were always running, always one step behind?

Frowning, she knelt beside her desk and swept the broken pieces of clay into a padded envelope, determined to work a miracle repair before Audra realized her first-grade masterpiece was damaged. As Cara studied the mass of broken pieces, she considered canceling her evening plans so she could help smooth the transition when the new nanny arrived. Her presence would make things easier for everyone, since Audra and Sophy had been extremely upset when Cara had announced the sudden departure of their longtime nanny due to illness.

At least that was the story they'd come up with for the girls and anyone else who asked.

Her door opened. "The DA needs you right away." Her assistant waved a folder. "Press leak on the Costello case. The details of his appeal have gone public, and we're already fielding press calls about possible tainted forensic evidence."

Cara checked her watch in disbelief. "Impossible. We only heard from his counsel ten minutes ago."

"That means it was public knowledge about eight minutes ago." Her gorgeous, rail-thin assistant smiled grimly. "Here's the authority you requested in the employee workplace privacy issue. Also, Senator Winslow's office has called twice to confirm your dinner tonight. Eight o'clock at the Fairmount. I told them it was firm, but they want to hear it directly from you. Pushy people, even though they try to be polite about it."

"Thanks. I'll call them back." Cara slid the padded envelope into her already crowded briefcase.

It was only after the door closed that she saw the small box on the floor under her desk. About the size of a cell phone, it was wrapped with brown paper and plain white string. Her name was typed on a label with the return address of the bridal shop where she and the girls had gone to look at dresses.

Probably some additional samples of trim for her to consider.

But when Cara pulled off the wrapping, her face went white. Inside the box was a single fragment of paper, torn from what appeared to be an old piece of stationery. There was one line of text on the sheet.

May 12, 1986. Los Reyes Clinic. Remember.

The words struck Cara like a physical blow. This time

the message wasn't about how she would die. In some ways, it was worse.

Moving like a sleepwalker, she shoved the box into her briefcase. Someone knew. After all these years, someone *knew*.

Voices echoed down the hall. She looked at the box resting on top of the broken pieces of her daughter's gift. She didn't have time to fall apart. She had to think, to act with her head, *not* her heart, or she would hurt everyone she loved.

She had hoped this day would never come, but now it had.

Slowly Cara stood up. She cleared her desk by habit, closed her desk drawers and locked them, then picked up her briefcase. By the time she reached the door, she had made a decision that no woman should ever have to make.

"Senator Winslow's office."

Cara sat tensely in her car, trying to stay calm. "Hello, Margo, it's Cara."

"Well, it's about time. The Great Man has been pacing around his office for the last hour, and every three minutes he comes out to see if you've called yet." Tate Winslow's veteran secretary laughed. "Since he's due out again any second, I'll put you right through."

Cara heard a *click,* and the deep voice of the man she loved filled the air. "Don't tell me something's come up again. You promised you'd pick out a dress tonight, Counselor, and I'm holding you to that."

No wonder he was called The Voice. Cara loved the rich bass roll of his voice and the emotion he'd never been afraid to show.

He would make a wonderful president, she thought numbly.

"We'll talk about the dress tonight, Tate. First I need to speak to you. Since I'm near your apartment, I was hoping you could meet me a little early." She prayed he wouldn't hear the lie.

"That's the best offer I've had in months." His voice fell. "If you're planning to spend the night, it will be the best offer I've had in a decade."

Cara tried to ignore the sharp stab of desire, mixed as it always was with the ache of tenderness. They were so perfect for each other—both overachievers, both products of tense households ruled by demanding mothers. Of course, Tate's home had been on an exclusive street in Pacific Heights and Cara's in a run-down row house near the Oakland docks. Tate had received a new BMW for his high school graduation, while Cara had received a bill for the first of many college tuition payments.

She closed her eyes. *Forgive me, Tate.*

"Honey, are you okay?" Tate Winslow's voice hardened. "I heard about the Costello appeal. Has something happened? If so, I'll send someone to—"

"I'm fine, Tate. I just—I miss you." This much was true, without question. If a whole day passed without the sound of his voice, Cara felt as if a physical part of her were missing. "So ditch the policy wonks and get yourself over here." She struggled for a tone of light seduction. "If you find a trail of lingerie scattered over the floor, don't worry. It's just another lovesick California constituent who's desperate for some hands-on advocacy."

"A smart senator always pleases his constituents. I'll be there in eleven minutes," he said huskily. "Assuming that I don't get pulled over by S.F.'s finest for a moving violation. Hold on a sec." He murmured a few words and she heard a door close. "Just cancelled two phone calls. Now I can be there in eight minutes. Honey, are you sure nothing's wrong? What's that sound I hear?"

Her heart breaking, Cara thought. Like dry stalks in a dry wind. "Just a truck going by. You really should tackle the urban noise issue, Senator. It would give you major voter points." She was crying as she got out of her car, tears cold and slick on her cheeks. A woman with spiky orange hair walked past, staring at her curiously.

"I'll pass your concern on to Greg. He sends his regards, by the way, and says he can't wait to see you and the girls."

"Your brother is far too smooth for his own good."

"Don't I know it. But with you, he actually means the compliments. And he really is crazy about the girls. So is my mother, who promises she'll drop by with that Ming Dynasty Chinese bowl for the reception." Tate sounded breathless. "Make that six minutes. It will be faster for me to walk in all this traffic. Add sixty seconds so I can stop for roses at the corner."

"No roses." Cara brushed vainly at her wet cheeks. "You've already given me too many gifts, Tate."

"The hell I have. You send them all back." The junior senator from California sounded out of breath. "Almost at Geary Street."

Cara had dried her face by the time she reached Tate's building. She waved to his doorman, then took the elevator up to the twelfth floor. In the sunny living room, she dropped her jacket and kicked off her shoes. *One more time,* she thought. *To remember him—and how close we came to happiness.* "I'll be waiting, Senator. I'll be the naked woman sprawled across your bed."

"Hanging up now." The phone clicked off. Minutes later a key rattled in the lock.

Tate Winslow opened the door and studied the trail of

clothes that led across the floor into his bedroom. "If these clothes belong to a prior tenant, I'm going to be extremely disappointed."

"Come on in and find out."

Cara's voice caught as he stood in the doorway, afternoon sunlight touching his ruggedly handsome face. She already saw changes there, lines of strain from too many late meetings and too many people who wanted a piece of his soul.

She raised one bare foot from beneath the covers. "I hope those phone calls you missed weren't too important."

"They're all important. Wetlands conservation. Dwindling tax base. My mother says all I do is talk on the phone, do you know that? But the right word at the right time can make all the difference when—" He frowned. "Hell, Cara, you don't want to hear about my problems now."

The silk comforter fell to the floor. She pushed to one elbow, all smooth skin and teasing eyes. "You have one problem that I'm going to take care of, Senator."

"In a minute you'll have me on my knees, honey." Tate tossed down his jacket, and his belt went flying. "I don't see you for two days and it feels like a year."

Cara considered the best way to distract him from his worries. "You mentioned a flower delivery?"

A huge bundle of roses appeared from behind his back. "Right here, ma'am. Do I rate a tip?"

"You bet." She gripped his tie and pulled him closer, all teasing gone. "I need you inside me. Right now." Her fingers dug into his shoulders. "Please, Tate." *One last time.*

She closed her eyes, hiding the sadness he wouldn't miss.

The force of his body came as a shock, pinning her

against the sheets while his hands circled her waist. Whispering her name, he shoved aside the sheet and studied
her full breasts. "God help me, I'll never get enough of
you."

She was already aroused, already slick and restless with
desire, and his fingers made her gasp with pleasure.
"Now," she said hoarsely, pushing up against him. "Don't
talk, Tate. Don't think. Just *do* it."

His clothes dropped in layers and then he pulled her
astride him. Cara closed her eyes as his fingers found her
with unerring skill. He pinned her hips and filled her in
one deep thrust, taking her with brooding urgency.

For one blind moment the threats were gone, the worries forgotten. She gasped his name, shocked at the speed
and intensity of the climax that ripped through her. She
was barely aware of him watching her.

When she finally opened her eyes, he began the whole
process again, until they both lay sweaty and exhausted,
with the covers tangled around them and the faint scent of
perfume drifting from the roses scattered over the floor.

"Do you have any idea how much I love you?"

Hard fingers trailed over Cara's face, but she didn't
open her eyes.

It was too soon for words. She needed to prepare, to
close her heart, which was still racing from the amazing
sex she'd just had.

No, not sex. Something far deeper and infinitely more
complex.

The skin at her neck prickled, and she looked down to
see three diamonds glittering against her skin, strung like
tears from a silver chain.

"For your wedding dress." Tate smiled uncertainly. "If
you want different stones or something bigger, you can ex-

change these. I already spoke to the jeweler about that. The girls thought they were just right."

"You showed them to Sophy and Audra?"

"I figured it was a girl thing. They know you better than anyone, plus they're brutally honest, the way only kids can be."

The stones were clear and bright, like the old yearnings Cara couldn't suppress. "They're perfect, Tate." Suddenly the diamonds felt unbearably cold. "But they're far too expensive."

"To hell with expense. I'm not getting married ever again—and neither are you, if I can help it."

Something tore at her throat. *Be hard,* she thought. *Do it now.*

"I can't take them." She pressed the chain into his hand and stood up. Behind her the phone rang, but neither moved. Tate cursed at the sound of his assistant's voice on the answering machine.

"Sorry to disturb you, Senator." There was a discreet cough. "I'm afraid that call you've been waiting for just came through from London."

Tate ran a hand through his hair. "I need to return this one, Cara. It will only take me ten minutes, then we can talk."

The call made it easier.

She nodded calmly and picked up her clothes. "I have to shower. Don't hurry for me."

He was staring at her, a puzzled look on his face. "What's wrong?"

Cara picked up her overturned shoes and studied them dispassionately. "Nothing." *Everything.* "It's been a long day, that's all. Make your call, please."

Standing beneath the hot spray of the shower a few minutes later, Cara locked her arms and took in long, shuddering breaths. It wasn't normal to feel so much, to know someone simply by the echo of a footstep or the brush of his hand. It had to be unnatural that the air felt charged and seemed to dance whenever he was close.

She tried to believe that. It helped her to steel her resolve.

She had locked the door, and it rattled now.

"Cara? Damn it, what's wrong?"

She was fully dressed when she opened the door. Her hair was brushed smooth, glistening where it was caught back in a rubber band, and her cheeks were pale beneath their careful makeup. "I have to go, Tate."

"Go?" He stared at her, taking in her fully buttoned suit, the purse on her shoulder. "I don't understand. You have to pick out your dress tonight. You know it's your last chance. Otherwise, they won't guarantee the work will be done in time."

Oh, the insidious stab of weakness.

The pain of letting go of so many dreams.

"It doesn't matter, Tate. I won't be needing the dress after all." Cara turned, drawing her hands behind her back. *Don't let him see,* she prayed. *Above all, don't let him argue.* "Not today. Not next week."

"I don't understand," he repeated. "Do you have to work late again? Is this something to do with the Costello appeal?"

"It has nothing to do with work." Cara hardened her voice, closed her heart. "It's over between us." She forced out the awful words like pits from a bitter fruit. "I'm sorry, Tate, but I can't marry you. The wedding is off."

chapter 6

When Summer reached the aquarium, Audra was nowhere to be seen.

Frowning, she checked with the nearest guard. "School group number three finished fifteen minutes ago, ma'am." He studied a column on his clipboard. "Their bus just left. Number twenty-three."

"Have you seen their student docent? Small girl, brown hair. She was wearing a red jacket and a black shirt."

"You mean Audra O'Connor? Sure, I saw her. She took group three today." The guard shoved back his hat. "Come to think of it, I haven't seen her around since the tour finished."

Years of training snapped into place as Summer motioned to Sophy. "Stay beside me, honey. Stay very close." She scanned the room, searching for dark hair and a bright red jacket. "We've got to find Audra." She held out an aquarium map to the guard, noting his name and badge number. "Please show me the route the tour took." Her voice fell. "And this is no rehearsal, Simon. I'll need three of your guards to patrol the other floors. Please give a radio description to all staff members, too." Her voice was crisp. "How many other exits?"

"Loading and Receiving. There's the rear deck facing the ocean, but—"

"Alert them all, and give them Audra's description." Summer was already shaping a field plan, sorting through her options. Most would involve approval of the aquarium director. "I need to speak with your head of security."

The guard looked worried as he traced the tour route and handed the map back to Summer. "You don't think— I mean, her mother told the museum director about what's been going on, but—"

Summer cut him off, glancing down at Sophy. "Call me on my cell phone with any news, Simon. And give your security director my number." She rattled off a string of numbers.

"Yes, ma'am."

Summer was at the far stairs when he called her back, his walkie-talkie raised to his ear.

"I'd better take you upstairs myself, Ms. Mulvaney."

"Did you find Audra?"

"No, ma'am, but we found her red jacket." His face was grim. "A guard noticed it behind a bench near the sea-otter tank."

"Simon, get people on the exit doors immediately." Summer had a cold feeling in her stomach as she tried Audra's cell phone. Again there was no answer.

"What's going on?" Sophy demanded. "Why is everyone frowning? Audra's late all the time."

"It's probably nothing, honey, but let's you and I check things out. Just like in *Mission Impossible.*"

"Cool. Let's go." Sophy skipped toward the stairs, too young and protected to understand that life didn't always deal out Hollywood-style happy endings.

Tate Winslow stared at the woman he had loved irrationally since even before their first date in law school. "What's wrong, Cara? Talk to me."

"There's very little to say." Her shoulders were a stiff, unrelenting line. "Several new cases are taking far more time than I imagined, and two of our staff are out on leave. The girls need me, too, with their new nanny coming."

She sounded exhausted, Tate realized. She'd been tired before, but never like this, as if she couldn't find enough energy to focus.

Fool that he was, he hadn't seen it until now.

"You can turn the Costello appeal over to Tony or Tristan. Either one would take it in a second."

Cara's eyes hardened. "The day I can't do my job is the day I quit."

"It isn't professional failure to step back and take a breather now and again," Tate said quietly. "Maybe it's time you dropped the pace a little. You've been working twelve hour days since I first met you."

She had been sorting linens at the college laundry, her hands moving fast and expertly. Her face was flushed, her clothes sweaty, and Tate had loved her at first sight. So had most of the male students in the law-school dorm. The linen service had had a huge run on towels that week.

She had created quite a stir when she had shown up with black boots and sleek black jeans in the front row of Contracts I the following Monday. The first week she had twenty offers for dinner and a study date, but she turned them all down—including Tate's.

After that, the queue in the linen service had wound down the hall and out to the street. Tate had been somewhere in the middle.

"Talk to me, Cara."

"There's nothing to discuss." She sounded calm, at least on the surface. "My decision is made."

"Last time I checked, there were two of us involved in this wedding. I'd say that gives me the right to ask a few questions when you try to call it off."

"I can't discuss this now. The girls are expecting me for dessert, summer school–homework check and bedtime stories."

Her face was pale. Did Tate imagine it or was there a hint of fear amid the exhaustion there?

"Is it your boss? I know he's been giving you hell. If so, I can make a few calls."

"I don't want or need special favors. You of all people should know that."

He shrugged his shoulders. "Hey, it was worth a try."

Cara didn't smile. "I've got to go." When she reached for the door, Tate cut her off. "I'm not letting you leave. You're working too damned hard, Cara."

"And *you* aren't? You're the one with back-to-back breakfast meetings, thirteen-hour days, and power naps in the limo on the way to another policy meeting."

"That's different."

"Why? Because you're a man and I'm just a little ole woman who belongs at home in the kitchen anyway?"

"You know that's not what I meant." Tate held down his anger. She was baiting him, but try as he might, he couldn't figure out why. "I only meant that you're worn out. No one works well in a state of exhaustion."

"You do."

"I get by," he said roughly. "And I get by because I'm thinking about a woman with soft skin and crooked eyebrows. A woman who tells me straight when I screw up. A woman I mean to make my wife, in front of our families and closest friends, then disappear somewhere and make love to her until neither of us can stand up and walk."

She closed her eyes. "Don't. This is already hard enough."

"Then talk to me, damn it." Tate gripped her shoulders, turning her to face him. "Tell me what you're afraid of, Cara. We'll work it out together, whatever it is."

"Not this time." The words were a whisper.

Tate heard the sound of regret—and terrible pain. In that moment, he realized he was losing her.

Her cell phone pealed twice from inside her purse. She still insisted on using the tune from *Gilligan's Island* so she could recognize her calls amid all the others in public places.

"Hello?"

Tate watched her face change.

"When?" Blindly she grabbed for the door. "I'll be there as soon as I can."

"What is it, Cara?" He put a hand on her shoulder, another on the door. "Damn it, tell me."

Her fingers trembled as she slid the phone into her pocket. "It's Audra. Today's her docent day at the aquarium." Her voice broke. "No one can find her. She's gone."

Tate pushed her into a chair and grabbed his shirt. "I'll drive you to Monterey."

"There's no need. My car's parked outside."

"Damn it, I'm driving you." Tate worked hard to hold back his anger. "There's no further discussion." He tucked in his shirt while he looked for his shoes. "I'll get a police escort to save time."

This time she didn't protest his interference.

"My car will be waiting in front by the time we get downstairs."

She nodded jerkily. "They're searching the aquarium

now." Her hands locked. "What if they don't find her? What if someone—"

"Don't." Tate pointed to the nearby phone. "Call Margo and tell her what's happened. Tell her I'll be in touch when I can."

He was dialing his cell phone as he disappeared into the bedroom.

"No sign of her on the third floor, Ms. Mulvaney." A guard with thinning hair met them at the stairwell outside the kelp tank. "I checked with people at all the exits, and no one saw her go out."

"What about the front?"

"That could be a problem." He looked down at Sophy and lowered his voice. "The regular guard was sick today. The replacement worker just left ten minutes ago, and no one's been able to reach him."

"Keep trying, please." Summer studied the floor plan. "What about the rooms over here?"

"Private offices, ma'am. Administration mostly."

"Has anyone checked them?"

"I don't believe so. I'll get someone on that right away." He turned away, his radio squeaking.

Sophy tugged at Summer's arm. "Why are you so upset? Audra's probably in the cafeteria sneaking a cup of coffee or flirting with that cool new boy who started working there."

Summer motioned to the guard. "Maybe you should check the cafeteria. Try the restrooms, too." She tapped on the map. "Meanwhile, we'll start here and work our way clockwise, room by room."

"You think Audra's hurt or something?" Sophy's eyes were huge and unblinking.

"Don't worry, honey. She was probably confused and

went to the wrong place." Summer checked her watch. "I have to phone your mom again."

"She'll be so frightened," Sophy said gravely. "She worries a lot lately. She tries to hide it, but we can still tell."

So much for fooling the kids, Summer thought. As they crossed the corridor, she dialed Cara O'Connor's cell phone.

Cara answered on the second ring, sounding breathless.

"Ms. Mulvaney here. We're checking the building now. So far no one has seen her leave."

"Thank God. Did you try the cafeteria? She sometimes sneaks coffee from a nice young man who works in there."

Summer smiled slightly. "Sophy just told me that, so I sent someone to have a look. Don't worry, ma'am. We'll find her."

"We'll be there as fast as we can. How is Sophy?"

"Just fine. Would you like to speak with her?"

"Please."

Sophy took the phone eagerly. "Don't worry, Mom. Ms. Mulvaney and I will find her. She's probably sitting on a bench somewhere playing her Walkman." Sophy listened for several moments, then nodded. "Yes, I'll stay with Ms. Mulvaney. She told me that, too." She looked up at Summer. "I like her, Mom. She's nice—and wait till I tell you about my ballet class. Okay. I love you, too. Bye, now."

She handed the phone back to Summer. "I'm glad the senator's with her. She sounds upset."

Summer smoothly guided Sophy behind her before she pushed open the door to the women's bathroom. A mother with a baby in a carrier was washing her hands at a sink, and two teenagers were combing their hair. Otherwise, the room was empty. After checking each stall, Summer headed to the next room. With every minute that passed, the possibility of foul play grew.

A woman in a museum uniform met them down the corridor. "Are you Ms. Mulvaney?"

"That's right. Any news?"

"No, this area's all clear. I covered every inch. One of the guards brought up her jacket for you."

Summer took the coat, shoving down a stab of disappointment. "Thank you."

"I'll carry it," Sophy said gravely. "Audra always leaves things lying around." She folded the jacket, frowning. "I don't think she was going down to the cafeteria or the gift shop, though." She ran a hand over the red fabric. "I think she was meeting someone."

Summer nodded at the guard. "We'll check, honey."

"No." Sophy didn't look up. "Not up here. I think she—"

Sophy was cut short by the whine of the guard's radio. "We have the girl. Repeat, we *have* the girl."

Summer said a silent prayer of thanks. "Is she hurt? Do you know her status?"

The guard nodded. "She's fine. They're on the way up now."

Audra appeared at the far end of the floor, looking pale and anxious, and Sophy immediately charged toward her. Summer followed, scanning the area for any undue interest shown by the half a dozen people scattered among the marine exhibits.

A female guard motioned to Summer. "She was in a restroom on the ground floor. Said she met a girlfriend after the tour. The two of them were in there talking, and she says she didn't realize the time."

Summer noted the woman's name and badge number. "Thank you for all your help. I'll call her mother, then have a word with your head of security. I'm sorry for the trouble."

"Just glad it was a false alarm. Everyone is jumpy these days. I'll call off the search."

Summer watched the two girls, leaning close in a bar of late-afternoon sunlight. Audra was as tense and closed off as her younger sister was full of innocent enthusiasm, but different or not, the bond between them was deep.

Audra waited stiffly as Summer walked closer. "I-I'm sorry, Ms. Mulvaney. I didn't realize how late it was. I didn't think that being a few minutes late would matter."

"Twenty minutes is not a few minutes." Summer was halfway into an angry speech when she caught herself. Punishment was for Audra's mother to set. Right now Summer had to handle damage control.

As the aquarium's security director appeared, Summer frowned at Audra. "You've made trouble for quite a lot of people. You could help by apologizing to some of them."

Audra flushed. "Oh, all right. Even though I think you're all making a big, stupid deal out of *nothing.*" She faced the security director squarely and made a credible apology, then thanked him for his concern. Summer was struck by her aplomb as she turned to thank two other guards.

When she was done, Summer pulled out her cell phone. "Why don't you give your mother the news that you've been found. She and Senator Winslow are on their way here."

"You called my *mother*?" Audra's shoulders snapped into a tight line of anger. "Why did you do that?"

"Lower your voice, please." Summer reined in her temper, aware that Audra knew nothing about the recent threats. "I phoned your mother as soon as you didn't appear with your group. It's my job to keep her informed."

"She treats me like a *baby*. Everyone does." Audra slung her jacket over her shoulder. "I hate it."

Then don't act like a baby, Summer wanted to say. Instead she held out her cell phone. "She's very worried about you, Audra."

"No kidding. She worries about everything."

Another reason to tell the girls the truth, Summer thought grimly. But it still wasn't her call. While Audra paced the room, phone to her ear, Summer sat down with Sophy.

"She didn't mean to cause any trouble." Sophy watched her sister pace. "She just likes to talk. When she saw her friend downstairs, they started gossiping and forgot the time."

"Then she'll have to learn not to forget. Audra inconvenienced a dozen people today and frightened her mother badly." Summer frowned, remembering that Sophy had been about to tell her something earlier. "What did you mean before when you said Audra was going to meet someone. How did you know that?"

Sophy looked away, fiddling with her backpack. "It was just a thought. It doesn't matter." Audra was still talking on the cell phone, arguing with her mother, when Sophy pushed to her feet. "Can we go now?"

Sitting beside Tate Winslow, Cara put down her phone with a sigh of relief. "They found her in the bathroom. She was talking with a friend and didn't notice the time."

"Thank God." Tate looked away from traffic and squeezed her shoulder. "Is Sophy upset?"

"Ms. Mulvaney says she's been wonderful. The two seem to have hit things off in grand fashion."

"That's the new nanny, right? How is Audra taking that?"

"Too soon to say. The girls loved their old nanny, even

though she was getting very lax." Cara laughed. "Maybe *because* she was lax."

"What was the problem again?"

"Appendicitis. It ruptured while she was shopping in San Francisco on her day off. She's still very sick, and I'm just glad I could find a dependable replacement on short notice."

"Where *did* you find Ms. Mulvaney, by the way."

"Oh, a friend of a friend," Cara said vaguely. "I have my own network, too, Senator."

"I don't doubt it for a second, Counselor." Tate smoothed a strand of hair off her cheek. "Now tell me what's really going on."

Cara stared out at the line of lights sprawling south toward Carmel. "Sometimes I wish you weren't so smart. And so damned stubborn."

"Same goes, Counselor."

"It was all a very long time ago. I thought it was finally over." Cara closed her eyes. "Buried deep."

"I haven't got a clue what you're talking about, honey."

"You aren't supposed to." The exhaustion was back in her voice. "No one is. I worked hard to be sure of that." Cara's voice wavered. "But someone found out, and they'll use it against me. Tate, I don't how to tell you this, but—" She stared down at her locked hands. "I was pregnant. It was years ago, back in a different universe. It was sordid and hopeless and I had school debts to repay, my mother to support, my sister to worry about. There was no way in heaven I could—" Her voice broke. "What could I give a baby when I could barely feed myself?"

"I'm pulling over—"

"*No,* keep driving. Otherwise, I won't have the nerve to finish."

She closed her eyes, swept back to the cramped student

apartment in West Philadelphia, with the trolley tracks right outside her window. She remembered the cold *clack* of metal wheels late at night, and she remembered feeling frightened, alone, and desperate. Then she'd gotten sick, and a simple bout of flu had developed into pneumonia.

A worse nightmare had followed.

"Who was the father?" Tate's face was set in grim lines.

"Do you really want to know?"

"Tell me his name. I know the rest already. If he didn't want the child, that makes him a coward as well as a bastard."

"Close enough."

He stared into a line of traffic. "I could kill him for leaving you like that."

"Forget him. He was—a mistake. A colossal, inexcusable mistake." Cara sat back stiffly. "I was taking a class with him, and we happened to meet at the library once or twice. It seemed so casual at the time. We did some research together, and the next thing I knew . . ." She gave a broken laugh. "What a pathetic cliché. He was my professor, Tate. Older, experienced, handsome. Like a fool, I fell blindly in love, right into bed with him."

chapter 7

Tate cut through traffic, then pulled off onto the shoulder. Before Cara could catch a breath, his arms were around her.

"Point number one: You have *never* been pathetic in your life. Point number two: *He* took advantage of *you*. As a professor, he was years older and in a position of authority, so don't tell me the mistake was yours," Tate said savagely.

She turned her face into his shoulder, trembling. "I knew it was wrong. Deep down, I knew it was just nailing a student. But I told myself I was different, that he would see what a valuable asset I could be. I was already doing research, writing papers for him, answering his letters. Then after three months I found out he was going back to his old position in Boston. He had a wife and four kids, and I was never pegged to be more than a diversion to get him through the school term."

Tate pulled Cara closer, muttering a graphic curse. "What did you do?"

"At first, I told myself it was a mistake. If only we could talk, everything would be fine. So I went to see him after hours at his office." Her voice fell. "I must have made a lovely sight—eyes red from crying, throat raw. I think I stopped eating for a while, too."

Tate's fingers tightened. "What happened?"

"Nothing, because I never saw him. I heard him inside, but he wouldn't open the door. I started pounding and . . . and the next thing I knew, I was sitting in a cruiser with a campus police officer, being threatened with arrest. My friendly professor had reported one of his female students was stalking him, and that she was mentally unbalanced. God knows I must have looked unhinged that night. My world was in pieces, and suddenly I had a child to plan for."

Tate kissed her damp cheeks, his face grim. "I only wish I'd known. I'd have killed him."

Neither noticed the roar of traffic streaming past. "And you would have ruined a wonderful career for nothing. I left school not long after."

"I remember. One Monday you weren't in class, and we heard that you'd transferred."

"Not true." After a long time Cara sighed, her face streaked with tears. "You're not going to ask me the truth?"

"The truth is that you survived. Now you have one of the most important jobs in San Francisco and two beautiful children. I have no reason to question whatever choices you made that day, since they brought you where you are right now." His voice softened. "Here in my arms."

"I'm glad you won't ask, because I did the only thing I felt I could, Tate. I have no regrets about that decision." Cara sat up straighter. "I went to a clinic in Mexico, and I was assured all records would remain sealed."

A car horn screamed. Two SUVs came perilously close to colliding as they changed lanes nearby.

Cara stared blindly at the passing cars. "I accept the responsibility for what I did, but I won't cause more pain to you or to my family. Dear God, if the press blows this up, it would devastate Audra and Sophy."

With a soft curse Tate turned her around to face him. "Someone found out." He cupped her wet cheeks, his expression as fierce as his touch was gentle. "Someone's threatening you with this, aren't they?"

Cara didn't move, didn't speak. Her whole body felt cold. After what seemed like an eternity, she nodded. "I'm afraid so."

"When, Cara? And why didn't you tell me sooner?"

"Because it's *my* problem. I'm not going to become a liability to you, Tate."

He cradled her face between hands that shook. "I *love* you. That's now and forever, and your problems are my problems. I also love your two girls, and you'd better get used to that, too, because I'm in your life to stay."

"You're not listening, Tate. This could *ruin* you." Cara took a raw breath. "You're a wonderful man—even more rare, you're an honest politician. This country needs you in the Senate and, God willing, at 1600 Pennsylvania Avenue. I refuse to involve you in this." She wiped blindly at her cheeks with the cuff of her jacket.

"Let me get this straight. The wedding's off," he said quietly. "To protect me, so I can be a force for fairness and decency?"

She nodded.

"To ensure my future happiness?"

"It's the right thing to do, Tate."

"The hell it is, because I have no chance at future happiness without you, Cara. What does it take to convince you of that?"

"I won't argue." She sat back stiffly. "My mind is made up."

"Do you love me?"

"What does that have to do with anything?"

His fingers tightened. "Do you love me?"

When she looked into his eyes, the pain she saw there almost made her lose her resolve. But Cara had seen enough lurid headlines to know that her secret could be twisted, blown up in a way that would shatter Tate's political future. If she married him now, it would cause more pain and harm. She would alienate his family and staff, and one day he would wake up hating her.

She couldn't bear the thought.

"Don't push me, Tate. What I feel for you—what I will *always* feel for you—is irrelevant. I need to do what's right, not what feels good."

"If you think Costello is behind this, turn his appeal over to a colleague."

"I can't be sure that he's the one. I have probably sixty cases on my desk now, and hundreds more already closed." She laughed tensely. "A lot of people hate my guts, you know. I'm certain Costello will always have a vendetta against me."

"Then I'll hire a private investigator. We'll fly down to that clinic in Mexico and see who's been sniffing around. We can start planning our strategy tonight at the house."

"Haven't you heard anything I've said? The wedding is *off,* Tate. For your protection, you shouldn't be seen with me."

"Like hell. Tonight we'll talk with my contact and decide what to do next." His voice was calm, utterly implacable.

"I won't ruin your future, Tate. The answer is *no*."

"In that case, I'll drop my plans for a presidential run."

"You *can't* do that."

"I can and I will. If you go, my presidential bid goes, too. I want you more than I want 1600 Pennsylvania Avenue."

"I won't let you bow out."

"Good, then help me find this bastard before he hurts anyone else."

Cara took a deep breath. "I'll give you one week. If we haven't found him by then, I'll inform the press that our wedding is off. I won't change my mind about this, Tate." Her voice shook.

"In that case, we'll have to work fast." He started the car and cut out into traffic. "Fortunately, I happen to know someone who's perfect for this kind of job."

"A private investigator, you mean?"

Tate shook his head.

"A policeman?"

"Something better. This man is as good as they come. I'd trust him with my life—in fact, several times I have."

"I don't understand."

"You will." Tate's eyes hardened. "He always gets the job done, no matter how nasty, and right now we need someone nasty on our side."

He sits in a parked car and watches them walk out of the aquarium, one striking woman, one attractive teenager, and a little girl carrying a pink knapsack. Sunlight strikes the middle one, who's wearing a red jacket. She looks angry, kicking at pebbles as she stalks ahead of the other two.

The tall woman is new, and he makes a note in a little book as she walks along the opposite side of the street. He sees her check the passing cars, the pedestrians nearby. Yes, this one is careful—maybe too careful.

He slides down behind the wheel of a rusty Honda Accord with Michigan plates. A Lakers cap covers most of his face, and the rest of his features are hidden behind a neat artificial beard. Always careful, he writes comments in a notebook between sips from a Thermos bottle. The book is full of timetables and maps, jammed with details of his eight months of surveillance. Who, what, where, and when—all are here, captured in neat, slanting script.

They are inside the parking garage now. His lip twitches as he watches the three of them slide into a white Lexus SUV with tinted windows and leather seats. Excellent car. Great power, tight handling, and zero to sixty in less than seven seconds.

The tall woman must be the new nanny. She drops something near the door and bends down to retrieve it. In the process she checks the underside of the car.

Very sharp, he thinks.

He frowns as she climbs into the Lexus, waits until the girls are buckled in, and pulls out into traffic, scanning the nearby cars.

People look at a BMW or a Jaguar, but no one looks twice at a rusty Honda Accord, and she is no exception. She is out in traffic in a second, unaware of him or the fact that this is no regular Honda. Thanks to his upgrades, the car can hold 160 on the straightaway.

Speed happens to be his second vice.

His lips curve in a smile as the Lexus passes, and he glances down, seemingly engrossed in the map of Monterey propped on his steering wheel. He lets a truck pass, then two other sedans. After that he follows, just another tourist on a sunny, crowded California street.

Near the dashboard, his telephoto lens clicks off a

dozen shots. He will print them tonight and they will reach their destination three hours after that.

The three people in the white Lexus are attractive, confident, oblivious. Soon he will change all of that.

He is very good at his job.

chapter 8

Neither Sophy nor Audra would eat. They wanted to wait for their mother, who was due in twenty minutes. Their rooms were clean, their homework done, their pet ferret fed. Now they sat uncomfortably in the big den that faced the backyard, while the clock ticked loudly.

Sophy drummed on the pine coffee table. "Let's play dominoes."

"Dominoes are for dorks." Audra gave a tight laugh and picked impatiently at a nail. "Forget it."

"How about Monopoly?"

"I'm going for a walk until Mom gets here." Audra swept up her red jacket.

"I'll come, too." Sophy shot to her feet. "You can come with us, Ms. Mulvaney."

Audra rolled her eyes as she shouldered open the door and hammered across the porch. "Bring the whole world, why don't you?"

Sophy skipped behind her sister. "Where are we going?"

"Into town."

"There won't be time for that," Summer said calmly, catching the door before it banged shut.

Muttering, Audra crossed the grass, heading toward the driveway, but Sophy stopped at the edge of the porch. "I don't want to go to town. I want to play baseball." She picked up a bat from an old wicker chair. "Please, Ms. Mulvaney. Audra never wants to play anymore, but she used to be the best hitter around."

"I still am," Audra snapped.

"Really? Why don't you show me?" Summer waited, hands on her hips. "Unless you'd prefer to explain why you set up that little surprise out in the gardening shed."

Audra stared back, stiff and defiant. "I don't know what you're talking about."

Sophy shuffled her feet. "You do know, Audra. You told me we had to teach her a lesson."

"Be *quiet,* Sophy." Audra kicked a pebble with her toe. "It was a mistake, okay? And I *don't* bat anymore. That's dumb kid stuff."

"I guess you've forgotten how," Summer said casually. It was primitive reverse psychology, but she was ready to try anything to keep the surly teenager from leaving the grounds.

Too bad handcuffing her to the front door was out of the question.

"I can still hit," Audra snapped. "And I happen to recognize reverse psychology when I hear it." Her eyes narrowed. "Do you play?"

"Not much. I think we should have our walk near the house, then go back inside to wait for your mother."

"You don't play?" Audra tossed the ball up and down, studying Summer. "Why not try a few? Toss her the bat, Sophy. I'll pitch."

"All *right.*" Oblivious to the undercurrents, Sophy raced toward Summer, bat in hand as the sun sank crimson into the ocean behind them. "We used to play ball for hours. It was so cool."

It had been fifteen years since Summer had held a bat, but some things you never forgot. The wood was smooth beneath her hands, and the curved end fit snuggly against her fingers. The air was clean, the wind still, a perfect time to feel the jolt of wood on leather.

Audra fired off the first pitch before Summer was in position, snickering when the swing caught dead air.

"She's a really good pitcher, too," Sophy whispered as she bent down to catch. "Watch out for her insiders."

Another pitch fired through the slanting copper sunlight. Summer tipped it and the ball flew right into Audra's glove.

"Throw another one," Sophy ordered. "She wasn't ready."

"Okay, fine." Audra leaned back. "Try *this* one on for size." A pitch fired past Summer's chest, but this one met the driving force of the bat and sailed high, a dark circle as it flew into the sunlight, over the redwood gazebo, over the pool and the lush tea roses, finally landing in a huge bougainvillaea.

"Hell!"

The plant shook wildly. Angry muttering drifted in the quiet air.

Summer's body tensed. "Sophy, stay behind me."

"But why—"

"Audra, come here, please."

"Would you look at that?" Grinning, the teenager watched the leaves shake. "You beaned him but good."

"Audra, *now.*"

"What's wrong?" She gazed back at Summer, her face tight with defiance.

"Please come over here." As she spoke, Summer gripped the bat and walked over the cool grass, putting her body between the girls and the unknown figure in the plants at the edge of the lawn.

A head appeared, silhouetted against the setting sun. Dark hair, broad shoulders, black shirt.

"Damned thorns." Gabe Morgan struggled out of the bougainvillaeas, rubbing his shoulders. Flower petals covered his hair and shoulders like red snow. "How about some warning next time?"

Summer didn't move. Had he been out here watching them?

Sophy started to run forward, but Summer caught her hand, holding her still. "What were you doing in the bushes, Mr. Morgan?"

Sophy moved restlessly from foot to foot. "But it's just Gabe. He works here."

Summer kept her body in front of the girls, bat held loosely at her side. "I'd like to hear your answer, Mr. Morgan."

"Hell, I'm bleeding here and the woman wants a job description." Metal rattled as the gardener hauled a roll of electrical wire out from beneath the bougainvillaeas. "For your information, I was replacing the lights back there. This whole row blew out last night and I just got around to fixing them. After this, I've got new path lights to install." He balanced a toolbox on one hip, looking sweaty, cranky, and dangerous. "In case you hadn't noticed, there's a wedding reception being planned, along with three parties here, two of them to be held outdoors at night." He waved a broken piece of wire in the air. "No lights, no party."

Sophy pulled free and charged over the grass. "She didn't mean to hit you, Gabe. We didn't even know you were there, did we, Ms. Mulvaney?" She peered up at his arm. "Is it bleeding?"

"Nah. Just hurts like—" He cleared his throat. "The dickens. You hit that one out of the park, Audra?"

"*She* did." There was unwilling respect in the teenager's voice. "No one *ever* gets a hit off my insiders, either."

"Looks like your new nanny did." Gabe studied the two girls. "Kinda late for baseball practice. Aren't you two supposed to be eating dinner?"

"We're waiting for Mom," Sophy said cheerfully. "Audra wanted to walk to town, only Ms. Mulvaney told her no on account of—well, I don't exactly remember why. But then I saw the bat and said we ought to play, then Audra threw one of her low insiders and Ms. Mulvaney *still* smashed the living bejeezus out of it."

Gabe's lips twitched. "The what?"

"The bejeezus. Tiffany Hammersmith says that all the time."

"Well, I don't think you should, honey."

"Oh." Sophy's eyes widened. "Is it rude?"

"Afraid so."

The little girl flushed. "Tiffany says a lot of rude words. She wears black thong underwear, too."

Gabe's lips twitched again. "Is that a fact? And Tiffany is what, nine?"

"Oh, no. She'll be eleven next month."

"Skirting middle age, in fact," Gabe murmured.

Summer felt her mouth slipping into a smile. With hard effort she summoned up a frown. "How long have you been out here, Mr. Morgan? Fixing the lights," she added dryly.

"About forty minutes, ma'am. I had to make a few calls to plant suppliers, then I grabbed a quick meal in the kitchen. Have you met Patrick yet?"

Summer shook her head.

"The boy makes a mean sourdough bruschetta. Compliment his dough and he's yours for life."

Something was wrong here, but for all her effort Summer couldn't put her finger on it. She looked at the girls. "I think we should go inside now." The sun was gone and the air was purple with the first hint of twilight. "You're shivering, Sophy."

"I'm not cold. It's not that." The girl looked back across the broad lawn. "For a moment I almost felt like . . ." She jammed her hands in her pockets. "Never mind."

Gabe knelt before her. "What is it, honey?"

She shrugged fragile shoulders. "Nothing, really. I guess Ms. Mulvaney is right. We should probably go in."

Gabe gave the girl a strange look. "I'll go with you and drop these lights off." As they walked back to the house, the girls in front, he fell into step beside Summer. "Did you get a confession out of them yet?"

"She admits nothing, but Sophy says Audra had it in for me. No surprises there," she added quietly. "I'll have to discuss it with their mother."

Gabe rubbed his neck. "Look, I'm sorry about what happened earlier this afternoon in the shower."

"I doubt it. In fact, I could swear you were enjoying yourself, Mr. Morgan."

"Call me Gabe. And you can put down the bat now. I'm trying to apologize here, not attack you."

Summer realized the bat was still hanging at her side. As she looked at Gabe, some of her tension faded. "How I feel about what happened doesn't matter."

"Of course it does." His voice fell. "I had some . . . disagreement with Susanne."

"The girls' old nanny? *That* explains why you were stark naked in my shower?"

"No, it doesn't. Audra and Sophy told me the new

nanny wasn't arriving until much later." Gabe shrugged broad shoulders that rippled beneath his well-worn tee shirt. "You weren't *supposed* to be in the guesthouse when I was there."

"Assuming that I bought your story—which I don't—I still don't see why they would pull a trick like that."

"They didn't want their nanny to leave. Susanne taught them all the cool new dances, shared her nail polish, gave them haircuts. Girl stuff like that."

Summer frowned. She wouldn't be offering any of those skills, not in this lifetime. They simply weren't in her repertoire. Kickboxing, definitely. Firearms safety, absolutely. But French braids and cool new nail polish?

No way. And she wasn't going to ask Gabe for details about his problems with Susanne.

"Forget about the old nanny. You seem to have won the girls over already—Sophy, at least."

"Sophy could make friends with Godzilla," Summer muttered. "But Audra hates me."

"Audra hates everyone, including herself. It's teenage angst."

"Maybe." One thing still bothered Summer. "Why weren't you surprised to see someone waiting outside when you came out of the shower?"

They were almost at the house now. The sky had faded to a rich molten purple. For long moments Gabe didn't answer, his eyes on the girls. "I had my reasons."

"Because you were expecting someone to be waiting," Summer mused. "Is that it?"

"Let's just say that Susanne had a way of turning up unannounced wherever I was." His eyes narrowed. "In my room. In my shower. Sometimes in my bed."

Summer frowned. "So you two were sleeping together."

"That's not what I said. Susanne was on the mend from

a broken relationship and looking for comfort and reassurance from a man—any man. I was within easy reach, so she chose me."

"Let me get this straight. She wanted sex, but you, being pure and noble of heart, turned her down?"

Gabe's voice hardened. "She told me no one would believe it."

"Did Ms. O'Connor know about this?"

"I didn't want to bother Cara. There was no need. I could handle myself around Susanne. I kept my mouth shut and my hands to myself. Things aren't always what they seem, Ms. Mulvaney."

"Probably not."

"So you believe me?"

"I'm thinking about it." Summer frowned. "You've got an accent. Were you born here?"

"Southern Wyoming. As beautiful a place as God ever set his hand to create." Gabe scanned the trees near the house. "My dad's work kept us on the move. Thailand, Singapore, Sri Lanka, we hit all of them. After that I spent ten years Down Under. People tell me I still have a bit of a roll with the arr's."

"Toss a shrimp ahn the bahbie," Summer said. "I can hear it now."

"What about you?"

"Oh, here and there," Summer said vaguely.

"East Coast." He crossed his arms. "Somewhere south of New York City, but north of Virginia."

Summer wasn't about to discuss her past.

Gabe held out one hand, studying her face in the deepening twilight. "Truce? Since we have to work in close quarters, feuding could be unpleasant."

Summer considered his outstretched hand. She wasn't fighting, but she wasn't ready for a truce, either. "I can live with unpleasant. Good night, Mr. Morgan." She moved past him, up the big stone steps.

"Tough, aren't you?"

"Tough enough." Summer wondered why she didn't quite trust the man. Was it because he had appeared from a perfect spot for surveillance or because of what had happened in her shower?

"Don't worry," she called over her shoulder. "You keep out of my way and I'll keep out of yours. No contact, no problems."

Gabe started to answer, but gravel shot over the driveway, and Summer spun around hard, verifying that the two girls were up on the porch in a position of relative safety. As lights cut across the darkness, she relaxed, recognizing the black Acura.

Senator Winslow turned off the motor, then moved around to the passenger side where Cara was gathering her briefcase, suit jacket, and a pair of killer heels that looked very uncomfortable. Up on the porch the girls let out a yell, racing to their mother, who dropped the shoes and caught them both in a tight grip.

In that moment Summer saw how strong the tie was that bound them. Despite Audra's bouts of sullenness, she was loose and smiling in her mother's arms, while Sophy's good humor flared into incandescence.

As the senator watched the noisy reunion, Summer registered his confidence and power. With his broad shoulders and rugged features, he was someone who would always be noticed. When he walked toward her, Summer saw the lines at his mouth and forehead that his easy smile couldn't conceal.

"Ms. Mulvaney, isn't it? Welcome to California. You've had quite an eventful first day."

When he spoke, Summer understood why journalists

on the Capitol Hill beat had dubbed Tate Winslow "The Voice." Every word rolled with deep resonance and a hypnotizing sense of candor.

A voice like that was a dangerous weapon for a politician, she thought cynically.

"It's a pleasure to meet you, sir. Yes, we had a little excitement. Thankfully, the problem was brief."

The senator nodded, then turned to Gabe. "Did you get those lights repaired?"

So much for her suspicions, Summer thought, grimacing at Gabe's I-told-you-so smile. "All but the last junction box, sir. I should have that one fixed in half an hour. After that I'll work on the new path lights."

"Good." The senator glanced toward the darkness of the beach. "More lighting should improve the security here. At least that's what the experts tell me." He watched a dark sedan pull into the driveway.

"Are you expecting company, sir?" Summer moved closer to Cara and the girls as a man and woman emerged from the car.

"That's Cara's police escort. Since these threats began, the state police have provided a detail for her protection," he said quietly. "For the moment it seems to be enough." He looked at Summer. "You know about the threats, don't you?"

Summer nodded. Cara O'Connor had kept Summer's real identity a secret from everyone, even the senator and his staff, until the source of the threats was identified. "When Audra vanished today, I shook out most of the museum to find her, sir. I'm afraid she suspects something is wrong."

"I'll pass the word to Cara." The senator grinned as the girls shot toward him. Sophy whirled in circles, pulling out her ballet shoes to show him, while Audra took his briefcase. With one arm around each girl, he walked toward the house, where Cara stood silhouetted in light from the big doorway.

They were a real, loving family, Summer thought. The kind of family she'd once had and lost so suddenly. She felt a moment of jealousy and forced it down hard.

Do the job, she told herself. *Forget the emotions, because they can get you fired fast.*

Or even killed.

She felt Gabe Morgan's eyes on her.

"You okay?" he asked quietly. "I saw something in your face. One second it was there, then it was gone."

Summer shrugged. Why did this stranger glimpse the emotions she usually kept well-hidden? "Just a trick of the light."

She started to walk past him, but he caught her arm. "What's wrong, damn it?"

"Not a single thing."

But the truth was that working with a family was different from Summer's usual assignments. She hadn't expected the intimacy, or how it would affect her. She had to stay aloof and unmoved to get the job done. Meanwhile, she had one more surreptitious search of the house to complete before the girls went to bed. After that came a detailed report on the incident at the aquarium.

"If you'll excuse me, I have work to do." She pushed past him, shoulders stiff, determined to lock down her emotions where they couldn't bother her—or jeopardize the job at hand.

chapter 9

Long curtains drifted at half-open windows. Summer would check each one later to be certain all were closed and locked, but for now it was pleasant to feel the sea wind on her face.

Sitting on Sophy's bed, with a book opened on her lap, Cara read quietly.

" 'It was late one winter night, long past my bedtime . . .' "

Sophy gave a little sigh and closed her eyes. Stretched out beside her, Audra wiggled once, then relaxed, her feet hidden in pink bunny slippers. Liberace was curled on Audra's lap, quiet for once.

" 'We walked on toward the woods, Pa and I.' "

Summer had vague memories of reading this same book long ago, but there had been no bedtime rituals such as this in her house. She had chosen her own books, alone at the public library, while her father had been off on some military posting too secret for details. And her mother?

She shook away cold memories and focused on the quiet bedtime scene before her, feeling like an intruder even though Cara had expressly requested her to stay.

As the words flowed, Audra closed her eyes, and even Summer felt the tug of sleep and peace.

What if there had been nights like this for her and her sister? How much better to grow up this way rather than within the tense silences of a household where people had forgotten how to communicate or even care?

There were no answers. No sense of resolution. But Summer hadn't expected any. You could never go back.

Cara continued to read from *Owl Moon,* her voice soft with emotion, easy with long experience at the familiar lines. The girls joined in for train whistles and owl cries as the story unfolded, and the sense of family became poignant and tangible.

If Summer had been the emotional type, the scene might have pulled out a few tears. Because she wasn't, she stood and slipped away. First she would check downstairs and make sure the cooking staff had locked up properly in the kitchen. With Cara's wedding approaching, kitchen activity had moved into fast-forward, and two pastry chefs were expected soon, to supplement the preparations made by the family's longtime chef. Cara had explained that Imelda and Patrick were excellent workers, but terrible about leaving windows open and doors unlocked, so Summer made a tour of the kitchen part of her security procedure.

On this trip she found a window cracked open off the pantry, wedged in position with a spoon. Annoyed beyond words, she planned a serious discussion of security with Cara as soon as the girls went to bed. Meanwhile, Summer continued around the house, jotting down problems in a little book. Finally satisfied that all doors and windows were secure and nothing looked out of place, she prepared to set the alarm.

A footstep in the hall stopped her.

"You left before we were done." Cara's face was calm but tired in the glow of the single overhead light. "I hope nothing was wrong."

"I needed to finish checking the house and grounds. I was just about to set the alarm before I went outside."

"Go ahead. Tate knows the code."

"Who else knows it?" Summer asked quietly.

"Only myself. And the girls, of course."

Warning bells clanged in Summer's head. How much would it take for a school chum to weasel the password out of Sophy, who trusted everyone? "You might want to consider changing the code on a weekly basis, just for safety."

"A sensible precaution." Cara rubbed her neck, wincing. "Why don't you set the alarm and finish your rounds while I make us some tea?"

Fifteen minutes later, Summer returned to find Cara curled in a window seat overlooking the rose garden, while tea steamed from the lip of a nearby kettle.

"I'm sorry about the tricks the girls played today. I've told them they're both grounded for a week. I trust that will stop the problems." Cara cut wedges of a frosted cake and shifted them onto plates of Royal Copenhagen china. "I thought you might like some of Patrick's beyond-decadent white-chocolate frosted carrot cake. I warn you, it's addictive."

Summer slid into the opposite seat. "Bad idea. I could barely fit into your leotard for Sophy's dance class today."

"She said you were wonderful, by the way. I'm sorry I couldn't be there. I've only made three classes this year." Cara frowned down at her tea. "There have been so many things I've had to miss since I took this job." When she looked up, her emotions were carefully tucked away. "You know, I haven't really had a chance to thank you for taking this assignment. You came very highly recommended."

"No need to thank me, ma'am. It was my chief's call. I have to admit that this part of California is gorgeous. So is this amazing house of yours."

"I've often thought we should sell it and move somewhere closer to the city, but the girls have spent most of their lives here and they would hate moving. Despite my long commute into San Francisco, so would I."

Summer watched her draw slow lines in her whipped cream. "The file said your husband built the house when you were first married."

"It was Howard's special project. He chose the granite, the wood, even the tiles for the roof. The two of us actually laid the flagstones for the fireplace ourselves when I was pregnant with Audra. There are a lot of memories here."

As she sat back, studying her teacup, something closed in her face, and Summer realized the personal details were over. Though Cara O'Connor looked delicate, Summer figured you didn't get to be an assistant DA without being tough and able to box up your emotions.

"I spoke to Audra about what happened at the museum. I explained how irresponsible it was and how many people she upset by her actions."

"But you didn't tell her that she could have been in serious danger?"

"No. I won't have my girls dragged into this man's sick game."

"It appears to me they already are," Summer said quietly.

"Tate thinks I should tell them. Now you." Cara pushed away her cake uneaten. "The girls have had too much to contend with already. There have been nuisance phone calls, day and night. We change the number and things are quiet for a few days, then somehow they get the number and it starts all over again. Sophy's friends want to know why she has police officers at her house and Audra's friends make fun of her because she can't go out for ice cream or a movie on a whim. *I'm* the reason," she said grimly.

"You're an important person. The work you do makes life safer for all of us."

"I used to think so. When I started out, you could have fueled whole cities with the strength of my zeal. Oh, I was going to make things different in San Francisco. I was going to be the tireless one, the incorruptible one, the prosecutor who would turn the tide." She took a long, harsh breath. "Lately, I don't know if I can pay the price. You can't have it all: job and family and sanity. Can you understand that, Ms. Mulvaney? That there is *always* a price, and usually it's the women who have to pay it."

Summer turned her teacup, understanding Cara O'Connor perfectly. The woman was clearly exhausted, clearly terrified about the threat to her children, but she still struggled to do the right thing. "I understand, ma'am. But it doesn't surprise me. Frankly, I never expected the world to be fair."

Cara studied her over the teacup, one brow raised. "There's a story there. It's written in your face when you think no one is looking."

Summer shifted uneasily.

"Don't worry, I won't probe. But I may make it my business to find out before your job is finished here."

Summer drummed her fingers on the table. "Be my guest."

She was cut off by the tinny melody of Cara's cell phone, the *Gilligan's Island* tune again.

"I've been waiting for news on a case." Cara touched a button. "Hello?"

Suddenly her whole body tensed.

Summer sat forward. "What's wrong?"

Cara stabbed at the phone, ending the call and tossing the phone onto the table. "Him. It's always the same metallic voice, wired through some kind of synthesizer." She closed her eyes, covered her face with her hands. "I've had a new cell phone number for two weeks, and some-how he found it. *Two weeks.* How does he know?"

Summer wished she could assure Cara that everything would be fine, but her gut instinct warned that the pres-sure was going to get worse. "What did he say?"

"That I'd be sorry. It's always been the same message."

"I'll have the call traced."

Cara nodded tiredly. "It's worth a try. But all the other times, he threw away the phones. He uses them once, then tosses them, and each time they've been stolen earlier the same day."

"Maybe he'll get careless, ma'am."

Cara took a breath. "Call me Cara, damn it. All my friends do."

Summer sat back, sensing that Cara O'Connor didn't let down her guard easily. "My pleasure, but only if you do the same."

"Agreed. There's something else, something that came today." With shaky hands the prosecutor reached into her briefcase and removed a clear plastic bag. Inside the bag was a brown cardboard box. "This was left under the desk in my office." Cara handed Summer a pair of latex gloves, then pulled on a pair herself before she lifted the lid.

Summer bent closer, reading the block letter words. " 'May 12, 1986. Los Reyes Clinic. Remember.' " When

Summer looked up, she was shocked at Cara's ashen features. "Maybe you should take a few deep breaths, ma'am. I think some whiskey would be a good idea, too."

"I said to—to call me Cara." She took a harsh breath. "And I don't drink. My husband had something of a problem, so I stopped keeping any alcohol in the house." She took a swallow of tea, then refilled her cup carefully, followed by Summer's. "I'll be fine. It was just hearing the words aloud after all this time."

Silently Summer covered the box, slid it back into the bag, and resealed the top. First thing in the morning she would forward everything to her forensic people. Maybe they could pull a partial print, a piece of hair or some other trace material.

"Do you want to tell me what the message means?" she asked quietly.

"It's the last thing I want to do." Cara gripped her teacup. "But I don't have a choice, do I?"

Summer didn't answer.

"Of course I don't. I know the date very well because in 1986 I—I went to Mexico. There was a small clinic in Los Reyes." Her voice wavered. "I'm not saying anything more. If you want to leave, fine." The teacup spun out of her fingers and turned on its side, brown liquid racing over the table.

Calmly, Summer reached across the table and blotted the spilled tea. "If you had an abortion, I'm not about to judge you for it."

"Everybody else would. God knows, I still have dreams about that day. Nightmares, actually. The ugliness of it all. The indecision."

"Have there been specific demands made?"

"Not yet, but it's only a matter of time." Cara closed her eyes. "I convinced myself the past was buried. Given my line of work, I should have known better." Slowly she reached for a new napkin, watching the brown stain creep over the white cotton. "I have a sample of Glenlivet in the pantry at the back of the top shelf. I told myself I'd keep it for necessity or a special occasion. I'm afraid this is it."

Summer found the small bottle, the size used on airplanes, and added half to Cara's tea. "Drink it. You'll feel better."

"No, I won't. I won't feel better until this person is found—and stopped." Cara's eyes were haunted as she took a sip of her tea and grimaced. "This tastes like battery acid."

"I'm told it's an acquired taste."

The assistant DA rubbed her neck with unsteady fingers. "You're not asking for any details?"

"I have the date and a location. You've given me what is necessary."

"I meant it when I said I wouldn't tell anything more. That's non-negotiable."

Summer nodded. She wasn't here to probe Cara's past. She'd make her own quiet inquiries and see what emerged. Meanwhile, security was her main concern.

"I'll have the box and paper analyzed first thing in the morning. We may get prints or enough DNA evidence to put this creep away."

Cara took another sip of her tea. "I don't think so. Whoever sent that box got past two sets of guards and my own assistant. This person is very good, Summer. That terrifies me."

"You think it's someone in the building, someone you know?"

"At first I couldn't accept that. Now I'd have to say it's possible. How else could they get into my office?"

"As of tomorrow, your door gets new locks, and you

keep it locked. No access without a call from your assistant. No one gets a key except the two of you."

"I was thinking along the same lines."

Summer made a note in her book. "I want to know everyone who entered your building today, along with who they went to see and when they departed."

"I thought of that. Security should have a list for me by noon tomorrow." Cara shoved a strand of hair from her forehead. "I asked my assistant for the names of people who came into my office while she was there." She pulled a piece of paper from her pocket.

Summer scanned the sheet. "Only twelve? Was she out for a long time?"

"She always goes for lunch at one. Anyone on the floor could have slipped in then, and most of them know her schedule." There was a note of weariness in Cara's voice. "Forty-two people work on my floor, and all forty-two were in the building today." She smiled grimly. "I checked with security."

"That gives us some kind of baseline, at least. Things could be worse." Summer refilled their cups. "Let's get to work." She read off the first name on Cara's list while opening a new page in her ever-present notebook. "How long have you known him and are you currently working on any active cases together?"

As Cara spoke, Summer took notes.

It was going to be a long night, she thought grimly.

They were halfway down the list when the back door opened and the alarm beeped.

"Only me." Tate peered around the corner, then punched in the security override code.

He looked rumpled and sexy with his shirt unbuttoned and sleeves pushed up. A man no woman could resist,

Cara thought. Heaven knows, she had tried vainly for years.

"Excuse me," Summer murmured. "I'll be right back."

She was gone before the other two realized it.

"That is one unusual young woman." Cara stood up. "Let me get you some tea."

"You stay put. Hopefully I can pour hot water without inflicting third-degree burns on myself." Tate slid into the chair beside her and traced her cheek. "You look like hell," he said huskily.

"So nice of you to tell me, especially since you look rumpled, but gorgeous as always. The world is unjust." Cara sighed. "What on earth are you doing with a boring workaholic like me?"

"Having the time of my misbegotten life." Tate spoke with a raw directness that stripped away the clever comment she had planned. "Remembering what it felt like to be eighteen and invincible, only now I'm a whole lot smarter. At least, I hope I am." He looked at the box, now carefully repacked. "Is this what you found beneath your desk?"

"Afraid so." Cara nodded, leaning against his chest. She needed to relax, just long enough for the names on her list to stop blurring and the panic to recede.

He smelled like oranges and aftershave and good leather, and she leaned closer, thinking that he had probably just showered and shaved. As she rested her cheek against his skin, she felt the old, racing heat, the slick sensitivity between her thighs.

Always the desire.

With a sigh she turned and focused on cutting a piece of carrot cake. "Patrick made this before he and Imelda left. No dieting allowed while that boy is in charge of the kitchen. Imelda said she's put on ten pounds since coming here." Cara sliced through rich layers of chocolate frosting and carrot-filled cake, then gasped sharply.

Tate shot forward and caught her hand. "You've cut yourself."

"It's nothing."

"Where's the alcohol, Cara? Otherwise, I run you straight to the emergency room." His face was impassive.

"Fine. The alcohol is beneath the sink, Dr. Clooney."

Tate muttered as he banged through the cabinets and returned with alcohol, paper towels, and a bandage. "This could hurt."

Summer appeared in the doorway, staring at Cara's hand. "What could hurt?"

"She cut herself. The woman's the worst patient on the planet, I warn you. Maybe you can keep an eye on this, since she's likely to forget." Ignoring Cara's protests, he put the bottle on the table. When he glanced at the nearby list, his eyes narrowed. "You were going over this together, weren't you? So Summer isn't your normal, everyday nanny." He took Cara's hand grimly. "Which is it, Ms. Mulvaney? Private investigator or undercover state trooper?"

Summer looked at Cara. So much for secrecy.

chapter 10

She's FBI, Tate. I didn't want to tell anyone until she had some hard evidence."

The senator's mouth set in a tight line. "I'm going to be your husband. I think that entitles me to full disclosure." When he dabbed at the wound, Cara sucked in a breath, and he pulled away with a curse. "Sorry. I didn't mean to hurt you."

"I hurt myself," she said softly. "You were never to blame."

Watching them, Summer realized they were talking on a deeper level, about things she wasn't meant to understand.

"I told her about Los Reyes. Enough, anyway."

Summer tried to read the senator's face. "Cara feels her past makes her a liability to you. What do you think, Senator?"

"Keeping secrets won't help my career," he said grimly. "And rumors about an abortion?" He shook his head. "I'd be kidding if I told you it won't make things rocky." He stared at Cara. "I'm not asking you for any details. Your past is just that, over and done as far as I'm concerned."

"Your staff and supporters may not feel the same way," Summer said quietly. "Does this new situation change your feelings toward Ms. O'Connor?"

Tate stood angrily. "Are you sure you want to ask me that question, Ms. Mulvaney?"

"I'm sure, Senator."

Seconds passed. Tate finally nodded. "I suppose your job means you have to ask cold-blooded questions like that, but the answer is no. This situation changes nothing, neither for me nor my staff."

"Good. And call me Summer, please. It's too early to rule anyone out, sir, so if Cara feels up to it, I'd like to finish going through this list. Tomorrow I'll start profiles on the people in her building and run a search for recent large bank deposits, trigger incidents, that sort of thing."

" 'Trigger incidents'?"

"Gambling problems, paid sexual partners, alcohol or drug use. Anything that could be a basis for blackmail." Summer had seen it before, too often to count. Again and again her job had taught her that private indiscretions didn't remain private, and secrets could become very dangerous weapons, indeed.

As Tate smoothed a bandage around Cara's fingers, a muscle moved at his jaw. "You're very efficient."

"Just doing my job, sir."

"Something tells me you're hitting hard, and I like that just fine, because I want this bastard nailed. We've postponed our wedding twice because of my career and Cara's schedule, but I'm not waiting any longer." He looked down at Cara. "If you try, I fully intend to shanghai you without benefit of clergy or wedlock, and there goes my political career."

"The senator shacks up with the assistant DA?" Cara's lips curved. "That might sell a few papers."

"A few million," Tate said dryly. "The tabloids are breathing down my neck already, so we do this by the book. You wear the garter and I get to take it off you in front of family and friends." Warmth filled his eyes as he stared at his bride-to-be. "Deal?"

Cara drew a slow breath. "These people won't let go of me, Tate. Things are going to get messy."

"Of course they are. Since when were you afraid of a good fight, Counselor?"

"Since you got involved. Since my family got involved, and I have to think of what this could do to Sophy and Audra. That terrifies me."

Summer cleared her throat gently, painfully aware of a ticking clock and all the work to be finished. "Sir, I have to ask you this. Do you know anyone who might be holding a grudge against you? A former employee or a disgruntled aide? Even a political opponent who might be unstable?"

Tate rubbed his jaw. "Can I count the Speaker of the House?" He smiled at Summer. "A joke, my dear. Not to say that I don't have a football field full of enemies, but our fights arc generally held out in the open, where everyone can watch. The game is called politics, and everyone's a Monday morning quarterback, you see."

Summer laughed dryly. "Just for the record, sir, I wouldn't take your job for a million dollars. I'd rather face down a bullet any day."

And she had, but Summer didn't mention that.

The junior senator from California flashed her the smile that had sent his female demographics right off the chart. "Glad to hear that my Senate seat is safe from you." His eyes hardened. "I'm going to tackle some tough issues like campaign spending, Summer. No more loopholes, no more cash delivered in brown paper bags. We've got a law with no teeth, but I'm going to give it fangs or die trying, and it won't make me popular," he said grimly. "But that's what America *should* be about, not privilege and cronyism."

If it were Election Day, he'd have *her* vote, Summer thought. How could you argue with the man's passion and candor?

Someone's cell phone made a muffled sound. Not hers, Summer realized.

Cara searched her pockets and pulled out her phone. After a moment her eyes brightened. "Amanda? Yes, we got here not too long ago. Tate's right here, and the girls are fine. Yes, I'm fine. The dress?" Cara cleared her throat. "Oh, everything went beautifully. I'm sure you'll be surprised." She looked at Tate and shrugged slightly. "No, I didn't choose the tulip skirt. No, not the *peau de soie,* either. That might be a little too formal for a ranch wedding, don't you think?" Cara smiled when Tate reached out to twine his fingers through hers.

"Tell my mother to bugger off," Tate whispered. "I don't give a damn what you wear, just as long as you're there and you say yes when asked."

Cara rolled her eyes at Tate, shaking her head. "Yes, Amanda, the girls' dresses are done. They're lovely. No, I didn't choose the strapless pink gowns."

As more questions flowed from the phone, Tate turned to Summer. "My mother always wanted to be a wedding planner," he whispered. "If she had her way, we'd have a white-tie affair, followed by a nice, cozy reception for about five thousand of her intimate friends."

Cara tried not to laugh when she heard his muttered comments. "Hold on, Amanda, I've got another call coming in." She pressed a button, transferring to the new call.

Immediately her body went rigid, her face fading to

stark white. "No," she said hoarsely. "It won't work. You don't frighten me."

Another threatening call.

With a curse, Tate lunged forward, grabbing the phone. "Who the hell is this?"

Summer shook her head at Tate, who ignored her.

"What kind of worm are you? By God, I'll—" The line went dead. "Why did you cut me off?" he snapped at Summer, who took the phone from his rigid fingers.

"You know the drill, Senator. They feed on anger and fear. Deny contact and you deny the gratification of any response."

"To hell with the drill. Cara's been hurt enough. This has got to stop."

"We're working on that, sir. But temper and emotion don't help."

Furious, Tate leaned forward, slamming a fist on the table. Then, just as suddenly, he recovered himself. "Fine. You're right, I suppose."

"What was the message this time, Cara?"

"How pretty Sophy was in her dance clothes and how Audra caused a scene when she disappeared at the museum today." Cara stared down at her rigid fingers. "He said I'd never see him, but he's always watching, always close. He said he's watching right now." She closed her eyes. "He wants to meet me."

Tate stifled a curse. "If you even consider it, I'll—"

Cara managed a wan smile. "I may be terrified, but I'm not crazy."

"You're not meeting anyone," Summer said flatly. "From now on, I'll take your calls at home when you're here. We need to sever all his links, rile him up, and then wait for him to make a mistake."

"What else do you suggest?" Tate covered Cara's hands carefully.

"I'd like to assign a monitored cell line so we can trace his calls in real time. He's fast at dumping phones, but if we establish a pattern of call locations, we'll narrow the field. If he calls often enough, we'll track him by his pattern."

Cara nodded slowly, though Summer could see how she hated to give up her privacy. "What else?"

"Tonight your biggest job is to rest. Your girls need you healthy and clearheaded. So does your job."

"Do you need something to sleep?" Tate asked. "If so, I can get you a prescription."

Cara shook her head and stood up. "Does anyone want to join me in some warm milk? It always seems to work for Audra and Sophy."

"I'll pass." Summer was glad to see Cara busy rather than pale and brooding. "By the way, Senator, you might want to phone your mother, since she was cut off."

"Damn, I completely forgot. I'll tell her I had an urgent call that came in on your phone, honey."

Summer got up to help Cara while he placed his call. "Are you okay with this?" she asked quietly. "I can get additional security here, if you want."

"Do you think that's necessary?"

"At this point, no."

Cara stirred the milk as it began to bubble. "Then don't. Your other ideas were good. Let's see what develops."

Behind them, Tate hung up. "World War III averted. Amanda will call you tomorrow, honey. She wants more details on your dress." He glanced out into the darkness. "And you might as well know that I've taken steps of my own. I've hired someone to keep an eye on you and the girls."

"You did what?" Cara frowned at him. "You should have asked me first, Tate."

"Maybe I could say the same thing about you calling in the FBI. But there's no use arguing. The man I've selected is a pro, and he'll get the job done."

Like a good prosecutor, Cara seemed to be sorting through every nuance of his statement. "Can we trust him?"

"Without question. I've known his family forever and his record is impeccable. They don't come any better."

"Having another stranger around will upset the girls terribly, Tate."

"Just hear me out. Then we'll decide what's best."

Summer didn't like the idea. Wild cards made her uneasy. "You've run a complete background check, sir? If you pick the wrong man, this could backfire badly."

"I'm aware of that." Senator Winslow watched Cara pour hot milk into a cup. "Don't worry, the girls will like him. So will you."

Summer heard quiet footsteps out on the porch. Three light taps came at the door.

Odd that there had been no sound of a car. Probably the senator had contacted an old law school crony with a few years in the reserves and a yen to play James Bond, but too many players put any mission at risk—especially when the players were amateurs.

She tried to think of a simple way to hatchet the plan without upsetting the senator. Because hatchet it she would, without question.

When Tate went to the door, Summer leaned forward, trying to see outside. The senator moved aside, clasping a broad shoulder encased in a worn gray sweatshirt.

The sweatshirt and the well-muscled shoulder belonged to Gabe Morgan.

Summer sat back, frowning. "But you told me that you were—"

"Gabe Morgan, landscape and general contracting. That was my arranged cover. Under the circumstances, the fewer people who know my real status, the better. But I've been watching you work and the way you carry yourself. I'd say you're a professional."

Summer nodded curtly. "FBI. We need another professional on the grounds, not an amateur." Summer watched Gabe's eyes narrow, growing frosty.

She ignored his scowl as small details fell into place. The memory of how he stood in a motionless stance, legs slightly apart, weight perfectly balanced. The way he always kept his left side to the senator, so his right arm was free. The way his sweatshirt bagged slightly at his waistband.

The man was carrying, she realized. And the man was a pro.

Even now he stood wary, powerful and silent in the doorway. This was no ex-law-school pal. Gabe Morgan was in prime physical shape, and he carried more than a few scars on those powerful shoulders she'd glimpsed as he emerged from her shower.

The cold professionalism in his eyes, gave away no secrets and Summer wondered how many men had stared into those cold eyes as they'd fought a swift, silent death. "Well, that little joke is on me." Summer's tone made it clear that no more jokes would get past her.

The senator motioned Gabe to bring up a chair. "Sorry, Cara, but we knew it would only make you more jumpy. When you told me about the box, Gabe and I decided it was time to bring you into the loop."

Cara's voice was icy. "So all this time you were working for Tate? How nice of you both."

"Gabe is here as a personal favor, honey." The senator took her hand. "I know how hard this is, and believe me, I know exactly how much it hurts to give up your privacy. But Gabe has plans on how to upgrade the security here. I've got to make some calls, and I'd appreciate if you'd hear him out before you snap off his head and mine."

Cara poured Gabe a cup of tea and held it out. "Nothing personal, but I'm trying to keep my head above water, and it keeps getting harder."

Gabe took the cup with a nod. "Understood, ma'am. You've got your job to maintain and your family to protect. I can help you do that, but you'll have to take precautions." Gabe looked at the senator, who nodded and left the room, cell phone to his ear.

"What kind of precautions?" Cara asked quietly.

"Tomorrow you have a new lock installed at your office." He sat back, fingers clasped. "Keys only to you and your assistant. I've had her checked out, by the way, and she looks clean."

Cara made an irritated sound, then shook her head. "Em would murder me if she knew. Go on, Mr. Morgan. Let's hear the rest."

"No one in or out of your office without your approval, and all visitors announced by your assistant."

"Ms. Mulvaney advised the same thing."

Gabe looked at Summer. "I'm glad to hear it. Next, I'd like a list of everyone entering your building today, along with everyone who works on your floor."

Cara tapped the paper in front of her. "Here's the floor list. I'll have the complete building roster tomorrow."

"I assume there are security cameras in place."

"Not that I know of." Cara frowned. "They may be hidden, of course."

Summer made a note in her book to rush a requisition of all security tapes for Cara's building.

"Possibly," Gabe continued. "Most public buildings have multiple levels of surveillance since 9/11."

"I can ask—"

"No need. I'll make a few calls tomorrow. The fewer people involved, the better."

The man was pretty good, Summer thought grudgingly. Was he CIA? Quantico HRT? Secret Service? With the senator's connections, he could be any one of the three. But even then, she didn't like the thought of turning over her responsibility for the family.

Gabe pulled a blueprint out of his black ballistic nylon bag and anchored the sheet with teacups. "The main points of access to the house are here and here. I've added an exterior motion detector by the rear kitchen door and put in an alarm to sound in my quarters. I also suggest glass-break sensors on all the downstairs windows. To be absolutely safe, the upstairs windows should be wired, too, but that's your call."

"Go ahead," Cara said tightly.

Gabe tapped six more points on the blueprint. "I'll install monitors on all your major downstairs windows. These should be operational by tomorrow morning."

The bushes outside those windows limited the range of efficiency for motion detectors, Summer knew. "Pressure plates, I take it?"

"Set to notify me wherever I am. I'll relay any information to you, of course."

Summer pointed to one corner of the blueprint. "There's a cellar on the west side of the house that needs to be blocked off. I checked earlier and found no interior access, but I want a more careful look tomorrow."

There was a hint of respect in Gabe's eyes. "So you noticed that. We'll check it out together."

Not a polite suggestion, but a command.

Summer frowned at Gabe. "What about these small windows near the pantry and the first-floor landing?"

"I'm setting up an interior motion detector to cover that area, but I doubt anyone will try for access there. The windows are too small."

"Second floor?" Summer shot back. "There are eighteen windows up there."

"A realtor's dream and a security nightmare." Gabe looked at Cara. "I'd suggest wireless monitors upstairs."

"Do it."

"That means no more sleeping with the windows opened."

Cara smiled grimly. "Summer has already given me an ultimatum about that."

"What about that big tree outside Audra's window?" Summer tapped the blueprint. "A well-trained intruder could be across a branch and inside in seconds."

Gabe's eyes narrowed. "I've got someone coming by tomorrow. He'll see to it that there are no branches with access to the windows or the roof."

You're good, Mr. Morgan, Summer thought. *But I'm better.* "There's also the small balcony off Ms. O'Connor's bedroom. Access is possible via the garage roof."

"Already noted. I'd like to nail that balcony door shut. Then I suggest we wire the porch and roof with motion sensors."

The senator returned and sat down next to Cara, who looked more tired than ever. "Do what you have to," she said. "I find I'm not in the mood to use the porch anymore."

Summer pushed aside her tea. "What else?"

"I've set up a surveillance camera on the front door." Gabe's eyes narrowed. "It's imperative that all of you check outside before opening the door."

Cara nodded slowly. "I'll talk to the girls. Thank God, tomorrow's Friday, and I'll have the weekend to explain to them. We're going to have to postpone the ceremony, too." She took a deep breath. "More calls to make and questions to answer."

Gabe glanced at Tate Winslow.

Uh-oh, Summer thought. *What next?*

"We'll discuss postponing the wedding later."

The senator cleared his throat. "I want to take you and the girls up to the ranch in Wyoming this weekend, Cara. You know how quiet it is and how much the girls love riding. It will be better if Gabe's team can tackle all these security upgrades without interference."

"Go to the ranch? But—"

"I'll fly us up." Tate slid his arm around her shoulders. "We can be there in time for a late dinner and my ranch hands will provide all the security we need. No one will get past Bud and his men."

Gabe's jaw worked up and down, which left Summer thinking he didn't like this part of the plan. "Sir? May I remind you that these men are not professionals."

"You've made your point, Gabe. But we'll handle this part my way."

There was a momentary silence. "Understood."

"Ms. Mulvaney can help the girls pack tomorrow so they'll be ready. After breathing in that clear mountain air and taking in a few world-class sunsets, you'll feel like a new woman."

"I hate it when you *manage* me," Cara said. "But the ranch sounds like heaven."

"One more thing. What if Gabe and Ms. Mulvaney take a little trip of their own?" Tate took her hands. "Down to Mexico."

Cara stiffened. "Absolutely not."

"We need them to check out the clinic. This is the best time, while we have a security team here at the house and the girls safe with us at the ranch."

"No." Cara frowned. "It could be very dangerous."

"We'll have a good cover story," Tate cut in. "Gabe had done some research on the place. Ms. Mulvaney could pose as his wife while he investigates the programs at the clinic. They will, of course, need to look around and scrutinize the facilities."

Gabe sat forward, nodding. "While we're there, I would plan to make contact with one of the clinic's staff, who may have information for us."

Cara closed her eyes. "Even in prison, Costello is a dangerous man. Assuming that he's behind this, he'll have people watching the clinic. Probably informers among the staff, too."

"Honey, you can count on Gabe to get in and get out without being detected."

"And Summer?"

"I'll see that she's safe, ma'am." His face expressionless, Gabe pulled a map from his nylon bag. "Say the word and we start our preparations."

Cara stood up slowly. "I wish I had another choice, but I don't."

"In that case, we'll leave you to it." Tate nodded at Summer, then followed Cara out into the hall, where their voices drifted away.

Summer drummed a hand lightly on the table. "Just for

the record, I'm not window dressing, Morgan. If this is going to work, you need my help."

"And I assume I'll get it." Gabe unrolled a map of Mexico. "But I also made a promise that you wouldn't be put at risk. You'd strictly be present as my cover."

"I'm releasing you from that promise. I'm trained, and I can protect my own butt perfectly well. Meanwhile, I've got security rounds to make."

Gabe followed in silence as Summer keyed the alarm for a delayed exit. The alarm light began to blink, and he remained at the door, waiting for her to leave first.

"Is this turning into some kind of infantile testosterone match?" Summer's voice was tight.

The alarm continued to count down.

"Well?"

"Not on my part." Gabe muttered something under his breath and walked out in front of her. "But when the testosterone starts flying, you'll definitely know it."

chapter 11

Upstairs in the small room at the north end of the house, Audra eased out of bed, fully dressed. Liberace raised his head as she passed, then settled back down in his cage. Down the corridor her mother was speaking quietly with the senator as they stood outside the master bedroom.

Funny, the way the two of them acted. Like lovers, only trying hard to hide it.

But Audra wasn't a kid. She saw how they looked at each other and how they kissed with a lot of tongue when they thought no one was watching. Audra was pretty sure they were sleeping together, but not here in her mother's house. Probably they went somewhere else, like maybe the senator's town house or even to a hotel.

Thinking about that made Audra feel hot and funny. She didn't like it when her friends asked her things about the senator, like wasn't he handsome and did she think he was a good kisser. For God's sake, he was going to be her stepfather, so what was she supposed to say?

But underneath Audra was curious, even though she didn't want to be. Her best friend, Tracey Van Doren, said that being curious about sex was no big deal. *Her* mother had been married four times and since each husband was younger than the last, Tracey had been curious a *lot*.

Audra wondered how it felt, having a man all the way, completely inside you. Sure, she'd done some experimenting with boys. Some of them were friends of Tracey's, and the kissing had been exciting and really cool. But the other stuff had gotten weird. Afterward, she'd felt—

Empty.

She frowned at the darkness, listening to her mother's door close. Were they finally going to give in and stop this stupid charade that they weren't *really* lovers?

Audra heard low footsteps in the hall, then the senator's quiet voice as he passed her door. Talking on his cell phone, probably to Washington or Paris or Bangkok. She had to keep reminding herself how *important* he was. And she liked him—*really* liked him, almost more than she could remember liking her real father, who had been a jerk. Especially when he was drinking.

Audra didn't want to screw things up, either. Her mom was pretty cool—for a mom. She deserved to be happy with an important man like the senator, who could actually sit and *listen* to what you had to say without smirking and being clueless like most grown-ups.

Down inside her jacket her cell phone chirped loudly. *Damn.*

Audra answered quickly, keeping her voice low. *"What?"*

"Hey, I've been waiting down here on this damned lawn for twenty minutes, freezing my butt off." Tracey sounded irritated. "Where the hell are you?"

"My mom just got to sleep, okay?"

"No shit. Is he banging her right there in the house?"

"Shut up, Tracey." It bothered Audra a lot when her friend said dumb things like that. Worst of all, it made

Audra feel like some kind of traitor. But they had been friends since they were three, and Audra was pretty sure Tracey didn't mean it. All the tough words were just a cover for The Fear.

Audra had it sometimes, too.

The Fear came when you were certain the other kids laughed about your clothes or your breath or the size of your butt. It came when you were certain your parents would do something ridiculously uncool and make *everyone* point at you and snicker.

Most of all, it came when you felt like Audra did now—alone.

Invisible.

Stupid and clumsy, like no one else had ever understood you or ever could, because you were like from Pluto and everyone else was from Muncie, Indiana.

"Ground control to space head."

"Shut up," Audra hissed into the phone, easing open the window next to the big tree on the lawn. "I'm coming out now. See you in two minutes."

"About time."

The line went dead.

Audra pulled out a black fire ladder and dangled it from the window, looping the metal clamps over the sill. The ladder was Tracey's, courtesy of stepfather #3, who had been in the insurance business and had a fixation about house fires, maybe because he hated to pay up afterward. He'd been a real cheapskate, Tracey had said, but he knew about how to get out of a house fast.

Like all the other times, the ladder worked like a dream, falling silently and unrolling to its full length. Audra shut off her cell phone and stuck it in her pocket, then worked her way over the sill. Turning carefully, she pulled the window almost shut and then began to pick her way down. Five feet from the ground, she jumped clear, then made her way along a little space behind the bougainvillaeas.

Tracey was sitting on the ground near a big jade plant at the edge of the garage. Huge earphones framed her face as she bobbed her head to unheard music.

"Let's go," Audra hissed. "And be quiet, because the senator hasn't left yet."

"No shit." Tracey brushed off the back of her skintight denim skirt. "Let's go pay a late-night visit. I mean, the man is *such* a stud. Even my mom says she'd be open to a little Oval Office sex with him."

"Shut *up,* Tracey." Audra stamped off toward the driveway.

"Hey, I'm sorry, okay?" Tracey caught up and grabbed her arm. "I keep forgetting he's going to be your *father.* Stepfather, anyway."

"It feels creepy when you talk that way." Audra jerked free. "Like you don't care about yourself or anyone else."

"Yeah, well, maybe I don't care much about other people because they suck, but we're best friends, right? We stick together no matter what." Tracey's face was pale and pinched in the moonlight. *"Right?"*

"Sure." Audra shrugged, feeling uneasy the way she always did when her friend acted odd and hyper like this. "Let's get out of here. If someone sees me, I'll be grounded for the next *century.*"

They picked their way behind another set of bushes, expertly avoiding the gravel. A few minutes later they came to a broad screened porch behind Tracey's house.

Audra sat down on a wicker chair in the darkness, fingering her cell phone. "I think I'll call that cute guy from my biology lab."

"You think he'll come out?"

Audra shrugged. "Maybe. Or maybe we could just talk for a while. I'm only staying thirty minutes, remember? My mom's still mad at me after what happened at the museum today. She's been so hyper lately," Audra said in disgust.

"At least your mom notices what you do." Tracey paced in the darkness. "Last night I didn't come home until almost five. Believe me, they don't give Girl Scout badges for the stuff I was doing."

Audra looked away, angry at the way the excitement had gone out of the night, leaving her empty again, feeling *guilty* though she'd done nothing wrong except sneak outside to keep her friend company. "Big deal."

Tracey dropped into a swing near the door. "*You're* no damned fun, that's for sure."

Audra shivered in the darkness, feeling more alone than ever. Facing The Fear.

Sometimes she almost wished she were a kid again, when her only worries were getting her braids straight and remembering where she'd hidden her Little Pony diary.

But mostly Audra wished she were completely grown-up. Then she'd never feel alone and afraid again.

"Want a cigarette?" Tracey tossed something through the darkness.

"Sure." Everything else so far had been a real bust, Audra thought. Her stomach growled, and she ignored it.

Twenty minutes later Tracey was in the middle of her third cigarette and a hectic story about the football player who had groped her after gym class.

Audra glared down at the fluorescent numbers on the watch her mother had given her for her fourteenth birthday.

To hell with Tracey and her stupid stories. She was going home. Sneaking out like this was dangerous—not that there had been any crimes on this street for ages, but Audra knew something was worrying her mom, making her hyper.

Probably some case at work. Though her mom never discussed her job, Audra knew she had to face down angry men and ugly crimes. Secretly, Audra was proud of her mom for doing stuff like that, for being so strong, because sometimes those men went to jail. Then they wanted revenge against the people who'd put them there.

That meant her mother.

They never talked about stuff like that, though. Probably her mother thought she was still a kid and wouldn't understand. Or maybe she didn't *want* her to understand, because understanding changed you.

Audra shivered a little, pulling her jacket tighter as she studied the darkness. She'd called the guy from her biology lab but he sounded odd, so she'd hung up. Probably he'd tell the other kids and they'd all laugh at her. On top of that, the cigarettes were making her stomach churn. She'd have to ditch her clothes and change, or her mother would smell the smoke.

Well, to hell with that.

Audra stood up, scowling—and when she did, someone grabbed her hard from behind, cutting off her breath.

chapter 12

Summer punched on the lights in the guest cottage. "I want to see exactly where you're installing the infrared sensors for the beach access."

Gabe dropped the blueprints onto her desk. "Be my guest."

Summer peered at the diagrams intently. "Along the main path?"

"For starters. More sensors will go near the garage. They're marked by the broken lines on the diagram."

Summer peered some more, then dug into her briefcase. Muttering, she slid on a pair of glasses.

"Reading glasses?"

"One more word and you're toast, Morgan."

Gabe sat down in an overstuffed leather chair and stretched out his long legs. "In that case, no comment from me."

"Good." Summer ran her fingers slowly over the diagram, as if feeling her way over possibilities and dangers. "This array should cover everything."

Gabe held back as long as he could. "Aren't you a little young for reading glasses?"

Summer ignored him. "We need more surveillance

cameras, one at the back porch and one along the path near the garage. The bushes make it hard to see anyone coming up from the road."

"I already asked. Ms. O'Connor nixed the additional cameras. The senator is going to work on her, but for now she says they're too intrusive." Gabe crossed his arms behind his head. "What gives with the glasses?"

"It's genetic." Summer shoved a strand of hair behind her ear, frowning. "My dad had the same thing. Hit him hard when he was thirty. He hated it." She looked off into space for a moment. "I was going to get the surgery, then this mission came up and everything got put on hold." She toyed with her wrist. "Who is the team handling the upgrades?"

"They're reliable, don't worry."

"It's my job to worry." Summer rubbed her neck. "Are they civilians?"

"Yes and no."

"What's that supposed to mean?"

"It means, the matter is taken care of. No more questions needed."

She swung around, staring at him. "In case you forgot, I'm a federal agent. It's my job to ask questions."

"Fine. You asked, and that's my answer."

"So he's really hush-hush." Summer nodded slowly. "In that case, it's fine with me. Just as long as he's good."

"He's so good that you've never heard of him. And you never will."

"Are you in the CIA? SWAT maybe?"

Gabe shrugged. "I'm a professional. That's all you need to know."

"Not by half. What are you looking at?"

Gabe steepled his fingers. "You. I'm trying to figure you out."

"Don't bother. I'm as dull and boring as they come, Morgan. I do the job and then I go home."

Gabe watched the smooth curve of her neck when she lifted her hair. He saw the muscles tighten at her thigh when she leaned over the desk. No, she was wrong. He had a ticklish instinct that she was far from boring once you got beneath all that spit-polish and edgy nerve.

Not that he'd ever get there or see her in anything but an ugly, plain-Jane dark suit.

Irritated that he couldn't seem to stop imagining Summer Mulvaney with her hair loose, her lips soft, dressed in something light and gauzy, Gabe stood up and checked his watch. "Time for a grounds check. I won't be comfortable until that new equipment is online. Right now a Russian tank battalion could probably get in here."

Summer pulled off her glasses. "I'll go with you."

Gabe opened his mouth to nix the idea, then stopped. She *was* assigned to Cara O'Connor and her family, and that made them partners.

Whether he liked it or not.

He pulled on a black nylon knapsack. "Let's get moving." He looked at her feet and nodded. "Rubber soles. Good."

"I know my job, Mr. Morgan."

Gabe smiled blandly. *We'll see about that.*

Audra's heart was pounding. She twisted hard, then gasped. "What are you *doing* here?" A small hand gripped her tightly, half-hidden in the bushes. "If Mom finds you outside, she'll kill us both."

Sophy held Liberace against her chest, shivering. "I heard a noise. When I went to your room you were gone, so I checked the window."

"I closed it," Audra snapped.

Behind her Tracey snorted. "Busted."

"The window wasn't completely closed, not quite. I saw the rope you used to raise and lower the ladder, too. It was still hidden in the tree branches. But I already knew something was wrong. And since I knew that Tracey sneaks out at night—"

"How do you know *that*?" Audra demanded.

"I just knew."

Tracey sprawled on a pink chaise, laughing. "Good work, Sophy. You ought to be a spy. Want a Camel?"

"Shut up, Tracey." Audra glared at her friend.

"*No.* I want to hear about Sophy and this stuff she knows. How does it work, Sophy?"

The younger girl chewed her lip. "I don't plan it, but it comes and goes. It's like the TV channels in a storm, you know? The picture can get wavy, but you can still see it."

"Let's go, Sophy." Audra was angry at her friend, but some part of her was still curious, unable to stop picturing exactly what Tracey and her mystery friend did when they sneaked outside at night. Was that abnormal? Audra wondered. Did you go to hell for having too much curiosity and too many bad thoughts?

"Chickens," Tracey called as the girls crossed the porch.

"I don't like it when you smoke." Sophy stroked Liberace's head. "I don't like Tracey very much, either. She's going to get in trouble someday. Besides, she's too old to be your friend."

"She's only a year older than I am."

"But she acts a lot older."

"Why don't you like her?" Audra demanded.

Sophy shrugged. "Just because."

"Did something happen?" Audra was seized by a flood of dark possibilities. "Did she do something to you?"

Sophy continued walking. "No, she just gives me the creeps. She doesn't like herself very much; you can see it in her eyes. One day I saw her talking to Uncle Tate, only she was acting odd."

Even though he wasn't their uncle, Sophy called him that. Audra thought it was stupid, but it was better than Dad, which just didn't feel right. "Talking about what?"

"I couldn't hear. But she was laughing and touching his arm, and then he looked mad and he said something back to her and then her face got red. She walked away really fast." Sophy looked up at her sister. "Uncle Tate just stared after her for a long time. He didn't look happy, either."

Audra had a cold, sick feeling in her stomach. Maybe she wouldn't see Tracey anymore. Maybe that was best.

"Come on," Sophy said impatiently. "It's late, but we can sneak down to the kitchen. Patrick left us some German chocolate cake."

"I don't want any," Audra said tensely. She couldn't stop thinking about Tracey and Senator Winslow. What if they were—

Without warning, Liberace wriggled out of Sophy's grip and shot along a low branch of the tree. Audra went after him while Sophy giggled.

Somewhere a clock chimed quietly in the depths of the night.

chapter 13

Mist swirled up from the beach as Summer walked down the flagstone path to the pool. The perfume of roses was intense here, reminding her of early summer nights back in Philadelphia.

There was no sign of activity in the outbuildings, or down the path to the rocky beach. All the ground-floor windows of the house were closed and locked.

Summer wasn't surprised to see Gabe pull out night-vision glasses and sweep the area a complete 360 degrees. "Everything nailed down tight," he said finally, stowing the glasses in his pack.

"In that case, I'm going inside. I want to recheck the windows in the kitchen and be sure the alarm is still set."

Without a word, Gabe turned, cutting across the tennis courts.

"You're not asking why?" Summer said quietly.

"I never question thoroughness."

Summer hid her surprise and rolled her shoulders, trying to work off some of her tension. "What time is it?"

"Almost one." Gabe moved with powerful grace, his footsteps silent on the damp grass. "I'll take the next circuit. We can rotate."

Summer raised an eyebrow. "You trust me to handle things?"

"You're the officer assigned. That means I have to trust you. It also means—" He turned suddenly, pulling her back against the corner of the garage as gravel skittered down the road. Car lights flickered through the mist, and Gabe's arm dropped to her waist, drawing her out of sight while the lights moved in a slow arc over the grass.

As the beams traced the wall only inches away from where they stood, Summer planned defensive scenarios in the event of gunfire from the car. At the same time she reached down, finding the handle of her service weapon.

If a door opened, she was ready to roll.

But no door opened. No footsteps crossed the gravel. The car moved slowly down the road, its lights fading back into the night. Summer felt the bushes twitch beside her and realized Gabe was gone. Releasing her handgun, she peered around the corner of the garage.

He emerged like a wall of shadow out of the fog, his expression grim. "I only got the last three letters on the plate, but I'll check it anyway. It could have been a local resident taking the wrong turn."

"At one A.M.?"

"Not everyone's a criminal." Gabe looked down, frowning. "Don't move."

Summer swung her head, assessing threat scenarios. "Did you hear something? Why are you—" Her voice caught in a gasp of pain as something dug into her scalp.

"Organpipe cactus. I didn't see it until you backed into it." Gabe leaned down, tugging gently to release her hair from the spines. "These things can be hell to get out."

Summer stood awkwardly, her hair caught in a dozen places. "Just get them," she said tensely.

"Slow is the only way. Otherwise they dig in deeper."

"Forget about slow. Yank them out." As she spoke, Summer twisted her head right and left, only to find her hair seized by dozens of new needles.

"Stop *moving.*" Gabe caught her hands, then clicked on a penlight with a red bulb and studied the damage. "Nice job, Mulvaney."

"What?"

"Your hands are going to be a problem. And your hair—forget working your hair free. I may have to cut it."

"Fine. It's just hair."

Gabe produced a big army knife. As he leaned over her, Summer felt his warm breath on her cheek and the brush of his hard thighs. "Don't get twitchy on me or you may end up bald."

She closed her eyes, stunned by the sharp awareness of his body pressed against hers. The knife moved, then tugged hard.

"Sorry if that hurt."

"I'm—fine. Just get it done." Summer tried to focus on anything but the rigid torso against her belly. Hair drifted onto her arm while he sliced down, strand by strand.

The silence of the night was suddenly far too intimate. "Can't you work faster?"

"No." Another hunk of hair fell on her arm. "I can barely see, so I'm going by feel alone. I'm *trying* to spare some of your hair."

"Forget about that and hurry. I want to go check the house."

Gabe made an irritated sound as he located another cluster of cactus needles. More hair fell onto Summer's arm.

She shifted restlessly, and Gabe gripped her shoulder. "I told you not to move."

"Fine, fine. I won't move. I won't even breathe, Attila."

More hair rained down, and then Gabe cradled her chin. "Last one. Hold still, because this could be the worst."

There was a sudden, sharp tug at her scalp. Muttering darkly, Gabe knifed through a tangle of hair and held it up gravely. "Cactus three, Summer zero." He dropped the hair on the grass. "All done."

When Summer turned her head, she was finally free, but her jacket was still stuck to the cactus. Impatiently, she shrugged off both sleeves and scowled when the jacket stayed right where it was, impaled on the sharp spines. Ragged pieces of hair hung above the jacket, making a ghostly doppelganger in the night. "I've got cactus spines everywhere." Shaking her head, she started up the flagstone path to the back door. "But at least I'm free for my round."

"You take the inside, I'll take the porch and roof." Gabe's voice trailed away as he vanished into the darkness before she could speak.

Summer inspected the ground floor, then headed upstairs. All the bedroom doors were closed and there was no sign of activity. After checking that the common windows were locked, she reset the alarm and left via the back door.

Gabe was waiting for her on the porch. "Any problems inside?"

"All quiet." Summer frowned. "Except for my skin, which is howling from those cactus thorns. I've got to get these things out before I go crazy."

"There's an old trick. I can show you."

I'll bet you know all the tricks, Summer thought dourly.

At the steps to his guesthouse she turned and kept walking. " 'Night, Morgan."

"You don't want any help?"

"If I can't handle a few cactus spines, I might as well hand in my badge. Thanks for the offer, but I'll see you in the morning."

She tried pulling them out with tweezers. She tried digging them out with a needle. Both ways were slow, painful, and largely ineffective.

The final blow came when she brushed back a strand of hair—and ended up with tiny cactus spines scattered painfully across her face.

Thirty seconds later she was hammering on Gabe's door with her elbow.

He took one look at her and stepped aside. If the man laughed, she was going to deck him.

"You were right; I was wrong," she muttered.

"Not a problem. Sit in the chair by the desk." Gabe vanished into the bathroom and emerged with a travel kit. He bent beside her and angled the gooseneck lamp, then shook his head. "You've got them everywhere. They must hurt like hell." His hands were gentle as he tilted her face back. "Close your eyes and relax."

Relax?

Summer took a deep breath, felt the light turn, warm on her face. Fingers brushed her brow.

"Better start with your hands." Gently, Gabe cupped her palm. "This shouldn't be too bad. Only a dozen here." Wielding a set of surgical tweezers, he worked methodically across her palm, pulling out spines of all sizes. When he was done, he cut a piece of electrical tape and pulled out the rest. "The tape's the old Arizona secret. Let's see your other hand."

As he spoke, Summer felt him wedge her body between his thighs. The man was amazingly strong, with defined muscles that made her just a little giddy. To make matters worse, when she looked up, his face was only inches away as he tackled an especially large spine.

Her hip bumped his groin. When she tried to turn away, she bumped him again.

His lips curved slightly. "If you're trying to distract me, you're succeeding."

Summer took a slow breath, keenly aware of his body holding her. "I'm not trying."

"You're still succeeding."

She didn't know what to say. The strange thing was that men's bodies didn't usually excite her. Usually intelligence and a sense of humor caught her attention first.

But very few men had bodies like Gabe's. He was dressed in well-worn navy sweatpants and no shirt, and Summer could feel every sculpted muscle like a blast of heat.

Which was absolutely *pathetic.*

She cleared her throat. "Aren't you done yet?"

"Three more." He bracketed her body with his locked thighs. "These two along your neck may hurt."

Not as much as seeing his abs only inches away.

"Hey." Summer winced as he pulled a nasty black spine free. "How come you know so much about these things?"

Gabe didn't look up, angling the light down for a better view as he extracted another long barb. "I was born in Arizona. My parents moved to Wyoming when I was seven."

"When did you meet the senator? He told us that he'd known your family forever."

Gabe looked up and flashed a smile. "He's got forty acres in Wyoming, right across the valley from the ranch where I grew up. He used to spend all his free time there. Of course, now he has no more free time left."

Summer tried to stop the odd, dizzy sensation of bubbles climbing up her throat. She found herself staring at Gabe's callused hands, which was even worse, because she realized how gentle he could be, calluses and all. "It's good that he's taking Cara and the girls away to the ranch for a few days. They could all use some R and R. So it's pretty nice, this valley of yours?"

"Spring-fed lake. Mountains and white-water rafting. You can ride for four days and not see a single road."

"Ride an ATV?"

Gabe gave an exasperated laugh. "A horse, woman. The *only* way to travel in the backcountry."

"Somehow I can't imagine a techno guy like you on top of a horse."

"Some things are best done the old-fashioned way. From a saddle, you can feel the wind and smell the sap rise in the pine trees."

"You miss it, don't you?"

Gabe didn't answer.

Summer felt a burning pain at the base of her thumb. "Ow."

Gabe held up his tweezers, gripping a long, barbed needle. "Got it."

"No wonder it hurt."

When she started to stand up, Gabe stopped her. "Let me clean you up." He opened an antiseptic wipe, dabbing it over her hands and neck.

"I, uh, appreciate it." Summer nudged him aside and stood up awkwardly. "Your help, I mean."

Gabe stood, too, cupping her chin. "Did you rub your face?"

"Maybe. Why?"

"You've got a needle on your lip." Frowning, he ran his hand along her cheek. "Give me a second."

Summer was intensely aware of every inch of his body as he bent closer. "Get it," she rasped.

"Don't move."

She closed her eyes as his finger skimmed the curve of her lower lip. Their thighs bumped and Summer's heart began to pound. "Can't you hurry?"

She heard his breath still. There was a quick, sharp prick at her lip.

Gabe cursed. "It's bleeding. Your lip must be—" He cleared his throat. "Sensitive. At your mouth, I mean." He leaned back. "Here's a swab. Probably you can handle that part yourself." His voice sounded strained.

Summer grabbed the square of white cotton and jammed it against her mouth, then gasped in pain.

"Watch it." Gabe pulled the cotton free and brushed her lip. "You always do things the hard way, don't you?"

"Not that I'm aware of."

"And you don't trust people very much, either."

"That's ridiculous," Summer said stiffly.

"Then why are your hands locked into fists right now?"

"I don't—" When Summer looked down, she was stunned to see that her hands were raised, fisted against his chest. She looked away. "Okay, so maybe I do have a few trust issues."

"Anything you want to discuss?" he asked quietly.

Summer felt more zinging sensations in her chest. She realized his hand wasn't quite steady at her mouth, and something shimmered to life, vague and powerful, drawing her closer.

Abruptly, Gabe stood up and tossed the strip of cotton into the garbage. "You'd better beat it. You've got security rounds in fifty-three minutes."

Summer ran her tongue across her lip, which still stung. To her irritation, the fuzzy, disoriented feeling was getting worse. "Thanks." Her gaze slid to his rumpled bed, where two pillows were pulled together in a mound, the blanket folded back in a crooked line.

She could imagine him sleeping there, one arm behind his head and the covers half-off. She wondered what he would be wearing beneath that single thin sheet.

Serious mental aberration.

She turned stiffly, certain that her cheeks were bright red.

"Summer?"

She didn't look around. "Yes?"

"Call me if you need anything tonight."

Only a fool would have found a double meaning in those words. "I'll be fine."

Summer closed the door stiffly. If there was one thing she had learned well, it was that relying on other people was a sure prescription for pain, and she had already had enough of that in her life.

chapter 14

Audra clung to Liberace, crawling along a high branch. She could see the wall, see her own window.

Sweat crept down her neck. She was grounded now, thanks to her tricks on the new nanny. But if she were caught tonight, she'd be grounded for the rest of her life.

If I don't get caught, she swore, *I'll never sneak out again. Never ever.*

She had already lowered the ladder via her rope, and as she crept along the branch she noticed a light in the new nanny's guesthouse. Gabe was still up, too, judging by the lights in his rooms.

What if they saw her?

Seconds later the window was open, and she helped Sophy cross the sill. After that, she set Liberace down, raised the ladder and stowed it away, then tiptoed across the floor, undressed quickly, and slid into bed.

Audra's heart continued to pound madly, but as minutes passed without discovery, she gradually began to slip into sleep.

She was dreaming about surfing when a hand circled her arm.

Sophy was standing near her bed, looking frightened. A big stuffed crocodile stuck out beneath her arm.

"*What?*"

"I can't sleep. I had bad dreams again."

Audra sighed and sat up. "What is it this time, the big orange worms or the green talking cats?"

Sophy stood very still. "This time it was a man. He was standing at the foot of my bed, watching me." Sophy clutched her crocodile tighter. "Just watching."

"Who?"

"I don't know."

Audra pulled back her covers. "Dreams don't mean anything, silly. Come on, let's go to sleep."

"But he was ugly." Sophy slid into the bed, shivering as Audra pulled the covers back up. "And this dream was different. *Important,* like a warning." She lay tensely, staring through the window at the mist. "Something's going to happen, Auddie. I know it."

"Go to sleep," Audra said impatiently. "Stuff like that doesn't mean anything."

But Audra lay awake for a long time, watching shadows move against the lawn. Sophy's dreams weren't like other people's dreams. Her sister's dreams—the ones she called *important*—had a bad habit of coming true.

With a curse, Gabe shoved back his blanket and checked his watch. Summer should be finishing her second security tour shortly, and then it would be his turn.

She was one hell of a woman, Gabe thought grimly. Spit-shined and buttoned-down, hungry for action and a chance to prove herself.

All job, she had told him. But there had been vulnerability in her face, just for a second, when he'd been working that damned cactus needle out of her lip. Gabe had found himself wanting to explore her lips slowly and see what it took to coax out a sigh of pleasure.

He shook his head, fully aware that Summer Mulvaney was off-limits.

Buck naked, he trotted to the shower and swung the elegant control bar until frigid water filled the air. He barely noticed the pain in his right knee or the stiffness in his leg. The scars from his last round of surgery were finally starting to fade, but he was still far from his full fighting capacity. With luck and some serious sweat, he'd be at eighty percent by the time this mission was done.

After a quick shower, Gabe cut the water and did a slow knee bend. Ligaments tightened and muscle burned, but he savored the pain like an old friend. At one time he had despaired of recovering his mobility, and a SEAL with limited capacity was bound for a desk assignment or training responsibilities. Both were crucial tasks, but not ones that Gabe had joined the Navy to carry out, and the sooner he regained his range of motion and full strength, the sooner he'd be reassigned to the dangerous work he did best.

Grabbing a towel, he dried quickly and dressed in black shorts. His knee burned as he pulled out a locked metal case, keyed the code, and located three documents. After studying two maps thoroughly, he unrolled a set of blueprints to the clinic in Los Reyes where Cara O'Connor had been a patient in 1986.

The blueprints were dated 1983.

He punched in a number on his encrypted cell phone and waited for the recorded message to click in.

"Yeah, this is Morgan," he said. "I need a large pepperoni with double cheese, so get your butt in gear and start cooking."

He glanced at the display and smiled when his phone rang five seconds later. "You're late, Teague. I could be a dead man in five. What kept you—a hot date with a smoldering brunette?"

At the other end of the line, Ishmael Teague flipped off the microwave communication prototype he'd been testing and said one gruff phrase in answer.

Gabe barked with laughter. "Same to you, pal. I'd say in spades, but you'd probably kick me around the block."

"Damned straight. And it only took me three seconds to call back." Izzy hesitated. "How's your leg?"

"Top-notch, compadre. No pain anywhere." The lie flowed easily, but neither man believed it for a second. "I need an update on the clinic blueprints. I don't want any surprises down in Mexico, so I need to know all renovations or structural changes that have been completed. And while you're doing that hacker-magic of yours, see if you can scout out the placement of any security cameras and alarm systems. I should be able to spot most of them, but I'm taking nothing for granted."

Izzy chuckled. "You don't want to be a guest of the Mexican Federales for the next ten years?"

"Sorry, I've got better plans. As soon as I wrap up this mission for Senator Winslow, I've got two weeks' leave and I'm chartering a boat in Tortola. Are you up for some sun, sangria, and a few adventurous ladies in search of a clothing-optional escape?"

"Name the place and the time. Just get that leg of yours in shape first," Izzy said quietly. "And you'll have your blueprints in an hour or so."

"Show-off." Still smiling, Gabe hung up. Ishmael Teague was a genius at finding things most people considered invisible. If any plans were available, he would find them.

Focusing, Gabe sank into another deep knee bend. Remaining crouched, he ticked off the seconds on his watch.

The burn grew to an angry throb as he approached two minutes, but Gabe gutted out the pain, blocking the memories of the high-altitude, low-opening jump that had gone wrong months before, landing him on a rocky slope rather than a deepwater lagoon off the coast of Australia. He'd nearly bought it on that jump, thanks to an inexperienced pilot.

But Gabe Morgan was an expert at knowing his own limits. He took everything right to the edge, and was pale and sweating when he extended his bad leg into a lunge position.

Experience had taught him that pain could be your friend if you let it, and his pain was going to get him strong again, back into the action where he belonged. With that thought in mind, he closed his eyes and kept right on counting.

"Cara?"

Pacing the room, Cara cradled her phone. She was too distracted to read and too worried to sleep. "I'm still here, Tate."

"Are the girls asleep?"

"For an hour." Cara stopped at a big glass table covered with photographs. She smiled at the picture of Audra tying her first fishing lure and Sophy riding her first bike. Memories washed over her in waves as she realized how soon her precious girls would be grown up, waving her good-bye.

"Honey?"

"Sorry, Tate. I've just been thinking that I may take some time off. The girls need me now and I'm always

missing some event or other. San Francisco can get along
without me for a few years."

"You love your job, Cara. It's not something you can
walk back into easily."

"I know that." She cradled a photo of Audra and Sophy riding horses on Tate's ranch in Wyoming. "But it's a
possibility."

"You know I want you and the girls with me. But if I
run, there will be impossible hours, endless stress, and
more impossible hours."

Cara closed her eyes tightly. "You *have* to run, Tate.
You'll be our best president."

"You and my mother keep telling me that, but I'm not
so sure." Tate sighed. "I should probably go. I have a six
A.M. conference call."

"Get some rest." Cara's voice was husky. "Think of me,
wrapped around you."

"If I think of that, I'll never sleep. By the way, I called
Amanda and apologized abjectly for cutting her off. She
suggests that you take the girls up to the ranch for a few
days. I didn't tell her that we'll be there this weekend."

Cara smiled. Amanda Winslow's charm was as legendary as her stubbornness. No mother had done more to
further her son's career or welcome a new woman into his
life. "I'll call her tomorrow and say we'll set a day. The
girls will love seeing her." Cara smiled. "Did she ask you
about my dress again?"

"Only a thousand times." Tate's voice fell. "Forget
about the dress and think about how much I love you. I
wish I didn't have to wait for breakfast to see you, so I'm
going to turn off the light and think about when we finally
stop this charade and sleep in the same bed."

The line went dead, and Cara put down the phone, listening to the silence of the house. For some reason the

stillness left her uneasy, filled with fears too vague for names.

Instead of sleeping, she decided to check on Audra and Sophy, then make sure that all the doors and windows were closed. FBI agents were trained, tough professionals, but no one could be as paranoid as a mother.

chapter 15

The next morning, clouds piled in from the west as Summer turned up the front drive. Audra dumped her backpack on the seat and slid in, making room for Sophy, who carried Liberace in a cage. She'd pleaded with her mother for permission to take the pet to class for show-and-tell, but Cara had explained that ferrets were currently illegal in California. Though the regulations were based on misinformation, it wouldn't do to flaunt them, and Sophy had finally agreed to take a stuffed corduroy ferret. It wasn't half as much fun—but at least it wasn't illegal.

She still insisted that Liberace go along for the ride, safe in his cage.

Sophy's pink gloves were back in place, Summer noted, a perfect match for pink flowered capris and pink sneakers. It was a fashion look that only a nine-year-old could carry off, Summer thought wryly.

"Everything stowed? Schoolbooks, lunch boxes, ferrets?" Summer took the muttering as assent and headed down the road to school. Cara and the senator had left an hour earlier after a hurried breakfast of oatmeal, croissants, and eggs with the girls. The senator had been joined by a secretary and a senior staffer, who were staying in Carmel to prepare for a benefit the senator was hosting for a local women's crisis center.

Because today was a half-day at summer school, Summer was scheduled to pick up the girls before lunch and make sure they were packed by the time Cara returned at five-thirty.

As she stopped at the corner, she saw Audra's friend waving to them.

"I forgot, Tracey needs a ride." Audra moved over to make room, her face unreadable.

Tracey was dressed in sequined flip-flops, a midriff-baring top, and a skintight denim skirt. Interesting school uniform, Summer thought, managing a cheerful greeting as Tracey scooted in next to her friend.

"Sorry, but I missed the bus, and our BMW is in the shop. Stepfather #4 says it's the brakes, but his car knowledge sucks, so who knows?"

Audra elbowed her friend, who shrugged, then produced a pack of cigarettes from her backpack.

Sophy's eyes grew huge as Tracey flipped open a heavy gold lighter.

"Please don't smoke in the car," Summer said calmly. "Sophy has allergies, and I doubt it's good for her ferret."

Tracey sighed, but pocketed the lighter and studied Summer. "So you're—what, the new nanny?"

"That's right."

"What happened to the old one? Susanne What's-Her-Name, who laughs like a horse?"

"Ms. Broyland had appendicitis, so I came to fill in for a few weeks."

"You don't look like a nanny." Tracey sounded querulous, like a sulky child.

Summer smiled slightly. "You never know."

"And what's with your hair? It looks—weird."

Audra sighed and rolled her eyes.

"This cut? It's all the rage," Summer lied calmly. "Back East, anyway." She glanced in the rearview mirror. "Tracey, isn't it? You live one street over?"

"Yeah, that's me." The girl drummed red-tipped nails on the window. "You come from San Francisco?"

"No, I live near Philadelphia. I taught at a small women's college there."

"No shit." Tracey frowned as Audra gave her another jab with her elbow. *"What?"*

"I think Audra doesn't like your language."

"Yeah, well, sorry and all that. So what did you teach at that college?" Tracey sniggered. "Crewelwork or something doofus like that?"

"I taught serial profiling."

"Huh?"

"Analysis of criminal psychology for female police officers." Summer had decided on this story with Cara. Staying close to the truth was always the best idea.

"No sh—" Tracey crossed her arms. "I mean, no kidding. So that's like murders and stuff?"

"You got it."

"Awesome. You dig into their minds, see what makes them tick?"

Summer nodded. "You look for patterns and try to recognize when they'll do it again."

"So you've met a lot of criminals and crazy people?"

"Enough." Summer swung neatly around the corner, pulling into a spot at the side of the parking area while little girls skipped past in bright shorts and bigger girls slouched along in miniskirts and peasant blouses.

A California education, Summer thought. Free and energetic, full of talk and creativity. Nothing like the cold,

Pine-Sol–scented halls of her schools back in Pennsylvania, dominated by the click of identical polished loafers, knife-sharp pleated skirts, and silent female hierarchies.

She passed Sophy her lunch box, and the girl took it carefully, then said good-bye to her pet ferret, who made short, *chirr*ing sounds. Audra was already outside, waiting impatiently, but Tracey was still studying Summer in the rearview mirror.

"You ever kill anyone?"

"I'm not in that kind of work," Summer said blandly. It was a lie. She'd killed once and clawed through gasping nightmares for months afterward.

Tracey started to say something else, but a car horn sounded behind them. Her face closed down, sullen and unreadable. "Yeah, well—see you." She closed the door and shouldered a red leather bag that probably cost a month of Summer's wages.

The honking came again, and this time a sleek silver BMW arrowed into the spot beside Summer. A man jumped out, his baggy brown uniform distinctly out of place among the sea of bright skirts and dresses.

He called to Tracey, looking expectant, but the girl tossed back her hair and shrugged, bored as only someone who is sixteen can look. The man in brown—Tony's Autobody, according to the back of the shirt—started to talk louder, leaning in with arms moving.

Tracey was completely unimpressed, shaking her head.

Summer rolled down her window, trying to pick up some of the conversation, but Tracey shrugged and raced off toward the front entrance, while Mr. Autobody stood glaring after her.

Summer locked the SUV and followed with Sophy, checking out the area for idling cars, loitering workers, or any other potential threats. Her route brought her past the man in the Autobody uniform, who made a rude gesture in Tracey's direction, then stalked back to the BMW.

Because Cara had insisted the girls' routine stay as normal as possible, Summer hung back unobtrusively amid the chattering crowd flowing down the hall. Sophy had a violin lesson first thing, and Summer watched Audra escort her sister to the music room, where Sophy was greeted by her teacher. Then Audra continued up the stairs, headed for the language wing.

After making sure Audra entered Intermediate Spanish, Summer circled back to the front steps, pleased to see a plainclothes security guard in position. The woman would make periodic spot checks on both girls, Summer knew.

She had argued for even more supervision, but no officers could be spared without clear evidence of intended harm. That left Summer on her own, which was generally the way she preferred to work, anyway.

She checked her watch, then trotted down the steps. There was still time for a slow circuit of the school grounds before she returned to the house.

A delivery truck was backing toward the garage when Summer turned the corner in front of the O'Connor house. The driver slammed on his brakes, cursing at a snappy silver BMW that raced along the driveway and cut around him on the right.

"You got a death wish or something, moron?"

The driver of the BMW—Tony's Autobody again, Summer noted—fishtailed hard, then shot out of the car. In seconds the two men were circling and trading insults that would have made a mobster's hair curl.

After more arguing, the Autobody poster boy waved his papers in the air and pointed toward the house.

The truck driver swung up his arms. "Not here. Can't you read? This is 1221, *not* 1251." The trucker gave an angry wave at the neat brass letters on the front porch. "Now get lost, because you're costing me time, which I ain't got any extra of."

The repairman slouched to the car, ground into gear, and raced back to the road, making a rude gesture.

Headed to Tracey's house, Summer concluded. Given his number-reading abilities, she didn't place much confidence in how long the repaired BMW would hold up.

She looked up to see Gabe leaning against her window, watching the BMW.

"Whole lot of activity for a Friday morning. Tony's Autobody?"

"Wrong house. He was returning the car to Tracey Van Doren's house."

"I thought the car looked familiar. Everything quiet at school?"

Summer nodded, gathering her purse and Liberace's cage. "I'd like to go over the plans for Mexico before I leave to pick up the girls." Summer looked up the driveway as the back door opened. A tall woman in a pink Chanel suit was talking with Imelda. "Who's that?"

"Amanda Winslow, Tate's mother. She charmed most of Washington in her day, and she still makes heads turn. I think she came by to drop off a silver urn and a painted platter for Cara, but it might have been a painted urn and a silver platter. She and Patrick were arguing about how to make the perfect sushi roll, the last I heard."

Summer had to admit that Tate's mother was striking. Her laugh was infectious as it drifted over the lawn. "Any strife there?"

"The mother-in-law part, you mean? Not a whiff. Her son's in love and she supports him two hundred percent.

She says Cara and the girls are the best thing that ever happened to him." Gabe looked at Summer and shook his head. "Relax, will you?"

"I must have missed that part of the job description," she said flatly. "Can we go over those plans now?"

Amanda Winslow turned as a short man in a denim chef's jacket and a red beret came to the back door, accompanied by Imelda.

"That's Cara's chef, I take it?"

"Patrick, the wizard with pastry."

The senator's mother appeared to be issuing a string of orders, which the chef listened to carefully, but he stopped nodding when the truck driver jumped down and began to unload produce boxes.

"But I need the organic," the chef said anxiously. "I ordered raspberries and basil."

The driver shrugged. "I got rounds to finish, Rodney. I can't stand here all day yapping."

"It's Patrick, not Rodney. And there must be a mistake. I didn't order these things."

The driver leaned closer and waved his clipboard. "Fratelli and Sons don't make mistakes, understand?"

"But—"

"Listen, Rodney, I need a signature, and one way or another, I'm gonna get it. You see what I'm saying?" Scowling, the driver headed back behind the truck while the chef stared glumly at the clipboard.

Gabe rubbed his jaw. "The man is a genius with pastry dough, but hopeless with pressure, I'm afraid."

"Why doesn't he order from someone else?"

"It's hard to find good suppliers. In San Francisco, he could pick and choose, but not here." Gabe rolled his shoulders. "I'd better go help him with those potato sacks. Come on, I'll introduce you."

Summer followed Gabe to the garage, where the young chef was struggling with a fifty-pound bag of russet potatoes, which he dropped when he saw Gabe and Summer.

"If you're here to cancel the prosciutto delivery," he said to Summer, "I may have to kill myself."

"Relax, Patrick. Your prosciutto's safe for the time being." Gabe pointed over his shoulder. "This is Summer Mulvaney, the girls' new nanny."

Instantly Patrick brightened, pumping Summer's hand. "Great to meet you. Ms. O has been really jazzed about you coming." His brow rose. "Do you like white truffle oil?"

If this was some kind of arcane test, Summer didn't have a clue to the right answer. "Sometimes."

Patrick rubbed his hands eagerly. "Great. I'm making focaccia with white truffle oil and caprese salad for lunch. Audra loves both of them. The girl has excellent taste, for a teenager. No fast food and Oreos for her." He took off his beret and wiped his forehead. "What am I going to do about baby artichokes? I need them for the benefit dinner Ms. O is planning."

Gabe hefted a bag of potatoes. "You're on your own there, Patrick. I've got two hundred roses and seventy-five calla lilies to worry about."

Up on the porch, Amanda Winslow turned, following Imelda back into the house. Summer heard something about organizing table skirts.

Meanwhile, Patrick frowned at the sunny yard. "It's going to be hell keeping the buffet placements warm for three hours." He ran his hand through long brown hair that stuck out in spiky clumps. "Will we have enough electrical outlets on the grass?"

"Ms. O'Connor asked me to work on it. I think I can guarantee you about six."

The young chef shoved up his sleeves and cracked his knuckles. "Not enough, but I guess I can come up with something. Chafing dishes," he muttered, lifting a box of Roma tomatoes and heading for the kitchen. "I can probably squeeze two hours out of a good candle. Back at the CIA, they told me there'd be days like this."

Summer watched him charge into the garage with the tomatoes cradled at his chest. "CIA?"

"Culinary Institute of America. He was their star grad five years ago." Along with the potatoes, Gabe picked up what appeared to be three boxes of white asparagus.

"I can help you with those."

"No need." His voice fell. "I'll be done here in five minutes. Then we can get to work."

As he spoke, a staple broke free on the asparagus box and white stalks flew in every direction. Cursing, Gabe grabbed for the broken end of the box, slamming against Summer's right arm, in the process.

She went pale, her whole body tense.

"Damn. Are you okay?"

"Fine." Her voice was low. "Forget it."

Gabe dropped the produce on the grass and reached for Summer's arm. "You may need ice on that. Let me have a look."

"I told you, I'm *fine.*" She turned away, shoulders rigid, her heart pounding. There were too many memories. "I'll—see you later."

"No doubt about it," Gabe said flatly.

Summer ignored the question in his eyes. She had to get away.

chapter 16

The flotilla of trucks arrived right on schedule. Within minutes a team of men in white uniforms poured onto the lawn with ladders, toolboxes, and long planks of aluminum siding, supervised by a tall man who bore a striking resemblance to Denzel Washington. After consulting a sheaf of papers, he motioned his crew to follow him over the grass to the back of the house, where he gave the doorbell two careful rings, then checked his watch.

Rubber soles squished over the damp lawn behind him. "Yes?"

"Triple-A Siding, here to see Ms. O'Connor."

"She's not in." Gabe Morgan surveyed the crew and their broad-shouldered supervisor. "That a problem?"

"We're scheduled to do roof and siding maintenance. Any sign of termites?"

Gabe ran his tongue across his teeth. "They've eaten away the whole south wall of the garage. In fact, things could get nasty out here any second." He motioned across the lawn. "I think you'd better come inside and fill me in on your plans."

Ishmael Teague, electronics genius, ace computer hacker,

and highly trained security operative, gave a wicked grin. "Happy to. And you would be . . . the gardener?"

"Among other things," Gabe said dryly. "Frankly, I like you better as the pizza delivery guy."

"I've delivered many things over the years," Izzy said, "but pizza has never been one of them." He made a quick gesture to one of his team, then followed Gabe Morgan down to his guest quarters.

Summer strode through her casita, railing at herself. So she'd gotten a bump from a wooden crate. There was no reason for her stomach to turn somersaults.

Feel the pain, but don't become part of it, the doctors had told her. Treat it like a difficult friend, then wave good-bye and close the door.

Easy to say.

She yanked off her jacket and tossed it on the bed. Next came the long-sleeved shirt. At least there was no sign of blood on the white cotton. At the worst, she'd have a few bruises where the staples from the crate had raked her arm, and that was nothing to whine about.

But when Summer walked to the floor-length mirror outside her shower, each step was an act of will, and her eyes, as she stared at her reflection, were filled with regret.

"We'll tackle the ground floor first." Izzy tapped the architectural blueprints spread out on the table before him. "Pressure plates outside the windows—here, here, here. Video camera hidden in the shutters near the front door, with full porch and front yard coverage." His long fingers moved slowly across the paper. "Wireless alarms upstairs and down, just in case someone decides to levitate over the pressure plates."

Gabe nodded. "Motion sensors?"

"Two of my people will handle that. Your suggestions on placement look good to me."

"What about cover?" Gabe snagged the coffeepot and refilled their cups. "We don't want to broadcast our new security."

"Officially, my crew will be installing new siding and trim, then checking the window frames and foundation for termite infestation. My people are damned good, so no one will notice the sensors that get inserted under the siding or the alarms on the windows."

"Good. Now let's talk about this cellar." Gabe tapped one corner of the blueprint. "There's a possibility of interior access."

"I brought materials to seal it up, if necessary." Izzy blew on his coffee, then took a long drink. "Anyone currently in the house?"

"The housekeeper is working upstairs. The chef is in the kitchen, too, along with an assistant. Tate Winslow's mother is with them. Prep work for the wedding."

"Anyone else on the grounds?"

"The new nanny." Gabe sat back, steepling his fingers. "The one I told you about."

"That would be Summer Mulvaney, our loaner from the FBI. How good is she?"

"Right on target so far. Audra slipped away yesterday at the Monterey Aquarium and she handled things fast while keeping a low profile. The little girl, Sophy, idolizes her already."

"You mean, she's a people person? Most of your garden-variety Feds are pretty weak in the social skills department."

Gabe laughed dryly. "I wouldn't call her Miss Congeniality. She doesn't trust anyone. I don't thinks she likes anyone, either." Gabe shrugged. "Whatever. Just as long as she gets the job done."

"I saw her this morning while I did a security check from the beach. What's with her hair? It's like Sandra Bullock on speed."

"You can thank me for that. She got tangled up in a cactus last night and I cut her free." Gabe shook his head. "Come to think of it, she and that cactus are a lot alike—prickly as hell and impossible to touch."

Izzy turned his coffee slowly. "Have you briefed her on today's installation?"

"She knows the general outline."

"Good." Izzy stared out at the green expanse of lawn. The sun had burned through the morning mist, and the ocean was ablaze with light. "Nice real estate. I didn't know you could live this well on an assistant DA's salary."

"You can't. The house originally belonged to Ms. O'Connor's dead husband. He was big in commercial real estate. Died six years ago."

"Hard on the kids. Hard on her, too." Izzy drummed his fingers on the table. "Assuming that she loved him."

"She did. According to the files, she's a regular straight arrow, professionally and personally."

"It's nice to know there are a few of them left." Izzy set a toolbox on the table and tossed Gabe a small key.

"Gee, are these the new Phillips screwdrivers I ordered?"

"Maps of Los Reyes. Blueprints and high-res photographs of the clinic. Complete bios and photos of key personnel, along with twenty thousand dollars' equivalent in Mexican currency." Izzy held up two U.S. passports. "*Don't* get caught. Don't even get suspected. Especially don't get yourself shot, because I hate to clean up blood.

We're skirting the gray area with this, and Tate Winslow's called in some favors, but you'll be working outside official jurisdiction."

"Not a problem. I've worked outside official channels before." Gabe rolled up the papers and slid them beneath one arm. "Gotta go. Mary Poppins is waiting to be briefed on our Mexico jaunt." He stood up as there was a tap at his door.

Summer was waiting right outside, her eyes narrowed. "Those men aren't replacing siding and I'm *not* Mary Poppins."

Across the room Izzy sized her up slowly. "Ms. Mulvaney, I take it?"

"Who wants to know?" She stood unmoving, legs apart, weight balanced.

Looking pretty damned dangerous, Gabe thought, and every inch a professional in spite of the color in her cheeks. "This is Ishmael Teague, Summer. He's on our side, and his people are handling the security upgrades at the house."

"Nice of you to give me some notice. I just handcuffed one of his team and locked him inside the cellar."

"Is that a fact?" Izzy looked delighted with this bit of news. "It will be my pleasure to ream him out for being so obvious and allowing himself to be caught."

"Oh, he wasn't obvious. If I hadn't worked a few summers installing aluminum siding back in Pennsylvania, I never would have noticed." Summer stared at Gabe. "What's in the toolbox?"

"Gear for our junket down to Mexico." Gabe put a steaming cup of coffee on the table in front of her. "Have a seat. Everything quiet at the house?"

"Except for some problems with pesto or pasta, I couldn't tell which. Patrick was talking to Amanda

Winslow and tearing out his hair." Before the other two could get a word in, she rounded on Izzy. "How many people on your team and how long before they're done?"

"Nine people and two—maybe three—hours."

"I want a personal tour and full briefing when they finish." She crossed her arms. "And I want all alarms relayed to a monitor in my guesthouse, of course."

Izzy glanced at Gabe, then back at Summer. "Of course."

"Who else will be wired into the system?"

"Mr. Morgan." Izzy smiled. "Of course."

Summer sat down at the sunny breakfast nook, pushing the coffee to one side. "I need to go over the plans for our trip to Los Reyes. The girls will be done at school in forty-five minutes, which doesn't leave us much time, so who gets to fill me in?"

"I do," Izzy said. "Money and passports are in this box, and Gabe has the clinic plans. You'll take a charter plane to southern Arizona this evening, and Gabe will meet you there. You'll be met at Los Reyes."

"Who's our contact at the clinic?"

"One of the lab workers. He's been approached by someone in the States, asking for information, but so far he won't say who."

"So we need to make him talk." Summer crossed her hands on the table. "What's our cover?"

"These days the clinic makes most of its money from cosmetic work and infertility cases. You and Gabe will be touring the clinic as prospective patients."

"So I'm infertile," Summer said coolly. "How nice."

"Who knows, maybe it's me," Gabe offered gallantly. "They'll want a whole gamut of tests, but first we have to tour the clinic and make certain it meets our high standards. That will give us access to our contact without any raised eyebrows."

"Sounds plausible." Summer glanced at her watch. "I'm still waiting for forensic results on the box Cara received yesterday. There's a chance that we'll have our man—or woman—sooner than you think."

"I never count on miracles," Izzy said dryly.

Summer frowned at him. "Neither do I, Mr. Teague."

"Glad to hear it." Izzy gave a two-finger wave and headed toward his van.

Summer stood up and walked to the window. "I don't like the feel of this. I've been assigned to safeguard Cara and her family, not break into a private clinic in a neighboring country."

"Senator Winslow has spoken with your boss, and everything's arranged. I'll be doing the B and E, not you."

"It's not easy to say no to a senator, I guess." Summer took a deep breath, feeling like a pawn being shoved across an invisible chessboard.

"When you get to Mexico, you should get a haircut. I'm no Vidal Sassoon." Gabe slid an uneven strand of hair off her cheek. "Clearly."

"It will be fine. Hair is hair."

"Can you do this, Summer?"

"Pretend to be married? Of course I can."

"Then stop tensing up whenever I get close." Gabe was right behind her, his voice low.

"Who's tense?" Summer took a step back, crossing her arms over her chest.

"You are."

"I'm tense?" Summer glared at him. After a moment of consideration, she moved closer, sliding her arms around his neck. Slowly she pulled his head down. "You think?" And then, without a pause, she kissed him.

Gabe stood motionless as her tongue slid back and forth over his mouth. He cursed when she bit him lightly.

"Is that convincing enough, *darling?*"

Gabe cleared his throat. "That should do for now." He started to say more, but she was already opening the front door.

"Glad to hear it, because—"

As they walked onto the porch, the leaded glass window upstairs in Cara O'Connor's bedroom disappeared in a hail of broken glass.

Gabe shoved Summer flat and fell into a crouch beside her while Izzy's handpicked team scattered in defensive postures throughout the backyard. "It had to come from the rocks near the beach," Gabe whispered. "None of the other houses face this direction, and there's no one in sight."

"No one in the gazebo. No one outside the garage. Let's go check the beach," Summer said tightly.

Gabe's hand tightened on her shoulder. "Stay here. You're not walking into a bullet."

"Of course I'm not. I intend to crawl to the far side of the porch, follow the path back to the service road, cross the dunes, and work my way up the rocks from the far side of the house."

"Let Izzy's people handle it."

"While we're arguing, the shooter could be getting away."

"Not likely with three of Izzy's men on his tail." As Gabe spoke, Izzy sprinted up. "What do you have?"

"There are kayakers all over the cove. Any one of them could have paddled to the rocks, taken a single shot, then vanished. The teacher has a bullhorn, so no one would have heard the noise." Izzy stared down at the beach. "My men are checking for footprints, but if our shooter stayed on the rocks, there won't be any."

"Cara isn't breaking fast enough," Summer said quietly. "No more phone calls. Now they're getting serious."

Gabe looked at Izzy. "Not a good sign. Let's take that back route down to the beach."

There were no fresh footprints on the path nearest to the house. Six people combed the rocks, but they found no trace of an intruder. Finally, Summer left the others and headed back to the house with Gabe, worried by this new level of threat. The closed expression on Gabe's face told her he had the same worries.

"We'll be a little late today," she said tightly. "I'm taking the long route home."

"You'll be checking for pursuit?"

Summer nodded grimly.

As they passed the garage, Patrick appeared with a towel slung over one shoulder. He seemed oblivious to the flour that covered the front of his denim tunic and the way his hair stood up in spikes. "Did either of you hear a noise out here? It sounded like a truck backfiring, but I didn't see Fratelli's produce people return."

Gabe nodded calmly. "We heard it. One of the workmen dropped his hammer and broke a window."

Patrick looked relieved. "When I heard the crack, I thought something had exploded in my oven. That happened to me once back in cooking school, and I got egg all over my face—literally." He brushed the front of his jacket distractedly. "Mrs. Winslow heard something, too, and I told her I'd check. She worries about everything now with the wedding coming up. I'll tell her what happened." He smiled crookedly. "Just as soon as she stops grilling me about the imported prosciutto." He brushed vaguely at his tunic, then vanished back inside.

"Nice car." Summer stared at the big silver Mercedes parked in the driveway. "It seems to me that Mrs. Winslow is calling the shots, not Cara."

"Mrs. Winslow is picky about things being done just right, but Cara doesn't agree to anything she doesn't want. It's fun to watch two pros maneuver for territory, believe me." Gabe turned to study the deserted path down to the beach. "You'll call Cara? She'll want to know about this."

"Next thing I do."

"I'll notify the senator." When Gabe turned, his eyes were hard. "Watch your back," he said quietly. "Otherwise—"

Izzy strode around the garage, his eyes hard. "We've got a problem," he said quietly.

They followed him into the shadows of the garage. The rear door of Cara's SUV was open.

"Take a look." Izzy turned on a penlight, casting a beam of light over the rear seat, and Summer felt bile fill her throat. A white rat was pinned to the leather, a large hunting knife planted through its head.

chapter 17

So they got tired of the threatening phone calls," Summer said tightly.

"Looks that way." Gabe glanced around the garage. "We need to preserve this somehow."

Izzy handed Gabe a piece of paper. "You hold him and I'll bag him."

"My God." In their concentration, they hadn't heard Patrick come into the garage. He was staring at the dead rat, a bunch of asparagus dangling from his flour-covered fingers. "Is that . . . thing a rat?"

Summer nodded. "Someone seems to be playing a crude joke here. Do you have any idea who would do this?"

"I—" The chef swallowed hard, looking as if he had to throw up. "Maybe Tracey from down the street? No, I don't think she and Audra would stoop to something like this."

"Patrick, do you have those white asparagus spears for me?" Amanda Winslow walked into the garage, her pink Chanel suit dusted by a thin streak of flour. "The pastry shells are almost ready and . . ." Her voice trailed away when she realized Patrick wasn't alone.

Coolly, Gabe stepped in front of the SUV, but it was too late.

Tate's mother stared into the car. "Is something wrong? What's that thing on the backseat?" She frowned, then took a jerky step backward. "It's—it's dead." She put one hand on the car, staring wide-eyed at the rat. "What in heaven's name is going on here?"

"Mrs. Winslow," Summer said quietly, "why don't we go inside? I'll make you some tea?"

"I don't want *tea.* I want to know why that—that dead *thing* is on the seat of Cara's car. It's revolting."

She tried to move closer, but Gabe blocked her. He turned and slid the cold body into a plastic bag.

"Keep it away from me. I have to call Cara." She dug in her pocket with shaky fingers and flipped open a tiny cell phone. "I think I'm going to be sick. . . ." she whispered.

Imelda and Summer handled Tate's mother while Gabe cleaned the seat and searched for any additional evidence or prints. Meanwhile, Izzy had faded away, taking the dead rat with him for a preliminary analysis.

In the afternoon sunlight, Amanda Winslow looked old and frightened. "I want Tate," she said in a shaky voice. "I want someone to tell me what's happening here."

"It is a very bad thing to see." Imelda patted her arm. "But it is like Ms. Summer says, a joke only. Drink some more tea, please."

The housekeeper looked frightened, too, despite her brave words, and Summer was relieved when the senator called back. After a few minutes she slipped away to pick up the girls, leaving Tate's mother to the housekeeper's care.

She made the drive with only minutes to spare. As the class bell rang, students spilled out into the hallway and down the front steps into the sunlight.

Laughter and color, Summer thought. So free, so California. She realized she was a little envious.

She found Sophy and then they went in search of Audra, who was outside her locker on the third floor, arguing with Tracey. When the two teenagers saw Summer, their faces turned stony.

Audra slammed her locker shut. "Let's go."

"Can I, uh, have another ride?" Tracey picked at a hangnail. "My mom's gone today." She looked up at Summer, her face tense. "Okay?"

"Of course, Tracey. It's no problem. You might need to move Liberace's cage into the back. Maybe Audra can—"

Tracey ignored Audra. "That's cool. I'm just going to the Java Jungle downtown. I'm meeting . . . some friends."

"You're sure?" Summer frowned. "Won't your mother be expecting you at home?"

The girl gave a snort. "Like—she is so *not* expecting me. I'll be fine, Ms. Mulvaney. Don't worry." She didn't look at Audra as she bent over to tug Sophy's pigtail. "Cool Hello Kitty purse. I've got one in silver and everyone always, like, tries to steal it from me."

Sophy looked worried. "They do?"

"Just because they're morons. Don't worry, no one will take yours." Tracey's face turned wistful for a moment. "You're lucky that way. You've got good friends. That's really cool." Then with a final glare at Audra, she started down the stairs.

Two miles from school something small and furry shot across Summer's lap.

"I thought you left Liberace in his cage," Summer said.

Sophy struggled to reach the ferret, which *chirr*ed loudly, climbing up Summer's arm. "I had him zipped in my backpack, Ms. M. He was okay until you turned that last corner."

"Sophy, I need to drive. Liberace isn't helping me."

"Sorry." Sophy produced a piece of smashed banana, but the ferret didn't budge. Two pieces of raisin, a chocolate chip, and half a carrot later, the ferret was still perched on Summer's shoulder.

She eased into a slower lane, scanning the traffic for a break, so she could pull off. She saw the car then, a dusty brown Honda hanging back, one lane over. Summer had seen the same car outside the school this morning when she'd dropped off the girls. "Anyone know someone who drives a brown Honda?"

"Not me," Audra said impatiently.

"I don't think so," Tracey said, after thinking for a few moments. "Why?"

"What's a Honda look like?" Sophy asked.

"It doesn't matter. I thought someone waved at us," Summer lied coolly. She tried to ignore the ferret nuzzling her cheek. "I guess I was wrong."

"There's the Java Jungle, right at the next corner." Tracey gathered her things quickly. "You can drop me in front. Thanks a lot." Tracey jumped out and looked at Audra tensely. "See you."

"Are you sure she's allowed to go off alone after school?"

"Come on, she's not a kid." Audra sat tensely, not looking at her friend. "She knows what she's doing."

Summer hesitated, and a car honked behind her, waiting for her parking spot. Behind that car, other cars began to honk. "Sophy, can you please put Liberace back in his cage?"

"I'm trying. Come here, Liberace." Sophy made a low clicking noise, holding out another piece of smashed banana. "Be good and come to Aunt Sophy."

"Oh, that's so stupid. Talking won't get him." Audra leaned forward, grabbing for the ferret, which shot to the floor, wedging its body in the narrow storage space beneath Sophy's seat.

A dozen cars were honking now. When Summer looked back, the dusty Honda was gone.

"If he moves, grab him." Summer eased out into traffic, looking for a quieter spot for a final showdown with Sophy's impossible pet.

The realization hit her suddenly. Liberace was white. The dead rat in the SUV's backseat had been white.

The message was that Liberace would be next.

"That was so cool, Ms. M." Sophy skipped over the driveway, carrying Liberace, who was now curled up in his cage surrounded by his favorite balls of aluminum foil. "You really *are* fast. For an adult, I mean."

Summer hid a smile. "So are you. Once I pulled Liberace out of the cup holder for the second time, you hustled him right into his cage." She raised one hand in a high five, and the two slapped loudly. "Nice reflexes."

Giggling, Sophy ran over to Gabe, who was carrying a flat of petunias up the path from the garage. "We almost had an accident on the way home from school, but Ms. M did this really cool driving thing, in and out of traffic, just like on *Top Cops*. Then we grabbed Liberace just in time, because this huge truck was changing lanes and he almost hit us."

Gabe looked at Summer, one eyebrow raised. "Almost?"

"We're fine." Summer frowned at Audra. "Patrick said to tell you he was making caprese salad and some kind of bread with white truffle oil for lunch."

"I'm not hungry." Audra stalked toward the house, and Sophy followed, deep in a rambling conversation with Liberace, who appeared to be asleep.

Sophy stopped at the porch. "Don't forget your suit, Ms. M. It will be cool to swim."

Gabe put down his flat of flowers. "Busy morning?"

"Death by escaped ferret, barely averted. Then I was nearly eyeballed to death by a sullen teenager." Summer sighed as she stared at Audra's retreating back. "Make that two sullen teenagers."

"Two?"

"We gave Audra's friend Tracey a ride. I have come to believe that mothers and nannies deserve hazardous duty pay." Summer rubbed her shoulder, which she'd banged against the door when she lunged for Sophy's pet. "Remind me not to travel anywhere with a ferret ever again."

"Liberace's a handful. So is Audra." Gabe's voice hardened. "What about the accident with the truck?"

"Sophy exaggerated. It was just a quick lane change. But I think there may have been a brown Honda following us back from school."

"Plate number?"

"First letters TR. I couldn't see the rest. I was more concerned with the ferret crawling up my shoulder and keeping the car on the road," Summer said tightly. "I'll be watching from now on." She studied the back lawn. "Everything finished here?"

"All complete. Izzy had to take care of something in

town, but he'll be back to give you a tour. What did Sophy
mean about the suit?"

Summer ignored the sudden pressure at her chest. "She
wants me to go swim with her. After that shot this morning, I don't want them exposed out here."

"I agree. Did you tell Cara what happened?"

Summer rubbed her arm slowly. "She went into full-
blown mother mode. She's terrified for her kids. She said
the sooner they leave for Wyoming, the better."

"Senator Winslow wanted to send in a SWAT team.
Under the circumstances, not a helpful move." Gabe
leaned against the side of the garage. "You don't swim?"

"Not if I can help it."

"Why not?"

"None of your business," Summer said evenly. "I have
to go. The girls need to eat, then pack."

Audra barely touched her lunch, and Sophy cut her focaccia into long, narrow strips, then ate each one slowly.
As the rich, earthy mix of flavors rolled over her tongue,
Summer decided that Patrick Flanagan was probably a
genius.

When she complimented the chef, he beamed, sliding
more handmade mozzarella onto her plate. "I consider it a
work in progress. I'm always trying different types of basil
and new olive-oil varieties. Experimenting is half the fun."
He looked anxiously at Audra. "You don't like the salad,
Audra? Caprese used to be your favorite."

"Uh, it's—great, Patrick. I'm just full."

Full from what? Summer wondered. The girl had con-
sumed two bites of oatmeal and half a glass of water for
breakfast.

Patrick hovered beside the table. "No, you're right. I

shouldn't have used that new basil. And the tomatoes that came today were crushingly bad." Muttering anxiously, he vanished into the kitchen.

"What's wrong, Audra?" Sophy frowned at her sister. "Do you want some of my bread?"

"No."

"Is your stomach upset again?"

"No," Audra snapped.

"Are you sure? Mom said to call her right away if—"

"My stomach is fine, okay?" As if to prove it, Audra grabbed the last piece of bread from Sophy's plate and shoved it into her mouth. "See. Are you satisfied?" she said around bites.

"Well, that's what Mom told me." Sophy sat in a tight ball, small and defensive beneath the sunny window.

"Audra, if you're sick, I can call your mother or take you to the doctor. You can tell me if anything's wrong."

"Nothing's *wrong*." Glaring at Summer, Audra shot to her feet. "I wish everyone would stop asking me that. I'm just not hungry, okay?" She took an angry breath, then flounced out of the room.

Summer stared after her. "Has she had this stomach problem before?"

"Once or twice." Sophy toyed with a piece of tomato. "Mom got really scared, and our doctor did a whole bunch of tests, but there was nothing wrong."

"Maybe I should call your mother."

Sophy's eyes widened. "Audra will get really mad if you do that."

All the more reason to call. Summer had heard that more and more teenagers were developing ulcers from stress. Maybe Audra was one of them.

"She gets really angry if you ask her how she feels."

Sophy brightened. "But maybe if she's okay, she'll come swimming with us. Even though we're grounded, we can still swim, right? See, I'm already dressed." She flipped up the edge of her sundress, revealing a Hello Kitty swimsuit. "Can I go sit by the pool?"

"Not yet."

"But Gabe is out there."

"Gabe is busy, honey. Why don't you help Patrick for a few minutes until I come back?"

Sophy studied Summer's navy pantsuit. "What about *your* suit? You'd look cool in a bikini. You know, one of the little knitted ones like Tracey's mom wears." She tilted her head. "Tracey says her mom *ought* to look great, after all the money she's spent on plastic surgery. Have *you* had plastic surgery, Ms. M?"

"Afraid not. All body parts here came with the original unit."

Sophy nodded, looking resigned. "Me, too. Someday I want to get my feet done."

"Your feet?"

"Melanie Jamieson says my toes are too big." Sophy sniffed. "Melanie is a creep, but she's right. And my big toe is crooked."

"Crooked is cute," Summer said. On impulse, she bent and kissed the top of Sophy's head. "It makes you an original. Don't ever let anyone ever talk you into changing."

"Okay," Sophy said simply, all thoughts of body defects forgotten as Patrick emerged from the kitchen carrying a three-tier chocolate cake crowned by white-chocolate roses.

"I need a taster. Anyone interested?"

"Me, me!" Sophy shot across the floor and danced around him.

"Audra isn't coming?" The chef looked crestfallen. "She loves my white-chocolate cake."

"I'll see if I can persuade her, Patrick." Summer suppressed a sigh.

When did evasive driving get supplanted by Adolescence 101?

chapter 18

Audra wasn't in the loft library or in her bedroom, but as Summer neared the end of the hall, she heard an odd noise coming from Cara's room. Standing at the open door, she listened intently.

The noise she'd heard was low, muffled sobbing.

What was she supposed to do now? She had absolutely no experience dealing with volatile situations like this. Kids were a complete mystery to her, and with her luck, she'd make everything worse.

Gradually the sobs began to fade. When the inner bathroom door finally opened, Summer was waiting, trying not to panic.

She tapped briskly at the door. "Audra, Patrick says he has chocolate cake for you."

"I'm not hungry." Fabric rustled. Audra sniffed hard. "Go away."

Summer opened the bedroom door slightly. "May I come in?" She took the silence for assent. "Sophy wants to swim, but Gabe says he has to do some repairs on the pump, so Sophy thought you could call Tracey on her cell phone and ask to use their inside pool."

Audra kept her back to Summer. "All Sophy thinks

about is swimming and ballet and Hello Kitty stuff. Besides, I don't want to swim."

"I'd consider it a huge favor if you'd ask. Maybe you could go in the water with Sophy, too. I don't swim."

The girl turned slowly. "Why don't you swim? Don't you know how?"

"It's been a long time, and I was never very good." A lie. Once Summer had been a natural, spending hours in the water.

No more.

She locked away the memories. "You've been crying," she said quietly to Audra.

"No way. I was just washing my face."

"I heard you, Audra. I know I'm a stranger, but if this is about food, about eating—well, there are things you can do."

Audra gave a defiant sniff. "I don't know what you're talking about."

"I'm talking about not eating anything but two spoonfuls of oatmeal this morning and not much more for lunch."

"I ate plenty. You just didn't see me."

"And then you came up here and tried to throw up."

"You're crazy." But there was desperation behind the words. "Why don't you just go *away*?"

"It never works, you know." Ignoring Audra's tense look, Summer sat down on the bed, speaking calmly. "You feel worse and worse, hungrier and hungrier. After a while your metabolism shuts down, and your body fights to hold on to every pound. Pretty soon you feel tired all the time, and you're obsessing, adding up the numbers, always counting the calories. After a few months you start digesting your own muscles and organs. Then comes the shortness of breath, the dizziness."

Audra spun around, her face pale and tight. "How would you know?"

"Because my sister had the same problem." Summer looked down at her locked fingers. "I watched her fade away week after week and there was nothing I could do." The words were hard, the memories even harder.

Audra stood uncertainly in the middle of the room. "So?" Her voice was very quiet. "What happened?"

"She nearly died. It was like watching a terrible disease cut her down a little more each day, only the real disease was in her head, not her body."

"What happened?" Audra whispered.

"She went away to a place with other girls who had the same problem. They talked about how they felt and the doctors helped my sister understand why she was obsessed with being thin. It took months, but she finally learned how to eat without throwing up."

Audra sank down on a chair near the bed. "I can't even throw up. Nothing comes up. Even a stupid, dumb thing like that, I can't do right." Her slender shoulders shook.

Summer put an arm around her, praying she would find the right words. "That's a good thing, honey. My sister—" The memories still clutched at Summer's throat. "Everything was damaged from what she'd done. Her throat, her stomach, all that took a long, long time to heal. So I'm glad you couldn't make yourself do those things."

Audra sank forward, braced against Summer's chest. Then she pulled away and brushed hard at her eyes. "None of my clothes fit. I'm fat and I hate it. Tracey says I'm a cow, and she's not the only one."

"You're no bigger than Tracey."

"She says—" Audra stopped. "I'm not? Really?"

"No question about it." It was a lie, of course. Audra was trim, with merely a hint of a curve at her hips and chest, while Tracey verged on skeletal. "She's probably jealous because you have some muscles from playing softball."

Audra wrinkled her nose. "I don't want muscles."

"Sure you do. Muscles and definition are very hot right now. Women in Hollywood kill to get muscles."

Audra digested this, then looked down at her thin arms. "What if I did want to get strong? How would I do it?"

"The best way I know is kickboxing. For speed, strength, and grace there's nothing better. Think Chuck Norris. No extra bulk there."

"You *know* that kind of stuff?"

"Enough. And yes, I could teach you how. In fact, we could start this afternoon." Summer glanced pointedly at the empty suitcase on the floor. "Right after you finish packing."

Audra picked at the sleeve of her jacket. "I don't know. I don't seem to have much energy." She took a deep breath. "I think maybe I need to eat something first."

Though mentally clapping, Summer forced her face to stay calm. "Probably that would help. Maybe a salad. Toast and a hard-boiled egg. Nothing heavy so that you couldn't exercise."

Audra jumped to her feet. "Could you ask Patrick for me? I've got to finish packing." She whirled around suddenly. "Did you mean that other stuff you said, about not swimming?"

Summer nodded.

"Why not?"

Summer felt Audra's intensity and realized a lie now could destroy the tenuous connection they had made. "It's a long story, Audra. It's . . . personal, too."

The teenager frowned. "Then you can tell me when we get to the ranch. We'll have time up there."

Summer didn't answer.

"It's something bad, isn't it? Big bad, not little bad. I told you my stuff, so I think you should tell me yours. That way it's even, right? Mom always says we should try to be fair and square."

"She's right, Audra. But I'd like to . . . think about it first." Summer stood up, smoothing her sleeve in an automatic gesture.

Then Sophy flew up the stairs with a towel around her neck and Liberace capering on a long red leash, and the subject was forgotten.

Clouds dotted the horizon as Summer watched Sophy tie Liberace's leash to a beach chair. Audra had called Tracey about using her pool, and in short order they were heading to a big Mediterranean-style villa nearby. Something about the sunlight made Summer try to remember the last time she'd taken a real vacation.

There had been weekend trips to visit her sister in Boston, a few hasty expeditions to buy furniture for her rental apartment in Philadelphia, but no real time off.

No barefoot, sun-and-sand excursions to Antigua or St. Croix. No hedonistic retreats to an isolated Hawaiian beach. After she'd lost her father, stability and economic security had been crucial to Summer, and she had pared her life down to basics: preparing for her job, doing her job, and worrying about her sister. Nothing else mattered. There was no circle of understanding friends, no string of cast-off boyfriends. Unlike her outgoing twin sister, Summer had no people skills, because she had never made time for things she considered nonessential.

When her loneliness hurt, she simply buried herself deeper in her work.

Sophy called to her from the far side of the pool, full of trust and almost frightening honesty. Even Audra was showing signs of good humor as she splashed her sister from the nearby steps.

"Ms. M, aren't you coming in?" Sophy kicked excitedly toward Summer, grasping a pink float shaped like a turtle on steroids.

"Not right now, honey."

"Please? The heater is on."

"It's still a little cold for me."

"But—"

"She doesn't want to swim, Sophy. Just leave it alone, okay?" Audra splashed her sister, then darted an uncertain smile at Summer.

So she'd remembered. Summer was stunned.

"But why *not*?" Sophy persisted.

The sun was beating down through the big glass windows facing the beach, and Summer pulled off her jacket. To circumvent further questions, she picked up Audra's Frisbee. "Catch this one, Sophy." She aimed a low pass across the pool, right into Sophy's hands. "Great. Now throw it back." As she spoke, Summer moved backward, arms raised.

She slammed hard into Gabe, who was carrying flowers as a gift for Tracey's mom—while he kept an eye out for anything unusual outside.

"Sorry," Summer muttered. "I didn't know that you—" Her breath caught as Gabe steadied her with one arm while he balanced two big geraniums with his other arm.

"Careful. You were about to fall into the spa."

Summer ignored the brush of his thigh. "Thanks."

"No problem," Gabe muttered.

Audra and Sophy studied them intently, and then Sophy kicked closer, scooping up a piece of dirt that had fallen into the pool. She frowned at Summer. "I still don't understand, Ms. M. Why don't you come in?"

"I can watch you better out here, honey."

Sophy turned on her float. "What about you, Gabe?"

"Can't. Soon as I drop off these flowers for Tracey's mom, I've got four dozen more geraniums to get into the ground at your house."

Pouting, Sophy rolled off the float, fast as a fish, and kicked away. In the process she doused Gabe, whose tee shirt darkened, clinging to his powerful torso.

Summer refused to look. She was already far too aware of the man.

Suddenly water pelted her, soaking her blouse and pants. Oblivious, Sophy continued to kick across the pool, singing happily. At the far end she climbed up the ladder and then saw Summer. "You're all wet."

"Thanks to you," Audra hissed.

Sophy grabbed her towel and offered it to Summer. "I'm really sorry, honestly."

Summer was about to answer when Tracey's cat raced underneath the beach chairs, hotly pursued by Liberace, who yanked his leash free in his wild dash. When the cat turned, the ferret followed, looping back and catching Summer's foot in the trailing leash.

"Be careful, Ms. M," Sophy called. "Liberace's right behind you."

Summer grabbed vainly for the leash while the cat and ferret circled her in a manic dance. Then Liberace arched his back and jumped onto a pile of towels, the leash snapping taut against Summer's ankles. Knocked off balance, she toppled sideways and landed in the deep end, with one ankle still wrapped in Liberace's leash. When she finally managed to kick free, her hair was soaked and her blouse billowed out around her.

"Wow." Sophy shot up in a storm of bubbles, grabbing Summer's arm for balance. "Are you okay?" Anxiously, Sophy clutched at Summer. "You *can* swim. Why did you tell us you couldn't?"

Then the little girl looked down. Her face went white beneath her freckles. "Why is your arm l-like that?"

Summer didn't look. She knew exactly what Sophy saw, knew exactly what her scarred skin looked like.

The leash slid off Summer's ankle. When she looked up, Gabe was holding Liberace. The pity she saw in his eyes was like an icy slap.

She yanked down her sleeve, a sick feeling in her chest. "Could you watch the girls for a few minutes, Gabe? I . . . need to change."

She heard his gruff assent and Liberace's nervous chattering, her whole body cold and numb. *Too late to hide now. Too late to pretend.*

She couldn't forget Sophy's look of horror.

Gabe's look of pity.

"What happened to her?" Sophy's tremulous voice echoed in the sudden silence.

"I doubt that's any of our business," Gabe answered quietly. "And I think swim time is over."

chapter 19

I t was one thing to face the ugliness with her own eyes. It was another thing entirely to see the shock and horror on someone else's face.

With shaky fingers Summer stripped off her wet blouse and slacks. If there had been time, she would have welcomed the oblivion of a long, steamy shower, but that was out of the question with the girls at Tracey's.

Because the job always came first.

After drying off quickly, she slid on a robe and searched through her clothes, settling on a gray suit and a blue blouse. Last came a pair of plain black walking shoes. She caught herself with a frown when her hand lingered on the gift her sister had given her for Christmas two years before, but what was the point of wearing a delicate silver bracelet when your arm looked like something from a Frankenstein movie?

"Summer, can I come in?"

Not Gabe. Not now.

She tightened the belt of her robe. "No. I'm getting dressed."

Behind her the door opened. "Too damned bad."

She felt him behind her, felt the heat of his powerful body, but she didn't turn around. "I need to dress."

"Don't stop on my account."

"Very funny." Her arms locked across her chest. "Where are the girls?"

"Next door at my place, watching TV. I can only stay a few seconds." His fingers brushed her chin, tilted her face gently. "I just wanted to be sure you were okay."

"I'm fine." She waited for more of the pity she had seen back at the pool.

"Don't brush me off," Gabe said roughly.

No pity there, she thought. Impatience and irritation, but no pity.

She pulled the towel off her hair, tossing it onto the bed. "I don't want to talk about it."

"Maybe you need to. Tell me what happened, Summer. Let me in."

She closed her eyes, hit with the need to pour out memories that wouldn't leave her alone.

Glass shattering. Voices screaming. The smell of gasoline, and then agony as flames swallowed her arm whole.

"Go away, Gabe. I—can't do this."

He bit back a curse, and then his hand settled gently on her shoulder. "You think I don't know how it feels?" He laughed grimly. "Trust me, you're wrong."

"How could you know? You're perfect, strong, every inch of you." Heat flared in her cheeks. "I've seen your body, remember? You were using my shower, and there wasn't anything I could miss." She shook her head. "I don't want to talk about this."

Maybe talking would help . . . at some point. But not now—not with this man who had a knack for reaching inside her and seeing what other people didn't see.

"Your call." His hand lifted from her shoulder. "But

I'm hoping you'll change your mind." He picked up a fresh towel and draped it over her shoulders. "By the way, which field office do you work out of?"

She didn't answer.

"I don't suppose Mulvaney is your real name, either."

"You know how this works." Her voice was suddenly tired. "Going undercover means just that. You keep the lies simple and everyone gets the same story. It's the only way you stay focused."

A muscle flashed at Gabe's jaw. "I know the rules, Summer. Hell, I wrote a few of them. But the trick is knowing when to break the rules."

She couldn't stop herself from searching his face. Something whispered that she could trust this man, and he'd never let her down. "The rules are made for a reason. Breaking them isn't an option."

His face was unreadable. "I used to think so, too."

She pulled the towel from her shoulders. "And now?"

"And now . . . I have to go." He shoved his hands into his pockets. "The natives are camped out next door and they're getting restless."

"Did you see her scars?"

"Of course I saw them."

Sophy leaned forward, hugging her legs. "How do you think she got that way?"

Audra went to the bathroom and found a dry towel for Sophy, who was dripping on Gabe's couch. She didn't have a clue where you got scars like the ones on the nanny's arm, but she knew it had to be from something terrible. "Gee, I don't know. Maybe I'll ask her," she snapped.

"You *mean* it?"

"Of course I don't mean it. You saw how upset she was

in the pool. That's why neither you nor I are going to bring this up again."

Sophy frowned, petting Liberace, who was curled up on her lap. "You're acting different. What did you talk about with Ms. M?"

"Nothing important," Audra said airily. "Just women stuff."

Sophy's eyes widened. "Like about boyfriends and thong underwear?"

Audra stared at her sister. "What do *you* know about thong underwear?"

"I know that Tiffany Hammersmith wears them, but I think they're stupid. I mean, when you sit down, they'd scratch like anything."

"They're not supposed to feel good," Audra said importantly. "They're supposed to *look* good."

"But they're under your clothes. Who'd see them there?"

Audra rolled her eyes but managed to bite back a sharp comment.

"Oh." Sophy sat up a little straighter. "So you call up your boyfriends and tell them what you're wearing. For underwear, I mean. Like in phone sex."

"What do you know about phone sex?" Audra demanded. "Don't tell me Tiffany Hammersmith told you about that, too."

"Only a few things. Most of them didn't make sense." Sophy chewed her lip. "I mean, why would you want to make moaning noises over the phone while you took off your clothes?"

"Never mind," Audra snapped. "And I don't want you talking to Tiffany anymore. Not ever, understand?"

"She has a pink Hello Kitty purse," Sophy said wistfully.

"Forget about her purse. Not *ever*," Audra ordered sternly, the way only an older sister can.

"Then you have to explain about phone sex."

Audra made a strangled sound. "Just watch Buffy and be quiet, will you?"

Sophy stared at the television thoughtfully. "Do you think Buffy has phone sex?"

Snorting, Audra pulled away Sophy's towel and wrestled her to the floor. Liberace shot out of reach as the two girls rolled around on the rug, tickling each other without mercy, which was how Gabe found them when he opened the door a few minutes later.

"Hey, what happened to the two sweet-tempered honor students I left in here? Did someone kidnap them?"

Sophy appeared from beneath a towel, grinning ear to ear. "It's us, Gabe. We're still here."

"Thank goodness. You had me scared. It's time for you two to get cleaned up and dressed before your mother gets home. I'll go up to the house with you."

Sophy's smile faded. "Isn't Ms. M coming?"

"Soon as she dries off, sugar."

"Is she . . . mad at me?" Sophy's lower lip trembled.

"No. But I'd say it's up to Summer to decide if she wants to talk about what happened."

"You mean, no more questions?" Sophy said slowly.

"I think that's fair. Don't you, Audra?"

Both girls nodded stiffly. Sophy studied her bare toes. "I guess I probably shouldn't ask her about phone sex, either."

Audra elbowed her sharply, while Gabe fought an awful moment of panic. He wasn't going to have to field questions about biology and dating behavior, was he?

He was saved by Sophy, who shot straight into a new topic. "Can we stay here until Buffy is done? She's about to nail a silver spike into this really bad vampire. Not the *good* vampire." Sophy frowned at Gabe. "Are there good vampires? I mean, if they're good, how do they—"

"Be quiet and watch the TV," Audra cut in briskly.

A sudden vibration in Gabe's pocket signaled an incoming call on his secure cell phone. Keeping one eye on the girls, he moved back to the foyer outside his small kitchen. "Morgan here."

"This is your friendly local pizza man." As Izzy spoke, Gabe heard a mariachi band and beeping car horns in the background. "I've got some news."

Gabe moved into the bathroom, pulling the door half-closed. "Hit me."

"First, the report on the box left in Cara O'Connor's office. The forensic team found traces of oil-based pigment mixed with hydrogenated soy oil."

Gabe frowned. "Translation?"

"The oil was a commercial hydrogenated variety generally used in fast-food production. There was a trace of mayonnaise blended with relish and spices."

"Special sauce?" Gabe chuckled. "You've got to be kidding."

"I'm doing my own tests to narrow the location. Each restaurant has a characteristic oil signature determined by local pollution, building age, and a dozen other factors. Do you have any idea how many Mickey D's there are in the greater San Francisco area?"

"I'm getting clogged arteries just thinking about it."

"So you understand why tracing this particular batch of frying oil and special sauce may take some time."

Gabe stared at the back of Sophy's head. "What about the pigment traces on the box?"

"It appears to be printer's ink, with a solvent used to enhance dispersal and penetration."

"Books?" Gabe mused.

"Newsprint. The range of fairly cheap oil-based pigments, as opposed to higher-end ink types, suggests a tabloid."

"So our mystery man—or woman—wolfs down a combo meal while scanning the latest story about celebrity liposuction and Martian babies? Not much to go on, Izzy, even for you."

"It's a start. I imagine Ms. Mulvaney should be receiving her preliminary findings shortly. Do me a favor and act surprised, okay?"

"Will do." Gabe checked on the girls, who were engrossed in the sight of Buffy decimating an army of undead, while their ferret backed in and out of a brown paper bag, tail twitching happily.

"How are the girls?"

"Fine. Liberace's destroying a sack and Buffy's about to nail the head demon, saving the world as we know it."

"A good show. Cara O'Connor's children have excellent taste." Izzy's voice hardened. "Which brings me to my next piece of news. Not everyone is thrilled about Senator Winslow's upcoming nuptials. One of his key fund-raisers resigned two months ago, ostensibly over salary issues, but office gossip says it was because he opposed the marriage."

"Why? You don't come with a better record than Cara O'Connor's." Gabe frowned. "Do you think it was personal?"

"Bingo. His sister was active in fund-raising, too, and it seems that she had romantic aspirations for the senator, with an eye toward sleeping in the main bedroom at the White House. I'm told a lot of women consider Senator Winslow prime marriage material."

"That would be motive. But did these people have access to Cara's medical history?"

"One more thing for you and Summer to check out while you're down in Mexico. I'm faxing through some pictures. Take them with you, show them around. See if anyone remembers them visiting the clinic."

"You got it." Gabe peeked out as he heard noises in the living room. "We'll have to wind this up, Izzy. Buffy just made hamburger out of the evil hordes. Liberace's doing a pretty good job on that sack, too."

"In that case, I'll give you the rest in shorthand. My sources tell me that one other person has been opposed to the senator's involvement with Cara. Winslow's brother, who happens to be his policy advisor, feels that Cara's record as an assistant DA is undistinguished and may harm the senator's presidential run. Greg Winslow was pushing for the senator to marry another woman four years ago—think old Virginia money and sterling pedigree. When the wedding plans were nixed, his brother almost quit."

Gabe watched Liberace race through the room, circling the paper bag. "I remember Greg Winslow was always a stiff neck. Discredited, Cara O'Connor would fit nicely with his current plans. We'll look into possible connections with him during our clinic visit, too. Meanwhile, see what you can dig up on him, like policy disputes with his brother, money problems, or alcohol issues."

"Senator Winslow isn't going to be happy if he finds out we're digging for dirt on his most trusted advisor."

"No kidding. Tate has always valued loyalty. This stays between us for now." Gabe rubbed his neck, listening to the final sounds of Buffy tackling the underworld hordes. "What about Cara? Does she know?"

"I doubt it."

"So how did you find out?"

"A few key sources and amazing electronic skills," Izzy said dryly.

"Hold on a minute." Gabe covered the phone and looked out, stunned to find Audra standing motionless just outside the door. "Is something wrong, Audra?"

"Sophy has to use the bathroom." Her hands were clenched tight. "Why were you talking about my mother?"

"I'm dealing with my toughest supplier," Gabe lied calmly. "He's opposed to roses, but your mom doesn't know that yet." He lowered his voice. "He's trying to push for hybrid lilies, mainly because it will cost twice as much."

"So you were talking about flowers just now?"

"Afraid so. What do you think, I'm a spy or something?"

Sophy appeared behind Audra. "I'm sorry, but I really need—" She winced, pointing to the bathroom. "You know."

"Sure, honey. Be my guest." Gabe stepped aside, then winked at Audra. "Go ahead and send me the price list for the lilies, but I can tell you now that Ms. O'Connor wants roses, so you're wasting your time."

"Got an audience, do you? In that case, I'll sign off. Watch for those pictures. You can download them via your cell."

Audra continued to stare at Gabe after he ended the call. "That's really all you were talking about? Just flowers and stuff?"

Gabe nodded. "Never underestimate the importance of good flowers. Now tell me why you're so worried."

"My mom is really upset about something. I hear her get up and pace at night. Other times she and the senator argue, but they change the subject whenever we come into the room."

"People who are about to be married have private things to discuss, Audra. That doesn't mean they're keeping secrets or that they're worried."

"Maybe." Audra studied her sandals. "Yesterday at the museum, Ms. Mulvaney went a little nuts, just because I was a few minutes late. Explain that."

"Your nanny was doing her job. Senator Winslow is a very important man, and since he's marrying your mom, that means *you* are important, too. Unfortunately, security has to be a part of your life from now on."

Audra's shoulders tensed. "You think someone would try to kidnap us?" She snorted. "No way. That stuff only happens on *Alias*."

"I wish you were right." Gabe chose his next words carefully. "If you're worried, you should talk about this with your mother. Talk to Senator Winslow, too. Get the facts, and you'll feel better."

Audra sighed. "I tried to talk to my mom once, but she got this stricken look. Like Bambi on the train tracks, you know what I mean?"

Water flushed inside the bathroom. "Does Sophy feel anxious about your mom, too?"

"Not really. She's just a kid, after all. Things don't seem to bother her."

The door swung open. Sophy peered from Gabe to Audra. "Is something wrong?" She glanced toward the living room. "Did Liberace do something bad?"

"He's fine," Audra said. "But we need to finish packing. Mom will be here in about an hour."

"I'm taking my ballet shoes," Sophy said as she clipped Liberace to a leash for the trip back to the house. "I'll find Mom's old dance costumes, too. Then we can have a recital at the ranch."

Audra sighed. "Count me out. I hated ballet. I'd rather

learn the tango. Or maybe I'll just try kickboxing." She nudged Sophy with her elbow. "Come on. Last one to the house is liverwurst pie."

Gabe followed them outside, scanning the lawn and wondering where on earth the stuff about kickboxing had come from.

Tate Winslow put down his phone with a frown. He had probably ten more calls to make before he left his office, along with five letters to dictate.

He knew he'd better thrive on the insane pace, because this was just the beginning. Assuming that he actually decided to run.

He sat back in his chair and picked up a small toy armadillo given to him by a colleague in Washington. The heavy shell made him smile wryly. Having body armor was crucial in a town that thrived on a high-octane mix of power, sex, and gossip. Over time Tate had learned to build his own protective shell.

But what about the future? Sophy and Audra deserved a father, and Cara needed a husband. God knows *he* wanted a family. It had been far too long since he'd lived in a house that rang with children's laughter and racing footsteps. Sharing a sink cluttered with perfume bottles and face cream seemed wonderfully exotic after years of camping out alone in hotel suites and expensive but impersonal rental homes.

Yet here he was, poised for the biggest political push of his life, a process that would swallow up almost all of his time and what little privacy he had left. It was an insane time to consider getting married.

But he had never wanted anything more.

The yellow light blinked on his phone. "Yes, Margo."

"Your brother's calling, Senator. Line two."

"Got it. When I'm done, let's knock out the rest of these letters. Then you can go." Leaning forward, he punched a button. "So, do we have our support for the wetlands conservancy or not, Greg?"

A chair creaked. Tate could almost see his chief political advisor dig into the pile of papers and press clippings that accompanied him everywhere. His ammunition dump, Greg called it.

"Better than I hoped. I've located two corporate sources ready to back your initiative, along with half a dozen grassroots conservation groups. It will make damned good press—more important, none of it will cost the public a cent. I've set up two interviews for you next week, but there's just one problem."

Wasn't there always? "Who's out for blood today? Sanders? Ashford?"

His brother gave a dry laugh. "Neither. This enemy is worse, Tate. It's your own lack of time. Your schedule is completely booked, and I don't know where to fit in anything else."

"You and Margo can find a way to shoehorn them in. Something else bothering you?"

Papers rustled. "I ran into another reporter from *The Wall Street Journal*. He asked when you were going to formally declare."

"And you put him off, politely but firmly."

"Of course." There was a brief hesitation. "He told me there's a feeling you aren't serious about becoming president. He was basically trying to bait me into an exclusive story, but it's worrisome nevertheless. He also said . . ."

"Go on, Greg."

"Damn it, he said a friend of his would double whatever salary I was getting from you."

Tate studied the stuffed armadillo. "Nice offer. I trust that you told him no."

"Of course I did. I'm not going anywhere, especially over to the media. We've had our differences, but that's ancient history now. This means there's more negative buzz about your presidential race. Someone could be trying to mow you down early."

"Nothing we can't handle. You're better at your job than you realize, Greg."

"It would be easier if you'd finalize, Tate. You've got a shot straight to the very top, and voters are ready for fresh ideas and new energy. I'm getting forty or fifty calls a day from people who want to volunteer for your campaign, even before it's officially announced. Mother called today and said your demographics are off the chart, according to one of her lobbyist friends. Our only challenge will be timing. You need to set a date for the official announcement before these negative rumors snowball. I know you're distracted with the wedding coming up—"

"My focus is hardly in question," Tate said impatiently. "I'm taking the minimum time off, exactly as we agreed. Damn it, this is August recess, my only time free." Why did he feel *guilty* for trying to have some semblance of a life?

"True enough, but the clock is ticking, remember that."

"I'll think about a date, Greg." Tate glanced at his watch. "Gotta go, bro. Five more letters to dictate. Is there anything else?"

"Have you heard from Mother? She left a message here and sounded upset."

Tate stared at the photo of his brother and his mother hiking in Alaska. "I spoke to her a while ago. She had to drop some things at Cara's, and apparently there was some kind of problem with a dead rat in Cara's car. Don't worry, it's nothing. She's probably stressed from all the wedding preparations."

"In that case, I'll see you at the airport later. I've got those health-care documents you wanted to review."

"If I don't hurry, I won't make it to the airport. Getting Cara to take three days off was no easy matter, either."

"She has that Costello appeal coming up, as I remember. Any problems there? You'd hope a conviction of racketeering, vice, trafficking in human illegals, and a few counts of murder would stick."

"Costello's going down and staying down. Cara and her people built a solid case against him, and this appeal has no merit."

"I heard one of the earlier witnesses wants to change his testimony."

Tate frowned. "Really? Cara didn't mention that to me."

"She probably forgot with all the distractions. Now get finished there and go meet her." Greg Winslow sighed. "As for me, I've got a date with two angry lobbyists. With a little luck I can keep them from strangling each other over Caesar salad and grilled chicken Florentine."

"Rock on." Smiling, Tate put down the phone. Then he picked up a file and started fleshing out answers to mail that couldn't wait.

Cara stood at her office window watching a layer of gray haze climb up from the Pacific. The shot fired at the house had left her terrified, and she was determined to get the girls away as soon as possible. She had always considered herself a strong woman with a solid moral compass, but the last weeks had begun to tear away her strength, filling her with doubts.

As the gray haze continued to climb, she thought about the girls. How could she bring her children into danger? How could she let them suffer for the difficult job she did? And how could she inflict her past on Tate if it could harm his career?

Audra's school gift was back in place on her desk, the clay body repaired. Unable to sleep, Cara had spent the hour before dawn gluing the fragile chips back into place.

Sighing, she picked up a photo of her girls laughing on a beach in North Carolina, and another of Sophy in a recent dance costume. Her throat tightened at the thought of one of them caught unaware in her bedroom.

Struck down by a bullet.

With tears in her eyes she picked up a family shot of her older sister outside her rustic house in Oregon, flanked by her three handsome boys of seventeen, fifteen, and twelve. Melody and her husband were ecologists with the forest service and their kids lived a life right out of *Wild Kingdom.* They were safe and sheltered, surrounded by beauty, and their boys had learned to paddle a canoe almost as soon as they could walk. It was still hard for Cara to believe that Mel's oldest son, Jordan, was heading off to college in the fall.

As she studied the photo, she made a mental note to call her sister and catch up on all the family developments this weekend. Too many months had gone by since she and her sister had spoken.

There was a low tap at her door, and her assistant opened it, elegant in gray pants and a gray cashmere sweater. "Tony called. He wants to talk to you about the Costello appeal. And you also have a visitor," she announced grandly.

"Who?"

"Me." Looking tan and very fit, Melody, Cara's sister, strolled through the door. "Since I never hear from you, I decided to swing by on my way back from a conference at Berkeley." After a tight hug, Mel moved back to study her sister. "So why aren't you sleeping?"

"Is it so obvious?"

"To me it is."

"The girls are fine. Sophy loves her ballet and Audra—well, she's going through some teen angst, but I'm sure it will pass."

"Don't talk to me about teens. Next year I'll have three of them, God help me, even if Jordan will be off at college." Mel sank onto a chair by the window, studying Cara. "You're working too hard. You and the girls should come up to Oregon and we'll take you camping. Jeff and the boys will get you unwound with some mountaineering. Since Jordan has his own canoe now, he'd take you on the ride of your life." She touched Cara's arm and held it. "We'd all love to have you. Don't worry about calling first."

"It sounds so wonderful, Mel. I'd love to, but . . ." Cara gestured at her crowded desk. "I'm locked in here."

"Think about it. The offer always holds." Melody took the family picture from Cara's hands. "The boys have grown since this was taken. Michael and Chance are giving kayak lessons this summer, can you believe it? And Jordan is busy getting ready for college." She handed the picture back to Cara. "Hard to believe how things change. It seems just yesterday that I met Jeff, and you graduated from law school." She stood up, pacing the small room. "I can't stay. I've got to be back at the airport by five for my flight. Besides, you have work up to your ears."

"You can't leave yet. Let's at least have coffee while you fill me in on the boys and all the news."

"Next time." Mel smiled wistfully. "I can see how busy you are. Your assistant had three calls on hold and by now there are probably five waiting. Take care of yourself, okay?"

Their eyes met.

"I owe you," Mel said quietly. "I'll never forget."

Cara hugged her sister. "Don't say another word."

"You never told, did you?"

"No. I made you a promise, and I'll keep it."

Mel slid the strap of her computer case over her shoulder. "Are you keeping Tate and his family in line?"

"Greg and Amanda have been very helpful in planning the wedding." Cara frowned. "You and Jeff and the boys are still coming, aren't you?"

"Couldn't keep us away. I always knew you'd marry someone important—the same way I knew you'd *be* someone important." Mel frowned. "Greg and Amanda haven't been making you jump through hoops, have they?"

"Of course not. Amanda has been wonderful about organizing the reception, and Greg put together the guest list."

"Just you, Tate, and four hundred of Amanda's friends," Mel said wryly. Then she shook her head. "Don't mind me. I'm just grumpy from traveling, and I miss my boys. Who knew I'd turn into such an old crone?"

"You're not a crone, you're wonderful. Give them all my love." Cara looked at the picture. "You look so happy together."

"We are." Mel smiled gravely. "Get some rest. I expect to see a serenely radiant bride when I get to Wyoming." She turned at the door. "It was the right thing to do."

Cara took a deep breath. "I know." Most of the time, Cara thought.

After her sister left, she stayed at the window for a long time, lost in thought.

The kitchen was gleaming.

Fresh salsa cooled in clay pots and beef strips were marinating for *carne asada*. Patrick Flanagan hummed as he finished pounding dough for the yeasty French loaves Sophy and Audra loved so well. He took great delight in the knowledge that he was very, very good at his work.

Imelda peeked inside. "I'm finished. Do you need anything before I leave?"

"Not a thing." Smiling, Patrick offered her a freshly baked croissant. "Take one for the road."

Imelda sighed. "You are very bad for me, Patrick."

"When you're in my kitchen, there's no willpower allowed." Flipping his towel over one shoulder, the chef leaned back against the granite sink. "Did you hear that truck noise earlier? Ms. Mulvaney told me one of the workmen dropped his hammer and broke an upstairs window."

"I heard the window break. It is like a gunshot, I am thinking. And so much glass in the bedroom. It is good that one of the workmen came soon after to help me clean or I would still be working."

"One of the workmen? Funny, I never knew one who was anxious to do cleanup."

"Oh, he is a very nice man. Very strong hands. If I am ten years younger . . ." Imelda smiled, mischief in her eyes. "But I am not, so I will drive home to my cats and my crossword puzzles instead. You are leaving soon?"

"In half an hour," Patrick said cheerfully. "Or I may wait until Ms. O'Connor comes home. I like to be sure the food is hot when they're ready to eat."

"Such a conscientious man." Imelda nodded approvingly. "Some woman will be very lucky to have a fine husband like you, Patrick."

"Oh, I'm too busy to get married. Give me the field any day." Smiling, he waved good-bye to the housekeeper, then went back to his perfectly rising dough.

The chemistry of making bread was always an intricate challenge, and Patrick Flanagan liked to test himself. It was pleasant to be close to his new family, too. For so many years he had been without roots or clear purpose.

But no longer. As he kneaded the soft dough, he thought about the powder in the jar he kept at the bottom of his leather satchel. The little bottle hidden on a shelf in his apartment.

His hands tightened, squeezing dough out through his fingers like strips of pale skin. All it would take was a few pinches.

Control, he thought sharply. No sudden changes of plan. There would be time for action soon enough. The gunshot had gone perfectly. His friend had left his kayak, climbed onto a rock out of sight, and fired as planned. The warning had been delivered.

The dead rat had been Patrick's contribution. He still had to smile at the look of sheer terror on Amanda Winslow's face in the garage. One minute she was snapping out orders, the next she was babbling in terror. *So delicious.*

As a boy he'd never been able to lie well. But now he was a man, and he'd discovered he had a real gift for shaping his lies to suit different people. He considered his next lie as he kneaded the dough one last time. At first, all that had been asked of him was simple surveillance, acting as a set of eyes and ears inside the house, but soon other assignments had come. It had been easy for him to read Cara O'Connor's personal mail, then pass on the information in his neat, detailed handwriting. It had been simple to hint to Audra that she was overweight and ugly, but of course he loved her anyway. How kind he had been, sympathizing with Cara O'Connor's busy schedule and her terrible regret at missing such a large part of her girls' day. He laughed when he thought how subtly he had fueled all her regrets.

Delicious, he thought. He loved being a chef, but his new career was so much more satisfying. He would receive another twenty thousand dollars soon.

"Bread's done," he said happily. "Now to the oven."

He stared around his gleaming kitchen. Yes, he'd have a lovely meal ready and waiting for his favorite family.

chapter 20

Audra and Sophy paced anxiously. Summer had tried to distract them with offers of food, television, and a Frisbee game, but the girls weren't interested. They were worried that their mother wasn't home yet, and soon Summer was feeling anxious, too. She was pulling out her phone to call Cara when a green Saturn raced around the corner and up the driveway.

When Cara emerged, clutching her briefcase, she looked rattled. "Sorry, my battery died, and I had to get a tow into Monterey. Thankfully they had a loaner." She hugged Sophy and smoothed Audra's hair. "No long faces allowed."

"You should have called," Audra said in a high, tight voice. "I was—we were all worried about you. You always tell *me* to call. And Patrick's been keeping dinner warm for hours and *everything.*"

Cara had a stricken look on her face as she leaned down to hug Audra hard. "I'm okay, honey. We're all okay. This weekend up at the ranch is going to be wonderful."

"You still should have called," Audra muttered. "And what was wrong with your car battery? Didn't you buy one two months ago?"

"I suppose the salt air took its toll." Cara rubbed her neck, frowning. "I'll ask when they bring the car back." She glanced at her watch and gasped. "Yikes, let's go see Patrick and have dinner. Then I need to pack. Who wants to help?"

"Me," Sophy said, waving a pink glove.

"I'd better help, too." Audra took her mother's arm. "Last time you forgot to pack any socks, remember?"

"I'm so glad I have you to keep an eye on me, honey." As Cara patted her daughter's arm, she glanced at Summer. "Are you packed, too?"

Summer knew the question was far from casual, considering her real destination. "Everything's ready."

Sophy skipped across the grass. "All you'll need at the ranch is jeans and boots—and more boots, Ms. M. There's a *lot* of horse poop up there."

Summer held open the door. "Thanks for the warning. I'll be very, very careful." Her cell phone began to vibrate. "Why don't you go ahead and eat while I check on Gabe? He's supposed to drive us to the airport, I believe." As the others went inside, Summer walked across the grass and pulled out her phone. "Mulvaney, here."

The news wasn't especially good.

The forensics report on Cara's box showed unidentified oil traces on the brown paper wrapper, along with a mineral oil–based ink, and further results would take a week.

"That's all?" Summer asked impatiently. "Unidentified oil traces?"

Her boss gave an impatient huff. "Cut me some slack, Mulcahey." A fiftyish Afro-American with a mind like an ICBM, Morrison Haley had grown up on the toughest streets in Detroit, always an inch over the line with the law,

which made him a damned hard man to fool. A determined local priest had helped him secure a football schol-
arship to UCLA, where he'd been a record-breaking
linebacker.

The special agent in charge of the Philadelphia field office was known as Mo to his friends, and Summer was one
of the select few accorded that privilege.

"Right now we're up to our ears in terrorist sight-
ings, most of them tips from whackos. Add in a string of
armed robberies and a counterfeiting chain and you'll
see why we're understaffed. I've already transferred your
box to Quantico for further tests, but it's not deemed high
priority."

"Look, Mo—"

"Sorry, but there's nothing more I can do. Ask Ms.
O'Connor to put in a word with the senator. He may have
the juice to get some action, but I don't. End of story." He
sounded disgusted, and Summer felt just the same.

"Without more tests, we've got zip, Mo."

"Stow it, Mulcahey. I sympathize, but that's my last
word." His voice tightened. "How's your arm? Any problems?"

Summer made her voice completely neutral. "No problems at all. Beyond the fact that I scare the shit out of dogs
and little children."

"You should have gone for reconstructive surgery three
months ago. Line of duty makes it Uncle Sam's tab."

"I had a case, remember." As she spoke, Summer un-
consciously fingered her arm. Though the sleeve of her
jacket covered all trace of her scars, she could sense them
with absolute clarity.

"Anything changes, you let me know. You took a
pounding, with no help from that chickenshit partner of
yours."

"Mo—"

"Don't Mo *me*. Riley screwed up big-time and I don't like putting the lid on it."

Glass shattering. Distant screams that sounded strangely like her own.

Then a sucking, snarling wall of fire rolling down her arm.

"Riley's dead, Mo. He had two kids and a pregnant wife. Let it be."

"I have and I will, because of his wife and kids. But damn it, I don't like it, especially when it leaves some people muttering it was your fault."

"I'll survive," Summer said tightly. "Riley's family needs full benefits. If there was a formal investigation . . ." She let the words trail off. They both knew what kind of red tape would result. A thorough investigation would reveal ongoing problems in field procedure, and Riley's benefits might be jeopardized.

Mo grumbled some more, then cleared his throat. "What about the letters you've been getting?"

"I don't know what you mean."

"Like hell you don't. Your sister told me about them."

"Jess? How did she—"

"Jess stayed in your condo for a few days. You were in D.C. being briefed, remember? While she was there you got two anonymous postcards in the mail. Nasty stuff, too. She called me, half-terrified, half-sputtering with outrage." He gave a dry laugh. "Not a woman to be messed with, your sister. My wife would love her." His voice hardened. "Any ideas who the bastard is?"

More than one, Summer thought. She had heard the muttered comments as she'd passed, but she had no firm names. "I can't say, sir."

"They're FBI, so they'd know the moves, but I may get something from the postcards yet. If so, I'll have their asses in a sling for this. I'm glad your sister thought to send me the postcards."

Leave it to Jess, Summer thought. "I see."

"Do you? I'm responsible for my jurisdiction, damn it. You should have told me about this," he snapped. "When did it start?"

"Two days after Riley died, sir."

Mo blew out a hard breath. "I expect you to inform me of any further harassment, in any shape or form. Is that understood?"

"Yes, sir."

He cleared his throat. "Call me Mo, damn it. *Sir* was what they called Sidney Poitier in that old movie. By the way, your sister said hello. She wants to hear from you."

By the time the line went dead, Summer's shoulders were tight with tension. She'd have to phone Jess and explain. She'd also have to . . .

"Something wrong?"

She jumped a good three inches, biting back an oath. "Make some noise, will you, Morgan? Otherwise, you might get yourself shot in that rugged jaw of yours."

Gabe simply smiled. "I trust your reflexes. Where are the Buffy fans?"

"Helping Cara pack." Summer slid her cell phone back into her pocket. "Everything set for Los Reyes?"

"Checked and rechecked. And you didn't answer my question. What's wrong?"

"What makes you think—"

"Because you look like you just took a bullet at point-blank range. So what's going on?"

"Nothing important," Summer said coolly. She started to walk past, but Gabe grabbed her wrist.

Dimly she noted it was her left wrist, not her scarred one.

"Let's get this straight. If something's stuck in your craw, it affects your judgment and response time. That affects the mission. So I'll ask you again: What the hell is wrong?"

Summer was surprised to feel her heart pounding. He smelled like shaving cream and some kind of lemon soap. Wet hair. Damp face. Must have come right out of the shower—

"Mulvaney, I'm waiting."

"Okay, there is something. I just had a call from my boss. The forensic analysis produced next to nothing. Mineral-based ink traces and soy oil of some sort."

He seemed to be watching her face intensely. "That's all?"

"My SAC sent the contents on to the lab in D.C., but don't hold your breath. Unless Senator Winslow makes a fuss, it could be weeks."

"He will," Gabe said calmly. "I'll talk to him today. Now what *else* is bothering you?"

She considered lying. Heaven knows, hiding the details of her life had become a habit. Then she looked into his eyes and decided lying would be about as useful as a raincoat on a June day in Arizona.

She looked out over the grass, watching a big trawler cruise south. To Baja? Or even farther, down to Puerto Vallarta or Peru?

She rolled her shoulders a little and realized she hadn't a clue where to start. "It's about work."

"The Philadelphia field office, you mean?"

Summer nodded. "My first partner . . . died a while back."

Seventeen months, two weeks, and four days, Summer thought grimly.

"What happened?"

"Routine surveillance. I was the FNG."

Gabe raised an eyebrow.

"Effing New Guy," Summer said grimly. "We were parked, watching the back exit during a low-priority search warrant entry, and suddenly—" The memories streamed in cold waves. "Three lunatics the size of Jesse Ventura on major steroids exploded out of a locked garage with opening fire. We were pinned down, and my partner, Riley, hadn't even put on his Nomex. I looked around, heard the windshield pop, and he's hit, crumpling hard." She took two sharp breaths, remembering what came next.

"Two of the guys race up to the car, and I see they have a red metal can. Everything happens so fast and Riley—my partner—had his window open. The next thing I know, they're dousing the seat, dousing Riley, dousing me . . ."

Her voice shook a little, so she stopped, awash in memories. She took another long breath. "In a second my clothes are burning. I try to get to Riley. Twice I try, but—"

Gabe's face was like steel when he reached out, gripping her shoulder. "So that's what happened. Bad break—especially for the FNG. You're still carrying it around with you, just like those scars carved into your arm. Let it go, Summer. Your partner screwed up, not you."

She shook her head, a quick, angry movement like brushing away flies. "Riley was right there beside me, joking one minute, bloody the next. Then burning like a torch because I couldn't get close enough. So don't tell me to let it go, damn it, because I *can't*."

"Point taken," Gabe said quietly. "Why didn't you check the garage first?"

Summer stared out at the ocean.

"It was your partner's job, wasn't it? But he was hungry, or impatient, or he got a call from his accountant."

"Call of nature," Summer said quietly. "He hit the bushes and said the garage could wait. When he came back, I asked, but he told me to shut up. I was the FNG, so I took orders. And then—" She shuddered. "Then it was too late."

Her fingers moved to her arm.

Gabe watched her cradle the scarred skin in an unconscious gesture that left him chilled, reliving the inferno through her motions.

She was right, of course. You never forgot a thing like that. You only thought about it slightly less than every hour of every day, wondering what you could have done differently so your partner would still be alive.

Gabe took in the closed expression on her face. "There's more, isn't there? It didn't end after the fire."

She made a sharp movement with one hand. "Look, Gabe, I really don't want to talk about—"

"What happened next, Summer? Did they collar you for the mistake, put you under suspension? The FNG takes the flack?"

Her fingers moved restlessly over her arm. "No. Nothing like that."

"Then what?"

He could almost see her muscles lock, refusing to form the words. She stared out at the horizon, where clouds piled up over broken layers of light. "Riley, my partner, had two kids. Nice kids." Her jaw worked back and forth. "His wife was pregnant with another one."

"It sucks, but I still don't see—"

"I covered up for him," she said tightly. "I said I screwed up and missed the men in the garage." She rubbed her neck wearily. "A formal investigation would have wasted precious taxpayer money, thousands of dollars."

"And blasted your pal Riley's death benefits, too." Gabe frowned. "So you took the fall for him."

"Damn it, I'm alive and he's *not*. It was the least I could do for his family. I can stand a little heat in return for knowing they'll be well cared for. Even if . . ."

She made an angry sound and shook her head. "Why am I telling you this? I haven't even told my sister or the staff shrink they sent me to afterward."

"You're telling me because I'm an outsider, a stranger who won't take sides and won't lie to you. Because I'm a stranger, I can say that what you're doing is pretty damned brave, Summer. Stupid, but brave. So who's giving you the heat?"

"Who said anything about—"

"It doesn't take a shrink to see that you're tied up in knots, guilty and angry by turns. Someone's gunning for you. Who?"

She ground one toe in the gravel. "I don't know. They leave nasty notes in my locker. Stupid stuff—old jockstraps, excrement." She took a slow breath. "Occasional letters."

Gabe made a harsh sound. "Threats?"

Summer turned away.

"Damn it, have they threatened you, Summer?"

"Yes," she said. The whisper of sound was so focused and contained that it left Gabe chilled.

"I'll kill them." He jerked out his cell phone. "What's your SAC's number?"

"*No.*" She gripped Gabe's arm, her hand trembling slightly. "He knows already."

"The bastard *knows* and he's doing nothing?"

"He's looking into who's behind this, but they're not stupid. Plus, they know exactly what he'll be watching for."

"So they wear gloves and wipe any prints," Gabe said flatly. "No licked stamps. Cheap, common paper that you can buy in any grocery store."

"That's about it."

Was this the reason she never asked for help, Gabe wondered, because she couldn't trust anyone around her? If so, it was a cold, brutal way to live.

Even as he fought the need to touch her, Gabe forced himself to stay very still, completely controlled. When had her emotions become so transparent to him? And what the hell had happened to his usual detachment?

Because the questions left him irritated, Gabe forced them out of his mind. "If they're cocky, they'll give themselves away. With a little help," he added grimly.

"How?"

"Let me work on a few ideas." He considered several scenarios to discuss with Izzy. Hell, there wasn't any piece of recording or surveillance equipment that Teague couldn't ramp up, hot-wire, or generally finesse into turning somersaults and backflips.

Which was exactly what Gabe had already put in place for Cara's safety. Now they'd rig the same thing for Summer.

But when they cornered the bastards who were hounding Summer, Gabe would be certain they spent a little quality time together alone with him in a soundproof room.

"Why are you smiling like that?"

"Nothing important."

"Gabe, I don't want your help." Her shoulders squared. "I mean it. This is my job, my problem. I can handle it."

"Sure you can. I'm just going to talk to someone who

happens to be good at electronics." Izzy would cut him off at the knees for such an underestimation of his amazing array of talents. "I'll pass on whatever he says. You can't object to that?"

"And you'll stay out of it?"

"Absolutely." Like hell, he would. "Satisfied?"

She gave an uncertain smile, which caught Gabe hard right at the middle of his chest, making him wonder when the air had been sucked out of his lungs. He cursed silently, aware that he'd just gone past simple sexual attraction.

Emotions were starting to get involved, and emotions always made things sticky. Worst of all, emotions had the potential to short-circuit his concentration.

Of course, he wouldn't let that happen. Gabe had stopped being a tongue-tied, sweaty-palmed teenager a few decades ago, and *these* emotions were going right into the garbage can.

"Now you're scowling," Summer said quietly.

He looked at his watch and shrugged. "It's getting late and we should go. I'll load the luggage, then give you a tour of the new security equipment."

"But your friend—"

"Izzy appears to have gotten tied up in town, and we only have fifteen minutes until we leave for the airport. I'll do the short version now and fill in the rest later, after I catch up with you in Arizona."

"What about the spent shell from Cara's bedroom?"

"We're checking for prints, but I doubt we'll find any. It's a standard purchase anywhere in the country, so no luck sourcing it, either."

Summer blocked his way. "What did you say you did for a living?"

"I didn't." Calmly, Gabe cut around her. "After I load

up, we'll start with the pressure-sensitive plates outside the back windows."

He hid a smile when he heard Summer mutter "hard-ass" and fall in behind him.

Izzy hated trim-layer chromatography techniques.

The need to use them didn't often arise, which was a good thing, because they left him in a foul mood. But since he was aware of how much competition there was for use of the expensive equipment at the FBI's central crime lab, he was happy to lend a hand, especially if he didn't have to run the tests himself.

Fortunately, a lot of people owed him favors.

He hunched over his computer, muttering. After careful deliberation, he picked up the phone and punched in a string of numbers.

"Forensic documents," an impatient woman's voice said.

"Sara, how are you doing?"

There was a brief pause, then a hiss of indrawn breath. "Izzy? Is that you?"

"Afraid so, Doc."

"So, are you drunk, in trouble, or in need of a favor?"

"So cynical. A man can't call up a sexy, gorgeous woman on a whim?"

The forensic document expert on the other end of the line gave a smoky laugh. "Oh, a million men could and would. But it's not your style, Izzy. You're too decent— and too damned smart—to get a woman's hopes up for nothing." She waited a beat. "Aren't you?"

Izzy wiggled uneasily. He'd forgotten the last time they'd met—and the unexpectedly intimate offer Sara had made to him. "My father taught me that the lady is always right. You can interpret that any way you want. So how many letters do you have after your name now?"

"Only three, but they appear to be adequate. Since I'm in the middle of an ink examination, I've got to be quick. That is, unless you want to take me out to dinner so we have more time."

Izzy laughed. "I wish I could, Sara, but I'm on an assignment."

"Now why doesn't that surprise me?" She gave a dramatic sigh. "So what is it you need? Watermark evaluation? Infrared ink comparison? Paper analysis?"

"Can I get the whole combo meal?" Izzy asked carefully.

"*Everything?* Do you have any idea what kind of backlog—" She stopped, took a breath. "Of course you know. Sorry about that. We're insanely shorthanded around here since several of our people were transferred over to counterterrorism. And I still owe you for setting up our network and connecting us to the federal DNA and fingerprint databases."

"It was my pleasure, Doc."

She cleared her throat. "Anything else you need, besides the combo meal?"

In for a penny, in for a pound, Izzy thought. "While you're at it, how about checking for hair and fiber, along with possible latents? Any impression evidence and static dust lifts would be nice, too."

"How about I give you the Hope Diamond while I'm at it?" the world-renowned director of the San Mateo County Forensic Document Division snapped.

"No need. Blue was never my color."

"If I didn't owe you—"

"You don't owe me a thing, Sara." Izzy's voice was

grave. "You're the best I've ever seen, and it was my pleasure to help you get the new lab computers online. I appreciate how busy you are, so it's no problem if you can't take the time right now. I'll find someone else to—"

"Like hell you will. Get me your documents and do it fast. I've got two vacation days coming and I'll cancel my trip to Martinique."

"I couldn't possibly let you—"

"A joke, okay? All I had planned was three George Clooney videos and some artery-clogging popcorn. Working for you will be a whole lot healthier."

Izzy smiled. "Now I owe *you,* Sara. It's a good thing I happen to have a source for that new Swiss electron microscope you've been lusting after."

She gave a yelp of pure delight. "You *mean* it? You wouldn't toy with me about a thing like that, would you?"

"Scout's honor."

"You were *never* a scout, but we'll overlook that for now. Get me your evidence and make sure it's uncontaminated. And just for the record," she added dryly, "the electron microscope isn't the only thing I've been lusting after."

Before Izzy could think of a suitable answer, she hung up on him.

chapter 21

Where's Liberace? I don't see his cage." Frantic, Sophy scrambled up the aisle of the small plane, looking for her mother.

"He's fine, honey." Cara smoothed her hair, looking frazzled. "He's right in his cage in the back."

"You're *sure*?"

"Tate put him there personally."

"Oh." Sophy took a slow breath. "Uncle Tate is careful. He wouldn't forget Liberace."

Cara studied her daughter, wondering where these new fears had come from. "Of course he wouldn't. Now it's time to strap in because we're ready to take off. Can you hear the motor change rhythm?" When all else failed, distraction was the best answer, Cara knew.

In the wing of the small airport north of Monterey, a technician in gray coveralls moved unhurriedly, recording equipment transfers and completed repairs.

With a new girlfriend who liked pretty things, Ray Markle had a salary that never stretched far enough, so the quiet offer that had come his way four months ago proved to be a godsend. All he had to do was note any flight plans filed for Senator Winslow's Cessna Grand Caravan, then make a call to an anonymous voice-mail box with all the details.

Ray had been able to take his astonished girlfriend to Acapulco the following month, and now they were planning a trip to Paris, thanks to payments wired directly into his new bank account in the Caymans. Ray accessed the account from an ATM card sent to him in an envelope with no return address, and he had no idea of the source of these payments, nor did he care. He told himself it wasn't breaking the law to jot down a few flight details.

As Senator Winslow and his group boarded the Cessna, the technician stood behind a wall of outbound cargo, dialing the phone number burned into his memory. When he heard the short electronic *click,* he rattled off the details of the senator's flight plan. Next stop for the Cessna was Elko, Nevada. Ray hadn't been able to track any stops beyond Elko, but he had a cousin near Vegas who worked weekends in Elko. In exchange for one month's payment on his new truck, his cousin would track the plane outbound to its next destination.

The whole arrangement suited Markle just fine— except for one detail. He wasn't an imaginative man, but the day the offer had come by phone, he'd been warned by a harsh, electronic voice exactly what would happen to him if he ever decided to discuss the arrangement.

The graphic description still made his skin crawl.

As the Cessna lifted smoothly from the runway, Ray was already on the phone with his cousin in Nevada.

"But I don't *understand?* Where is Ms. M? Why isn't she going with us?"

"Lower your voice, Sophy." Cara was sharper than shc

intended, all too aware of the airport crew scattered nearby. "I told you we'd discuss this at the ranch."

"But why—?"

"Stow it, Sophy." Audra bent down beside her sister, glaring. "Can't you see this is important?" she hissed.

Sophy swallowed. "Important how?"

"*Later.*" Gripping her arm, Audra walked Sophy to the front of the plane. "Look, Mom brought Liberace's cage up here."

Instantly distracted, Sophy let out a yelp and crouched down to chatter nonsense at her pet ferret, which answered with noisy indignation at his incarceration.

"Thank you, Audra." Cara put a hand on her daughter's arm. "Sometimes she wears me out. We'll discuss everything, I promise, just as soon as we get to the ranch." She squared her shoulders. "I shouldn't have waited this long to tell you the truth, either. Now maybe you'll share something with me." She softened her tone. "Like why you believe you're fat."

Instantly Audra flushed bright red. "She told you?"

"Of course Summer did, darling. And we can work this out, I promise, but only when we stop keeping secrets. That goes for me as well as you."

"You're worried about something bad, aren't you, Mom? No offense, but you've been a little hyper lately."

Looking at her suddenly mature and thoughtful daughter, Cara felt a crazy urge to laugh. *They grow up,* she thought in amazement. They argue and they yell, but then they grow up, and one day they actually give you great advice.

Life couldn't be all bad.

"We'll talk about that, too, honey. I promise."

"Cara, can I talk to you a moment?" Tate Winslow

made a small gesture toward his pilot, who was walking down the aft stairs.

"Of course. Audra, will you stay here with Sophy for a second?"

"Sure, Mom."

Cara followed Tate outside, where he scanned the nearby runway. Seeing no one within hearing range, Tate nodded to his pilot. "James tells me there's a storm front running through southern Wyoming. Things could get bumpy up there."

"Is that dangerous?" Cara asked the pilot.

"No, ma'am. Mainly uncomfortable. I suggested we alter our route to avoid the turbulence, but it may involve an extra stop and more airtime."

"I'd like to make it easy on the girls." Cara looked up at the open door to the Cessna. "Audra gets airsick, I'm afraid."

"No problem. I'll arrange it." The pilot nodded and headed off across the runway.

Tate moved closer to Cara as a small Jeep lumbered past, loaded down with cargo crates. "There's a tropical storm heading toward the Pacific Coast of Mexico, too. Bad time for flying."

"But Los Reyes is—"

Tate cut her off, frowning. "No names, honey. Our travelers have been informed. They'll be considering alternate routes."

Cara rubbed her neck as another cargo transport lumbered past. "I'm having second thoughts about this plan, Tate. It's going to be very dangerous if they question the wrong people." Her voice fell to a whisper. "There must be an informant there at the clinic. No one else could have known about me or the date." She hesitated for a moment.

"What's wrong, Cara? Did you tell someone else?"

"No." Cara took a breath. "It could only be the staff at the clinic."

"Then let our friends call the shots. They're professionals, and they won't be sloppy."

Cara closed her eyes and ran her hands over her face. "Maybe we should call everything off. Both trips."

"You and the girls need to be somewhere safe now. Trust me, no one can get within ten miles of the Lazy W without Bud and his boys running them to ground."

Cara touched his face gently. "I never could resist a glib-tongued politician with an agenda."

"Damned right," the senator said, in no way taking offense. "Now let's get this bird back in the air. Bud has four barn-sized strip steaks waiting to slap on the grill. Three minutes up, three minutes down."

Cara wrinkled her nose. "That's barbaric. You may as well hear them *moo*."

"No, ma'am. That's beef the way it's meant to be served." Chuckling, Tate took her arm and guided her toward the Cessna, where a man in khaki work pants backed down the stairs carrying a metal box filled with cleaning supplies. He nodded politely as he moved aside to let them pass.

If either Cara or Tate had looked closer, they would have noticed that the worker's bright identity badge read "T. Markle, Maintenance."

At the other side of the airport Summer was waiting to board a small cargo plane. The painted sign on its wings read "Almost, Arizona—there's only one way to get closer to heaven!"

"Ms. Mulvaney?" A lanky man with a grizzled face and a big clipboard sauntered toward her. "Just got you on under the wire. Had to remove a skid of extra virgin olive oil to do it, though."

Summer blinked at him. "Who are—"

The man stuck out a dusty hand. "Name's Grady. Deputy sheriff of Almost, Arizona, and editor of the *Almost Gazette.*" His eyes narrowed. "Don't reckon I can interview you for the next issue. Not when I was told to keep this all quiet like."

"I'm afraid so, er—Grady." Summer followed him across the tarmac, trying to keep pace with his long strides. She'd been told by Gabe to expect a deputy sheriff named Grady to meet her in Elko, but the rest of the details of her trip were vague. "Is that the plane we'll be taking?"

"Sure is. And you're in luck, ma'am. The sheriff is piloting today. One of his favorite things when he's got a day off, which is next to never."

Summer followed Grady up the stairs, where two young men were nearly done loading boxes of high-end food products. When she turned, her breath caught.

The man in the cowboy boots and well-worn Stetson was the spitting image of Mel Gibson, right down to the devilish grin. "Welcome aboard Almost Air, ma'am. I'm T.J. McCall."

Summer shook hands, trying to conceal her surprise.

"Don't worry about trying to hide the shock," Grady drawled. "T.J.'s used to it by now. If you come with me, I'll show you to your seat."

"Enjoy your flight, ma'am." The sheriff/pilot gave a two-finger wave and headed to the cockpit. Summer was barely settled and strapped in when the small plane began to taxi across the steaming tarmac.

"Next stop, Arizona," Grady said proudly.

"I *know* that, Ray. But I'm positive they said Mexico. The woman mentioned a place called Los Reyes, or something close to that." Terry Markle cupped his cell phone, speaking quietly in the stairwell just off the Elko staff lounge. "She was arguing with him, Ray. And I'll be damned if that wasn't Senator Tate Winslow *himself* she was arguing with." His voice rose with excitement. "Her two girls were real polite, even introduced me to their pet ferret—"

"To hell with their pet ferret," his cousin snapped. "What I need are their flight plans and ETA."

"I'm on my way to check now."

"Did anyone leave the plane in Elko?"

"A woman. Tall, with dark hair. A real looker, or she would have been if she hadn't been wearing such a gaw-dawful ugly gray suit. Hell, women today—"

"Stow it, Terry. Get me the flight plan and the names of all the passengers. Then see if you can find out where the other woman went."

"I've been trying to tell you where she went. Hell, you never listen to—"

"*Where?*"

"She took a cargo plane south. Almost Airlines."

"Almost what?"

"Almost, Arizona," Terry said impatiently. Clouds were piling up on the horizon. Storm coming, he figured. "They're a small carrier south of Phoenix. *Way* south," he added.

"Okay, good work. Gotta go, Terry."

"Wait. You'll wire me that money, right? My new truck—"

"Consider it done," Ray snapped. "And keep your damned mouth shut."

Terry shook his head as the line went dead. His cousin

was a real jerk, but who couldn't use a little extra money? Smiling, he sauntered off to finesse the Cessna's final flight information from an old friend he knew in administration.

Over the next half hour four calls were made to the anonymous voice-mail number. Strategies were devised, maps consulted, money discussed. Within twenty minutes, wheels began to turn on both sides of the border, greased by vast amounts of untraceable cash. The world was full of secrets, but if you had enough money, as Ray Markle's employer did, no secrets were safe.

Patrick Flanagan smiled as he put down the phone. Life was good.

And it was about to get even better.

chapter 22

The Lazy W Ranch straddled fifty acres of some of the prettiest grazing land in Wyoming, bordered by dark waves of fir and oak. A river wound through the rolling hills, alive with rainbow and brown trout.

But the ranch's value didn't come from mineral rights or long-term investment potential. Though his family had a number of residences scattered over the country, the Lazy W was really home to Tate Winslow—the place where he'd learned to hoe an irrigation ditch, tie a fly lure, and lay down a barbed-wire fence. The clean, rugged hills of the Lazy W held his heart, fed his dreams, everything that Washington, D.C., was not.

Which was why, for Tate, even an hour spent here wiped away months of exhaustion, cynicism, and doubt.

He smiled as Sophy charged past, running straight into the arms of Bud Fowler, ranch foreman for over thirty years. The old cowboy caught the little girl tight and swung her around in a circle.

"How about we get Peaches ready for a dawn ride, Sophy? We can head up north and watch the sun break over the mountains."

A well-briefed and trusted family retainer, Bud was too polite to comment on the pink gloves Sophy was wearing. Instead he swung the little girl up onto his shoulders, then beckoned to Audra. "You been working on your casting arm, Audra? A lot of fat trout are waiting in that stream, you know."

"I don't have so much time right now, Bud. Not with school and . . . everything."

"Darlin', even a grade-A student's got to take some time off. Just wait till you taste a nice, fat trout grilled on the fire, minutes from the water. Add a little cornmeal, a pinch of salt, and cook it up real fast in olive oil. Heck, no fancy restaurant's gonna come close to that."

Audra smiled shyly. "I packed my fishing gear, just in case."

"Well, you trot on down to see me tonight after dinner and I'll work on a new move with you. You'll have a trout in no time."

"Can I try, too?" Sophy demanded, bending forward over Bud's head and blocking his view.

"Sure can, honey. And my Elly just may have some fresh peach ice cream hidden somewhere." He glanced at the senator. "Fresh chocolate chip cookies, too. Assuming anyone is interested," he added dryly.

"You tell Elly her last shipment of cookies was well-received." Tate grinned at his old friend. "Only problem was that I made the mistake of taking them out of my office. My campaign spending bill got more support that one day than it had for the six months preceding."

"In that case, I'll advise her to lay in more flour and sugar, Senator. By the way, your mother called twice and your brother called three times. Nothing that was an emergency, they said." With Sophy still riding firmly on his shoulders, Bud turned to Cara. "Good to see you again, ma'am. I've got a nice mount ready for you tomorrow, if you've a mind to join the girls."

"Can I tell you later?" Cara resolutely avoided Tate's eyes—and the flush that threatened. "Dawn may be a little too early for me."

"No problem. Me and the boys'll wrangle these two cubs just fine. You can take things easy up here. I hear that big trial is keeping you busy as a gopher in quicksand. No court dates or dockets here, ma'am." He tickled Sophy's leg. "Just mile-high sunsets and nights so quiet you can hear the aspens growing."

"Bud, can you really hear—"

Audra cut her sister off, but her laugh was light, freer than Cara had heard it for weeks. "Of course you can't, silly. It's a—a figure of speech. Right, Bud?"

The old cowboy rubbed his jaw. "Hard to say about that, honey. Last night it was so quiet, I cudda sworn I heard a coyote cough over in the next county."

Even Audra laughed in delight at this example of a tall tale, for which Bud was justly famous.

"And that was with my earmuffs on," the old cowboy added, all honesty. "But just you tell me about this new beast you brought with you. What do you do with a ferret, anyway?"

Excited, the girls held up Liberace's cage.

"Stop worrying, Cara. They'll be safe here. So will you," Tate said quietly, touching her cheek.

"I know. At least, the rational part of me knows. But I'm worried about Gabe and Summer. Have you heard anything yet?"

"Still too soon, honey. Gabe should check in when they arrive in Los Reyes. Don't worry, they won't be working alone down there."

"You still haven't told me—"

Tate slid his arm across her shoulders. "Later, Counselor. If we don't hurry up, that steak I was telling you about is going to get up and amble back to the herd."

Up ahead, Sophy lowered her voice. "Look, Bud, he's kissing her again."

"That bother you, honey?" Bud's tone was casual.

"Not really. It's just—I mean, I don't get why grownups do that stuff all the time. Phillip Howland kissed me once and it tasted like crayons. *Ick.*"

Bud kept a carefully straight face. "Boy oughta be horsewhipped and no mistake. What about you, Audra?"

"Yeah, do *you* like kissing?" Sophy demanded.

"Actually," Bud cut in gently, "I was asking if the senator and your mother kissing bothered her."

Audra toyed with the strap on her backpack. "No. Why should it? The senator—well, he's great. I think it's really cool he's gonna be our father. Well, our stepfather," she said thoughtfully. "And any fool could see that Mom thinks he's, like, a major *babe.* So, yeah, I'm cool with it."

Bud nodded. "Glad to hear that. Now, why don't we get the Jeep loaded and then you can introduce everybody at the ranch to Liberace?"

The sky was streaked with long fingers of purple beneath racing clouds. Cara sank down on the bent-twig rocker on the Lazy W's broad front porch, watching far-off lights twinkle from the nearest town, fifteen miles away.

"All this unimaginable peace." She took in a long, delicious breath of clean air. "And stillness everywhere. Why do I always forget how good it is to be here?" She looked up at Tate, who was leaning on the split-rail porch, cradling a cup of coffee. "Thank you for reminding me."

"My pleasure. We all need some time out of the pressure cooker. How's that cut on your hand?"

"Fine. I can't believe I was so clumsy."

"Stress, honey. It can hit you in ways you don't expect. Believe me, I know." Tate sipped some coffee. "Audra's growing up. She's looking a little tired, too. I'd like to spend some time with her, if you don't mind. Maybe we'll go fishing one day."

"She'd love that." Cara frowned. "And you're right, she does look tired. Also, she's not eating enough. Apparently someone's been telling her she's fat. We'll have to ply her with food while we're here."

"Don't worry, Bud and Elly make feeding guests a prime mission in life, so Audra won't know what hit her." He stared off over the peaceful valley. "And Sophy, dear Lord, was there ever a child so bright and amazingly honest? She makes me feel a year younger for every minute I'm around her."

"She adores you," Cara said softly. "So does Audra." She stuck out her tongue. "According to Audra, I think you're a major babe."

"I'm glad to hear it, Ms. O'Connor." Tate set down his coffee and moved behind Cara, expertly massaging her tense shoulders. "What about those pink gloves Sophy's taken to wearing?"

He felt the instant jerk in Cara's shoulders, but continued to rub gently.

"I thought it was a fashion thing at first. You know, like the Hello Kitty purses and the big, fuzzy slippers. But I'm not so sure. Sometimes when I touch her, she looks so—so odd. Surprised, shocked, maybe a little afraid. I've been meaning to ask her, but things have been so busy and—" Cara closed her eyes. "That's no excuse. I've let too many things slip with the preparation for the Costello appeal."

"I hear one of the witnesses may recant his story."

"It's possible."

"Forget about it for now." Tate worked his hands slowly up and down her back. "That's why we're here, re-member?"

Cara gave a groan of utter contentment. "Do that again and I'll do indecent things for you, Senator."

He did it again, chuckling. "Can I have a written depo-sition to that effect, Counselor? Or shall we simply move to adjourn?"

He kissed her neck and the tender skin behind her ear until she shivered, her breath turning husky. "Tate, the girls—"

"Are down with Bud and Elly, who will keep them en-grossed in tall tales over chocolate cookies and peach ice cream for at least three hours." His lips curved as he found the top button of her blouse. "If we hurry, we could join them."

Cara eased her hands under his shirt and laughed darkly when he groaned. "Senator, the very last thing I plan to do tonight is hurry."

Their fingers entwined as they crossed the porch. As one, their shadows joined and then disappeared into the quiet house.

Grady started talking on the runway in Elko and didn't stop until the cargo plane cut its engines in Arizona.

"Hell, Grady, let the lady rest." Sheriff McCall ap-peared from the cockpit, shaking his head. "You'll have to forgive him, Ms. Mulvaney. He's imagining you're a bank robber or a movie star. Why else would you hitch a ride at the last minute?"

"Now wait just a minute, T.J. I never said—"

"Don't have to, Grady. It's written all over your face."

The sheriff picked up Summer's small suitcase and grinned. "But we're neither one asking any questions." He trotted down the stairs with lanky grace. "Jeep's over here."

Walking outside, Summer was hit with a wave of heat so solid it jerked her breath out of her throat. On three sides of the small airfield low trees and dense shrubs climbed toward jagged mountains. The sky shimmered in the last rays of the setting sun, burning the nearby red cliffs. Summer had never been in the desert before, and the smell in the air surprised her, a complex mix of sage, rosemary, and primal earth.

She had a dozen questions to ask, but experience had taught her that words were usually not the best way to measure people, so she slid into the Jeep beside the sheriff and waited, already sensing she could trust him.

As much as Summer ever allowed herself to trust anyone.

"Don't talk much, do you?"

She shrugged. "Enough to get the job done."

T.J. McCall angled his hat back on his head. "A part of me is mighty curious what that job is, but the police officer in me is damned sure it's none of my business." Without looking away from the road, he reached beneath his seat and pulled out a padded envelope. "This is for you. It came about twenty minutes before we left."

He made a point of keeping his gaze steady on the road as Summer opened the envelope.

The forensic report inside was neatly typed and amazingly detailed. Cara O'Connor's box had produced traces of a cheaper quality, mineral oil–based pigment, consistent with tabloid printing materials. The paper also contained evidence of hydrogenated soy and safflower oil, cellulose gel, monosodium glutamate, smoke flavoring . . .

The list of chemicals and additives went on for four lines, followed by the final terse analysis: "fast food hamburger, fast food fries with ketchup, mustard, *and* special sauce." Summer frowned as the report continued.

Distinctive types of petrochemical distillate traces suggest the proximity to a major airport, while salt admixture indicates proximity to the ocean. Additional cross-tracking by menu selections narrowed the outlets, and when coupled with the air pollutant profile—

Summer stopped reading for a moment. In all her time at the agency, she had never come across such a detailed report. Clearly big strings had been pulled to accomplish this in such a short time. The senator's involvement would certainly have been behind some of those strings.

She continued to scan the notes, mentally reviewing the data for flaws or omissions, but the work seemed bulletproof—right down to the secondary geographic analysis of superimposed probabilities, which yielded seven high-priority candidates: two in Oakland, and five near San Francisco International.

Impressed, Summer filed away the street addresses in case they triggered additional connections, then slid the report back into the envelope.

Surveillance teams were already in place. Patterns were being noted, especially for any suspects with clearance into the Justice Building where Cara worked.

"Everything okay?" the sheriff asked casually.

"Looking better every minute." Cara studied the reddish landscape dotted by towering saguaro cactuses. "It's beautiful here. Not in a typical green suburban way, but the colors are amazing."

"The desert grows on you." T.J. downshifted and

bumped onto a dirt road. "People come to Almost bound for someplace else, and a lot of them end up staying."

"Because of the beauty?"

"And the peace. And the way people stick together here. The world can be a low and unworthy place," he said gravely. "But not Almost."

There was pride in his voice as he turned at a stand of cottonwood trees, then slowed before a house that rose in sinuous walls of reddish-brown adobe. Lights gleamed through punched-tin lanterns outside a pair of massive wooden doors.

"Welcome to my house, Ms. Mulvaney."

Summer could only stare at the magnificent structure on the hillside, its windows ablaze with the last colors of the sunset. She was still gawking as she followed the sheriff through the courtyard, past a fountain that spilled over weathered stones.

"You can relax in here," the sheriff said, showing Summer to a lovely room with peach-colored walls and French doors that opened onto a private desert garden.

She sank down on the bed, trying to shake the travel from her mind. Where was Gabe? She needed to see the maps of the clinic and review their cover before . . .

Weariness struck her in a wave, but she forced it down with sheer willpower. The sheriff was right, she needed to clean up, and the idea of food sounded wonderful. She closed her eyes, rubbing the knot of tension at her neck, wondering yet again where Gabe was.

Something hit the bed beside her. Summer sat up sharply, staring at a pair of red boots and an ornate red belt with silver buckles. An exquisite lace blouse and long silk skirt flashed through the air and covered her lap.

Not exactly FBI-approved dress style.

She looked up, raising one eyebrow. "Am I missing something here?"

"New clothes." Gabe filled the doorway, a long unbroken line of black. "Bathroom's in there. Let's see if I pegged you about right."

chapter 23

Gabe's first thought was that she looked exhausted. His second thought was that she'd never admit it in a thousand years. Even if she did, the painful truth was that they didn't have time to rest, because they had to be in Mexico that night.

"While you change, I'll go over the schedule."

Summer looked uncertainly at the expensive cowboy boots on the bed. "You didn't tell me my cover included experience as a rodeo rider."

"Very funny. We'll pick up a few more things tomorrow in the hotel. Meanwhile, these will get you into character." Gabe handed her the skirt and belt. "We're Mr. and Mrs. Walker and we just got back to the States after four years in Asia, where I built heavy industrial sites for a Texas oil company and you—"

Summer stuck her head out of the bathroom "—danced in country and western bars?"

"Where you ran a small but highly profitable interior design company. Your work included corporate living quarters as well as private beach homes for the diplomatic community."

"I'm impressed."

"You should be." Gabe heard clothing rustle.

"Except I couldn't tell you the difference between Palladian furniture and Neoclassical even if you had a hunting knife at my throat."

Gabe purposely looked away as fabric swished with a sexy whisper. "Hence the cram course." He opened the file that Izzy had handed him at the airport. "All you have to do is memorize a few key themes. If anyone asks you a question, tell them you suppose that some people may disagree, but you've always thought the Spanish Colonial Revival is the most livable aesthetic."

Summer stuck out her head. "Huh?"

"Repeat after me." Gabe ran through it again, while Summer dutifully followed suit. "Good. You hate pointless ostentation, but you strongly support a period attention to detail. Your turn."

Inside the bathroom, silk rustled, and Summer repeated the words mechanically.

"You are also a firm believer in proper proportion and Old World craftsmanship."

As Summer repeated the line, she pushed open the door.

Gabe swallowed, pretty sure that someone had pulled half the air out of his body. The skirt clung to those long legs, peeking over sexy boots, while the silk blouse hugged high, perfect breasts.

"I don't like silk," Summer snapped, fiddling with the back of her blouse. "And this stupid thing buttons all wrong. How am I supposed to—"

"I'll do it." Gabe walked behind Summer, who was glaring into a floor-to-ceiling mirror on the closet door. "And you don't look like an idiot."

"Easy for you to say. You're not wearing a skirt that

may rip if you sit down crooked and a blouse that shows every God-given detail."

And those God-given details were amazing, Gabe thought. "You look good in Western clothes, so stop fidgeting." He smoothed the blouse, nudging the first button closed. "You're perfectly dressed, Mrs. Walker. The general idea is for you to look expensive and feminine, and you do."

Summer glared at her image in the mirror. "Feminine? I look ridiculous. I've never worn a silk blouse like this in my life."

Gabe's fingers brushed her warm skin. "Maybe you should start. With your dark hair, this blouse is a knockout." He realized his hands were tracing small circles on her back, and cleared his throat. "Even if it is a little tight."

"A little? If I take a real breath, every button will go flying."

Gabe frowned, realizing she was right. "I must have gotten a size too small. How about we leave a few buttons open until we reach the airplane, and tomorrow we'll get you something more comfortable. Not that I don't like how you look in this."

She stood frozen, staring at him in the mirror while his hands rose slowly along her back, opening on her shoulders. They stood body to body in the twilight, her hair stirred by a warm wind from the nearby window.

"Gabe?" Her voice was low and uncertain.

"Yeah." He touched one dark strand, uneven where he'd chopped it free of the cactus. Hell, she should have looked awkward and ugly, but somehow the uneven cut only made her look innocent and unforgettable.

"Gabe." This time there was a hushed certainty in her voice.

"Hell," he said, not sure why he did it—and then not caring as his lips brushed hers, even though he knew it was unprofessional.

But her mouth was full and soft, warm as if it held the last of the day's heat, and when he turned her in his arms, she made a small sound that could have been his name. Then she moved in against him, soft as sunlight.

His senses filled with her. He closed his eyes on a curse and drew her closer, nudging her mouth open with his lips until she shivered and her hands slid around his waist, the pressure of her body making his brain fog up.

He'd always enjoyed kissing, and Gabe fell into the sensations now, holding her still for a long, intimate exploration that left them both unsteady.

When he opened his eyes, she was staring over his shoulder, looking confused and flushed and a little stunned. She tried to speak, then drew a raw breath. "What was that about?"

"Hell if I know." With a surge of possessiveness that shocked him, Gabe drew her back into his arms and ran his hands slowly down the perfect line of her back until they settled against her hips.

Desire hit him, sharp and sudden. It was the same feeling he'd felt too many times to count, except something was different about it this time.

Damned if he could figure out what.

Summer took a jerky step backward. "That was—" She waved a hand. "Something." She took another breath. "I'm still trying to find the right word."

"You and me both, honey." Gabe wanted to stay here all night, tasting the smooth skin of her mouth, listening to the breathless little sounds she made when he bit her bottom lip gently and pulled off her blouse.

Hell.

They had work to do.

"What are you thinking?"

"That I must be losing my mind." Angry at the lust he was feeling, Gabe released her and grabbed the file he hadn't remembered dropping. "Let's get on with the job and go over these notes like nothing happened."

Summer ran her fingers slowly along her arms. "*Did* something happen?"

"No. Yes." Gabe jabbed a hand through his hair, muttering. "Damn it—*no*." He opened the file and slapped it down on his lap. "We're working together, watching each other's back. It's not a normal situation and—that means control can slip." He nodded, pleased with his cool, sensible explanation. "It's nothing we can't handle. We're smart and we're strong, which means the curiosity is over now. Back to work." Confident, he checked Izzy's careful notes, tracking the next part of their wholly fictional biography. "Proper proportion," he muttered. "Old World craftsmanship. Your favorite building is St. Peter's in Rome," he said. "And your favorite painter is Delacroix, because he—"

He looked up and every sane thought flew out of his mind. Summer was frowning as she yanked at the fine silk, trying to free her arms while she clutched the blouse to her chest. He coughed hard. "Did I miss something?"

"I'm taking this *stupid* thing off. The buttons are just about to pop." One arm came free. "Being partially naked isn't a good way for me to start our visit." Summer pulled her other arm free. "I'll wear my own white shirt."

"It makes you look like a banker—or an FBI agent," Gabe said hoarsely. He pulled off his jacket and tossed it to her. "Put this on and I'll see if Sheriff McCall's wife has something that will fit you."

"You want me to borrow clothes from a complete

stranger?" Summer pulled Gabe's jacket up, her arms stabbing up and down beneath the leather. A moment later her blouse drifted to the floor.

"Thank God, that's done. I couldn't even breathe."

His jacket opened, and Gabe saw the pink swell of one nipple beneath her sheer bra.

He felt the air leaving his body again. "Could you stop that?"

"Stop what?"

"Moving around. Making me nuts."

"Am I making you nuts?"

"Close enough."

She pulled Gabe's leather jacket closed. "Then finish it."

The air was leaving the room again, and his pulse was annoyingly loud. "Finish what?"

"The biography. The one you're crushing in your hands."

Gabe rubbed his neck, trying to make sense of what he'd been reading before Summer had pulled off the lace blouse. "You like Delacroix because of his vibrant colors and sheer emotion. Got all that?"

Summer rattled off the details flawlessly, which impressed the heck out of Gabe, because he could barely talk. "Okay," he went on resolutely. "Now for tonight. After registering in the hotel as Duke and Marie Walker, we'll stroll a bit and make ourselves visible in the lobby. Holding hands will be expected, as will a few overt signs of affection."

Summer stopped struggling under the jacket. "How overt?"

"Whispered comments. Knowing laughter and a few hot kisses. We're supposed to be madly in love, desperate to conceive a child, remember?"

Summer gnawed ruthlessly at her lip. "Fine."

"So who's your favorite painter?"

"Delacroix." When Summer handed Gabe his jacket, her old blouse was back on. "After that comes St. Peter's in Rome. And proper proportion. And Spanish Colonial Revival."

"Clearly, you were one of those all-A front-row students I hated in high school." Gabe's smile faded as he took out a stack of photos. "These are shots of the clinic and the offices."

"Who's our informant, one of the doctors?" Summer mused. "A disgruntled nurse?"

"A researcher who's been with the clinic for six years."

"Can we trust him?"

"We don't know yet. But even if he bails out, we can still pump the staff."

"Not as useful as a trustworthy contact on the inside." Summer held up the photo of a slender man with wire-rim glasses.

"That's our man, Terence Underhill."

Summer thumbed through three other photos of the clinic grounds, stacked them neatly, and handed them back to Gabe.

"Don't tell me," he said irritably. "On top of everything else, you've got a photographic memory."

"You've been watching too many movies. There is no infallible ability to process visual information. Mostly, you need reference points. With faces, you look for the details that can't be changed, like eyelid shape. Space between lip and nose. General jaw outline. Just about everything else can be distorted, colored, or reshaped."

"Something tells me you've seen through a few disguises."

"Enough." She turned away, frowning. "The one that

really mattered was the one my partner didn't bother to check for."

"That wasn't your fault," Gabe said quietly.

"No? Maybe I could have argued a little harder, insisted a little longer. I didn't put up much of a fuss when Riley hit the bushes without checking out the garage first."

"You can't go back."

"I let things slip once—I told myself it was fine to bend the rules, that nothing would go wrong." She stared at Gabe, her eyes filled with regret. "I won't make that mistake again."

Gabe started to argue, but she raised her hand. "A man died because I should have made him go by the book, Gabe. End of story." She shook her head once. "So I'm going to second-guess every single thing you tell me and everything anyone else tells me, too.

"When do we meet Terence Underhill?"

"Our contact is working on the details right now. I'll tell you more as soon as I know for sure."

There was a light tap at the door. "Dinner's ready, folks."

"Coming right out." Gabe held out one arm. "Ready, Mrs. Walker?"

"Just as long as I don't have to call you Duke," Summer said dryly.

After two servings of grilled salmon with anchiote peppers and corn salsa, T.J. McCall's wife, Tess, appeared with a tray of chocolate desserts that left Summer groaning. Sipping strong coffee out on the porch was a strange experience, the air heady with sage and mesquite smoke that seemed to catch in the long hollows of dry arroyos.

When it was time to leave, Summer felt a pang of re-

gret. The sheriff and his wife had been affable hosts, asking no questions, and Tess had loaned Summer a soft
blouse to replace the damaged one.

Again with no questions asked.

"Mrs. Walker?"

Standing in the small airport, Summer stiffened, realizing her fictitious name had been called. A smiling staff
member directed her to the plane, where Gabe met her a
few moments later, after a final conversation with the sheriff. Then the doors were locked and the engines throbbed
and they droned down the runway.

Summer turned to study Gabe's face in the dim cabin
lights.

His hand was open on his knee, rubbing idly, and
though his face held no expression, Summer sensed he
was in pain. Something to do with his knee, she guessed.
How had she been so preoccupied that she hadn't seen it
before?

There in the snug, humming darkness, she caught a
sense of secrets, closely held things that skated just below
the surface of this man she hardly knew. Not that his secrets held any importance for her. She *was* the job, that
was the pure, absolute truth. She could play at being a loving wife all day, but at night, back in the privacy of their
room, all warmth and affection would fade until they
turned away from each other, strangers once more.

The thought left Summer with a sense of emptiness. Or
it would have, if she allowed herself to dwell on what
might have been.

But habit had its uses, and habit kept her to the work at
hand, whispering that it was better to be cool and unat-
tached. Without distance, people started to matter—and
for Summer, the people who mattered always went away
and didn't come back.

"Something's *wrong*."

"What do you mean?"

Cara sat up, gripping the sheet tangled beneath her flushed body. "I can feel it."

Frowning, Tate checked his watch, then grabbed his cell phone.

No questions asked. Cara realized this was one of the reasons she loved him so completely and absolutely. Few men would have understood Cara's gnawing fear that her professional life would one day cross over to harm her children. Fewer men still would have made no complaint when that fear interrupted them in the middle of sex.

She watched his face, greenish-gold in the LCD from his cell phone. "Bud, it's Tate. Everything quiet down there with the girls?" The senator listened in silence, then nodded. "That's just fine. We'll be down in about forty-five minutes. Save us some peach ice cream."

"Well?" Cara demanded, still struggling with an odd, drifting certainty that something was wrong.

"They're safe and bone-deep happy. Elly's feeding Audra ice cream by the pint and Bud's showing Sophy how to tie her first fishing lure. No one has seen anything odd anywhere, except for two shooting stars."

"You're sure?"

"Bud's a careful man, honey. He knows what's at stake—in general terms, at least. Now you really can stop worrying."

"Let me check my voice mail." The sharp, discordant sense of danger persisted as she dialed her number back in California.

Three calls. One from the cleaner, one from her chef, and one from the local League of Women Voters, inviting Cara to speak at a fund-raiser in six months.

Nothing else.

She put down the phone and closed her eyes. "Maybe I'm losing it. Maybe it's one big game and Costello is finally winning. I can't stop worrying, Tate. I close my eyes and I see the girls at that window, just before the bullet hit."

"No one said you had to stop worrying, honey. The trick is to have a break now and again. Each time you do that, you take back a piece of life." His hand skimmed the warm line of her back. "Of course, I could offer to distract you."

Cara made a husky sound as he leaned down to kiss the spot where her shoulder curved to meet her neck. "If I don't stop feeling distracted, I may miss something that allows Costello to walk, or my girls to be harmed. I'll be one of those bad mothers who wasn't there when her kids needed her."

"Costello won't walk," Tate whispered, pulling away the sheet. "Your girls are safe, and you're a great mother. But right now, I'd like to do a little more research on some of your other abilities."

Cara shivered as his hands skimmed her breasts. Need left her throat dry. "As a litigator?"

"Not exactly." His thigh slid between hers.

Cara turned, pulling Tate down against her. "You mean, as a taxpayer and civic-minded resident of the great state of California?"

He studied her face in the darkness. "Forget California. Forget everything outside this room. I'd walk away from it in a second if it meant protecting you and your family, Cara. Do you believe that?"

After a long time, she nodded.

"Then say it out loud. You've been hurt before, and I need to know that you can trust me with what you value most." There was an edge to his voice, bound with a note of fear.

"I wouldn't be here if I didn't trust you, Tate. And my girls certainly wouldn't be running free as if this were their home."

"Damn it, it *is* their home—yours, too. At least it will be, just as soon as you marry me."

"We'll discuss that later."

"No, now."

"Later," she said. "After Summer and Gabe return."

He started to protest, but she put a finger on his lips. "I trust you with everything I am and everything I love. But the rest of the world?" She shivered though the room was warm. "Not them, not in a thousand years. There are a lot of Costellos out there, and they'd eat us alive if they could. So don't ask me for promises, Tate." There was desperation in her voice as she pushed him down and slid her body onto his. "That way I won't have to tell you any lies."

chapter 24

The car was waiting at the airport, just as promised. A small man with a straw hat carried a sign that said "Walker," and when he saw Gabe wave, he hurried to take their bags, speaking in broken English. Gabe responded by switching to fast, colloquial Spanish.

The man looked at Summer and said something low, which made Gabe laugh as he shot back an answer.

"What was that about?" she murmured, once their old Ford taxicab was bumping along the road toward the center of Los Reyes.

"He says the *señora* can't be my wife. You're too—" Gabe cleared his throat. "I believe the word he used was *juicy*."

Summer smiled at the man, who was watching her in the mirror. She leaned closer to Gabe and toyed with his hair. "Just call me a devoted, loving wife, Mr. Walker," she murmured.

Gabe's eyes went dark. "You're doing one hell of a job, Mrs. Walker."

Then he bent his head and ran his mouth slowly over hers, pinning her against the seat while he tasted her with his tongue.

Hunger shimmered between them. Summer's heart did a sharp jackknife and ended up somewhere near her ankles.

When she was able to focus again, Gabe was back on his side of the seat, smiling possessively. "You're blushing, Mrs. Walker."

"Like hell I am." Summer looked down, pretending to straighten her blouse in case he was right.

"Looks good on you. You could stand some color."

"Cosmetic advice? What next, fashion tips?"

She couldn't read his face as he ran his thumb gently along her cheek. "Only one thing would look better than what you're wearing now."

Summer crossed her arms stiffly. "And that would be?"

Gabe smiled faintly. "You wearing a smile and a promise, nothing more."

She bent close, smiling sweetly. "In your dreams, Morgan," she whispered.

His laughter was rich and dark, and in response, the driver looked back and nodded, pleased to see that the two Americans were very much in love.

When the bellman left, Gabe turned on the shower full blast. "Come here and kiss me," he said loudly. "No talk. There may be bugs," he whispered as he pulled Summer into his arms.

Summer nodded, but an inner demon made her drape her body over his and slide her arm around his neck. "What's the hurry, darling?" she purred.

Something flashed in Gabe's eyes. If it was a challenge, she noted it and then ignored it. Some part of her wanted to be . . . what was the word the driver had used?

Juicy.

A juicy woman.

She let the words drift in her mind, enjoying their dark thrill. All her life she'd been too tall, too plain, too studious. No one she knew in high school or college would ever have called her sexy.

But she felt sexy now, smoldering in the balmy night, wrapped in Gabe's arms. Which was why she threw caution to the wind, pulled down his head, and opened her mouth over his, tasting him slowly.

When Gabe pulled away, a pulse hammered at his jaw. "You do pick your moments, Mrs. Walker."

"All part of the therapy, Mr. Walker," Summer said sweetly.

Gabe pulled something out of his pocket and palmed it. She watched him move to the bathroom door and flip off the light.

In case there was a camera hidden in the room.

"Can you get me a clean shirt, honey?" His voice was casual as he pulled off his jacket, then held the small, countersurveillance device out of sight while he swept the bathroom, top to bottom.

Summer let out a little breath when he shook his head. "Here's your shirt."

Gabe moved back into the plush bedroom and took the clean shirt she had removed from his bag. "Nice place. There's supposed to be an outdoor hot tub, in case you're interested."

"Sounds wonderful." Summer forced a smile as Gabe flipped off the light and moved carefully from one corner of the room to the other, glancing down frequently to check for a reading.

Finally he nodded at her. "Unless they've got something so damned high-tech we've never heard of it, this place is clean." Gabe slid his equipment back into his pocket and swung open the heavy glass door to the porch.

Instantly the air was filled with honeysuckle and jasmine. But Summer was thinking about security as she headed to the bathroom, pulled down the shower rod, and held it out to Gabe.

His brow rose. "It's a little late for golf."

"But not for security." Summer reached behind him, then closed the slider and dropped the shower rod into the track. "No one will be coming through there without a battering ram."

"Good call." Gabe closed the curtains and pulled out a phone. "Underhill is waiting to hear from me. With a little luck, we may be able to hit the clinic tonight and be long gone before our appointment tomorrow."

Summer wasn't counting on it. In her experience, things inevitably went wrong when you least expected them to.

"Where does he keep the material he has for us?"

"In his lab on the clinic grounds. But he's convinced someone on the staff is watching him, so he's being very careful."

As he spoke there was a short *click.* The slider rattled.

"Get the lights, then hit the bathroom," Gabe ordered. "Stay out of sight."

Summer knew he had command rank and she didn't waste time with questions. She flipped off the main room light, and eased the bathroom door closed behind her.

Gabe walked to the sliding door, and a small cone of light bored into the darkness outside. She heard the door open.

"I hope you're not here to sell me a *National Geographic* subscription."

The other voice was tight and breathless. "You asked for *Gourmet,* sir."

"Right on time." Gabe's voice leveled out. "Come in, Mr. Underhill."

Hidden in the bathroom, Summer saw the curtains swing out as a man moved through the darkness. "Your room is safe?"

"Passed with flying colors." Gabe closed the door and pulled the curtains back into place. "You'll understand if I don't turn on the lights."

"Of course." The man turned, scanning the room, and Summer had a glimpse of white linen pants and a white tropical-weight jacket. "Are we alone, Mr. Walker?"

"My wife should be back in ten minutes. If you don't mind, I'd like to be done before she gets here. She knows nothing about any of this."

He was protecting her, Summer realized. Just in case something went wrong.

"You're prepared to turn over your evidence?" Gabe asked flatly.

"We have to discuss several things first. You have my money?"

"It's in my account. I'll make a wire transaction as soon as you've given me what I need and the material has been verified."

"All of the money?" Underhill blurted.

"One hundred thousand, ready and waiting for your creditors."

Underhill's sigh was audible even to Summer, hidden behind the door.

"Good. That's very good, Mr. Walker." Underhill rubbed his neck nervously. "I can't go on like this, working for Costello. He could turn on me any second."

Summer bit back a breath. Cara's instincts had been right.

"Tell me about this man Costello," Gabe said calmly.

"He works out of California and Arizona. Drugs, protection, illegal aliens—that and more."

"How did he get a piece of you?"

"I can't tell you that."

"Then the deal is off. Good-bye, Mr. Underhill." Gabe walked toward the patio door.

"No, wait. You know that I—I owe some people money. A lot of money."

"So?" Gabe's light moved again, picking out Underhill's pinched features.

"I gamble, Mr. Walker. Sometimes I win, but usually . . ." The scientist laughed bitterly. "Who am I kidding? I always lose. Every night I swear I'll make up my losses, but I end up digging myself in deeper. When I reached forty thousand dollars, I went to the casino owner and said I'd do anything. The next night I heard from Richard Costello."

"I see. He paid your gambling debt. What did you do in return?"

Underhill stared down at his expensive shoes. "I did whatever he asked. Sometimes I delivered messages. Sometimes I carried money to one of Costello's colleagues. I've paid off Mexican politicians and American ones, too. But mostly Costello has been interested in one thing— information on a patient who was here many years ago."

"Why would he want something like that?" Gabe asked blandly.

"Who can say? His people simply tell me what to do, and I send the information to a P.O. box in Oakland. My bank account is then credited within twenty-four hours."

"Easy money," Gabe said dryly.

"It was at first. Then Costello was indicted, and his people wanted me to dig deeper, to find out more and more. This patient could be involved in his indictment, maybe as a witness, not that I would ever ask." Underhill shifted tensely. "Last month they told me if I didn't produce more information, they'd mail pieces of me back to my wife." Underhill shook his head. "I've documented everything—the calls, the visits, the trips I made for them. I can tell you the name of every politician I had to deliver money to, with dates and amounts. I also have copies of the patient information I was able to dig up. The information is in a secure safe in my lab, Mr. Walker."

Gabe stared at Underhill in silence. "Fine. We'll go in tomorrow."

"That's not possible." The scientist shot to his feet. "Tomorrow's too late. We have to get inside and make the transfer *tonight.*"

chapter 25

Gabe cursed softly. "Out of the question."

"I wouldn't ask if I had any choice, damn it. The director is concerned about staff theft and I got wind of a wall-to-wall inspection to begin tomorrow afternoon. I can't be caught with these files. Costello has spies among the staff."

So much for smooth and easy, Summer thought grimly.

"Tell me exactly what you have for me." Gabe's voice was curt, impersonal. "It has to be damned important or this conversation is over."

"I can tell you everything Costello wanted done and how much he paid to do it. You can bury the guy with these records."

"I believe Costello's already in jail."

"Then my records will *keep* him there. I also have photographs of the people he sent to deal with me, so you'll be able to track his organization. That's got to be valuable."

"Perhaps. How would we receive this information, Mr. Underhill?"

"I asked for a SEAL." The scientist squinted at Gabe, trying to read his face. "I know they're professionals and they're trained to get the job done."

"My background isn't important."

"To me, it is. Tell me, damn it." Underhill was sweating, his voice jerky.

"You've got what you wanted," Gabe said quietly.

Summer felt a little punch of surprise. So Gabe was a Navy SEAL. Senator Winslow had chosen his backup well.

"Good. But I repeat, you need to go in tonight. I'm being watched, and this inspection at the clinic means I have no more time to remove that information for you."

"Why didn't you move the files to a safer place?"

"I planned to, but I don't trust my staff at home, and anything else local would have been too obvious. Last month we started new clinical trials on several products and I haven't had time to leave Los Reyes, so the files stayed locked in my safe."

Underhill tossed a rolled up paper on the bed. "Here's the map of the clinic with your entrance and inside route marked. I need to know whether you'll go tonight, Mr. Walker, because I'll have preparations to make, and I'm due back for tests on a new drug for male pattern baldness."

"Based on rats?" Gabe asked dryly.

"Mice. Then humans three months after that, if all goes well. Of course, I won't be staying around for the results."

Gabe crossed his arms, watching Underhill fidget. "This man Costello you mentioned won't be happy to lose his prize pigeon. One day he might decide to come after you. What happens then?"

"I won't give you names, but a small Asian government is desperate to acquire biotechnology for a toehold in the international market. I'm going to help them with that, in exchange for protection and a new identity."

"Very neat. Singapore?"

"No comment. Are you in or out, Mr. Walker?"

"Sri Lanka?"

"No." Underhill's hands flashed to his face. "And forget asking me any other questions."

Gabe shone the small light on Underhill's face, and Summer saw beads of sweat dotting the man's forehead. "I'm in," Gabe said finally.

"Alone?"

"One other person."

Underhill started to ask a question, then shrugged. "Fine. I'll meet you at two o'clock this morning at the north end of the old market near the clinic." He opened the slider, dodging the curtains. "You'd better be damned good, because we'll have only one chance. If you fail tonight, I'll destroy my evidence and make it appear to be a lab fire. Costello and his men are killers, and I'm taking no chances on a mistake." The door closed with a soft *hiss*.

Gabe crossed the room and opened the door to the bathroom. "All clear. Did you hear him?"

"Enough. So you're a SEAL."

Gabe nodded.

"Do you believe him?"

"Not completely, but most of his story checks out. Just the same, we're doing things my way, not his way."

Summer rolled her shoulders, hit by a wave of exhaustion. "What now?"

Gabe flipped on the light. "You're going to rest while I go over this map. We'll also keep Underhill under surveillance, just in case his offer turns out to be a setup."

"We?" Summer fought a yawn. "I don't understand—"

There was a light scratch at the sliding door to the patio.

"Right on time." Gabe flipped off the light again. "I told you we wouldn't be down here alone." He opened the door quietly, and when he stepped aside, a tall figure emerged into the darkness of the room. Without a word Gabe closed the door, pulled the curtains, and hit the lights.

Summer was surprised to see the same man who had installed the new security at Cara O'Connor's house. Tonight he was wearing all black, and he looked more like Denzel Washington than ever.

"You saw Underhill?" Gabe asked him.

"I was waiting in the bushes when he came out. No one followed him, and I tracked him to his car to make sure no one was waiting there."

"Underhill was lying about one thing," Summer said carefully. "He knows more than he's saying about Costello, and his actual destination is Sri Lanka."

The new arrival frowned. "A hunch, Ms. Mulvaney?"

"Call me Summer. And it's body analysis, not intuition. When you mentioned Sri Lanka, he covered his mouth with two fingers. He also locked his ankles and leaned back on the bed. It's a classic gesture-cluster."

"Want to try that again?" Gabe muttered.

"Gesture-clusters," she said impatiently. "Grouped nonverbal communications that signify predictable attitudes. Underhill was showing a textbook stress posture reinforced by the concealment gesture of his hands covering his mouth. Since he was denying that he was going to Sri Lanka, there is a substantial chance he was really indicating the opposite."

Their visitor raised an eyebrow. "I'll pass that information on to the right parties." The visitor held out his hand. "Izzy Teague. We didn't meet properly before." After they shook hands, he continued. "So what do you make of the rest of Underhill's behavior?"

Summer reviewed Underhill's conversation, focused on

his gestures and body positions. "When he mentioned his drug research, he was facing Gabe directly, his head tilted the same angle as Gabe's. These are fairly straightforward signs of openness and lack of stress." Summer frowned. "The part about the lab fire was different. When he mentioned that, he brushed his nose. Taken alone, the gesture can be ambiguous, but with a stiff posture and averted eyes, I'd say that he was lying."

"So he doesn't plan to destroy the evidence in a fire?"

Summer sighed. "I'm an FBI agent, not a psychic, Mr. Teague."

"Izzy, please. And you're acting pretty damned close to one, from what I can see."

"It's behavior analysis, not trickery. All I know is that Underhill didn't believe what he'd just said. Either he'll keep the evidence or he'll destroy it in a different way. I can't say more without additional observation."

"Hell." Izzy sat on the bed and opened a sleek black briefcase. "I don't know about you two, but right now I'm fifty-fifty for scrapping this whole mission."

"Neither of you has to worry," Gabe said quietly. "You'll strictly be backup. I'm the only one going in. I gave Tate my word."

"The senator wouldn't expect you to walk into an ambush," Izzy said flatly.

"I'm not going in blind or unprepared, despite Underhill's suggestions. You're going to check the clinic walls and find me a cold spot, Izzy."

"Already done. I just finished shooting every foot of the exterior. There are cameras and motion detectors, but I managed to find you a few safe access points."

"You've been busy." Gabe checked his watch. "Here's how we're going to handle things tonight. With a little luck we'll be long gone by daybreak, drinking coffee back in Carmel."

At five minutes to one, well before Underhill's planned meeting time, a rusting Taurus cruised the dark walls around Los Reyes Clinic.

From the front passenger seat, Izzy scanned the darkness through night-vision goggles. "No sign of Underhill or guards. What do you have, Gabe?"

Gabe continued his own survey. "Nada, but let's take one more loop. Summer, slow down at the back wall, near the service entrance. If Underhill is here with hostiles, I want to know it."

Summer nodded, following the elegant limestone wall that circled the clinic. A skilled driver, she was credentialed in both speed and evasive techniques, and she had already memorized the layout of the clinic. "Front guard gate coming up in twenty feet." The warning gave the men time to close their eyes, so that the heavy lights near the entrance didn't disturb their night-adapted vision. "Okay, we're clear."

The car purred on, passing two rows of adobe guesthouses for visiting patients. The high fences were screened by azalea and oleander, which hid a narrow border of electrified wire at the top of the wall.

"There's part of the old market. Underhill expects you here." Summer pointed to a small brick embankment. "That's the drainage tunnel he marked on his map."

"Forget the drainage tunnel." Gabe adjusted the angle of his glasses. "I'll be going in somewhere else."

Summer laughed. "Score one for the visiting team. Remind me not to tangle with you."

"I wouldn't advise it," Gabe said from behind his

glasses. "We're going to let Underhill think he's got a sucker right in the palm of his sweaty hand."

Suddenly Summer slowed. "Get down!"

The two men hit the floor as a black van approached. Through the back windows Summer made out several men dressed in dark uniforms. One of them was gesturing as he spoke on a shortwave radio.

"Police," she said quietly.

"Armed?" Gabe's voice came low, down behind her seat.

"Hard to say." The van's motor growled and without warning the driver pulled out in front of Summer. "Looks like four, maybe five men in back. I can't see if—"

Suddenly, the van's back door burst open.

Three brawny men in full combat uniforms jumped down from the van, running directly toward her.

chapter 26

Beneath a Wyoming sky full of stars, Cara stared out over the river. Even surrounded by peace and beauty, she couldn't relax. Turning on her twig porch chair, she saw Audra talking happily with Bud about fishing lures and spawning seasons. Her teenage daughter's cheeks had regained their color, and the hollows were gone in her face.

"You okay, Mom?" Sophy leaned closer to her mother, twisting rope in the intricate knot Tate had just taught her.

"I'm fine, buttercup. Too much coffee, I suppose." Cara sighed. She owed it to her daughters to relax. They had so little time together that it was criminal to waste it on groundless worries. She peered over Sophy's shoulder. "Nice knot."

At least her daughter wasn't wearing her habitual pink gloves. Maybe that fashion statement was over.

"It's harder than it looks. Bud can do one behind his back." Sophy frowned when her mother leaned closer and turned Sophy's hands, admiring the knot.

"You . . . shouldn't worry so much." Sophy took a sharp breath. "We're all going to be fine. And you haven't let us down."

Cara turned sharply. "What do you mean? I didn't say I'd let you down."

"You thought it." Sophy frowned at the knot gripped in her fingers. "Sometimes I know . . . stuff like that. The way I knew about Gabe's training accident. It usually happens when I touch someone."

Cara stared at her daughter. "I don't understand."

Sophy took a sharp breath and flung her body against her mother. "I don't want to know things, but it happens anyway. First I feel strange, sleepy almost, and then everything goes kind of quiet. That's when I know. It happened to me a minute ago, when you touched my hands." Sophy's body shook. "At first it was like a game, but n-now I want it to go away. Please make it stop, Mommy. I just want to be normal. No more waiting for people's thoughts to flash inside my head. No more of their ideas that get tangled up with my ideas."

"But I don't understand, Sophy. This doesn't make sense."

"I know that, but it still happens, don't you see? And I don't want to be afraid of touching people." The girl's voice broke. "Especially you."

Dear God, what to say, what to do? Cara stroked her daughter's hair, deeply shaken. Was Sophy's imagination out of control? Was this why she wore her incessant pink gloves and had trouble sleeping, because of some illusion that she could see into the future? "It's okay, buttercup. Trust me, everything will be fine." Tears burned Cara's eyes as she held her sobbing young daughter. Why hadn't she seen Sophy's fear sooner? How could she have become such a bad mother?

"We—we'll go see a doctor, but I'm sure there's a simple explanation. Maybe you're allergic to a certain food.

Or maybe you have a low-grade infection. The mind can do funny things."

Sophy struggled away from her mother, her eyes red and swollen. "It's not like that. And stop thinking you're a bad mother, because you're not."

Cara felt panic kick in. "What did you say, honey?"

"I said to stop thinking that you're a bad mother."

Cara shook her head. Her daughter had to be making all this up. She'd always been so bright, so creative. Maybe too creative, Cara realized suddenly. "Sophy, this is serious. You shouldn't say things that aren't real."

"But it *is* real. I tried to tell Audra, and she laughed at me, too. I told her I knew about how she was afraid to eat, so she dumped her food when you weren't looking. And I told her I knew how she went into the bathroom and made all the food come up."

Cara could only stare, stricken by this new revelation. Not Audra, her dear daughter. *I don't believe it,* she thought. *It can't be true.*

Sophy flung herself back stiffly, away from her mother. Her eyes were haunted. "See? You don't believe me, either."

Cara swallowed hard. "I'm trying to believe you, but it's just—hard." She desperately wanted to believe her daughter, but none of this made sense. "Try to explain it to me, honey."

"I can't. It just happens, that's all. Usually with someone I know well, but not always. Like last week, when Grandma Winslow came by to drop off the linen tablecloths. Do you remember?"

Cara nodded, unable to speak.

"She gave me a hug. A long hug." Sophy stared down at her dusty sneakers. "And I could see how she was confused, wondering if she'd forgotten to take her heart medicine. I couldn't see clearly, but I know she was worried about something else. I think it was about Uncle Tate, something to do with a big building. It looked like . . ." Sophy hesitated. "Like the White House."

Cara tried to cling to reason and logic, but she knew how much Tate's mother wanted to see him in the White House, a goal she had shared with her late husband for two decades. But Sophy hadn't known about Amanda Winslow's detailed aspirations for her son.

"Go on, honey."

Sophy took a deep breath. "Remember a few days ago when Tracey came to stay over with Audra?"

Cara nodded tensely.

"Tracey was acting funny and she bumped into me in the garage." Sophy clasped her arms together tightly. "And I saw things. Bad things."

"Like what, honey?"

"Fighting. Crying. A car at night." Sophy closed her eyes. "Tracey was with someone in the car. They were doing strange stuff."

Cara felt her heart begin to hammer loudly. "You . . . saw Tracey in the car? One night when you and Audra were outside?"

"No. I saw it in my head. It was like everything tilted, and then suddenly I was looking through Tracey's eyes, not mine."

Cara hugged her daughter fiercely, more frightened than she had ever been in her life. "What do you see now, buttercup?"

As she spoke, Cara willed her mind to one thought.

Sophy gave a low, hiccuping sob. "You. How you love me. I can feel it around me, bright and warm. You want me to feel it, don't you?"

"Oh, yes." Cara held on to her precious daughter. "I do

love you, buttercup—more than forever, longer than always." Cara brushed at her tears, sensing that nothing would ever be the same after this moment, that all their lives were going to change. As soon as possible, she had to talk to Audra about her weight worries, and something would have to be done about Tracey, too. Cara would ask their priest, Father O'Neill, to talk with Sophy about her visions. They would also find a child psychiatrist and maybe an internist who—

With an effort, Cara closed down the logical part of her mind. Sophy needed the deeper, primal part of her now. Most of all, her daughter needed honesty and the certainty of her unconditional love. "I believe you, honey. I'm just sorry it took me so long to understand."

Sophy clung tightly. She didn't ask any questions. With her mother's arms locked around her and her love a deep, almost tangible force, no more questions were necessary.

Tate found them there on the dark porch, arm in arm. "What's wrong?" He stared anxiously at Cara. "Did you fall? Is Sophy hurt?"

"We're going to be fine," Cara said fiercely, brushing her daughter's wet cheeks, then wiping her own. "We weren't before, but things will be different from now on. Won't they, Sophy?"

Sophy nodded, leaning against her mother. Suddenly she shivered. "Aren't you afraid?"

Almost by habit, Cara started to lie, but then she realized there could be no more soothing lies, no more evasions of any sort. Not with this unusual child who seemed to glimpse the truth in all its painful clarity. For Sophy's sake, Cara would have to be honest, even if it cut into the established fabric of their lives. "Yes," she said softly. "I'm

afraid. I don't want things to change, but they have to."
She looked at Tate. "For all of us, like it or not."

He put his hand on Cara's shoulder. "You two are starting to frighten me."

"I'll explain later." Cara managed a crooked smile. "I
promise."

"I'll hold you to that." Tate put one arm around her
shoulders and the other around Sophy.

The girl stiffened.

"Tate," Cara said quietly. "Maybe you shouldn't—"

"It's okay." Sophy took a deep breath and stared up at
the stars. Her face tightened, as if she were grappling with
ideas she couldn't express or even understand. "I want it
to be okay, and that means starting right here. I remember
Summer told me that we all have to listen to the voice we
don't want to hear, the one that's very quiet. She said usually that's the most important one." Sophy eased closer to
her mother, but didn't pull completely away from the senator. Her brow furrowed in a mask of fierce concentration.

Was she trying to block the outside thoughts, working
desperately to be a normal, nothing-special nine-year-old
in pink shoes and pigtails? Cara felt a stab of pain as she
watched her daughter struggle to cope, facing a reality
that seemed far beyond comprehension. There in the
darkness Sophy was growing up fast, learning to listen to
her heart.

Cara could only watch in awe.

chapter 27

We've got company," Summer murmured. "Stay down." She pulled a big poncho over Izzy, who was pressed against the floor of the car's front seat. When she checked Gabe, she was relieved to see him sliding beneath a blanket. As long as they didn't move, the darkness should conceal them.

Her headlights picked up the dull glint of the weapon slung over the approaching officer's shoulder. He waved his hands, speaking a torrent of Spanish.

Summer didn't understand a word.

"Roll down your window," Gabe whispered behind her. "I'll tell you what to do."

Summer took a deep breath. "He's got a Heckler Koch MP5." She rolled down her window and summoned a smile as the officer drew up beside her.

"He says your front light is broken," Gabe whispered. "Just nod and smile."

Cursing her high school decision to pursue French instead of Spanish, Summer followed Gabe's directions, nodding vigorously.

The officer bent and pointed to her front fender, speaking again.

"He says he won't make trouble for you this time. Not if you understand the seriousness of the problem." Gabe spoke quietly. "Which means he wants a bribe. What color is his uniform?"

"Gray pants, light shirt."

"*Caminos.* Federal Highway Patrol. Okay, that's good." Gabe's voice was low, soothing. "Take three bills out of the envelope beneath the front seat and hold them under your hand just outside your window. No need to say anything."

Still smiling, Summer palmed the bills, exposing them as the officer walked toward her.

A new torrent of Spanish followed. Summer felt a cold stab of fear to see the man frown, then trigger his walkie-talkie and step back from the car. What had she done wrong?

A second man sprinted across the road. Short and stocky, he fingered the rifle slanted over his shoulder as his partner's walkie-talkie buzzed harshly. He looked at the car, then walked a few steps away, complaining angrily.

"This one is the boss," Gabe whispered. "He gets the first cut of any bribe. Just keep smiling, honey."

Summer kept her mouth stretched in a tight smile as the new arrival pulled the three bills from her hand, then studied her in the dim light.

Summer lowered her head as if shyly avoiding his eyes, befitting a modest young woman in difficulty.

"*Americano.*" The man said something meant for his companion, who nodded and laughed vigorously.

Summer was sure her smile was starting to crack. Why didn't they just leave now that they had their money?

She moved her foot, feeling her purse on the floor. There was a Colt in the outside pocket, but the way things were going, she wouldn't have time to reach it. Shooting a

Mexican Federal Highway officer wouldn't help her FBI performance rating, either.

The two men stared at her, laughing and making no move to leave. Summer felt her palms start to sweat.

Without warning, their walkie-talkies exploded in noise, and the older man spun around, headed back toward his van, with the second officer close behind.

"What's going on?" Gabe whispered.

"The older one took the money. Then his walkie-talkie started to chatter." Summer swallowed hard, rubbing her sweaty palms. "All clear, thank God."

As the van roared away, Gabe pulled back the blanket and raised his head. "Nice job."

"Ditto." Izzy appeared from beneath the poncho.

Summer managed a laugh. "Yeah, except I'm drenched in sweat." She looked back at Gabe. "What did the boss say when he was laughing with his friend?"

Gabe's eyes darkened. "He was speculating on your, er, figure. Trust me, you don't want to know the details."

Summer drove past a row of buildings that looked like offices, with small balconies beneath elaborate Mediterranean tiled roofs. Next to them was a parking area dotted with cars and a few small trucks.

Abruptly, a flashlight beamed down from the top of the wall.

Gabe glanced at his watch. "Guard rotation, right on time. Underhill's lab is inside a fireproof facility straight down that path, about thirty yards to the north. What do you think, Izzy?"

"No sign of guard activity."

"Slow down, Summer." Gabe rose slightly, scanning the darkness.

"Nothing in sight," Izzy muttered. "So what's your call?"

Gabe put down his night-vision glasses and stared into the darkness. "Let's do this thing and get the hell out of Dodge."

Izzy arranged his earphone and rechecked his heavy backpack. "The tree is about twenty feet from the car, right through that row of bougainvillaea bushes. I can set up a temporary power outage for the electric fence, but it can't be longer than ten seconds or they'll go on alert. Short problems with power are the norm here, so we should be okay."

"Ten seconds is all we need." Gabe adjusted his black tactical vest over his black shirt, checking his attachments and D rings for secure fit. He slid a long knife into its holster, then clipped the holster to his belt and looked at Izzy. Both men wore dark balaclavas, hiding their features. "Ready to party?"

"Bring it on."

Gabe checked the street, then opened his door. "See you in ten minutes," he said to Summer.

"Break a leg. And, Gabe, don't go for any fertility tests without me," she said sweetly.

His chuckle drifted back to her through the darkness, and then he was gone. A few seconds later, the lights in the clinic compound flickered, and Summer saw the tree leaves sway above the wall.

They were over.

It had been six long minutes since the men had left the car. One small truck blasting disco music had passed Summer, but the driver paid no attention to anything but the woman with her arms locked around his neck.

Suddenly Summer saw the tree branches shake. Gabe loomed up out of the darkness.

"Change of plan. Our blueprints were wrong. The lab access has been upgraded with new insulation, and I can't fit through the damned ventilation hole."

"What about Izzy?"

"No go, either. It's the shoulders."

Summer realized what he wasn't saying. "But I could fit."

He nodded, his face hard.

She didn't waste time with questions, stripping off her cardigan and pulling on a black nylon jacket. "Where's Izzy?"

"He'll stay in place near the wall until we're through. After you let me in, Izzy will bring you back here, while I hit the ventilation shafts down to the lab."

"Too much time wasted. You need Izzy monitoring the guard post and radio communications, not running cover for me. I'll come back alone."

"Forget it."

"This is no time for chivalry, Gabe. I know the route and I'm armed. I'll be fine."

"Our intel isn't ironclad. Izzy goes with you or you don't go."

Summer slid her lip mike into place and pulled a bala-clava around her face. "You need Izzy right where he is. Trust me, I'll call if I need him. Let's go."

Gabe muttered something that sounded like "hard-ass female," then motioned Summer to follow him into the darkness.

The main security center for the clinic had unpainted stucco walls and probably a dozen power lines running into the roof. One guard stood outside smoking a cigarette and talking to his partner, who was busy relieving himself in the bushes.

A few feet away, just across the wall, Summer crouched motionless on the ground, trying to ignore an itch at her nose.

Finally the men walked away. Gabe tapped her shoulder once.

Time to move.

Without a sound, Gabe swung up into the overhanging tree, following a branch over the fence. Summer followed in silence, grimacing when a twig snapped back into her face. The wall and the electric wires were directly beneath them as they crouched tensely, waiting for Izzy to work his magic a second time.

"Hold tight." Izzy's voice rippled through Summer's headset. "One more wire to go. *Bam,* let's kick it up a notch."

Once again the lights flickered. The air-conditioning coughed and the big waterfall in the pool stopped flowing over a cliff of man-made boulders. Gabe tapped Summer's arm, moving out along the branch, and a moment later she heard him drop lightly onto the clinic grounds.

As Summer was crossing above the fence, a phone rang inside the security center. She heard a man's angry tirade as she swung down and dropped.

She hit harder than expected. Standing up, she felt a sharp twinge at her ankle. Gabe pulled her back into the foliage just before the lights came back on. Once again the air-conditioning kicked in and the water feature began to spill over the boulders.

Izzy's voice crackled through her headset. "You have thirteen minutes and ten seconds until the next security check. Get moving."

Gabe hit his power button once in reply, then nodded

at Summer. He had his game face on now. Summer realized that she probably did, too.

Amid more cursing from the security office, the two headed toward the small shed beyond the pool enclosure and stopped beside the ventilation hole leading to the roof. Braced against the wall, Gabe held out his hands to Summer, lifting her up so that she could remove the grate, which Gabe had already unscrewed. Once in place, she swung her legs down through the open hole, but got only as far as her thighs.

Izzy's tense words broke the silence. "You've got company at six o'clock. I make out two men and both are armed as hell."

Major problem.

The grate was off, and Summer was now stuck tight, completely visible.

"Yes, Amanda, we're fine. The girls are telling tall tales with Bud and the boys. Tate and I were just about to join them." Cara glanced at Tate. Her eyes filled with mischief as she snapped his naked backside with a towel, earning a soft bite at the curve of her breast.

Her voice caught in a soft gasp as Tate moved lower, finding soft, yielding folds of skin.

"No," she said hoarsely.

Tate smiled darkly and ignored her.

"No, not you, Amanda. I was talking to Tate. He—he wanted me to have some more wine and I—"

She gripped Tate's head, her eyes closing as a wave of pleasure tore through her.

"What? Oh, you know Tate." Cara took a sharp breath. "You can't tell him no. He always gets his way."

"Damned straight." Tate grabbed the phone. "She'll

call you back, Mother," he said tightly. "Yeah, later. No, I don't want to hear about the dead rat again."

Tate's hand moved, his thumb climbing between Cara's legs until she went rigid, digging her nails into his back. "Have to go, Mother," he said. "I've got another call. That's right, it's an emergency. Could be a nuclear issue. Definite meltdown possibility," he said hoarsely as Cara pushed him against the wall.

Her mouth closed over him and he bit back a dark curse. "Where? Closer than you'd ever imagine."

He flipped off the phone and twisted, gripping Cara against the rough log wall of the bedroom overlooking forty miles of pristine forest.

"Meltdown, Senator?" Cara's eyes glinted.

"Any damned second."

The phone dropped. He was inside her, her legs wrapped around his waist, before the phone hit the floor.

chapter 28

Summer kicked her legs, feverishly shoving against the roof, but each time something held her back. She heard the *click* of metal against tile and looked down. Her belt buckle was stuck.

Somewhere a bird cried in the night, and flashlights moved over the lawn. Any moment she would be caught in their beams. Sweat dripped down her face as she unhooked the belt and yanked the leather free. With one kick she was down, plunging through the ventilation hole.

She couldn't let go, not with the guards close enough to hear her fall. Ignoring the burn in her fingers, she clung to the ventilation frame, suspended in the hot darkness while a steady stream of Spanish continued a few feet away, and sweat dripped in her eyes.

Keep on walking, she prayed.

When she heard the sound of a bullet being chambered, her heart thrashed up into her throat. Somewhere the bird cried again—then its cry was swallowed by the harsh report of gunfire.

The guards laughed as the bird fell to the ground in front of them, and then their footsteps passed.

Summer held out as long as she could, then fell, landing

on the shed's bare concrete floor. Biting back an oath, she flipped on her penlight with a red beam.

The walls around her were covered with torn *Baywatch* posters and a *Gilligan's Island* poster. On the other wall of the shed the key was hanging exactly where Gabe had said it would be, behind a small wooden picture of the president of Mexico. She hit the transmit button once, signaling all clear to Gabe, then grabbed the key, flipped off her light, and opened the door.

Gabe shouldered inside a moment later. "Got it?"

Summer pressed the key into his hand.

"Izzy, what's the status outside?"

"Two guards at the main entrance. One more near the lab entrance. Except for that, it's quiet as a convent at midnight."

"Moving." Gabe tapped Summer's shoulder and pointed to the roof. They made their way outside, around to the back of the shed. Gabe turned his back to the exterior wall, ready to help Summer up when a burst of Spanish stopped them cold.

Gabe pushed Summer down behind an oleander shrub seconds before a uniformed guard appeared. As the man's voice grew angry, his rifle climbing to level position, Gabe continued to speak calmly.

Summer inched away in the shadows and crawled around to the far side of the shed, then circled back through the darkness.

She needed a distraction to get in closer, so she tossed her penlight through the darkness. As it bounced off the far wall, the guard spun, and when he did, she circled in from behind and toppled him with 600,000 volts from her stun gun before he could make another sound.

Gabe confiscated the guard's gun and wrapped his arms and mouth with duct tape. "Thanks," he muttered.

"No problem."

Gabe dragged the guard into the shed and finished securing his legs. Summer was right behind him. "Let's get you back," he whispered.

"No way. I'm going with you."

"She's right, Gabe." Over the headset, Izzy's voice sounded tense. "You need backup, and I have got to stay here for the electric interrupts."

Gabe didn't argue further, though his eyes were hard with anger as he tapped his transmit button once for affirmative. The night was suddenly very quiet, disturbed only by the restless *hiss* of running water. There was no going back, Summer thought.

"They're bound to notice a guard missing," Izzy said quietly.

"Who cares, just as long as we're way the hell gone by then." Crouching near the wall with a penlight between his teeth, Gabe explored the unpainted floorboards and picked out a thick set of electric wires with his light, following them until they vanished behind a piece of plaster. "Here's our lab access." He nodded at Summer. "Noise discipline from here on. According to Underhill, it's about six feet down to the air vents for the lab. How long until the next guard rotation?"

Silence.

"Izzy?"

"Sorry." Izzy sounded breathless. "Had to duck some police. Our pals in the van are monitoring the area."

No one said the obvious. A police presence was one more strike against the success of the mission. "You've got less than eight minutes."

"Copy." Gabe worked several planks free, revealing a dark hole beneath the shed's floor.

He tapped Summer's arm and then started down. He

appeared to be in a power and ventilation conduit, the flat metal walls dense with wires.

At Gabe's signal, Summer swung down after him. The conduit appeared to stretch twenty yards in both directions, which matched the information in the blueprints Gabe had been studying at the hotel. When he pointed forward, Summer nodded, following him on all fours along the heavy frame at the inside edge of the conduit.

Sweat dripped down her face, and her knees ached. She was starting to slip into the jittery place where you made mistakes that could blow an assignment and get you killed.

Silence spread out around them. Summer forced her muscles to loosen and her breathing to slow. Staying relaxed was crucial, in order to prepare for any kind of response.

Gabe pointed down, then tapped his watch and held up two fingers.

Summer knew the drill. He had two minutes to get into the lab and open Underhill's safe, which was hidden behind a row of glass beakers near his mainframe computer.

If they were being set up, now was when they'd find out.

Summer nodded at Gabe, who smiled faintly, blowing her a kiss. She had to admit, the man had guts and attitude to burn. In any other time and place, she might have developed a serious case of lust for both his body and his bravado.

But not when they could get shot or arrested at any moment.

"Izzy?" Gabe waited tensely.

"Our distraction's almost in place. Give it a few more seconds."

Summer didn't know how Izzy had planned to pull the guards away from their security cameras, but she was sure it was ironclad.

"Okay, you're ready to rock. *Go, go, go.*"

Gabe slid away a square of wire mesh and vanished into the lab while Summer clocked his time. First he had to unlock the door to the inner room, she knew. Then would come the safe itself.

Glass struck glass, then more silence. Had Underhill lied? Was the code correct?

Sweat trickled into her eyes, but she didn't move to blink it away.

Noise discipline was a bitch, she thought grimly. At least she wasn't hunkered down in a wall of bushes near the Schuylkill River, surrounded by hungry mosquitoes, like her last assignment. She still had marks from the mosquito bites, along with a nasty knife scar at her ankle as a memento.

She tried to relax. Gabe was damned good, judging by what she'd seen so far.

Air hissed across her face as the air-conditioning kicked in.

One minute left.

Peering down through the open grate she saw Gabe shove something inside his nylon vest. When he looked up, she gestured sharply.

Get up here. Now.

He nodded, checking the flap pocket on his tactical vest. He was below the ventilation grid when booted feet approached, echoing loudly in the night. Something moved at the edge of Summer's vision—not a uniformed security guard, but a pair of dusty feet.

A boy with crooked teeth and a torn Arizona Diamondbacks shirt slipped out from behind a lab table, staring warily at Gabe. The boy's eyes widened when he looked up, seeing Summer and the open grate at the ceiling.

The thought of knocking out a kid was repugnant, but Gabe wouldn't have much choice with a guard coming.

She looked down at the boy and managed a smile, then held a finger over her lips. His dark eyes grew even wider as he stared first at Gabe, then up at her. Summer realized her jacket had shifted, revealing a line of jagged scar tissue above her wrist. The boy looked at the skin gravely.

A dog barked somewhere nearby, the sound low and angry, rumbling through the lab, and Gabe took a step back, blocking the boy and motioning for him to run.

Protecting him from the dog, Summer realized, even if it cost Gabe precious seconds. But the boy's crooked teeth flashed in a sudden, wide grin, and he shook his head, pointing to Gabe, then up at the ceiling.

He was telling Gabe to go, Summer realized.

The barking grew louder. But the boy shook his head hard, pointing up, never saying a word.

Gabe did a smooth pull up off the table, swinging into the open hole while the unseen boots hammered closer. Quickly he leaned down and slid the mesh back into place while the boy stood below them, his face grave.

A guard's shoulders appeared. A big Doberman hurtled into view, its paws planted firmly on the boy's shoulders. The guard laughed and nudged the boy with the butt of his gun, showing no surprise at seeing him in the lab.

Suddenly the dog's tail began to wag, and the walkie-talkie screeched again. Impatient, the guard fiddled with the unit, barking a question at the boy, who shook his head gravely.

Gabe and Summer waited tensely. If the boy talked . . .

The guard asked more questions, and the boy shrugged, snuggling up to the dog, who lapped his face

with barely contained joy. Finally the guard shoved the
dog with one foot, then moved out of sight, speaking impatiently into his handset.

As Summer watched, the boy looked up once, smiled,
and vanished in the other direction, the dog at his side.

The silence seemed to clutch at them as Summer and
Gabe crawled back toward their access point. Gabe scrambled up, then reached down for Summer, his penlight
gripped between his teeth as he pulled her up after him.
Inside the shed, the bound and gagged guard was writhing
vainly against the wall, but he froze at Gabe's muttered
command.

Low voices drifted toward them in the night. A truck
engine growled.

"Izzy, sit-rep."

"Path is clear. *Go.*"

Gabe tapped Summer's shoulder and opened the door.
Immediately humid air washed over her, and Summer
realized she was soaked in sweat. She followed Gabe outside, staying close to the building and then cutting across
the lawn, retracing their steps toward the back wall.

Gabe tapped his mike button twice, signaling Izzy.

"Glad you made it. Okay, you've got guards near the
patient quarters." Suddenly Izzy's voice tightened. "Holy
shit."

Summer looked right and left, but saw nothing. "Guards?"

"Worse."

Summer's foot slipped in the grass, and she caught an
unpleasant canine odor. She tapped Gabe's shoulder, trying to warn him as a growl came out of the darkness. A
moment later it was echoed by a deeper growl.

Too late for warnings.

Directly in front of them two snarling Dobermans
stood blocking their exit route.

chapter 29

As Gabe stepped in front of her, Summer dug into her pocket. "I've got the Taser gun."

Gabe opened one of the pockets on his vest and pulled out a similar unit. "We may not have much time. These things are tested on people, not dogs."

The two animals edged forward, their growls menacing. Somewhere a man shouted, and Gabe stretched out his hand. Two visible lines of current shot through the air. The bigger dog whined, his body going rigid. But when Summer directed a blast at the other dog, he barked sharply and kept coming.

"You're losing charge." As Gabe turned and aimed at the big head, a twig broke behind them. Suddenly the second dog dropped to the ground, his tail banging on the grass. To Summer's surprise, the boy in the torn shirt walked out of the shadows and touched Summer's arm, then pointed to the top of the wall.

Who was he, Summer wondered, and why was he here at the clinic?

When the boy leaned over, petting the big dog's head, Summer realized that his left sleeve dangled free. Just below the shoulder, his arm ended abruptly.

A rope ladder hit the ground in front of her. Gabe pushed her forward, and she clambered up the ladder, bumping her head soundly on an overhanging branch.

At the top of the wall, she turned.

The little boy was still on the ground, rolling happily with the dog. He stared up at Summer, put his finger to his mouth and smiled.

Frowning, Summer moved past Gabe and crossed over the wall.

Underhill emerged from the darkness even before the car. "You were supposed to be waiting for me on the other side of the clinic at two, damn it. Your man brought me here or I wouldn't have found you."

"Change of plans."

"That's it? I'm waiting here terrified and you change the plan?" Underhill's hair was mussed, his eyes wild. "I want answers, Walker. Did you find the safe? Did you get my disk and files out safely?"

Gabe pulled off his headset. "Get in the car." Gabe opened the front passenger door and motioned Summer inside.

"Damn it, I need to know—"

Gabe gripped Underhill's shoulder and shoved him into the backseat while Izzy slid behind the wheel.

Gabe stared at Underhill as the car began to move. "We've got a problem."

Underhill sat up stiffly. "Someone saw you?"

"A little boy was in the lab when we got there. He saw us."

"Crooked teeth. One arm gone?"

Gabe nodded.

"Don't worry, that's just Felipe. He lives on the grounds."

"What if he talks?" Gabe said. "He knows that we were in your lab."

Underhill shrugged. "Felipe cares about nothing but animals. Since he has a way with the animals, the director lets him hang around. Don't worry about it." Underhill sounded impatient.

"But the boy may talk," Summer said. "He seemed . . . different somehow."

"He can't talk, even if he wanted to. His family was taken by the police during a strike and his parents and brothers were killed. Felipe was just three, so they took his arm, then cut off his tongue. His father talked too much and to the wrong people, they said. Now the boy will never talk again," Underhill finished flatly.

Summer turned away, feeling sick.

"A nun in the neighborhood got him decent medical care. Now he lives with her in an orphanage to the south, when he's not at the clinic helping with the lab animals. The boy is amazing. You name it, he can calm them down, even if they're twice his size."

Summer remembered how the little boy had stared at her arm. He knew the trauma of being scarred. Was that why he had helped two strangers? Or did he simply dislike the guards?

Underhill stared into the darkness. "My car's down that street, so I'll get out here. Check the disk tonight, and you'll see it's valuable. I'll expect a wire transfer to my account within the next hour."

"We can do that."

"You won't be keeping your clinic appointment tomorrow, I imagine."

"Now that we have your evidence, the sooner we get back to the States, the better."

Underhill nodded. "Remember, I'll be watching for my

wire transfer." He took a last look at Gabe, then opened his door. "By this time tomorrow, I should be long gone, too."

By the time Izzy reached the hotel's broad courtyard, their dark clothes and surveillance equipment were safely stowed in the trunk. To all appearances, they were simply three happy tourists returning from a night on the town.

"So how about it, Izzy? What was the secret distraction you engineered for us tonight?" Gabe crossed his arms. "Something high tech, no doubt."

"Low tech, Morgan. But very high volume." Izzy held up a tiny digital camera and triggered a movie clip on the LED screen.

Summer watched a voluptuous woman in a skintight red dress wobble up the clinic driveway in high heels and begin to remove her clothes, singing loudly. By the time she was down to her black lace underwear, six guards were crowded close, cheering her on.

"Red gets them every time," Izzy muttered. "Must have been twenty guards in the courtyard by the time she finished."

Summer hid a smile. "Where did you find her?"

"One of the local cantinas. She was paid very well, believe me. Once you two were out, I sent a fake police car to pick her up for drunk and disruptive conduct. And it was *very* disruptive, right when we needed it."

Gabe shook his head. "I hate to say it, Teague, but you're the man."

"Damned straight, Navy. Don't you forget it." Izzy grinned as he pulled around to the back of the hotel. "Keep your powder dry, folks. I'll check back at Gabe's call, and we'll be on our way." After a two-finger wave, he drove off.

Summer frowned as Gabe started for the nearest path. "This way will be faster," she said.

"Don't tell me you memorized the hotel plan, too."

"Not the whole plan," she said defensively. "Only the important parts." She pushed past Gabe. "If you have a problem with my work, you can—"

He caught her arm, pulling her back against a wall covered by white flowers that filled the night with fragrance. "No, I *don't* have a problem with that. For the record, I don't have a problem with anything you've done. You were as good as it gets at the clinic tonight, and I couldn't have gotten in without you."

He was still wearing his game face, Summer realized. Pressed against him in the darkness, she listened to the noisy pounding of her heart, wondering why his opinion mattered so much to her. After all, they were just partners.

"I don't care if you—" She stopped, staring at him. "You don't have a problem with that?"

"Hell, no. Why should I have a problem relying on you when your excellent judgment saved my butt?"

"Because I'm—" *A woman,* Summer started to say. "A complete stranger. And I'm younger than you are."

Gabe's fingers opened on her arm. "And because you're a woman?" He cursed softly. "Who did the number on you, Summer? Was it your partner or an old lover?"

His touch was too gentle, his eyes too intent. None of her lies seemed to work with him.

"Tell me," he said grimly.

"Why does it matter?"

A man and a woman appeared, walking from a nearby building, and Gabe pulled her back behind a jasmine hedge. There in the darkness, pressed against his chest, Summer felt the heat of his body. His muscles were clenched, his hands rock steady, and she was anything but immune.

No wonder she had fantasies about waking up beside him, feeling his hard body sink into her while the covers went flying.

The couple walked closer, talking quietly. Gabe leaned in close and kissed her, hard and unyielding, almost angry. "I don't want it to matter, but it does."

She felt the tension in his body. "We should go." She swallowed hard. "They—they're gone now."

But Gabe didn't move, didn't release the muscles locked against her. "Tell me, Summer. What happened to you?"

"Everything and nothing," she said softly. *Seeing too much of the world and too little kindness there.* She tried to move away. "I don't want to talk about this."

His hands opened over her hips. "It wasn't a lover?"

She took a sharp breath. "No."

"I'm glad to hear it. One more thing, just for the record." His lips brushed her forehead, her cheeks. "I want you like hell, Summer. Not just because you've got great legs, and you're smart as anyone I've ever worked with. You may as well know that scar on your arm doesn't make one bit of difference. I want you naked in my bed, being bossy and honest and unpredictable. Hell, I can't walk for thinking about it."

Summer felt the world tip at his words.

Because of the warm air. Because of the jasmine blossoms scenting the night wind and the moonlight that peeked between racing clouds. Or so she told herself.

Not because of trusting or believing. Not even because of the raw desire that was making her breasts tighten and her heart hammer. She had given up on things like trust long ago.

She managed a light laugh. "You mean, you're in the mood for a little postgame R and R?"

Gabe didn't laugh back. He didn't even smile. "I'm asking for more than a little, and I'm in a dangerous mood, honey. The kind where I just might take it. Right now it would be damned easy for me to pin you against this wall and hammer your brains out, so don't push me." His fingers climbed, cupping her breast. He circled her nipple, which instantly hardened.

Summer closed her eyes, feeling the nudge of his erection. She wanted to tell him to stop, but her heart was beating and the words wouldn't come.

What if she took a chance, just this once?

Summer stared at the white blossoms swaying against the wall. What were you supposed to say to a declaration like that? "If you want me, it's only because of the adrenaline," she whispered. "It wouldn't mean a thing."

Except to her. Summer was shocked to realize how much.

"I know that. I've done enough field time to know that the adrenaline can be a real bitch, messing you up bigtime when you come down." Gabe's voice hardened. "I don't want morning-after regrets, Summer, and I don't want to hurt you. But that's the *only* reason you've still got your clothes on."

Nothing seemed to have been touched inside their room, but Gabe carried out the same thorough inspection he'd conducted upon their arrival. Satisfied that all was clear, he offered Summer first shot at the shower.

The steam made her remember the first time she'd seen him—emerging from her shower, humming an off-key Beatles song, his grin as easy and smooth as sin itself.

Irritated at the memory, Summer finished washing her

hair, dried off quickly, and slipped on a white hotel robe. When she opened the door, Gabe was putting away his cell phone. "Any news?"

"Izzy's been monitoring all the radio bands, and he says they found the guard we left tied up. The man couldn't give a useful description, and he doesn't know where we went. We should be safe for a few hours while I finish up here."

"Any mention of our lab visit?"

"All quiet. Apparently, our friend with the dog didn't alert anyone."

"That's good news." Summer sat down stiffly on the bed. "The shower's all yours."

"Thanks." Gabe picked up a towel from the desk. "Get some rest. I'm going to finish checking out Underhill's disk and file."

"I could help you with that."

"No need."

Summer glanced at the sofa and saw that he'd laid out an extra blanket and pillow. Even at a distance she could see that the sofa cushions were thin and lumpy. "You're not really planning to sleep there, are you?"

"Trust me, I've slept on a whole lot worse than a lumpy sofa."

"Well, tonight you're not. This bed is big enough for an army, and that's that. So get moving."

"Why, Summer?" He was wearing his game face again, she realized. The man was completely controlled, absolutely unreadable.

"Because we have to be up soon to meet Izzy. And because you didn't push me when you could have. So I guess that means I . . . trust you." She gave a crooked smile. "Coming from me, that's saying a lot."

She lay down and looked away, afraid he would see the

conflicting emotions she was trying to hold in check. She definitely didn't want to think about him standing a few feet away in the shower, naked and covered in steam.

Or stretched out beside her in the bed.

She closed her eyes and punched at her pillow. " 'Night, Morgan."

She was relieved when he muttered an answer and walked past her into the bathroom.

His knee hurt like Godzilla had swallowed him for breakfast.

Gabe winced as he pulled off his shirt. He'd gotten a nasty scrape when he'd dropped down that access tunnel, and now a jagged gash ran from the top of his calf up to his upper thigh. But it was the big bruise covering his knee that worried him. Whenever he turned his leg, he felt a popping sensation.

Not a good sign. After two extended knee operations, his last surgeon had warned that excessive trauma could tax the tendons beyond hope of repair. For that reason he had ordered an unusually long recovery period.

After that had come Tate Winslow's request for help.

Gabe sure as hell didn't want to end up in the hospital for more surgery, possibly even a knee replacement. On a mission in the middle of Mexico, he had no options for treatment, anyway.

Shucking the rest of his clothes, he sank into the steaming tub, trying to keep his knee straight. When the heat hit him like a wall of bliss, he groaned out loud.

"Hey." Someone tapped on the door. "You okay in there?"

Gabe muttered an oath. Did the woman have super hearing, along with everything else?

"Just fine," he called. "The water's great." He twisted in the tub, repositioning his leg with a grimace. "Go to sleep, Summer."

There was a long silence. "Sure. Whatever. As long as you're okay."

"No problems here." Gritting his teeth, Gabe leaned back and closed his eyes. As hours of travel and stress took their toll, he felt sleep reach out, enveloping him.

He jerked awake and sat up sharply, sloshing water all over the floor. The bruise had turned dark blue, covering most of his knee and reaching down his calf. Stiffly, he maneuvered to his feet and grabbed a towel, then opened his travel kit.

Thank God for heavy surgical tape, Gabe thought grimly.

Gabe had finished wrapping his knee and was almost done reviewing Underhill's files on his laptop when his cell phone vibrated a silent alert. "What?" he snapped.

"And the top of the morning to you, too."

Izzy sounded disgustingly chipper, Gabe thought. "Yeah, yeah." He studied the two open files on his screen. "I'm checking Underhill's data now." More entries filled the page. "Let's see, we've got payments to police officers in Nogales, bribes to an assemblyman in California, payments to three DEA agents in Mexico and two more in Canada. Our pal Costello is a one-man World Monetary Fund. There must be a hundred or so entries in this file alone." Gabe stretched out his knee, wincing a little. "Underhill was right; this is solid stuff. Costello won't be going anywhere after this gets into the pipeline."

"Glad it was worth the trip." Izzy's chair creaked.

"Cara and the senator will be delighted."

Izzy didn't answer.

"Got something on your mind, Teague?"

"I've got information on Summer." Izzy waited a beat. "She isn't there with you, is she?"

"She's asleep, the way I should be," Gabe growled. "What did you find out?" He sat down on the edge of the tub, intrigued.

"In a minute. How's your knee?"

Gabe winced as he tried to find a more comfortable position. "Just fine, so stop worrying like a mother hen and tell me what you found."

"I couldn't get a hit under Mulvaney, so I checked all FBI field offices for women with the initials S and M."

"Run that by me again."

"Those are her real initials," Izzy explained. "Didn't you see the inside of her watch?"

"Can't say as I did." Figure Izzy to pick up a detail like that. Gabe stared at the white bandage covering his leg, which was starting to feel slightly better. "How many matches did you get?"

"127. Then I cross-checked by age. I'd put her somewhere between twenty-five and thirty."

"Sounds about right."

A chair squeaked. Gabe could almost see Izzy hunched over a small and breathtakingly expensive laptop that was probably on loan from a top-secret government program. The No Such Agency was Gabe's best guess.

"That was more manageable. Only twelve this time." Izzy's chair squeaked again. "I ruled out all the agents from California, because they wouldn't use someone local. Too much risk of recognition."

"And?"

"Bingo. Her name is Savannah Mulcahey. Her friends call her Summer."

Savannah.

Damn, it suited her. At least, it would if she ever let go and forgot about her job for more than sixty seconds at a time. Gabe let the word slide over his lips, savoring the slow vowels. "What else did you find?"

"She works out of the Philadelphia field office. There was a problem with her partner last year. Summer was hurt then."

Gabe listened to Izzy's description of the attack that had ended in the death of Summer's partner. Izzy had come up with far more than Summer had revealed, including details of the harassment that had come after her partner's death.

Someone was definitely going to hear about this, Gabe vowed. He'd start with Tate Winslow. Let a senator rattle their cage and see how long it took to get action.

"Gabe, you still there?"

"All ears. What else?"

"Not much. There's no husband and no parents living. Just one sister. That's it for family."

"Nice job. Next you'll be giving me her medical records and grocery list."

"I didn't realize you wanted them."

Gabe felt his eyes drift closed. "Very funny. Better hit the sack, Teague. We'll meet you near the back parking lot."

"One more thing." Izzy cleared his throat. "Summer's a nice lady. Excellent moves and good judgment, too. In case you're interested, I hear that she hasn't been involved with very many men. No one at all in the last two years."

Gabe frowned. "Who said I was interested?"

"No need to snap, Morgan. You asked for information and I got it. To continue, according to her supervisor's last performance rating, she's one of the best he's ever seen and she's married to the job. Sounds a whole lot like you, come to think of it."

Gabe ignored the curiosity in Izzy's voice. "Didn't your mother ever tell you that gossip is downright crude?"

"Only every day." Izzy chuckled. "Then she proceeded to nail the whole neighborhood and half my teachers at school. Man, the woman was inexhaustible. Made my life hell." Izzy was still chuckling when he broke the connection.

After putting away his phone, Gabe checked his elastic bandage. The compression was helping to control the swelling already. Next step, pajamas.

He didn't usually wear them, but he wasn't about to let Summer see his knee in this shape. There would be no stopping her questions then. More important, he needed all the distance he could manage with her warm, sexy body only inches away from him in the bed.

Not that a pair of pajamas was going to be much help, he thought grimly.

chapter 30

She was sound asleep, her foot dangling from beneath the covers. She sighed, one leg shooting off the bed, giving Gabe a view of excellent thighs beneath a blue nightshirt.

He ignored the desire ratcheting to his groin.

He told himself it was simple, uncomplicated lust, the kind any normal male would feel finding a beautiful, complicated, prickly-as-hell female asleep in his bed. He ran a hand through his hair and smiled to see that she'd left his side of the bed empty, with the covers neatly turned back.

Something worked into his chest, but hell if he could put a name on it. Not simple lust, not mere male curiosity. Something jarringly protective.

Hell, again.

All thoughts of sleeping on the sofa vanished. How could a man resist an invitation like turned-down covers when he was dead on his feet?

Gabe woke up with his hand on Summer's hip and her leg wrapped around his thigh. For long moments he didn't move, feeling his blood slam down to places he shouldn't have been thinking about. How the hell did a man stay oblivious when a woman's half-naked body was wedged against him?

Grimacing, Gabe tried to disentangle himself, but Summer gave a throaty sigh and burrowed closer, her soft breasts thrusting against his chest. Gabe figured she was having a nice fantasy of her own, because her nipples were hard, clearly evident through her cotton nightshirt.

Gabe closed his eyes as her fingers slid across his chest, settling below his waist. When her hand started to move lower, he gripped it hard, biting off a curse. In her exhaustion, Summer seemed oblivious to her movements. Her breath puffed softly as she lay facing him, her hair a dark curtain on his pillow.

There was a gut-wrenching intimacy to sharing a pillow, Gabe realized. Though he'd never thought about it before, it felt more personal than sharing sex. Or maybe it was the way Summer lay, completely trusting, her body relaxed and vulnerable beside him.

Sleeping Beauty had a few thorns, Gabe thought wryly. She had trust issues the size of Texas, her relaxation skills were abysmal, and she was married to her job.

But he wouldn't have it any other way. Simple women got boring, and Summer was anything but simple. Stubborn, secretive, meticulous, and abrasive came to mind, but she was also brave, supportive with the girls, and smarter than most men he'd worked with. Gabe would trust her guarding his six o'clock anyplace, anytime, which surprised him because a military career didn't exactly breed gender equality.

She rolled onto her side, her lips nuzzling his neck. Gabe took a harsh breath as desire broadsided him. Cursing softly, he tried to pull away, but Summer followed him when he turned to his other side. Within seconds she was wrapped around him again.

And this time her hand was between his thighs and her cotton nightshirt was pushed halfway up her chest. Gabe closed his eyes as he felt her nipples against his back. With tense fingers he tried to pull her hand away from his thighs, only to hear her murmur irritably and push closer.

He took a deep breath, fighting primal temptation.

The woman was completely trusting in sleep. Only a jackass would take advantage of the situation to open her legs and slip inside her.

Even if it did make for one hell of a fantasy.

Summer turned sleepily, saying something about prank mail. More fallout from her partner's death, Gabe realized.

She muttered again, tossing restlessly. This time it was something about her sister and an old broken swing. Gabe shook his head. He'd had his own share of bad dreams filled with memories of faces and places he'd worked hard to forget in his waking moments.

"Have to go." Summer sat up stiffly. "Have to check house, test the alarm. See if girls are okay."

Before he could move, she pushed away the covers, her shirt bunched above full pink breasts. The sight hollowed a path right to his erection, but Gabe didn't try to hold her back or touch her in any way.

She was still sound asleep, he realized.

"Go back to sleep," he said hoarsely. "The house is fine and the girls are safe."

"You sure?" she murmured.

"The girls are fine." Gabe tugged her shirt down. Though he ached to touch her perfect breasts, he ignored the urge. He had never taken advantage of a woman and he wasn't about to start, not that Summer would ever appreciate his nobility, since she fell back onto the bed, her arm thrown to one side, sound asleep instantly.

She was one hell of a woman, Gabe thought wryly. And if he didn't have her soon, he was going to lose his mind.

She was hot, restless. The sheets felt heavy, scraping against her naked skin. Something was pressing her back, rubbing her hips, pinning her to the soft bed, and she murmured in pleasure, welcoming the weight between her legs, welcoming the hands that were giving her so much pleasure.

A fine sheen of sweat covered her breasts.

She tugged up her shirt, trying to cool off.

But the heat didn't stop as she tossed back and forth, searching for heat and contact.

And she sighed when she felt the muscled shoulder press against her chest and callused fingers stroke her breasts.

"Gabe," she whispered.

Summer came awake in a rush.

Gabe was right beside her and he was naked—or half-naked, wearing pajama bottoms that rode low on his hips. To her mortification, she was spread over his body like confetti after an out-of-control party.

Her tangled up shirt revealed all of one breast and most of the other.

Red-faced, she shoved down her shirt and inched back to her side of the bed, praying Gabe wouldn't wake. When his steady breathing didn't change, she closed her eyes in relief.

One problem solved.

With sleep out of the question, she pulled a book off the nightstand. Unfortunately, it was a lurid male action-adventure.

Book in hand, she dug out her reading glasses and a penlight and tried to focus on the macho hero being groped by a sultry female spy. The text was leaving her cold even before Gabe's hand slid onto her thigh.

She gulped as heat spiraled through her body, then targeted her nipples.

The man was a threat to her sanity.

Firmly, she moved his hand and went back to her book, where the hero was now cramped in the backseat of a taxi while the exotic spy probed at his zipper. As if real women acted that way with a stranger, Summer thought irritably. What was the author's idea of foreplay, saying hello?

Gabe muttered in his sleep, and then rolled sharply, his leg sliding over Summer's thigh. Her throat went dry as she felt his erection drill against her stomach. The man was built, and he smelled wonderful, a mix of lemon and cloves and old leather.

She tossed her light and book on the floor, fed up with the improbable coupling in the backseat of the taxi, but as she moved, Gabe's hand closed on her breast. Summer sucked in a stunned breath as her body went liquid with need.

He rolled again, pinning her beneath him. When Summer tried to talk, only a croak emerged, and his hands tightened, pulling her over onto his chest, so there was no way she could avoid the wonderfully insistent bulge at her stomach. It irritated her that she didn't want to.

"What are you doing?" she rasped.

"Umhh."

"Gabe, wake up."

His fingers slid into her hair. "Dreaming. This has got to be a dream." His eyes opened. "Maybe not. Nice glasses," he murmured. "Very sexy."

"Yeah, right."

His lips curved. "Honey, you could wear duct tape and work boots and I'd still have trouble zipping my pants."

Summer felt heat fill her face. The rough edge in his voice was making her toes curl, and his hands were doing things that left her nipples aching and tight.

Gabe smiled crookedly. "If this bothers you, just shout."

Summer considered shouting, but the thought was blocked by a stunning wave of lust.

You've got to trust someone, and it may as well be me.

His words came back to her, and Summer realized they were dead right.

She didn't stop to think or plan. In a burst of movement, she circled his neck and pulled him toward her. Unfortunately, at the same moment, he was reaching for her, and they collided midway.

Gabe yelped as her teeth scraped his cheek. "Damn, Summer. There's no need to bite me."

She stared at him, flushed and mortified.

He traced her cheek and smiled crookedly. "Not yet, anyway. Not until you're wrapped around me and we're both ready to scream. Which, at this rate, should be in about three minutes."

"You really want to—"

"Of course I do. You want to stop now?"

"But why—"

"How about you quit telling me all the reasons I shouldn't want this, because none of them are going to change a thing." He pulled off her glasses and put them on the nightstand. "These glasses of yours should come with a warning: hot sex may occur if used indiscriminately."

Summer still couldn't believe this tough, gorgeous man was holding her hungrily, but she wasn't going to change her mind. Before she could lose her nerve, she wriggled up his chest until she was stretched out across him.

"You're definitely going to kill me, honey."

Her panties went flying. Summer smiled, amazed at how fast his control was being battered down. To help things along, she reached tentatively between them until she found his straining erection. She couldn't resist a sigh of pleasure when her fingers found their goal. Suddenly bold, she tightened her hand, imagining how he would feel inside her.

"My turn, damn it."

Suddenly she was flat on her back and Gabe was kissing his way over her tight nipples while she wriggled restlessly. Her ribs were next, then her navel and flat stomach were treated to a slow, wet exploration that left her breathless as he whispered erotic promises and approached the spot no man had ever touched so lovingly.

Gently Gabe nudged apart her thighs, stroking her with his tongue, pulling her sensitized body fully awake. Then he did something amazing with his tongue that made her stare at him in confusion and light up like a city block on the Fourth of July.

She was fairly certain she called his name hoarsely as the pleasure roiled through her. Gabe's dark laughter told her that he had heard, too.

She had never been so close and connected to someone, and the feeling was pure freedom, giving her the confidence to try anything, to share everything.

Gabe moved over her again, making her body weep,

making her back arch as another blinding climax tore through her.

Even before her pleasure peaked, she wanted him again. She closed her eyes. "Gabe, please—"

"Coming, honey."

The blanket went flying, landing near her panties in the middle of the floor. Summer watched him kick free of his pajamas.

Amazing and hot and ready for her.

Then he pressed against her, and Summer felt the shivery aching begin again, before their skin had done more than slip closer. She climaxed wildly, scratching his chest, panting his name.

"God help us both," Gabe muttered, hands on her hips, not moving until her shudders stopped. When she opened her eyes, he pushed down, trapping her, giving her time to feel the slow power of his body filling her. There was nothing left that separated them, and as she stared into his hard face, watching his focused intensity, she felt the heat snap through her again.

She moved restlessly, her body on fire. Gabe thrust once, withdrew, and filled her in one hard stroke. She clawed at his back, driven by a need she'd thought only happened to other people.

Yet now with her body molded perfectly to his, she was open to a flood of amazing sensations, poised at the edge of something totally new that she wanted more than breath itself.

"Let it go, honey." Gabe's jaw hardened as he pushed up on his forearms, licking the tip of her breast and then biting down gently. "Let me feel you now."

The shock of his restless fingers made her gasp and spiral out of control while he gripped her tight, driving rhythmically inside her. She felt his penis, hot and huge, and she came to the edge and slipped over, her nails digging into his back while the force of his release filled her.

But of course by tomorrow they would both be gone, their job complete.

And Summer knew that after this night, she would never be the same again.

chapter 31

G abe's cell phone alarm woke him at six-fifteen.
Next door the shower was running and Summer was singing. He eased out of bed, wincing when he stood up. His leg was stiff as he rewrapped the bandage that he'd removed in the night.

Gritting his teeth, he bent into a careful stretching routine.

After three minutes he was cursing silently.

After eight minutes, his leg began to recover its old flexibility.

He checked the bandage again, then reached for his pants hastily as the shower stopped, and Summer emerged in a fluffy robe. Her hair was wet and her cheeks were flushed, making Gabe remember how they'd spent the night.

He was all set to reach for her when sanity returned.

Everything that had happened was an illusion fueled by risk and adrenaline. It was time to put the emotions away and finish the mission.

He sat down and buttoned his shirt. "Sleep well?" Thank God, his voice sounded steady.

"Fine. You?"

"Well enough." Not for one damned second. Her body had been too warm, rubbing against him and denying him any rest. "You finished in there?"

"Gabe, we need to talk." Her voice wavered. "About last night." Before he could speak, she dug her hands into her pockets and turned away. "I just want you to know that I appreciate what you did and why you did it."

"You do?"

"Of course. And I understand how a man like you would feel about what happened last night."

Gabe felt a spark of irritation. "A man like me?"

"Someone who's confident and handsome, with an amazing body. You probably have to beat women off with a stick, while I—" She stared out at the bright red bougainvillaeas lining the patio. "That part doesn't matter. What matters is that I won't turn last night into a mushy melodrama. We had sex, okay? It was just hormones. Adrenaline gone amuck." She ran a hand through her damp hair, frowning. "Just because we had simple, sweaty sex, don't think you owe me anything, because you don't."

"I see." Hell if he did. Who was she to call what had happened between them *simple*?

"I knew you would. And you're right, it's better this way. The work has to come first and we've still got Under-hill's disk to squire back to safety." She dropped her robe, revealing a sheer lace bra and panties that hit Gabe like a body blow. "I'll dress and get out of your way, then we can both focus."

Focus. Gabe drew a hard breath.

Right. Just as soon as she pulled some clothes over those long legs and the pouty nipples he'd savored thoroughly in the night.

Summer pulled on dark slacks and a dark sweater. "I'll

order breakfast for us while you shower and dress. Be careful with your knee."

"My damned knee is fine," he said irritably.

"You don't have to lie about it," she said calmly, slipping on her shoes. "I'm just glad we're both taking this in stride. Last night was . . . a nice illusion, but now it's time to get back to reality. So what can I order you for breakfast?"

Her eyes were guileless, her smile soft. The combination nearly knocked him off his feet. "I'm not hungry."

"You need to eat." She swept a swift, almost unwilling glance over his body. Her cheeks were the color of crushed raspberries as she studied his chest. Gabe knew he had welts where her nails had scratched him.

"Don't worry, the scratches don't hurt."

Her cheeks turned even brighter red. "I-I don't know what came over me."

"Great sex came over you," he said roughly. "Not *simple* sex, *great* sex. That's two different things. And I'll have *huevos rancheros,* along with coffee black enough to make my hair stand up. Toss in anything else that looks interesting."

She smiled faintly. "Anything else I can do?"

"Yeah. You can leave before I pull that lace underwear off and see if you can put more welts on my chest."

She frowned slightly. "There's no need to pretend this is . . . important, Gabe. You won't hurt my feelings."

The woman truly didn't have a clue, Gabe realized. And to his dismay, his body was responding vigorously to all this talk about sex and lace underwear. Gabe wanted her again, hard and deep, right against the bedroom wall.

And she was worried about ordering him the right food for breakfast.

Men were from Mars, all right, but women were from

the Horsehead Nebula. Gabe realized she was waiting for his answer, a frown on her forehead. He wished they had time for explanations, but they didn't.

"Forget about what I said." His voice was rough. "You're right, the work is all that counts." He turned away, gathering his clothes in a nylon travel bag. "Let's wrap this up and go meet Izzy."

"No problem. I'm packed already. My bag's on the bed."

"Too bad we didn't get the clinic tour after all," Gabe muttered. She was taking this whole thing far too calmly. For some reason he wanted to shake her up. He leaned closer, wrapping a strand of hair around his finger. "But we probably wouldn't have convinced anyone that we were passionately in love and trying to have a baby."

"Why not?"

"Because you're distracted, and I'm trying to ignore the fact that you're distracted."

She bit her bottom lip, leaving Gabe in a sudden state of arousal. "You think I can't focus?"

"Yeah."

"I can do whatever's necessary."

"There's no need to shout, Summer."

"I'm *not* shouting." Rising to her toes, Summer slid her hands around his neck. "I'm not distracted now. I'm thinking about having more sex with you."

"*Great* sex," Gabe said hoarsely, pretty sure the top of his head lifted free when she pulled him down and bit his lip hungrily. Her hand slid around his back, settling possessively on his butt.

The woman was *good,* he thought dimly.

Without breaking the kiss, Gabe pulled her between his legs. Purely as a test, he told himself. To see how convincing she could be.

She tilted her head, studying him intently. "I'd like having more sex with you." She traced his lips slowly with the tip of her tongue, and that one amazing move almost made Gabe forget this was purely a performance.

"Does that feel like I'm distracted?"

"I'll tell you in a minute or two," he said hoarsely. Despite all his control, his hands rose to her breasts, coaxing her nipples to hard points.

She made a ragged sound of pleasure, and Gabe kept right on touching her until she moaned again and her fingers dug beneath the waist of his pajamas.

He managed to stop her hand before it found its mark. They needed distance, he thought grimly. Anger would make her back off.

"Not bad," he said hoarsely, "but your emotional tone was all wrong. You kissed me like a freshman on a first date."

Summer stared at him. "I kissed you like—"

"No one in their right mind would believe we'd had sex before."

Her eyes narrowed. "You big, arrogant—"

"But it doesn't matter. We're leaving in less than an hour."

She took a sharp breath and glared at him. At least she didn't look vulnerable and uncertain now, Gabe thought. That was the good news.

The bad news was she looked as if she might shoot out both kneecaps if he said another word. He made a production of checking his watch. "I have to shower, then I'll meet up with Izzy and see you downstairs."

"You want to know what you can do with your emotional tone, Morgan?"

"Sorry, no time." Gabe closed the bathroom door

quickly and heard a *thud* as her shoe hit hard. The outside door slammed shut a moment later.

He ran a hand through his hair. Thank God she'd gotten angry. One more gut-wrenching kiss and he'd have stripped her naked while they took the long road to oblivion all over again.

All the way down the hall, Summer kept waiting for her heart to stop pounding.

Had she lost her mind? This was work, and emotions had no business intruding.

In a blur she walked through the lobby, dodging bags and early arrivals while she continued to berate herself. In all fairness, it wasn't Gabe's fault that she'd tangled her body around him in sleep all during the night. It wasn't his fault that she'd practically melted all over him during one of her steamier fantasies.

She took an angry breath, sidestepping a group of American tourists who were awaiting a tour departure. Why did the wretched man refuse to admit that his knee was bothering him? Summer was certain his movements had been jerky when she'd first come out of the shower.

She smiled at the waiter, who showed her to a table overlooking the crowded lobby. After a cursory glance at the menu, she chose oatmeal and coffee for herself, then placed Gabe's order, explaining that her husband would join her shortly.

Her stomach tied up in knots. She had no experience with relationships or the kind of passion she'd experienced with Gabe. Her coworkers back in Philadelphia called her coolheaded, even stoic, but behind her back they called her a variety of nasty names that involved the word *ice.*

Yet Summer felt anything but cold remembering the

things Gabe had done to her in the night. In fact, every nerve clamored for her to go back upstairs and maneuver his lean, hard body exactly where she wanted it.

Hammering her brains out.

She closed her eyes and made a hopeless sound. Maybe she was just punchy from adrenaline and lack of sleep.

Summer realized that a man at a nearby table was staring at her. She looked away, avoiding his eyes, and noticed that two tables away another man was showing equal interest.

Why? Was her sweater crooked? Did she have food on her face?

Bewildered, Summer checked the mirrored column near her table, stunned to see a stranger with glowing cheeks and sexy, mussed hair. All of it came courtesy of Gabe and the amazing sex that had kept her up half of the night. That was no illusion.

But what happened to them now?

Torn by indecision, Summer watched the waiter arrange plates on the table. She couldn't pretend what she felt for Gabe was limited to their work. Her breasts still stung from his stubble and her thighs ached from the force of his slow, powerful possession.

But Summer was a woman who never, ever lost control. She didn't groan men's names and claw their chests in the middle of hot, out-of-control sex.

Until last night. Until Gabe.

She closed her eyes, remembering how she'd sprawled over him in her sleep. She'd bit him and clawed him, but afterward she had curled up against him, feeling absolutely secure and protected in his embrace.

Though they were barely more than strangers.

Light-headed, she stared at the eggs and oatmeal cooling on the table. She had to end this emotional turmoil

now. She refused to confuse good sex with lasting commitment or love. Only a fool would make a mistake like
that.

Gabe knew that, too. That had to be why he'd criti-
cized her, to remind her they were playing a role and nothing more. He was right, she realized sadly.

But it hurt. Oh, how it hurt.

Gabe appeared in the doorway and spotted Summer.
Awareness punched him in the chest even though he'd
seen her only ten minutes before. They'd just have time to
eat before they met Izzy, and he realized he was ravenous.

Summer's face was unreadable as he sat down.

A few minutes later his cell phone rang.

"Yes," he said tersely, while he monitored traffic at the
front of the hotel.

"It's me." The voice was Underhill's, low and shaky.
"They discovered the guard you left tied up in the shed,
and now all the staff is being watched. I have new information for you, but the only way I can make contact with you
is if you keep your morning appointment. Understand?
Have your driver go around and wait at the loading dock
behind the lab. I'll meet you for your tour."

"Impossible."

"It's vital information about Costello—and someone
else in your government. A senator."

"Keep talking," Gabe said coldly.

"I can't. There are people here."

"You can't get away?"

"Don't you think I'd try if I could?" Underhill's voice
broke. "I need your help. No one will question a hotel limousine carrying prospective clinic patients. If you don't
come here, I—" He stopped suddenly. His voice changed,
all flat and businesslike. "Yes, I'll be right there. Of course

I remember the staff meeting." Underhill cleared his throat. "And you'll have those beakers and pipettes ready for me by tomorrow morning? Excellent. I'll be over in a moment."

The phone went dead. Underhill had company, it seemed.

Gabe put away the phone. "Change of plans. We need to keep our clinic appointment after all. Underhill has new intel about Costello's connections. One of them may be a senator. Underhill can't get away and we need what he knows, so we get ready to move." Gabe glanced at Summer. "Any problems with that?"

She frowned. "Let's go change so we can meet Izzy and then finish this."

Izzy was sitting on the back fender of a dusty Jeep Rubicon with 32-inch tires and a gouged hood.

Gabe checked out the rugged car with interest. "Nice wheels, Teague. You do much off-roading?"

"You better believe it. This baby has skid plates, front and rear differential wheel locks, and reinforced driveshafts. I could take a rock wall without spilling my coffee."

"No kidding."

Summer cleared her throat loudly. "Before you two get swept up in the passions of engine torque and gearing ratios, I'd like an update on Underhill."

"Coming right up." Izzy produced a sleek PDA and pushed a few buttons.

"What's that?" Summer asked, peeking over his shoulder.

"High-res satellite shots of the clinic. We happen to be in luck, because there are no clouds today."

"Those are real-time high-res shots?" Gabe shook his

head. "I don't want to know how you got clearance for that."

"That's right, you don't." Izzy zoomed in on an image, frowning. "Something's going on. There's a hell of a lot more activity at the clinic than when I checked last."

"What kind of activity?"

"Two Mercedes, a Hummer, and three delivery trucks. More workmen from the electrical company that was working on-site at the clinic yesterday. No sign of Underhill, but something's definitely happening over there."

"Not good."

"What do you say?" Izzy asked quietly.

Gabe sat down on the opposite fender of the Jeep. "Stay ready to move, but let's give it ten minutes. I want to know what's happening at the clinic."

chapter 32

Gabe was wearing a perfectly tailored Armani suit as he watched Summer move through the sunlight. She was elegant and sexy in a gray silk dress that fit her like a second skin. When they walked through the lobby, half a dozen men turned and stared.

The thought hit him that Summer *could* be involved with someone, despite Izzy's research.

The possibility left him scowling.

"What's wrong?"

They were almost at the front entrance to the hotel. Gabe considered the casual, roundabout approach and scrapped the idea. "Are you seeing anyone?" he demanded.

"What?"

"Involved, Mulvaney." He almost slipped and used her real name. "Having sex in a committed consensual relationship with another adult, be that male or female."

"None of your business."

They walked outside into a perfect day. The sky was a blinding blue, and the sun shimmered on her hair, picking up glints of bronze and auburn. The scent of her shampoo, a subtle mix of apples and cinnamon, was driving Gabe crazy. "Damn it, Summer, just tell me if—"

"No."

"No, you won't or—"

"No, there's no one."

"Good," he said harshly. He'd already heard it from Izzy, but he wanted to hear the answer from Summer.

"Why is that good?"

"Because if you were involved with someone, you'd be thinking about him instead of the job." *And I might have to kill him,* Gabe thought. "If you're distracted, you're more likely to make mistakes."

"What about you? How many women are penciled in to your date book, breathlessly awaiting your return?"

"I don't keep a date book." Gabe frowned, scanning the dozen cars parked in front of the hotel. Only one woman had ever distracted him from his work. Right now she was six inches away, smelling like apples on a summer day and driving him crazy.

"You look wonderful, so relax."

"I've never been much good at relaxing," Summer said irritably.

"Start trying. We're supposed to be crazy in love, re-member? Looking tense doesn't go with our profile."

"So?"

"So lean in closer and touch my shirt. Laugh softly and look into my eyes. The act has to be solid."

Summer slid an arm slowly around his neck. "Like this?" She leaned into him and took his mouth in slow, hungry nibbles. When he groaned, she tongued his lower lip.

Gabe's hands slid to her waist. "That's convincing enough," he growled.

She bit his lip again, then smoothed the spot with her tongue. "Are you sure?"

He cursed softly and turned away as three police officers

appeared at the entrance to the hotel, struggling with a European businessman in a white suit. The man was belligerent and frightened in turn, switching from French to German to Spanish.

The police officers paid no attention, ignoring his demand to speak with his lawyer.

"What's going on?" Summer muttered.

"I'll find out." Gabe spoke quietly to a nearby bellman, then returned as the police van pulled away. "I couldn't get anything concrete, just that he was a businessman with many debts. He had checked out and was leaving the country today." Gabe looked down at the hotel's front steps. "Forget about him. Izzy's here with the car."

Across the driveway a man in a black uniform was holding open the door to a big silver limousine. Now Izzy was wearing a rakish hat and a devilish smile.

Summer took a deep breath and looked at Gabe. "Ready, Mr. Walker?"

"Absolutely, darling." Gabe nodded and took Summer's arm.

Summer tilted her head and traced his cheek slowly. "I'm sure it will be a very instructive morning, *darling.*" In the backseat, she leaned closer to Gabe. "But for the record, if anyone tries to give me a pelvic exam, I'll use my service revolver on them."

Tracey Van Doren was bored and depressed.

Damn it, where was Audra when she needed her? Vanished with her mom and sister, of course. Just Tracey's luck.

She picked up her old Girl Scout binoculars and stared idly through the bright kitchen windows at Audra's house. There were two people inside, and then one of them disappeared. Only Patrick was left, doing something near the

table, then opening drawers and searching through canis-
ters.

Tracey saw that there was a pile of opened letters on the
table near him. She figured it was a little odd that a chef
had so much mail.

She moved to get a closer look, then saw him turn and
stare up at her, frowning. A sudden wave of fear went
through her. Why was he staring at her? And why did he
look so angry?

chapter 33

The first thing we'll need today is a sperm sample."
Gabe took a step in front of Summer. "I'm afraid that we're not here to—"

"It's standard procedure, Mr. Walker." The medical assistant smiled brightly at Gabe. "You and Mrs. Walker can share the patient room. If you need . . . inspirations, you'll find appropriate magazines in the drawers near the door."

"There's been some sort of misunderstanding." Gabe smiled coolly. They had only been at the clinic for five minutes, and so far there had been no sign of Underhill. "We're here for a tour, not for treatment."

"Trepidation is quite normal, Mr. Walker, but there's no reason to delay specimen collection. We'll need to examine your wife, too, of course. After that you can tour the clinic and speak with our director." The medical assistant set a plastic container on the counter in front of Gabe. "Your specimen goes in here. Write your name on the white label before you return it, please." She smiled pleasantly at Summer. "Your wife is free to accompany you."

"We are *not* here for specimens." Gabe pushed the plastic cup back across the counter. "Check your records. We're here for a tour."

The assistant looked up as the door to the office behind her opened, and two men in gray uniforms emerged, carrying a roll of cable between them. They paid no attention to patients or staff, muttering as they ran cable along the bottom of the room and out into the hall. "But your name is right here on my list. Sperm sample for Mr. Walker. Physical exam for Mrs. Walker."

Summer's eyes narrowed. Anyone who tried to get her *near* a chair with stirrups wouldn't be able to sit down for a month. "Why don't you check with the director? We have a tour scheduled. I even have a confirmation letter."

"Oh, dear, the director will be gone for at least another hour. Waiting for him would put us behind schedule, and the examination rooms are booked solid from eleven o'clock on." Smiling but resolute, the receptionist pushed the specimen cup back toward Gabe.

Barbie in a white coat, Summer thought. At least Barbie had longer legs.

Gabe scanned the woman's nametag. "Ms. Jorgensen—" He smiled confidingly. "Molly." He leaned down, completely nonthreatening. "How about you check your schedule again?"

"But Dr. Teller says—" Molly stopped abruptly as the door opened behind Summer. "Eva, thank heaven you're here. These patients say they're not scheduled for specimen collection. Maybe someone made a mistake on the schedule." Molly was becoming more flustered with every word.

Across the room, one of the uniformed workmen looked up briefly, shook his head, then returned to his cables.

Eva was clearly in a position of authority. Taking charge, she peered at the scheduling book, then frowned at Gabe and Summer. "You are Mr. and Mrs. Walker?"

"Yes, and we're still considering several other clinics."

Gabe slid his arm around Summer's stiff shoulders. "We are supposed to have a tour, then speak with the director. Are you sure that nothing is scheduled for us?"

The woman peered at the appointment log. "You're right. See, Molly? The evaluation was for the Wiltons, not the Walkers, and the Walkers are to meet Dr. Underhill, not the director. I remember seeing an e-mail about that change early this morning."

The receptionist frowned. "I didn't get that e-mail."

"Never mind, I'll handle it, Molly." The woman smiled at Gabe. "I can take you down to meet Dr. Underhill, one of our senior research scientists. If you're certain you don't want to get started with an evaluation, that is."

"Absolutely," Summer said sweetly.

"In that case, let's take this door."

One hurdle crossed, Summer thought grimly.

Now all they had to do was pick up Underhill and get the hell out of Dodge.

Los Reyes Clinic spread over five gorgeous, wooded acres, and in the daylight, Summer could see that no expense had been spared in its design. Every inch of space suggested a world-class spa rather than a medical facility.

While their guide rambled on about an eighteenth-century colonial governor who had lived here with various mistresses, Summer checked surreptitiously for signs of extra security or surveillance, but, unlike the night before, the cobblestone courtyards and green lawns seemed completely peaceful. Nothing disturbed the international roster of patients who demanded state-of-the-art medical care in a luxurious setting.

Each residence had its own outdoor spa, private garden, and balcony; inside were stone fireplaces and high-tech computer data ports. To Summer's relief, no guards were anywhere in evidence.

She smiled at their guide as they walked past the power shed where she and Gabe had gained entrance the night before. "Everything looks state-of-the-art. How long has the clinic been in operation?"

"About forty years. When Dr. Teller purchased the clinic, he updated the facilities, focusing on infertility, though the clinic used to handle a broad range of medical problems. Right now we're in the middle of scaling up our research and data-storage areas. As you know, we have an international staff and patient base now."

As they passed the pool, Summer saw two women on teak lounges reading novels. She realized that the things in their mouths were thermometers—the only sign that they were at a medical facility, not a Four Seasons resort.

Not too far away, two more men in gray uniforms were stringing cable and installing new wiring.

Gabe took Summer's arm. "My wife and I definitely want to see the labs. We may not be scientists, but we want to be certain that safe, hygienic conditions exist for the sake of our child."

Their guide smiled. "Dr. Underhill is very knowledge-able. He doesn't give many tours, but I'm sure you'll find him helpful. When you're finished, he can escort you back to the office."

"Don't worry about us, Eva," Gabe said pleasantly. "I'm sure Dr. Underhill can point us in the right direction when we're done."

" 'Safe, hygienic conditions'?" Summer murmured as they followed their guide across the courtyard into the fenced lab area.

"I'm a responsible father-to-be." Gabe scanned the

high fences and the halogen security lights scattered around the lab complex. "Someone paid a bundle for this setup. Making babies must be big business."

"For this clientele, at least." Summer watched Eva slide a plastic ID card through a security scanner. There was a discreet *buzz,* followed by a synthesized voice that said "Eva Breuner. Entrance approved."

"Very nice."

"There were no checkpoints like this anywhere else," Summer pointed out quietly. "Tighter security here."

Gabe leaned closer to Summer. "Heads up," he whispered. "Underhill at three o'clock."

Terence Underhill was walking toward them, looking rumpled and cranky, like a man who'd spent most of the night fighting bad dreams.

He stopped beside Eva, frowning. "Sorry, my last experiment hit a snag. This is Mr. and Mrs. Walker, I take it?"

"Yes, Dr. Underhill. They were worried about whether we have safe, hygienic conditions here."

"Nonsense, we have the best equipment and the finest staff available." Underhill stared at Gabe. "Are you a scientist, Mr. Walker?"

"No, but my wife and I are willing to pay for the very best."

Underhill pulled out an ID card. "I'll escort them from here, Eva. And I'll be sure they finish on time." The scientist turned and slid his ID card through the security scanner. "After you, please."

Inside the lab, Summer noticed low-profile surveillance cameras mounted above the molding all along the corridor, and Underhill was limiting his conversation to generalities. When they came to an inner set of double doors, he slid his card into a small slot, and a green light flashed on.

"This is our hormone test center. You may find it interesting."

As the doors slid open, Summer had a sudden whiff of something different about the air.

Underhill glanced back at her. "So you noticed that, did you? Because of the chemicals we work with, we have our own closed ventilation system in here for safety. We take advantage of that technology and generally maintain the oxygen at twenty-two percent."

"You pump in your own mix?" Summer's eyebrow rose. "That must be expensive."

"Not as expensive as losing months of work due to human error caused by muddled thinking." Underhill pointed down the corridor. Neat, printed signs warned workers to wear goggles when using lab facilities and to clean up and store all chemicals before they left the premises. "Safety is very important to us." He pushed open a heavy metal door and waited for Gabe and Summer to precede him. Once they were inside, he closed the door and stood against it, his face haggard and strained. "We don't have much time. We'll walk through two more lab areas and then leave."

"This additional information of yours had better be good," Gabe said flatly.

"Trust me, it is."

"A senator?" Voices drifted from the hallway. Underhill motioned Gabe to silence as the big metal door rattled behind him, and then two men walked into the neighboring lab, visible through a high window. "Later. Is your driver parked in the back?"

Gabe nodded.

Underhill swallowed. "As soon as those workers leave, we'll detour through that lab and take the back door outside."

Behind the window, one of the uniformed men bent down, reaching for something near the floor.

Underhill frowned. "They shouldn't be there." When the man didn't look up, Underhill knocked loudly on the Plexiglas.

"What's going on?" Gabe moved beside him.

"That's the ventilation panel they're working on. But it's not right." He licked his lips nervously. "They're too soon." The scientist shoved Gabe aside and hammered on the window. "Stop," he ordered angrily. "This isn't right."

Summer realized the air smelled musty, like wet animals. Given the kind of tests that must have been done in this room, maybe extra oxygen was a good idea.

Suddenly Gabe jerked on the doorknob, banging loudly. "Open up. Damn it, somebody get over here!"

The sound echoed in the empty room, but next door the workers didn't seem to notice.

"They can't hear you in there. Even if they could, they wouldn't care." Underhill sank against the wall, his face pasty white.

For some reason Summer's pulse felt fast and unsteady as she walked toward Gabe.

The air.

Underhill had mentioned the lab's high-tech ventilation system. She realized the air had probably been tainted. "Gabe, do you smell it? Gas?"

"I smell it. Help me find something to break the window."

Summer noticed a small storage chest on the far wall. She fumbled open the biggest drawer and found a fire extinguisher, but when she tried to lift it, she was struck by a wave of dizziness. Swaying, she braced her shoulder against the wall while the floor tilted wildly.

Gabe was working on the doorknob with a penknife,

and Summer watched his face blur, then split into two identical images. Seconds later Underhill slumped onto the floor.

Gabe's mouth moved, but Summer couldn't make out the words. "Use this." Fighting to breathe, she held up the fire extinguisher.

"Hold on, honey." Gabe caught her as she swayed.

"Feel sick. It hurts—to swallow." Summer took a jerky step, then collapsed against Gabe's chest.

chapter 34

Gabe's wrists were on fire. Cursing, he opened his eyes and squinted into darkness. He was face-down, his cheek pressed against vinyl, his wrists bound at his back.

He twisted upright, and pain shot through his head. A little gift from the gas in the lab, he figured.

"Summer?"

No answer.

He had a knife secured in his boot, but his legs were bound, too. He would have to—

Something bumped his shoulder.

"Gabe?" Her voice was unsteady, inches from his head.

"Right here. Keep talking."

"I feel like throwing up."

He had to smile. "Me, too, honey. Feels like the mother of all hangovers, believe me." Gabe felt her leg and then rolled sideways, working his hands upward. The movements were difficult because his wrists were bound. "Are you hurt?"

"My head feels like a merry-go-round on fast-forward, and my elbows ache. Otherwise, I'm just chipper. Where in the heck are we?"

"I think we're in the backseat of a truck." Gabe refused to think about the grinding pain at his knee. "Are your hands tied?"

"Tight." Summer laughed grimly. "Duct tape, I'm afraid."

"No problem. I've got a knife stashed in my right boot, but I can't reach it with my hands bound behind me like this."

Summer wriggled closer. "Okay, I can feel your boot." Her bound hands covered his leg, digging beneath his boot. "No luck. I can't get any lower. I had a razor and a nail file in my purse, but it's gone now. How about your belt?"

The prong, Gabe realized. "I knew there was a reason I liked hanging around with you. Other than your great legs, of course." He grimaced as her fingers slid upward, digging at his waistband. "Watch where you're jabbing, honey. You may want that part of my anatomy fully functional sometime soon."

"Promises, promises." But Summer's voice was grim as she struggled to free his belt from its clasp.

Gabe vowed it was no idle promise. Once they got the hell out of Mexico alive, he'd prove that to her, preferably until they were both sweaty with exhaustion.

Metal clanked somewhere nearby. Was it machinery? Before Gabe could be sure, the sound faded and Summer went back to work, driving her taped wrists onto the prong of his belt. Each time her hands scraped against his groin, Gabe savored a few choice mental curses.

"Pass go and collect two hundred dollars for not complaining," Summer said tightly. "That's got to hurt."

"I'll live."

"How's your knee?"

Gabe didn't want to think about it. "Not a problem."

"How about the truth this time, Morgan?"

"Okay, it's pretty stiff." The truth was, his whole leg hurt like something important had pulled loose, but there was no point in telling her that.

"What happened to you?"

"A training exercise. My parachute screwed up." Gabe didn't elaborate. How did you describe the shock of plunging out of the sky in a dead drop, with your chute damaged and your guts knotted in terror?

"HALO?"

So she knew about high-altitude, low-opening jumps? Points for the Feeb. "Bingo."

"If you weren't fully recovered, why did you agree to come and handle this situation for the senator?"

"This is a piece of cake compared to what I usually do. Besides, I couldn't turn down Tate Winslow. I owe him and his family too much for that."

"Anything you care to discuss?"

As Summer's hands slid back and forth over his belt, Gabe felt her breath, warm and moist on his cheek. "I'm not sure." He cleared his throat. "By the way, it's a good thing you aren't married or I might have had to arrange a mercy killing."

"Mercy for whom?" she whispered.

"For me, damn it."

"Homicide won't be necessary." Summer took a breath. "I'm not married. Never even came close."

All they had to do was stay alive for the next few hours, Gabe thought. When they didn't check in on time, Izzy would initiate an immediate search, using the imbedded transmitters in Gabe's regular cell phone and the small backup phone, which was hidden inside his boot.

No way to reach it with his damned hands bound.

Wedged together as they were, he felt Summer's heart pounding against his chest. "Any luck?"

"Not yet. The tape is too thick. Your belt prong keeps slipping."

Gabe glared into the darkness, with something hard pressing at his back. He wanted to help her, but his hands were useless.

"Okay, I just made a small hole at one edge," Summer said quietly. "How about telling me how you know Senator Winslow."

There was no noise or movement around them, and Gabe decided distraction was a good idea, considering the current position of her bound hands. "My father and Senator Winslow's father met in the army. My dad saved his life a couple of times, and Randall Winslow never forgot. Afterward, Randall set my parents up on their first fifty acres." Gabe shifted restlessly. "Can we stop talking now?"

"No. Are you married?"

"Not now."

Summer's hands stopped moving. "But . . . you were?"

"A long time ago." Gabe sifted through painful memories. "We met in high school and got married that same summer. We had a daughter by Christmas." It hurt to remember, even now. He was sure it always would.

"And?"

"And it only took a shit-for-brains drunk driver twenty seconds to kill them both." Gabe glared into the darkness, assaulted by bitter memories. "One moment they were laughing in the snow and the next they were caught in a ball of burning metal when the driver jumped the curb."

He heard Summer's breath catch. "I'm so sorry, Gabe. I—didn't know."

"Not many people do. Rosalita—well, she was full of joy and wonder, the hardest worker I ever met. I was young and reckless, but I loved her, and our baby girl was the most beautiful thing a man could ever hope to see. Both of them always loved the snow. Funny, I forgot that until now." Frowning, he pulled his thoughts back from images of dark eyes and soft laughter. "Afterward, I got in my car and started driving, with no particular plan. Two weeks later I ended up in a beachfront bar in Mexico, stone drunk and robbed blind." After a moment, Gabe went on. "That night Tate Winslow's dad came down and dusted me off, literally and figuratively. Three days later I was in basic training. If he hadn't tracked me down at that bar, I'm not sure where I'd be now."

"Randall Winslow sounds like an interesting man."

Gabe laughed softly. "Yeah, he was that, all right. The man just kept coming, working at you until you saw his way of thinking. He and Amanda, Tate's mother, always believed in getting involved and staying involved. When Tate needed my help, there was no way I could refuse."

"Because it was personal." In the cramped space, Summer dug her hands against his belt. "Sorry if this hurts."

"Do what needs to be done. Forget about me." Without warning, light burned into Gabe's eyes. As he'd guessed, they were inside the extended cab of a battered pickup truck, and two people were walking toward the truck.

The woman in front was the receptionist who'd argued with them at the clinic. The man beside her had been running cable.

"Company," Gabe whispered. "Stay down."

"Almost free," she said breathlessly.

As the uniformed man headed for the driver's side door of the truck, light struck the revolver holstered beneath his shoulder. "Do it fast," Gabe whispered. "Our options may be starting to dwindle."

chapter 35

Answer your damn *phone,* Gabe."

Muttering, Izzy broke off his latest attempt to rouse either Summer or Gabe. When his pager was equally unsuccessful, he opened the big metal case on the car seat beside him and powered up his GPS, praying they still had their phones.

He'd watched them enter the clinic's main reception building, then emerge with a woman in a white uniform. From his vantage point in the loading area behind the lab, Izzy had seen them enter the lab building with Underhill. Ten minutes later they still hadn't reappeared, and a guard had come by, politely but firmly telling Izzy to return to the main parking area at the clinic entrance. Though he'd taken his time, Izzy had complied.

At twenty minutes, Izzy knew things had gone south, because Gabe hadn't answered his cell phone at the pre-arranged time. When he'd checked with the receptionist, he was told that Mr. and Mrs. Walker had taken a taxi back to their hotel.

Of course, they hadn't.

Now with his laptop open, Izzy tried to locate Gabe's

phone. A digital map appeared on-screen, with an arrow flickering inside the lab. So Gabe was still inside.

Izzy sat back slowly. Or *was he?*

He opened a new screen on his computer, taking a different tack. Senator Winslow had made it clear that the three of them would be on their own here in Mexico. There would be no consular backup, no cavalry charging in with guns blazing.

Izzy's face hardened.

Not that it mattered. He made a damned good cavalry regiment all by himself.

Summer's hands were on fire, her skin abraded and raw up to her wrists. Though she was bleeding, she kept twisting feverishly, trying to free the last remaining piece of tape. She felt the truck moving while the motor throbbed noisily beneath them, coughing occasionally.

"How are your hands?" Gabe said, his mouth near her ear.

"I felt another piece of tape break," she whispered back. "My hands are slippery, which should help."

"Slippery from what?"

"Sweat." And blood, Summer didn't say. She bit back a curse as another layer of skin tore free.

A bump sent them flying a foot into the air, then slammed them back down.

"As soon as I can, I'm going for the driver," he whispered.

"How?"

The truck backfired, swerving hard. Tree branches scraped the metal body like clawing fingers.

Gabe didn't answer. Silently, Summer reached up to check her door, but the latch was frozen, rusted all the way through.

No chance of getting out that way.

She felt Gabe shift, then pull his hands apart, slamming her on the chin in the process. "How'd you do that?" she whispered, her voice barely audible above the hammer of the old motor.

"I found a rusted nail on the floor, caught in an old piece of rope. Thank God for garbage." Gabe dug into his boot, then pressed a knife against her fingers. "Use this. I'm going for the driver."

Summer gripped the knife awkwardly between her knees. She was still bleeding and the knife slipped, cutting her thumb. Ignoring the pain, she went to work while Gabe snaked his arm around the driver's throat, squeezing hard.

The driver yelled Spanish curses and the truck twisted. Summer heard a hissing noise, and Gabe's body went tense as he took a burst of pepper spray directly in the face, but even then he didn't let go of the driver's throat. She shoved the knife down again, and the tape on her hands broke free. Gabe was struggling blindly with their frenzied driver. She lunged over the seat, pulled up the driver's door latch, and pushed open the door. Gritting her teeth, Summer pulled the man sideways, and with a brutal shove from Gabe that knocked the revolver to the seat, they pushed the driver outside.

He hit the road with a cloud of dust and an angry yell.

As the truck kept moving, Summer saw that Underhill was slumped down on the passenger seat, still in his rumpled suit. The driver's revolver was on the seat next to him. Gabe was still half-blinded by the pepper spray, and the truck was fishtailing wildly as they twisted along a narrow mountain road.

Summer leaned over the seat, grabbing the wheel. "I doubt we'll see the driver again anytime soon," she rasped.

"Fine by me."

Summer managed to climb into the driver's seat without letting go of the steering wheel. Underhill gasped out a tortured breath and began to struggle, his arms striking her in the head.

Summer tried to dodge Underhill's flailing arms. "Hold him. He's waking up."

Gabe managed to grip the scientist from behind and hold him steady. "Terence, can you hear me?"

The scientist gasped an answer, and the next swerve pitched him hard against Gabe's arm.

"Blood on the Armani. I hate it when that happens." Gabe shifted to find a better grip while the scientist twisted, oblivious. "Terence, hang in there, pal."

Summer tried to decipher Underhill's guttural ranting. "What's he saying?"

"Can't tell. Something about a panda?"

Summer saw a green van racing through the dirt behind them. One of the men in the front seat looked like the driver she had tossed out of the truck minutes before.

The road was dangerously narrow now, with almost no room to maneuver, but the van kept coming, and slammed hard against her back fender.

Summer veered to the left, racing along the very edge of the road, fighting to hold the truck steady with the van right behind her, ramming her bumper.

Below her she saw a flash of silver from the ocean, and then the road twisted sharply. To the north, weathered stucco houses dotted the hillside, and after a steep descent the road split in two.

The van hammered them again. Summer's head snapped backward and she nearly lost control of the truck. Dust swirled through the window and she coughed hard, spit out a mouthful of grit, then drove the accelerator back to the floor. "Can you see yet?" she shouted to Gabe.

"Still blurred as hell."

"The driver's gun is on the seat."

Underhill was muttering brokenly, but Summer couldn't look away from the road.

Something struck the rear window, cracking the glass.

"We're taking fire here. Give it some juice."

Trying to ignore the van riding her bumper and the sheer drop to her left, Summer floored the accelerator again while Gabe knocked a hole in the cab's rear window.

Squinting, he squeezed off four shots and then cursed. "You need to hold us straight! I'm guessing here already."

Summer gritted her teeth. "In case you hadn't noticed, this road is bumpy as hell."

"I noticed, trust me."

A bullet cracked against the roof.

"There's a split in the road ahead." Summer measured distances and calculated speed. "Get ready, because I'm turning hard."

"Hold on." Gabe's first shot shattered the van's windshield, and their pursuers slowed abruptly. As Summer barreled into the turn, a mother and three children walked onto the road, directly in front of the truck. Breathing a silent prayer, Summer jammed the brakes hard and spun the truck ninety degrees. With dust flying wildly, they careened into a skid.

She flipped on the wipers, half-blinded, watching the van roar past her with no break in speed. Amid a stream of curses, the driver swerved into a rock, and the van soared into the air, crash-landing against a huge cottonwood tree.

Before Summer had time for relief, the road twisted sharply to the right and she saw a cement overhang twenty feet away, part of a new irrigation canal. They were headed directly toward the unfinished edge.

Summer stared grimly down the hill, her options fading. "Brace yourself, because this is going to hurt like hell," she shouted.

Then there was nothing but brown, rocky soil stretching out below her.

chapter 36

Amanda Winslow closed the trunk of her old silver Mercedes and smiled at Cara gamely. "I told Tate to prepare to be supplanted." She held up a dozen bags with bright bows and ribbons. "We have serious work to do, my love. Not that you aren't gorgeous, but a bride can always use a little extra glow for her big day."

Cara put her arm around Sophy, who was staring wide-eyed at Tate's mother. "What a lovely idea. But you really shouldn't have gone to all this trouble, Amanda."

The slim, white-haired woman laughed in delight. "The only trouble was negotiating that dirt road to get here. The day spa treatments become trouble is the day I draw my last breath. Do you know, Tate and his brother used to tease me that I should open my own spa since I was already an expert." Her head tilted. "And I actually considered it. I even signed a contract on a lovely little property in Georgetown near Tate's old law office." She winked at Sophy. "Thank God, I came to my senses in time."

"What happened?" Sophy demanded, in awe of her future grandmother.

"I realized that I would have been appalling as a masseuse, my dear, and even worse as a business manager." Shaking her head, Amanda juggled two bags and took her son's arm. "Are the reporters leaving you alone here?"

"So far we've managed to fly below their radar. I've promised Audra a fishing expedition today." He grinned at his mother. "Don't suppose you'd want to give up exfoliation for standing waist-high in frigid water?"

"Blasphemy, my love." Amanda handed one of her bags to Cara. "I think we should start with the algae rinse. After that comes the loofah scrub and the warm mud wrap. When I'm done, you'll look like a teenager—not that you aren't close to being thirteen already, my sweet."

Sophy giggled. "What about me? Can you make me look older, Grandma?"

"Are you staying with us, Sophy? If so, I think you'll fall in love with my strawberry mousse face cream. I even brought a pair of little red spa slippers, just for you."

Beaming, Sophy took a skipping step. "Audra will be *soooo* jealous."

"Then we won't tell her, will we?" Amanda's voice was low and conspiratorial.

Sophy hesitated. "Grandma Amanda, what's blas— blasma—"

"Blasphemy. That, my love, is an act of irreverence toward something sacred."

"Will I know a lot of big words like that when I grow up?"

"When you grow up, you will walk on Mars," Amanda Winslow said gravely. "You will own a huge international corporation and rule it with an iron hand. Who knows, you might even decide to become president." As they crossed the porch, she glanced across at Tate, who was walking beside Cara. "Forgive me for arriving unannounced, but when Bud mentioned you were coming, I couldn't resist. Now, is there anything I can do to help you two? Any calls to return, food to order, reporters to badger?"

"We're all set," Cara said. "All you need to do while you're here is relax."

"Relaxation always bored me. Let's see, I packed all kinds of good things for lunch." Amanda frowned at Cara. "Audra was looking pale when I saw her last. Has she been sick?"

Cara swallowed. "She's been under some stress lately."

"You should help her with that, darling. Let's both try." Amanda turned to her son and waved airily. "Off with you, Tate. Go find your frigid stream and cast away. We women have *serious* work to do."

"Anyone for lemonade? It's my special recipe, brought all the way from San Francisco, made with lemons, blood oranges, and all the pulp you can squeeze in." Amanda Winslow poured three glasses and handed one to Cara, then placed the iced pitcher on a lacquer tray. "Sophy, be a love and bring me the little suitcase from the front seat of my car. I must have left all my brushes in there. You can have your lemonade when you return."

"Okay." The little girl stopped in the doorway and looked back. Sunlight was spilling through the big window in the upstairs bedroom, and her mother was sitting in a chair, her legs curled, looking very happy.

I want her to look like that all the time, Sophy thought. *Maybe if I'm very good, I can make that happen.*

Grandma Amanda was refilling her mother's glass as Sophy skipped down the stairs, thinking about red spa slippers and strawberry mousse. She dawdled crossing the front porch, enjoying the sun on her shoulders and the stillness all around her at the ranch.

It was good to feel safe.

When she walked back with her grandmother's little case, she kicked up dust with her sneakers, just for the fun of seeing the brown clouds dance around her. Then she heard her mother's voice carried through the open windows above the porch, and she smiled.

At the front door she saw something on the floor behind the big leather chair her Grandma Amanda liked best, and for a frightening moment Sophy thought it was her diary, the one she never showed anyone. How had it fallen out of her knapsack?

When she remembered she had left her diary at home, locked in her desk drawer, Sophy walked closer and saw a big blue envelope, the kind that came from foreign countries. Since she collected foreign stamps, Sophy knew this stamp was in Spanish and came from Mexico.

It must have fallen when they came in, Sophy thought. The letter from Mexico probably belonged to her Grandma Amanda, who got letters from all over the world for her international charities. Sophy bent down and picked up the colored envelope.

As her fingers touched the paper, she swallowed hard. She couldn't say why, but something about the envelope felt strange.

"Amanda, I don't understand."

"No? I should think it was entirely clear." Amanda Winslow put down her Prada purse on the big, rustic dresser and turned. "I can't allow you to destroy my son's future, even if you're too selfish to see that's exactly what you're doing."

"Why are you saying this? What makes you think—"

Cara blinked, rubbing her face. Suddenly she clutched her stomach.

"Exactly, my dear." Tate's mother smiled faintly. "I know all about your sordid visit to that little clinic in Mexico. Los Reyes, wasn't it?"

"But when . . . how did you find out?"

Amanda lifted her shoulders in an elegant shrug. "Really, Cara, do you think I'd let him marry just anyone? I had you investigated, of course, just as I had his other women investigated. You were the best candidate for Tate, I have to admit, and after the first date I knew he was serious about you. He wanted marriage and a family, something he'd never considered with any of the others." Her lips pursed. "I sent a man to do some research in California. When that was done, I sent a different man to your old law school and another to that apartment you had in college. Well, guess what? Your old landlady remembered that you'd been sick one term and had to drop out of school. She also said you'd made a trip to Mexico with your sister." Amanda stared coldly at Cara. "The next part wasn't so easy. You covered yourself well, as any good lawyer would." Tate's mother moved around the bed, watching Cara closely. "Then I had a bit of luck, and the last part of the puzzle fell right into my lap, so to speak." She smiled. "Richard Costello."

Cara couldn't speak. A terrible weight was squeezing her chest, driving all the air from her body. She looked at the lemonade glass, her head pounding. "No."

"Yes, Cara. I worked out all the details about six months ago. It was Costello who gave me the idea." She smiled very elegantly, the perfect smile that Washington reporters had seen for years. "And then those terrible threatening letters began to arrive at your office."

Cara struggled to her feet. "A-Amanda, you didn't. Costello is a criminal. You can't know what you're saying."

The old woman laughed tightly. "I know *exactly* what I'm saying. It's all your fault, after all. If you hadn't been so selfish, you'd have seen your duty sooner, and none of this would have been necessary. But you aren't feeling so well, are you? What a pity."

Sophy gripped the envelope, shivering.

Trust your heart, Summer had told her yesterday, while the surf rumbled in the distance. Sophy thought about her ballet class and about Summer's words, while she held the colored envelope, her body shaking.

Something was wrong. She felt the way she'd felt those other times, when bad things were about to happen. She'd never been wrong so far.

She looked around at the quiet house, filled with the sudden knowledge that her mother was in danger. Maybe they all were.

Trust your heart, Summer had told her.

Sophy found her backpack and dug inside it.

Apple-cinnamon lip balm. Two Scrunchies. Half of a Snickers bar. Hello Kitty bag. Hello Kitty two-way radio.

Her heart began to pound louder. She took a deep breath.

Trust your heart.

She opened the screen door, then closed it gently with both hands, careful not to let the frame bang. Gripping the radio, the one she and Audra used to play with for hours before Audra started acting so grown-up, Sophy flipped on the power button.

"Audra, can you hear me? Please, Auddie, it's Sophy. You have to come *now.*"

"Right here looks good." Tate pointed toward the stream, silver in the clear morning light.

"But I left my fishing stuff near the horses."

"Don't worry, Bud will bring everything down." Tate took Audra's arm. "Besides, we've got all morning. Let's go see what's biting."

chapter 37

A udra, can you hear me?" Sophy gripped the handset, running toward the stables. "Is anyone here?"

Tears streaked her face as she ran past the empty stalls. "Auddie, please, please hear me. Mom and I *need* you."

No one answered.

"Here are some pills to move things along," Amanda said coldly. "Fifteen should do the job. Probably even six or seven would work."

"Amanda, you can't mean what you're saying."

"Shut up for once. You're not in a courtroom now." Tate Winslow's elegant mother, dignified in a gray silk jacket and skirt, pulled a bottle from her pocket. "I've thought it all out."

Dizzy, Cara stumbled back toward the door, only to find Amanda moving to cut her off. "Tate wouldn't want this," Cara whispered. "He'll hate you."

"His career means everything to him—and to me. I won't let one silly woman ruin all that he's worked for. I'm only glad I finally realized how dangerous you are."

Cara closed her eyes, trying to focus. No, none of it made sense. Amanda wasn't rational.

She clutched her stomach as another wave of nausea hit. Something in the lemonade, she realized. The pain came again, bending her double.

Amanda pursed her lips as she unscrewed the top of the bottle. "The girls are absolutely wonderful, even if you do persist in coddling them beyond permission. But I'll see to it that they're given some spine. No more pampering. They'll go off to the best schools in the East, since Tate and I won't have much time for them. Once the news of your suicide from a drug overdose hits the papers, he's going to be terribly busy doing damage control. But I'll make certain he looks heroic. A sad man hoodwinked by an aggressive and unstable woman. His female demographics should skew right through the roof," she added gravely. "All *you* have to do is swallow a few pills. As a matter of fact, you might be the final thing that puts him into the White House."

"Keep your hands off my girls," Cara said hoarsely. "You're s-sick, Amanda. You're twisted."

"Actually, *you* are the one who is sick. The nausea can be quite awful, I understand."

With trembling steps Cara wobbled toward the door. She had to get help, but the phone was downstairs. She'd never make it that far.

"Nasty, right to the end. A good prosecutor and a wretched choice for a wife." In the sunlight, Amanda's manicured nails looked like perfect drops of blood as she poured a handful of pills into her palm. "I suppose I should call Patrick to help me with this part."

Cara tried to focus. "Patrick Flanagan? Patrick, our chef?"

"Didn't you know? Patrick has been working for

Richard Costello for a long time now. I'm afraid he hates you greatly, my love."

Summer's lacerated wrists were on fire.

Dust flew up in angry brown sheets, and then the truck tilted sharply, slamming her back against the door frame.

Not *panda,* she realized.

Not a panda at all.

She knew now what name Underhill had tried to give them, but it was too late to help. Gabe threw his body over the seat—over Underhill and over her—to protect them, and there was a loud *BOOM!* like overhead thunder and she was tossed straight forward, glass clawing at her head.

Then there was only pain and a flat wall of darkness sweeping down around her.

"Auddie, where *are* you?"

The handset crackled against Sophy's ear. "I'm right here. Why are you shouting, Sophy? You're scaring all the fish."

Sophy almost dropped the radio in her panic. "S-something's wrong, Auddie. You've got to come back to the house right away. Have them call the police."

"What are you talking about? Sophy, if this is a joke—"

"It's not, Auddie. I saw something and it was horrible. Mommy's in danger, and you have to come here now. Hurry, and be sure to bring the others with you."

"What do you mean? Why—"

"I have go back now. *Hurry.*"

Sophy shoved the radio back in her pocket. She found what she'd been searching for, then raced back through the stables.

A strange car was parked at the back of the house now. Sophy didn't question the instinct that made her zigzag through the trees and enter quietly from the small side porch, where no one would see her.

The phone was ringing downstairs, but Cara could barely hear it. She sank onto her knees, holding her stomach as more cramps hit. Amanda's hands blurred in front of her, shoving her onto the floor.

Downstairs the phone stopped ringing.

Cara thought of her girls. She refused to fail them. She wouldn't miss their driving tests and proms, their graduations and beautiful weddings.

Her vision was getting worse, and sharp nails dug at her mouth, trying to work the big capsules past her locked teeth. Cara shook her head, fighting hard, but she was losing strength fast.

She remembered there had been something bitter in the lemonade, something that didn't taste like pulp. Amanda's shadow fell over her.

Amanda.

As she wobbled back to her feet, Sophy ran into the room. Cara tried to protest, but her daughter dug in her pocket and pushed Amanda back against the wall.

There was something small and gray in Sophy's hands, Cara realized. Cats? But Amanda was desperately allergic to cats. They made her skin break out and her throat swell up. Sophy knew that.

Of course. Smart, brave Sophy was frightening Amanda with two of the stable cats, defending her mother. As she crawled across the floor, Cara heard Amanda cough, shouting at Sophy. Cara gripped Amanda's legs and held on tight, forcing the old woman to drop her hands.

One by one the pills scattered, hitting the floor.

Downstairs the phone began to ring again and there

were loud footsteps on the porch, followed by a man's voice, tense and angry. Patrick, here in Wyoming?

The front door banged hard and Cara threw up in waves of torment that seemed to go on and on. Sophy pressed close, burrowing against her while the cats meowed between them.

Cara pitched forward, her body shaking. She didn't hear Sophy cry out or call her name. She didn't even feel Tate pick her up, cradle her head, and carry her carefully down the stairs.

The sirens were deafening.

The noise barely registered with Izzy. Considering the kind of work he did, he had seen all manner of deaths. He'd watched men gurgle away their lives from throat wounds, choking on their own blood. He'd seen men rub their eyes, only to find that their faces had been shot away. He'd even spent his own private stretch of time in hell, beginning on a perfect summer day in Thailand many years before. The scars he still carried served to remind him how men could stoop to acts of violence that no animal would commit.

He watched a team of men with stretchers carefully lift Summer's body off the front of the mangled truck, where the village women had found her. No one in authority was saying much, despite all his questions, and Izzy's training as a medic told him that Summer's condition would be touch and go.

Thank God, he'd been able to trace them through Gabe's backup cell phone.

He turned and looked at Gabe. The man was still recovering from a HALO jump that by all rights should have killed him, and since that hadn't done the job, the damn SEAL had to get himself thrown around inside a runaway truck.

And on top of everything else, Izzy couldn't reach Tate Winslow or Cara O'Connor at the ranch in Wyoming.

Izzy punched another number on his phone as two medical techs passed him carrying another stretcher to the crash site for Gabe, who had blocked Summer's impact with his own body. Flung across the dashboard, he had twisted hard, one shoulder pinned under the steering wheel while his knee punched right through the rusted front dashboard.

One of the medics whispered that he would never walk again. Seeing the unnatural angle of Gabe's knee and two inches of exposed bone, Izzy knew it was a grim possibility.

In the distance a chopper droned closer. About damned time, Izzy thought. He had pulled a whole lot of strings to arrange fast transport across the border to a U.S. facility where Gabe and Summer would receive expert care.

As the big bird thundered in, Izzy stood motionless, squinting into the dust and wishing like hell that he could do something more to help.

But he was fresh out of miracles, so he stabbed his cell phone and tried Tate Winslow in Wyoming one more time.

chapter 38

Tate stood on the porch shouting into his cell phone as Bud roared up in his big pickup. They'd take the fastest route to Laramie, where the ER staff had been notified to expect them, with a possible diagnosis of poisoning.

Tate hadn't believed it when Audra ran along the river, shouting at him, her face white as chalk. He'd ridden with her back to the house, convinced it was some kind of a joke, but then he'd seen Cara, curled up on the floor, fighting to breathe.

With Bud's help, he lifted Cara into the backseat while the girls got in front. Tate covered Cara gently with a blanket, desperate to do something, anything at all, to help her. She was too pale, her body shaking, her breath labored.

Suddenly everything he'd accepted and dreamed about seemed to slide away from him. If what Sophy said was true, and his mother had truly argued with Cara, then tried to give her some kind of pills . . .

Amanda was headstrong and painfully determined when she had a goal in mind, but Tate couldn't believe she would hurt Cara or the girls. She had told Tate once that

Cara was the best thing that had ever happened to him, and she valued the strength of family as much as he had, even if she had been quick to calculate the political points a family would score in a campaign. "Being happily married with two adorable children never hurt a man who wants to be president of the greatest country on earth," she had told him confidently.

Impossible to think of his mother snapping completely, turning into a murderer.

Tate closed his eyes. The truth was that he hadn't spent much time with her in the last year. His brother had mentioned that she had some health issues, but they'd been minor, according to Greg, mainly a problem with one of her medications. But that, too, had been resolved, and just last week Amanda had assured Tate that she felt better than she had at thirty.

The truck pitched and swayed along the bumpy drive, dust kicking up in an angry cloud. Cara's eyes closed and her head lolled.

Tate felt as if his whole world had tilted off course. The girls looked almost as bad as he felt.

Leaning forward, he put his arms around Audra, then Sophy. "I thought it was a joke. Dear God, I was so sure." He closed his eyes and worked to pull himself together. He owed the girls that much.

He owed Cara that much.

"She's going to be fine, you two. The people at the hospital have everything ready for us." He struggled a moment, then forced a smile, the strong, confident kind that he used to forge coalitions and build grassroots assent.

Neither Audra nor Sophy responded.

Tate frowned at a sudden thought. "Sophy, honey, did you see where Grandma Amanda went? Did you hear a car?"

Sophy gave him an odd look, and for a moment her eyes were a stranger's eyes. "I heard her leave, Uncle Tate. I think I heard her car. I—I can't remember." Her lip started to tremble as she looked down at her mother. "Patrick was there, but he left, too."

"Patrick, your chef, here at the ranch? Well, never mind. I'm sure my mother went to get help." Tate tried to put the best spin on matters as he glanced at the rearview mirror and met Bud's eyes. It was like a kick in the chest when his ranch foreman frowned and shook his head.

So it was true. Bud had seen something Tate hadn't. How long had Amanda been planning this, hating the woman he loved?

Wind churned across the road, scattering leaves and dirt over the windshield, so they drove blind.

If he lost Cara, nothing would matter. Tate choked the thought down like ashes. No way was he going to lose her. He'd badger and bribe every specialist in the country until someone found a way to help. Then he'd badger and harass Cara until she got well, just because she would be sick of seeing his face all day, every day. And he'd damned well take care of her girls until she was strong enough to take care of them herself.

It was the least he could do. Even if she hated him after this, hated the thing his mother had tried to do.

With Cara in his lap, he gripped Audra's hand, pulling Sophy against his shoulder, and stared out at the roiling dust, trying to think about life, not death.

Dirt blocked the road, making the Mercedes skid wildly.

Amanda stared at the cloud for a moment, forgetting why she was here. Then she remembered.

Because of *her,* the beautiful, scheming woman who had

stolen her son and destroyed his future—what would have been Tate's and Amanda's magnificent future together.

She was glad she had let Patrick drive. Her nerves were shot and she was still having trouble breathing.

He slanted her a questioning look. "Did you do it? Was she frightened?"

Amanda shuddered. "Sophy came, but I'm sure Cara got the message."

Patrick slapped the wheel happily. "Better and better. Her own daughter sees her terror. That's perfect."

"Don't be coarse, Patrick."

"Shut up, Amanda. Business is business. So did she agree to help out with the appeal? Will she get that forensic evidence we need?"

"Not exactly." Cara had been curled up on the floor struggling to breathe when Amanda had left. With any luck she would soon be dead. But Patrick and his vicious employer didn't plan on losing their inside informer. Their goal was her complete compliance, not her death.

The poison had been Amanda's revelation. She had to free her son from his obsession with Cara before the woman distracted him from his crucial political mission. It was Amanda's simple duty as a mother.

"What did she say?"

"Not much. She was too . . . upset."

Patrick turned, glaring at her. "You did something, didn't you? What *was* it, old woman?" Patrick gripped her arm. "Tell me, damn you."

"I did something I've been thinking of for months." Amanda felt a ragged laugh escape, then another. "You never knew. You thought you would use me, Patrick, but *I* used you."

Amanda stopped suddenly. She had been a certified

beauty for fifty years, and she was still held to be the yardstick for charm and elegance. Now it was all crashing to an end.

"Forget about Cara and drive," she said acidly. Her head was aching and she couldn't think straight. Every detail had been meticulously arranged, from the contact in Mexico and the threatening letters to the kidnapping at the clinic when the wretched nanny and Gabe Morgan had checked in. No doubt both of them were dead by now. A pity, since Gabe had always been a respectful boy, but Costello's men would have seen to that.

Just as Cara should have been dead by now, thanks to the ground seeds Amanda had mixed in the lemonade pulp. The botanist at the National Arboretum had described their action very thoroughly while giving Amanda's garden club a tour six months ago.

She remembered his discussion of toxic glycoproteins, whatever those were, but all that really mattered were the small scarlet seeds, which concentrated the main toxin of the plants. The botanist had assured his fascinated audience that even one seed well-chewed could cause fatal poisoning.

Amanda had used five seeds, taken from plants scattered about the gardens of her sprawling estate back in South Carolina. The same plants now grew in Cara's backyard, thanks to Amanda. Of course, Tate wouldn't care to make public the sordid details of Cara's suicide, so it would be termed an accidental overdose, possibly influenced by Cara's fear of scandal, resulting from the discovery of her visit to Los Reyes Clinic.

A yellow sign flashed by the side of the road, blurred by the dust, but Patrick didn't slow down. Amanda coughed, hard, struggling to breathe. Sophy knew she was allergic

to cats. Why had the girl turned on her that way, screaming and unrecognizable?

In growing confusion Amanda thought about her
meticulous plans for Christmas at the White House and
fireworks on Independence Day, along with select little
dinners perfectly orchestrated to make Tate the most powerful president in history. And her files full of secrets
would be carefully held in reserve, in case anyone dared to
cross her precious son.

But what would happen now? Sophy would tell Tate
what had happened, and then Tate would turn against her.
If the truth ever leaked to the press, the scandal would
destroy him.

Amanda closed her eyes in confusion. She couldn't allow Tate to be harmed. There had to be some other way.

Patrick was staring at her again. "You're starting to an-
noy me, old woman. Stop rambling and tell me what Cara
said when you left. Costello will want to know."

"She said that I was twisted and I needed medical help.
She told me to keep my hands off her girls." Amanda
searched the rocky landscape, looking for an answer that
would protect her son. If Costello found out what she had
done, he would never let Tate go. He would blackmail
Tate and bleed him dry, destroying his glorious future.

Dear God, what to do?

The answer came to her, a bright light in the midst of
her terrible confusion. She recognized the turn ahead.
When Bud had mentioned something about the road being washed out, she hadn't paid much attention but now it
made all the difference. Sitting beside her, Patrick was
oblivious to the danger as her expensive Michelin tires
dug in hard, then kicked free and swerved across the
gravel.

It was time.

It was her duty—to her son and to her country. A Winslow never forgot the importance of duty.

Through the racing dust, she saw the turn flash before her.

Amanda Winslow took a deep breath and yanked the wheel, closing her eyes as Patrick screamed and the road vanished beneath them.

chapter 39

She's pretty banged up."

Gabe stared through the windows to the emergency room unit where three doctors worked on Summer. She was shoving away their hands, groggy but complaining loudly, demanding to see Gabe and Izzy. "Give me the details, Teague."

"You want the technical stuff, I can throw that on you. Trust me, it won't amount to more than this. She has a head wound, substantial blood loss, but nothing invasive. She narrowly missed a broken rib, and she has a broken arm, which they're preparing to set right now." Izzy smiled slightly. "If she stops raising hell long enough, that is. She's also got extensive lacerations on the chest and neck from breaking glass."

Gabe swallowed. "How bad?"

"She's going to need some cosmetic surgery. Nothing crucial that has to be sewed back on, if that's what you mean."

Gabe closed his eyes. "Yeah. That's what I meant." He forced away nightmarish visions and told himself sternly that she was alive. That was the bottom line. "Anything else?"

"Mild concussion. Some evidence of shock. Significant blood loss, which is being managed aggressively. The good news is she has no sign of hemorrhaging, no sign of internal injuries. If you hadn't been airlifted to the hospital and stabilized so fast . . ." Izzy shrugged, letting the words trail away.

Gabe knew it was true, but seeing Summer pale and struggling didn't seem to be cause for rejoicing. "What about Underhill?"

"He didn't make it. Never regained consciousness, I'm afraid."

After a moment Gabe shook his head. "So we didn't get that name he promised us, after all."

"Summer did. It was the first thing out of her mouth when she woke up in the chopper. Not *panda*, pal. Underhill was *trying* to say *Amanda*."

Gabe stared at Summer, his leg throbbing in spite of the massive amount of painkillers the orthopedic specialist had ordered for him. "Tate Winslow's *mother*? What does she have to do with this? The woman's got to be seventy years old."

"And sins are confined to youth? I just spoke to the senator in Laramie. Right now Cara O'Connor is in intensive care undergoing treatment for leptin poisoning induced by ground-up rosary pea seeds, courtesy of Amanda Winslow. None of us saw it coming."

"That's crazy." Gabe rubbed his neck. "What's Cara's prognosis?"

"Too soon to say. She threw up fairly soon, which limited the amount of toxin she ingested. The ER team gave her gastric lavage and now she's on IV fluids to stabilize her blood chemistry. So far, there's been no sign of convulsions or cardiac involvement. The big question is whether she'll lose kidney function, and that's going to take time to assess."

Gabe still couldn't imagine the charming and stately Amanda Winslow planning anything like this. "I still can't get a grip on this. I've known the Winslows forever, and they're a great family."

"From what Cara told Tate, his mother was irrational, afraid that news of Cara's abortion would destroy his shot at Pennsylvania Avenue. To her, that meant everything. But it's over now. Amanda and Patrick spun out on a mountain road. By the time they were found, both of them were dead."

Gabe was silent for a long time. "I still don't see how Amanda knew about Cara's visit to Mexico."

"You ready for this? She was working with Costello." Izzy's face hardened. "The chef was one of Costello's people, too."

"Patrick?" Gabe couldn't hide his disbelief. "The man had the disposition of a pet rabbit."

"A good actor, and hardly tame. Costello had every detail of Cara's past researched during his trial. Eventually he discovered those missing weeks she spent in Mexico and he planned to blackmail her into working for him. That meant probing the evidence and testimony of key prosecution witnesses. The scary thing is, he might have succeeded, too. Apparently, the old forensic lab in San Francisco was a nightmare, because a leaking roof contaminated dozens of lab samples, invalidating some of the evidence actually gathered in the case. Thanks to Costello, two key witnesses also announced they wanted to change their testimony. Yes, he might have walked away, free and clear."

"If Cara O'Connor hadn't stayed tough," Gabe said quietly. "How are Sophy and Audra?"

"Shaken up, scared crazy, but physically fine. They're not leaving their mother's side."

"And the senator?"

"I spoke to him briefly. He told me exactly what he knew and exactly what Sophy had told him. None of it was pretty, considering that his mother appears to have arranged a complicated plan to murder his bride-to-be. The media is already on the scent, and they still don't know the half of it."

"Let's hope they never do. Amanda's dead and so is Patrick. I suppose they've paid their price." Gabe grimaced as the wheelchair he was sitting in brushed the wall. "Damned chair. Damned knees." He stared impassively at Izzy. "How much did they tell you?"

"That you're going to be immobilized for two, maybe three months. After that there's an experimental bone implant technique they want to try out."

"The relevant word is *experimental.*" Gabe turned away, looking through the window at Summer, who had finally stopped arguing with the nearest doctor. An IV line hung from her arm and she was fighting to keep her eyes open.

Stubborn, difficult woman.

Wonderful woman.

"Don't tell her about me, Izzy. I don't want her to know."

Izzy frowned. "What do you mean?"

"It was time to leave, anyway." Gabe's hands tightened on the arms of the wheelchair. "This makes things cleaner."

Izzy glared at Gabe. "Cleaner for *who?*"

"For both of us," Gabe said quietly. "You think I should hang the hell around? Hold her hand and act warm and fuzzy? Sorry, but I don't *do* warm and fuzzy."

Gabe's jaw worked up and down. "I may not walk again, Teague. We both know that changes everything."

Izzy crossed his arms in stony silence.

Gabe snorted. "I figured you'd say that."

"I said nothing, Morgan."

"That ugly, beat-up face of yours said it for you. You think I'm some kind of shit for cutting things off with her, and that's too damned bad." Gabe gripped the big wheels and started down the hall, moving awkwardly in a wave of unrelenting pain.

"That's right, you *are* a first-class shit. Even more, you're a fool. Now stop trying to run into a wall and let me help you."

As Izzy took charge of the cumbersome chair, Gabe glared down at his legs, immobile in horizontal hip-to-ankle casts. "You're wrong, Izzy. For once in my life, I'm being smart. And for the record, I can manage just fine."

"Sure you can. I hear they're holding a spot for you in the Boston Marathon, too."

Gabe's face was dotted with sweat. His hands fisted in his lap as he fought through a wall of dizziness and pain. "Damned straight they are. I just might win."

At the end of the hall, a Navy orderly was waiting. He saluted Gabe smartly. "The helicopter is ready, sir."

Gabe looked back at Summer. For a moment the silence hung heavy, and then he cleared his throat. "Take care of her," he said hoarsely. "If she asks, tell her you don't know where I am. Tell her I dropped out and started a new religion down in South America somewhere."

Izzy shook his head. "You're a real hard-ass, Morgan. I'll tell her, but don't ask me to like it." Izzy hit a button on the wall, and the automatic door opened with a *hiss*. "And just for the record, my face may be busted up, but it still looks better than *your* ugly-as-sin mug."

A hint of a smile brushed Gabe's mouth.

He turned back for a last look at Summer, motionless in a white bed, a monitor beeping beside her, and his smile faded. "She'll forget about me in a week, anyway. Couple of clean-cut young suits will whisk her back to Philadelphia, give her flowers, take her out to a fancy restaurant, and I'm history."

Guys with whole bodies, Gabe thought grimly. *Guys who can still walk. Young guys with some kind of future to offer a woman who didn't need more pain and uncertainty in her life.*

"In fact, I'm probably history already," he muttered. His jaw locked hard as he gripped Izzy's hand for a moment. Then the orderly pushed him over the threshold, out to the waiting military transport.

chapter 40

It was hard to breathe, harder still to stay. Every nerve was screaming for her to put a thousand miles between herself and this silent room.

But Summer Mulcahey had never been a coward or a quitter. Losing her father too young had made her tough; living with a mother who generally ignored her and often resented her had done the rest. So instead of bolting, Summer locked her hands in her lap and waited.

Mariachi music drifted through the open window of the second-floor apartment. She closed her eyes, breathing in the sea air scented with jasmine and lavender, thinking about Mexico. Thinking about a room where Gabe had made her feel cherished and unscarred, powerful in her choices and honest in her passion.

But a truck hurtling down a winding road had changed them both. She still awoke at night shuddering with terror from the memory—and from the knowledge that Gabe had bought her protection by covering her with his own body.

When she had resurfaced after surgery in Tucson, groggy and disoriented, Izzy had answered every question except those that involved Gabe. As the drugs wore off and her mind cleared, she had pelted him with demands for any piece of news about the SEAL, but Izzy had stood firm. Eventually Summer had returned to Philadelphia to continue her treatment nearer to home.

After weeks of rehab, her arm was weaker than normal, but she had recovered most of her range of motion in the elbow and her scars were no longer obvious. The good news was that she would be fit to return to work in a few short days.

The bad news?

Trying to decide if she wanted her old job back. Knowing Gabe had changed her, making her softer in some ways and harder in others. For the first time in years, Summer had examined her life objectively, and she hadn't been thrilled by the sight. It was painful to realize that she had no friends, zero hobbies, and an apartment with all the warmth of a budget residential hotel.

Just as she'd told Gabe, she *was* the job. 24/7.

Her sister Jess had tried to hammer the same point home for years, but Summer hadn't listened. Now, after a brief, intimate relationship with Gabe, she was suddenly hungry for more, not because she felt incomplete without him, but because a door had opened for her, revealing a side of herself she hadn't glimpsed before. Summer was ready for the unexpected, and even if the prospect left her painfully vulnerable, she had to know if she and Gabe had any future together.

Which was how she came to be sitting on a beat-up leather sofa in a silent apartment on Coronado Island, watching the sun set in bloodred splendor over a beach she didn't know the name of. She had dug and delved, berated Izzy and questioned Cara until she finally had Gabe's address. Thanks to Izzy, she even had a copy of his key.

If only she could ignore an instinct to creep out the door and keep running, right back to Philadelphia and her old, familiar world.

But she wasn't running. She wasn't a quitter. She had to know, and for once in her life she was going to take a chance on her heart.

She heard a door open.

Slow footsteps crossed the hall, and Summer's breath backed up like cotton in her throat as she watched the doorknob turn slowly.

He was as rugged and tall as she remembered, but his face wore new lines and his eyes looked tired. She couldn't speak, afraid of the questions she had to ask. She should have called first, but what could you say in a phone call?

Gabe dropped a set of keys on a painted pine table and walked to the window without turning on the light. Against the drifting curtains Summer saw his dark silhouette as he stared out at the fading sunset and the red Victorian roof of the Hotel del Coronado.

Abruptly he turned, his eyes searching the darkness until they locked on her face. Summer realized he was carrying a cane, gripping it hard with gloved fingers.

"Why did you come?"

The blood drained out of her face.

Because I missed you like I'd miss part of my own body. Because I probably love you, but I've got no yardstick to measure by, and if it's true, the possibility terrifies me.

But now that she was here, inches away from him, with every word so precious, Summer couldn't think of one that was true enough for the storm of emotions she was feeling.

Trust your heart, she'd advised Sophy once, and the advice may have saved Cara O'Connor's life. Summer decided to follow her own advice now, even if it terrified her. "I came because I had to. It wasn't finished, Gabe."

"For me it was." His voice was harsh.

Summer stared into his eyes, unflinching. "I don't believe you. Being a good liar must go with being a SEAL."

"SEALs are good at a lot of things," he said grimly.

"What happened to your hand?"

His gloved fingers tightened on the cane. "Skin grafts." He didn't look at her, his shoulders stiff. "How's your head?"

"My quantum physics research is on hold, but otherwise I'm fine. The headaches aren't so bad anymore."

He turned at that. "What headaches?"

"It doesn't matter." Summer felt dizzy just looking at him, overwhelmed by emotion. Odd, because she had always prided herself on being perfectly controlled, completely logical.

But that was before Gabe.

That thought left her terrified, too.

"Izzy didn't tell me about the headaches." Gabe stared at her, unmoving. "You okay otherwise?"

"Fine. Don't expect me behind the wheel of a car, though. When I try to drive, I get a little crazy. Remembering, you know? Details about the road, the cement at the end." Summer forced a smile. "I should be going back to work in a few weeks."

Something crossed his face. "Glad to hear it."

Silence fell. Why were they talking about everything but what mattered? Summer wondered.

"You got those cuts taken care of?" Gabe turned away, back to the window. "The ones on your neck and chest. Izzy told me about them."

Summer shrugged. "He pulled some strings. So did Tate Winslow. The specialist they found did a great job.

He wanted to take a few extra nips, make me into Julia Roberts, but I told him the cosmetics didn't matter."

"You don't need to be made into anything else." Gabe's voice was gruff. "You hear from Izzy a lot?"

"About once a week." Summer managed a smile. "How do you think I got your address and your key?"

"I figured something like that."

Summer summoned her courage, standing up slowly. "I keep remembering something you told me, Gabe. You said that I had to trust someone, and it might as well be you."

"I say a lot of things." Gabe stared out at the boats hugging the curve of the shore. "Most of them are pure stupidity."

"No, I learned to trust you then, and I trust you now. That's a new experience for me." Summer laughed tightly. "Of course, my dance card hasn't exactly been over-booked, if you know what I mean."

"Summer, you don't have to—"

"Let me get this out, Gabe. I came to find you because I needed answers and finality." Summer took a breath. "I wanted to see if—"

He cut her off, gripping the cane as he turned. "Look, you may as well know this up front. I've got someone coming over tonight. She should be here any second."

" 'Coming over'?" Summer tried to smile. "As in, cleaning your apartment? Delivering your groceries?"

"No. Not like that."

This pain was worse than what she'd felt waking up alone in the emergency room, and she had a sudden sense that it was never going to get better. "Oh."

Funny how the world could shatter around you and all you could say was *oh*.

"I'm sorry, Summer. I should have told you sooner."

"No problem." She closed her eyes. Gabe was entitled to his choices, just as she was entitled to hers. There had been no commitments made, no declarations, no vows of any kind. "That's wonderful, Gabe. Actually there's . . . there's a man back in Philadelphia. Someone I met in the hospital."

"A doctor?"

Summer nodded. "Surgeon. He took care of my arm. Talk about a cliché."

"No." He cleared his throat. "That's—good, Summer. That's great."

He needed to be free, Summer thought. He had someone else, and she was determined to be happy for him. "So we're clear about everything."

"Sure. Absolutely. He's a lucky man."

Summer's chest ached, as if someone were drilling slowly right down through her skin and into her heart. "Thanks."

There was a knock at the door. "That must be Nickie." Gabe turned as the door opened. A tall woman in cutoff blue jeans stood in the doorway, carrying a bag of groceries. She had very white teeth and perfect abs beneath a cropped yellow polo shirt.

Most of all, she had Gabe's key. Things were definitely serious between them.

Another drill went down into Summer's heart.

The woman—Nickie?—looked from Gabe to Summer. "Sorry, Gabe. I didn't know you had company." She smiled at Summer. "Are you from the Navy?"

"No." It hurt to breathe, hurt even more to smile, but Summer managed it.

"Well, don't let me rush you. I'll just put these things in the kitchen."

Summer watched her walk away. She was young and

nice and looked very competent. "I'd better go, Gabe. You're busy."

"Summer, I'm sorry."

"No problem. I just wanted to see for myself that you were okay. Hey, one minute you're crashing in an out-of-control truck, and the next minute you're on the beach. Life manages to go on, doesn't it?"

Whether you wanted it to or not.

"Summer, I—"

"Great to see you, Gabe." She didn't wait, couldn't bear another second. She fumbled her way out to the hall, moving blindly, desperate to escape. Only outside on the street did Summer jam a hand to her mouth. Unshed tears burned at her eyes as she flagged down the first taxi that passed. When she rode away into the fading sunset, she didn't look back.

Some risks hurt more than others.

Gabe watched her from the window, watched her without moving.

"Why did you do that?"

He didn't answer. His whole body felt numb.

"Gabe, that woman loves you, damn it."

"Her loss."

Dr. Nickie Evangeline was his downstairs neighbor. Though still a medical resident, she had become his unofficial rehabilitation mentor. She stared at him impatiently. "You love her, too."

"Now that's downright delusional, Doc." When Gabe turned, his face was hard. "How about we get to work?"

Her lips pressed into a hard line. "Your rehab can wait. Right now I'm more concerned with your ass-backward mental state."

"Hey, I'm fine. All systems go. I could bench-press three hundred fifty pounds."

"I get it now." Her eyes narrowed. "You told me to dress this way. You told me when to come. You knew that she was going to be here, didn't you?"

Gabe didn't answer.

"What happens next?"

"Not a single damned thing."

"You won't be this way forever, Lieutenant. You should tell her."

Tell her what? Gabe stared at his leg. There was more reconstructive surgery the next day. Maybe he'd come out of it with a brace and two pins, and a knee strong enough to run on again.

Or maybe not.

He was doing the right thing, Gabe thought grimly. Life went on, as Summer had said. In the grand scheme of things, what could have been carried no weight. At least she had recovered beautifully. He'd never seen her more calm and confident, although for a moment there had been something uncertain in her face, something wistful in her voice.

Just your imagination, fool.

Gabe heard the door close behind him. Nickie was disgusted with him, but of course she didn't understand.

Frowning, Gabe took something out of his pocket and turned it slowly in his palm. It was the simple blue rubber band he'd taken from Summer's hair back on that night she'd been caught in the cactus. He took it out sometimes and looked at it, touched it, slipped it over his fingers.

In the last months he had carried it everywhere. Even into surgery.

Down on the street the taxi began moving. Gabe couldn't pull his eyes away.

He had read once what it felt like to walk on the moon. One astronaut had said that you felt rootless, unspeakably alone, cut off from Earth with its blue seas and all you knew and loved. Gabe felt that way now as the lights of Summer's taxi flickered, then vanished into the twilight.

wyoming

chapter 41

The Laramie Airport was quiet at this late hour. A few tired travelers waited for their baggage, glancing out at skies that promised snow.

Didn't it just figure that they had lost her bag, Summer thought. After two delayed flights and ten hours of non-stop traveling, she was dead on her feet, and now her bag was gone.

She shouldered her backpack and headed to the information desk to file an inquiry. With her luck, they wouldn't find the bag until she was back in Philadelphia on Monday.

What was she doing here, anyway?

Frowning, she backtracked through the last month, beginning with the news that Cara was completely recovered and she and Senator Winslow were finally tying the knot. But Summer was in the middle of a tough case and she still had five rehabilitation classes to complete. She didn't have time to fly out to a ranch in the middle of nowhere. Despite her protests, Summer soon found out that San Francisco's assistant DA was a hard person to refuse—and her two winsome girls were even harder to refuse than their mother.

Audra wanted to show Summer how her kickboxing moves were coming along.

Sophy needed to display her latest ballet technique.

Despite her exhaustion, Summer smiled at the memory of that last, hectic phone call. The deciding point had come when Cara mentioned that Gabe wouldn't be attending because of his Navy duties. Summer still remembered the sharp, stabbing pain of hearing his name again.

Not that the pain wouldn't heal, because it would.

Maybe in twenty or thirty years. Meanwhile, she had a wedding to attend.

A television echoed in the deserted airport coffee shop, blaring all-night news. Summer noticed that her current case was mentioned briefly, with the facts largely garbled. She shook her head as a weatherman in a string tie pointed to a colorful map, warning that bad weather was headed in over the Rockies.

Just her luck. First her bag bit the dust, now a major snowstorm was roaring straight toward her.

The man at the information desk was courteous and efficient when Summer gave him her name and hotel address. He seemed to study her for a moment, then handed her a receipt, explaining that her bag would be delivered directly to her hotel, assuming it was found before the storm hit.

"Gonna be a bad one," he added gravely.

Not overly optimistic, Summer asked for directions to the nearest store. She couldn't go to a wedding in blue jeans.

Summer was just picking up the rental car Senator Winslow had arranged for her when her cell phone rang. Izzy's voice boomed out, energetic as always. "So how's Wyoming?"

"Do you have a tracking device on me, Izzy?"

The woman at the rental desk looked up and shrugged. She'd probably seen and heard everything, Summer thought.

"Nah. I checked the national flight database, confirmed you were on board, and tracked your arrival time. Nothing major."

Summer nodded at the rental agent, collected her papers, and headed toward the parking lot to find her SUV. "Glad you're on our side, Mr. Teague."

"That's Izzy to you, ma'am." Papers rustled. "I thought you might like an update on the Winslow case. I've got some interesting news about our not-so-friendly family chef."

"You mean Patrick Flanagan?"

"Patrick Flanagan, aka Patrick Cash. When the police searched his apartment they found a key to a storage facility. Yesterday it was finally located and opened."

"And?"

"And they found a shitload of files and photographs, begging your pardon."

"No problem. What kind of files and photos?"

"Surveillance stuff, records of phone calls Cara O'Connor had made and received. Notes on the girls, on their school schedules, and details about Audra's friends."

"Including Tracey Van Doren?"

"One and all. Tracey told her mother that she had been involved with Patrick for about six months, sneaking out secretly at night. Apparently, he was using her to get inside information about the family. Her self-esteem was pretty shaky, so it wasn't hard for him to use her."

Summer stared at the darkening sky. "Bastard."

"No doubt about it. We knew he was involved, but not

how carefully he had planned every move. He toyed with Tracey's head, but now she's in therapy, and that's helping to straighten her out."

"Therapy has helped Cara and Audra quite a bit. Cara's sister and her family have been involved, too. They're all going to be at the wedding, I hear."

"Nice people. I spoke to Cara's sister several times about some media concerns."

Summer heard something in his voice. "What is it, Izzy?"

"Nothing."

"I still can't believe how Patrick conned everyone. He seemed so helpful, so unthreatening." Summer sighed. "I should have read him better. The man was too good to be true."

"Forget feeling guilty. He was a master of manipulation, but his cooking skills were real. He was also involved in Costello's protection rackets and smuggling down in Mexico. A real credit to his employer, you might say."

He'd been there all along, right under their noses. Summer blew out a long breath. "How do you hear these things first?"

"Must be my charming smile." Izzy laughed. "That and my superior surveillance skills."

"What about Patrick's involvement with Amanda Winslow? Won't that all come out now?"

"Maybe not. With Patrick and Amanda dead, everything changes. Costello's still trying to prove he's a stand-up guy, completely reformed, and he won't be anxious to have his connection with Patrick revealed, since it will harm his appeal. In fact, I doubt that Patrick planned the murder. My guess is, the assignment from Costello was to frighten Cara into helping with the case."

"So the poison was Amanda's idea?" Summer considered the pattern. "It makes sense. Costello wouldn't want Cara dead until his appeal was granted."

"That's how I figure it," Izzy said grimly. "But Cara and Tate will have to live with the possibility that someone else may surface who knew what Amanda had planned."

Summer rubbed a knot at the back of her neck. After his mother's funeral, Tate Winslow had postponed his presidential run indefinitely. The discovery of Amanda's dementia had left him shaken, determined to spend time mending fences and taking a long, hard look at his future.

Whatever he decided, Cara would be at his side.

Izzy cleared his throat. "So how are you holding up?"

"Fine, except that my suitcase is lost."

"Anything I can do to help?"

"Buy me some lingerie? Hack into the national airline database and find the missing bag?"

"I could try."

"That was a joke, Izzy. I'll be fine. I may simply head for the nearest store and shop till I drop."

"Then you'd better pick someplace close, with that storm front rolling in. There's a nice place about six miles away, I see. You want driving instructions?"

"Is there *anything* you don't know?"

"Nothing of any value," Izzy said calmly.

Silence fell. Summer watched two sleepy boys in cowboy boots and miniature Stetsons cross the lobby with their father, a tall cowboy who was waving at a woman with snow dusting her hair.

So the storm was already here.

Izzy cleared his throat. "I'll tell Gabe I spoke to you."

Summer gripped the cell phone tightly. "There's no need. He's too busy to be interested in me." She ignored the burning pressure at her throat. "I have to run, Izzy. It's starting to snow and I don't want to be stranded."

"Sure. Drive carefully. I'll tell Gabe you said hi."

The phone went dead.

Summer took a hard breath. No more remembering. Gabe had moved on, and so would she. She was halfway to the front doors when she heard her name called.

"Ms. Mulcahey?" It was the woman from the rental car desk.

"Yes."

"I'm afraid I forgot something." The woman held out a long box. "This came tonight and was to be held for your arrival."

Frowning, Summer took the box and opened the cardboard lid. Inside a single red rose nestled on white paper. "For me?"

"Yes, ma'am. It was prepaid. Somebody knows how to be very romantic."

Probably Izzy, Summer thought. Trying to cheer her up. The man was unbelievable. "Did he leave his name?"

"I'm afraid not." The attendant glanced out at the white flakes dancing over the entrance road. "Enjoy your rose. And drive carefully. It's getting pretty nasty out there."

One hour and two aspirins later, Summer stood in one of Laramie, Wyoming's, few dress shops. A long red dress and a lacy bra lay on the bench beside her as she stared in the long mirror. Her current selection, a dress of blue silk with a clinging skirt and a beaded hem, was nice. Either this dress or the red one would be perfect for Cara's wedding—except that Summer wasn't in the mood for a wedding.

They said when you fell off a horse, the best medicine was to climb right back on. Maybe she should check out the unmarried men and find a nice tall cowboy to carry her off into the Wyoming night.

Except there would probably be six-foot snowdrifts by this time tomorrow, and even if there weren't, Summer couldn't summon any enthusiasm for snuggling up with a stranger, no matter how handsome.

She unzipped the dress and pulled it over her head, wincing as the silk caught in her hair. Pain stabbed down her forehead from half a dozen beads tangled in her hair.

Just great. A predawn departure, two delayed flights, and a food quota of four bags of salted peanuts. Life just wasn't fair.

Cool air brushed against her legs.

She turned around slowly. "Is someone there?"

There was no answer.

"Hello?"

The dressing room curtain rustled behind her. "Why don't I help you with that?"

Summer's heart skipped against her chest like a small, frightened animal.

Gabe.

She took a step backward and banged hard into the wall, the dress still stuck over her head.

"Stop before you hurt yourself."

As if *he* cared. "I don't need your help. Just g-go. What are you doing here anyway? You're *supposed* to be somewhere working."

Summer couldn't seem to breathe. It wasn't supposed to happen this way. She was supposed to be cool and aloof, so beautiful that she broke his heart. Not caught like an idiot with her dress tangled around her and tears on her cheeks.

"I lied," he said.

"G-go away."

"I can't. You break my heart," Gabe said quietly, bending to untangle the beads from her hair.

Summer peered through a gap in the silk. He looked good, she thought. No, he looked fabulous, lean and dangerous in a black turtleneck and a black leather jacket.

She forced down an instinct to touch his cheek, to comb back an unruly strand of dark hair. Did the man think he could wander back into her life after months of silence, as if the awful scene in San Diego hadn't happened?

"Fine, Morgan. One night. Decent sex and nothing else. That's all I'm interested in." He'd never expect this answer from her, Summer thought grimly.

He stared as if he hadn't heard her correctly. "You want sex?"

"Yeah, you know sex. That thing two people do when they get naked and make hot, panting sounds. You've got one night. And in the morning, you take a hike."

"I know what sex is, damn it, but you're out of luck."

"In that case, good-bye, *adios, sayonara.*" Summer shoved the dress down, wincing as another clump of hair pulled free, along with three crystal beads.

Cursing, Gabe yanked her into his arms. "Okay, it's a deal. But it will be one night of *incredible* sex. *Decent* won't even come close."

Summer felt a dangerous stab of desire and realized the mistake she'd just made. "But you're not interested. Not in me. Back in San Diego you said—"

"I know what I said in San Diego, but I've changed my mind," he said grimly.

"Too bad. I've changed my mind, too. I'm not in the mood for sex after all."

"Sure about that?" He traced her lips slowly, and Summer fought not to betray her slamming pulse.

"I'm sure."

He stared at her, his face unreadable. "If it's sex you want, I'm your man, honey."

"Do us both a favor." Summer tilted her chin, summoning every bit of cold, angry willpower. "Go take a long hike in the snowstorm—right up to the top of the nearest mountain. And *don't* come back."

Summer headed out of the department store lot into a solid curtain of white flakes. She was still a little shaky and some of the blur in her windshield was from tears, but in spite of that she felt surprisingly good. She had seen Gabe and survived. He was just as rugged and handsome as she remembered, with the same dark intensity that made women turn their heads and stare in avid appreciation.

But Summer hadn't caved. She'd kicked him out of her life, which was just where he belonged.

Feeling calmer, she peered through the snow and flipped on the radio. Dear God, no more advertisements for Viagra or used truck parts, she prayed.

A hand touched her shoulder. Gasping, she almost shot through the roof. Her hand was on her service revolver when she saw Gabe leaning over from the backseat of the big SUV.

"Get out," she snapped.

His hand curved, cupping her cheek. "I was a fool, Summer."

"Damned straight you were. *Are,*" she added fiercely.

"Let me make it up to you."

"Not interested, Navy. And how did you get into my car?" she demanded.

Gabe waved a key. "Izzy has connections you wouldn't believe."

Summer spotted an abandoned gas station down the road and pulled beneath the overhang. "If you're not out of here in two minutes, I'm calling the local FBI field office."

As she clutched the wheel, she saw her arm, pale in the moonlight cast off the snow. The scars were small now, barely visible, but to Summer they were just as glaring as ever.

You didn't see yourself the way the world saw you. The truth in your head was always different from the truth everyone else saw.

Only with Gabe had she managed to forget her scars and bad memories. But she wasn't going to risk being stupid and naïve like that again.

Teeth caught her ear gently. Callused fingers eased down, opening her coat and tracing the collar of her blouse. "How about I explain? Then we can have that amazing sex you wanted. Hell, with this storm moving in, you can punish me for hours."

"Dream on, Morgan." But his fingers were doing something unforgettable, and her body was remembering Mexico, coming alive in hot, reckless ways. She moved out of reach. "For the record, I'd rather cough up fur balls."

"No, you wouldn't."

On the radio, a man's voice droned on, announcing plays from a baseball game recorded earlier on the East Coast. "Line drive to center field."

Gabe's tongue brushed her ear. "I love you," he muttered. "I was afraid to tell you that when I had no future, Summer. The woman in my apartment in San Diego was a friend helping me with my rehab. Call me stupid or call me a coward, but the surgery on my knee took weeks, and it might have failed. Hell, it still might. You need to know that up front."

Something softened in Summer's heart. "You'll pull through."

"Will I? Look at me, Summer. I've been rough with you, partly because I lost someone I loved once and I was afraid to go through it again. If I left you first, the problem would never arise. I regret how that hurt you, and I hope you'll give me another chance. Even if I am a big, stupid, overbearing—"

Summer turned around. "I never said you were stupid," she said shakily as Gabe's arms wrapped around her. "All the rest will depend on you." Her lips curved. "On how amazing the sex is."

Gabe studied her with a look of sheer, focused wickedness. "Snow's getting pretty bad, I think we'd better stay here for a bit." He was already tugging at her coat and freeing her blouse.

Summer took a shaky breath and reached for the wheel—then yelped when she felt her blouse go flying. His fingers freed one breast and teased her already aroused nipple to a tight, hard point. "*Stop* that."

Laughing softly, Gabe kissed his way along her jaw and bit gently on her lower lip. "Afraid I can't. You're just too damned—juicy." He leaned closer, and his hand slid to her waist and below, cupping her through too many layers of cloth. "God, you feel good. This is definitely going to take all night."

Snow dusted the windshield as her bra fell and she attacked his sweater, desperate to feel the heat of his skin. "Incredible sex, remember? Nothing less counts." She refused to think about tomorrow. Tonight she was going to trust her heart and believe it hadn't steered her wrong.

Gabe pulled her down onto the seat beside him, his eyes

very dark. "I'll do my damnedest, honey." He frowned. "It's been a while, though, and my knee—"

"Forget your knee, Navy. Tonight you won't even know it exists." Summer felt her heart in the words, knew her vulnerability.

The radio droned on as Gabe pulled off his shirt. His eyes savored every inch of her body.

"That's a solid hit. Line drive to center field," a male voice shouted.

Summer gasped as Gabe stripped off his pants and buried himself inside her, hot and huge and *hers*. Reckless or not, she never wanted to go back to the 24/7 workaholic she'd been before Gabe. Their hands joined, their fingers locked. Summer realized she was different, and that the change had started the moment she'd seen his naked body in her shower. Someday she'd tell him what a great body it was, too.

"Another slam to center field," the disembodied voice announced on the radio.

Summer watched Gabe while pleasure took her up, fast and hard.

"And the crowd goes wild," she whispered.

She wore a dazed smile and not a hint of anything else. Her body still tingled from the hot pull of his mouth.

As her pleasant exhaustion began to lift, Summer realized she was going to have beard burn in all sorts of interesting places in the morning.

She trusted him. She trusted herself now and how he made her feel. The combination was heady.

She felt his strong body turn beside her as he slipped one arm beneath her head. Given that they were wedged into the backseat of a Jeep Grand Cherokee, the fit was tight.

"You still alive?" she whispered.

Gabe stirred. "Possibly." He propped his head on his hand. "Of course, the night's not over yet." He traced the pinkish mark on her upper breast. "Did I do this?"

Summer nodded smugly. "You need a razor."

"Sorry."

"Apologize and I'll have to shoot you, Navy."

Gabe's lips curved. "Don't suppose that I did that any-where . . . else."

Outside the highway was white with newly fallen snow, but inside the car, they were warm and snug, body to body. Summer stretched slowly. "A skilled operative like you could probably find out."

"Is that a challenge?"

"You bet."

"I always like a good mission plan." Gabe shoved away scattered clothing, Summer's cherished rose, and the blan-ket he had brought with him all the way from California as part of his careful plan. "One on your hip. It looks un-comfortable." He whisked it lightly with his tongue. "One on your elbow. Another one on this pink and very beauti-ful nipple." This area received his particular scrutiny, fol-lowed by the loving rasp of his tongue.

The car was warm, the motor idling. Outside the win-dows, snow continued to veil the night. A red motel sign blazed across a white-swept field, less than a mile away, but neither had been able to wait. Summer still couldn't believe she was having wild, reckless sex in the backseat of a rental car with her clothes in a crazy tangle around her.

Life was good, she thought weakly. When Gabe turned his attention to her other breast, life became even better. "Arkh."

"I beg your pardon."

"It's code. It means that you were—amazing."

Gabe drew her closer, running one hand gently along her cheek. "Good."

"Was it—what I mean is, were you disappointed?"

"What do you mean?"

"You know. With me. With us." Summer cleared her throat, frowning at the roof of the car. "As a good . . . well, whatever you men call it."

Gabe's eyes narrowed. "A good lay?"

"Or whatever."

"Mulcahey, I could barely move when you finished with me. And when you straddled me and took me in your hand . . . Disappointed? Hell, I almost had a coronary."

Summer flushed. "That's not an answer."

"You want to know how it felt?" Gabe nudged her up onto his chest, so that their legs intertwined and Summer was seated firmly on his thighs. "Let me think."

"Amazed?" Summer murmured.

He moved slightly, and their bodies slid into an intimate fit. "Engorged. Amazed, too."

"This is important, Gabe." She stared at him gravely. "I mean, we both know I'm not exactly Dream Date material. I'd probably be the first to get voted out of the tribe—"

He cut her off with a curse, holding her perfectly still. "You keep me up at night. You make me smile when it's the last thing I want to do. You are the bravest woman I've ever met, especially if you're willing to take a chance on a hard case like me."

"In a second," she said softly.

He traced her breasts with one finger, smiling when she shivered, her nipples going taut. "I forgot to mention that you're so damned responsive you take my breath away."

"Only with you," Summer whispered, shocked that he could make her feel this way again so soon.

"Glad to hear it. At least I won't have to kill anybody."
His voice filled with something low and primitive.

His hand slipped between their bodies, exploring her
slowly. "You're wet, honey."

Summer felt a delicious stab of heat as his fingers
moved deeper. "Hard not to be, with you wedged naked
against me and gorgeous muscles everywhere I look." She
wiggled against his chest.

"That old man in Mexico was right," Gabe said huskily.
"You are definitely juicy."

"You think?" Summer licked her dry lips, remembering
how he'd felt inside her, slow and relentless, so hard she'd
screamed when he'd driven her up to a mind-shredding climax. "Why does this keep getting better and better?"

"You mean this part?" He pushed slowly inside her until
her muscles tensed, clutching around him. "Or *this* part?"
As he spoke, he moved again, seating himself higher.

Summer panted, unable to answer, her nails digging
into his back. The car windows were completely fogged
up, and some part of Gabe's mind found that amusing.
Another part couldn't have cared if everyone in Wyoming
was camped outside to watch.

He was beyond caring.

He shifted, holding her motionless above him while
snow drifted cool and silent against the fogged windows.
His eyes were dark, holding unspoken promises. "This
is once in a lifetime, honey. It's never been this way for me,"
he said savagely. "There have been a lot of others, Summer.
After Rosalita, I wasn't going to take a chance on caring too
much. But then there was you, and God help me, I can't
stop thinking of you or wanting you like this."

He rose without warning, driving deep. He felt her
stiffen, watched her lovely eyes darken with surprise, then
blur as she shot to a panting climax that left her nails raking

his back. As she gripped him, it was all Gabe could do to keep from throwing himself over that jagged edge along with her, but the sight of her pleasure was too damned erotic to miss.

He held back, opening his senses to the amazing experience of her body riding him while he hoarded the memory of her hoarse, throaty cries. If she wanted reckless, she could have it—morning, noon, and night. If she wanted long, slow cherishing, she'd have that, too. And if any of her fellow agents tried to harass her, he'd see that they turned up with a few broken bones. They'd already received indirect warnings to that effect, delivered through her SAC, who sounded like a stand-up guy. Better still, Summer had been officially cleared of any involvement in her partner's death.

Of course, Summer had no idea that Gabe had made a call to Tate, who had handled the matter discreetly. If she found out, she would probably murder them both.

Gabe dragged in a breath when he felt her body shift, her hands moving down to cup the most sensitive part of him, taking him between her fingers. Slowly she explored him, testing the smooth curves, lifting gently.

"Damn, honey, if you do any more of that—"

She did, rising slowly.

Sliding down onto his rock-hard erection.

Gabe sucked in a breath as his control shredded to confetti. She took him with hungry urgency, drawing him deep, her hands an exquisite torment.

To hell with waiting.

Gabe growled her name and poured himself inside her.

Someone moved.

Gabe smiled up into the darkness. "If a fire starts inside the car anytime soon, don't bother to wake me."

A slow, sated laugh was Summer's only reply.

"Come to think of it, I just saw sparks. They were right above your . . ." He showed her where with skillful fingers.

Summer shivered. "Static electricity, Morgan."

"Oh." He traced her hip slowly. "Is that what they call it?"

She gave another husky laugh.

"I've got one thing to ask."

"Sorry. Too tired." Her hand moved down his thigh. "All your fault."

Gabe didn't hide a possessive smile. "Just one, I promise."

"You can try." Summer moved her thigh sleepily across his leg. "I may not remember anything beyond the last twenty minutes, I warn you."

"Tell me something you've never told anyone else. Something that only I will know."

Summer opened one eye slightly and considered. "I have a freckle on my left thigh, just below my . . ." She raised one leg in the dim light. "There."

"Nice, but not what I had in mind. Tell me something personal."

"Is this some kind of weird test?"

"Call it a beginning. We're building things here. New things like trust, understanding. Hell, Summer, I want to do everything right with you."

Another arrow slid painlessly into her heart. She couldn't fight her happiness any longer. Love had crept up on her and she wouldn't hide from it. "No complaints from this side of the seat." She took a breath, her body tensing just a little. "Here's my thing. I don't know how to dance. Even the thought scares the heck out of me. And to do it in public—" She blew out the breath she'd been holding. "Sheer panic."

"But you helped with Sophy."

"Kids and their moms. That doesn't count."

Gabe kissed her shoulder. "I think you'd be great."

"Never. Don't even think about it. I mean that." She pushed up onto one elbow. "Your turn, hard case."

Gabe frowned. "I'm not—"

"Yeah, you are. I'm waiting."

"Singing."

"You don't like music?" Her brow rose. "Frank Sinatra? Jon Bon Jovi?"

"No, *me* singing. In front of someone else, damn it."

Summer traced his mouth. "As I recall, you were singing the first time we met."

"That was different. I didn't know you were there and my leg hurt, so I was trying to distract myself from the pain."

"I thought you were just being a jerk." Summer laughed softly. "For a jerk, you had a world-class butt and abs to die for."

"You looked? You made such a big deal about ignoring me."

She'd looked, all right. No woman alive could have ignored that amazing body. Even Mother Teresa would have stolen a quick peek. "So sue me. What happens now that we know each other's deep, dark secrets?"

"Nothing. It's enough to know, and feel safe that someone else knows. It's about trusting, not necessarily about doing."

Another arrow zinged deep into Summer's heart.

"Smart guy." She slid her leg across Gabe's body. "If I had any strength left, I might just—"

Gabe cut her off, frowning as a dark shape moved out of the snow. "Hell."

"What?"

"We've got company."

Summer stared over his shoulder. "Just a snowplow. See, he's turning in the opposite direction. Life has to go on, I suppose."

"Not for me," Gabe muttered. "I may just change my address to the backseat of this car."

"Good plan." She collapsed against him, scattering provoking kisses over his chest until he pulled her down and stilled her with a tongue-to-tongue, openmouthed kiss that started the whole dizzy madness all over again.

An hour later Gabe could barely move and his knee hurt, but he'd never felt so alive in his life. He owed it all to Summer.

Not because she didn't have a clue how graceful, gorgeous, and sensual she was. Not even because of her focus and intensity, which he found more sexually arousing than any low-cut lingerie.

It was because of the bond that had grown, unshakable between them. Because of their trust. Either way, it added up to a four-letter word he hadn't had the courage to use for years.

His parents' marriage had been rock stable for fifty years, and they'd held hands right up to the day his father had died of a massive heart attack. Gabe had figured they were some kind of freak of nature and had long ago stopped hoping to find the same kind of intensity in a relationship. The women he met usually wanted a few drinks and a night of gritty sex, no strings attached.

And when they waved good-bye, Gabe had always felt a sense of relief.

But Summer had stirred a different reaction right from the start. He'd needed to know more about her, wanted to get closer, from the second he'd seen her glaring at him outside the shower.

She wasn't bouncy and perky. Her nose was slightly crooked, her shoulders were a little too wide, and she had a mouth that could raise welts. But he found her blindingly irresistible. The sex was incredible, too, but this went way beyond sex. Staring into the darkness, Gabe smiled.

Her eyes were closed, and her breath skimmed his cheek as she slept, curved against his chest. Even the slightest friction of her thigh against his groin rocketed down to his growing erection.

It was happening again. She made him feel fifteen again, awash in hormones and sheer lust.

But she had to be tender after all they'd done. Ignoring his need, he pulled the blanket over them and drifted off to sleep while snow whispered muted promises in the night.

"You asleep?"

"Mmnrah."

"Summer?"

"Wmmmm."

Gabe shifted her sleepy body, peering through the gray, predawn light.

A motor raced nearby.

Gabe pulled the blanket up over her breasts. "We've got company."

"G'way. Not on duty," she rasped.

He almost smiled. What had happened to the 24/7 work-obsessed field agent he'd met a few months ago? "It's Gabe, honey, not work."

"Gowaywannasleep."

The blanket twisted free, hitched across her shoulder. Her lovely breasts glinted up at him in the dawn light.

Cursing, Gabe covered her up, then reached for his pants. "I think you need to wake up, here."

Sighing, she pulled the pillow over her head.

Gabe dug under the seat and found his jeans. After digging through more clothes and Summer's dropped cell phone, he found the weapon he'd stashed during the night. Not that he expected trouble, but Gabe had learned that trouble usually came when you had your pants down.

Metaphorically speaking.

Car lights flashed through the swirling snow, and a voice drifted toward him.

Gabe eased the gun into his palm as a figure loomed out of the snow, bending toward the window.

Gloved hands brushed off a wedge of snow, and dark eyes flashed in a dark face. "Damn it, Morgan, don't you ever answer that overpriced cell phone I gave you?"

chapter 42

As snow piled up on the windows, Gabe cursed softly. The expensive cell phone in question now showed six missed calls.

Leave it to Izzy to track him down in the middle of the season's biggest snowstorm.

After checking to be certain that Summer's blanket was secure, Gabe rolled down the window. "Sorry, didn't hear your calls. Things got a little hectic." He cleared his throat. "With the storm and all."

"The windows look pretty fogged up, pal."

"Stow it, Izzy. What's the emergency, did some D.C. bureaucrat misplace a box of paper clips and trigger an audit?"

"That was last week," Izzy said dryly. "This morning I got a call from Senator Winslow. He was upset when you and Summer didn't show up at the motel last night, so he called the local police, in case you were stranded in the snow. But the police hadn't seen you, which made him even more worried. That's when he called me."

"False alarm. As you can see, we're both fine."

"Summer's in there with you?" Izzy's head tilted slightly as he took a step closer.

"Back off, partner," Gabe growled.

"No need to shout."

"Who the hell's shouting?"

"You were." Izzy tried to hide a smile. "They probably heard you over in Casper. Besides, I can't see anything in there because it's too dark." He muttered something that sounded like "damned shame, too."

Gabe grunted as snow whirled through the window and dusted his shirt. "Something else on your mind?"

"Wanna tell me why you're parked out here when there's a decent motel right over that hill?"

"Not really. Anything else?"

"In case you forgot, the wedding is supposed to start in a few hours." Izzy crossed his arms. "The girls have been asking for Summer."

Gabe closed his eyes, rubbing his neck. "That late already?"

"Afraid so."

Where had the night gone? "What I wouldn't give for some stomach-scouring black coffee right now."

A steaming cup appeared at the window.

"I'm not even going to ask how you did that." Gabe took the cup gratefully. "But God bless you and Mrs. Starbucks, wherever she might be."

"No Starbucks open in two hundred miles, not with this snow. I made it myself. Any complaints, keep them to yourself."

"No complaints from me." Gabe took a sip of the strong, steamy brew and sighed. "Nice job, Teague. You're going to make some lucky woman a fine, strapping husband one of these days." He ducked the punch aimed at him through the window. "You waiting for something else? I'm on officially authorized leave, in case it escaped your notice."

"I'm well aware of that." Izzy cleared his throat as Summer muttered in her sleep. "As it happens, Senator Winslow asked me to hang around and escort you two to the ranch. The snow is pretty bad along the last stretch of interstate north of town."

So the world was about to come roaring back to life.

Gabe frowned at his coffee. He was insanely proud of Summer for the difficult job she had carried out. He knew that her sense of duty was just as inviolable as his was. But he was going to see that she took more time off. He even had the perfect plan for how she was going to spend it.

In the backseat of a Jeep Grand Cherokee, blowing off the top of his head and making him thank his ragtag team of guardian angels for seeing that he got the stupid assignment of protecting a senator and his fiancée.

Meanwhile, Izzy was waiting and Gabe's cell phone was blinking with a text message. There would be no more delays, no more holding the world at bay.

No more reckless sex in the back of a Jeep.

"Understood, Teague. You can go on ahead."

"No can do. I'll just hang right here, freezing my butt in the snow while you finish waking up."

"Do you have any idea how obnoxious you are?"

Izzy's lips twitched. "They tell me it's a gift."

Gabe tugged on his sweater and boots, then swung open the door and turned to glare at Izzy. "If a word—even a syllable—about any of this gets out, you are history, Teague. She's had enough razzing from those chimp-brains back at her field office."

"My lips are sealed."

"They better be." Gabe handed back his empty coffee cup and slid into the front seat. "We're going to the motel to clean up. We'll be out in twenty minutes. You can follow us, if you feel the necessity." Gabe slammed his door and revved the motor. When he looked out, Izzy was standing in the snow, chuckling. "You still there, Teague?"

"Hell, yes. I wouldn't miss *this* for the world."

chapter 43

What happened to my other earring?"

"Right here, Mom."

"Now I've lost my *shoes.*"

"They're over here." Sophy giggled at her sister. The girls had never seen their cool, efficient mother looking so giddy and distracted, and they were secretly thrilled. Cara's face was flushed and she looked radiant.

But her hands were shaking.

"Relax, Mom." Audra patted her mother on the shoulder and handed her the missing pair of sinfully beautiful Jimmy Choo pumps. "You look great. Uncle Tate is going to swallow his tongue when he sees you."

Sophy giggled. "He told me last night that you were the most beautiful woman on Earth. And me and Audra are next," she added proudly.

"I, not me," Audra corrected. But she nodded calmly. "He's right. So stop worrying about everything, Mom. Sophy and I are fine, your wedding's gonna be totally cool, and Summer and Gabe should be here any minute."

"I still don't understand what happened to them." Anxiously, Cara brushed the soft curls that trailed from beneath a spray of bright pink roses. "They should have been able to find the motel last night."

"Maybe they didn't want to." Audra smiled knowingly at the driveway, where an SUV had appeared amid swirling snow. "They were probably a little distracted."

"You mean, they stopped to kiss?" Sophy studied her sister intently. "Maybe they wanted to have phone sex?"

"Sophia Marie O'Connor!" Cara looked shocked. "What in the world do you know about phone sex?"

"Not very much," Sophy said wistfully. "No one will talk about it with me. I asked Gabe, and he told me I'd find out soon enough. Uncle Tate told me to ask you, and Audra just tells me to shut up because I'm still a kid."

"Well, you are," Audra snapped. "You wouldn't understand, anyway."

"I know all about thongs." Sophy glared defiantly at her sister.

Cara breathed a prayer for guidance and stopped searching for her lost glove. "Darling, we're going to have a talk, you and I. We'll talk about anything you want, all right? Even . . ." She grimaced. "Even phone sex."

Audra started to giggle, and then Sophy joined in. Within seconds all three were laughing, until they collapsed together on the sofa.

"You'll ruin your dress," Audra managed to say.

"Oh, phooey on my dress. It seems like forever since we've had a good laugh together." Suddenly Cara looked down at Sophy. "Did you find your new pink shoes, honey? I thought I saw them in the bottom of your suitcase."

"Oh, no, everything's fine, Mom. My shoes are cool." Sophy squirmed off the sofa and shot toward the door. "I hear Summer and Gabe downstairs!"

As she spoke, there was a knock on the door. "Anyone in here getting married?"

At Sophy's burst of laughter, Summer opened the door wearing a parka and hiking boots. Snowflakes dotted her hair, and her cheeks were bright.

"You came!" Sophy hurtled toward her. "See my new dress? I even get to wear earrings. Little ones, that is. Where's your dress?"

Summer gave Sophy a hug, then held up a big box. "I'm ready to rock and roll."

Audra studied Summer's face, noted the flush, and looked pleased. "I take it that Gabe found you."

Summer cleared her throat. "He's with Senator Winslow now, getting dressed. I could probably use some help, too."

"Sophy, get all our stuff from the bathroom. Mom's done, so now we can start working on Ms. M."

Sophy shot off. *"Cool."*

As snow swirled around the big picture windows, no one talked about Tate's mother or Patrick Flanagan, or how death had stalked this house one day at the end of summer. But the memories hung in the air like spiderwebs, invisible and chilling.

In the weeks following Amanda's death, Tate Winslow had announced he would not pursue his bid for the presidency. For two years Amanda Winslow had hidden her deteriorating state from her family and friends, and Cara was convinced the experimental medications had hastened her decline.

But Summer refused to think about death as Sophy opened the big box on Cara's bed. The dress she'd chosen for the wedding was long and full, rich silk that made her skin glow. When she looked at the matching shoes with four-inch heels, Summer winced. Running shoes were more her style, and she prayed she wouldn't disgrace herself by falling onto her face when the ceremony began.

A few minutes later she was transformed, trying to keep from toppling in her killer Jimmy Choo satin mules.

"Wow," Sophy whispered.

"Sheesh." Audra gave a long, silent whistle.

"You look lovely," Cara said.

Summer tugged at the front of her dress, which was lower than she had realized in the store. "I don't know," she said uneasily. "If I bend over, everything will—what I mean is, it would be a disaster."

"Then don't bend over," Cara said with a mischievous smile. "Not unless you're with Gabe. Otherwise there will be a stampede by the men in the room. By the way, give Gabe our love."

Summer felt heat fill her cheeks. Were her feelings so transparent?

But as she stood tottering in her four-inch heels, she felt something loosen inside her, stirring on powerful wings, weightless like the reckless teenager she had never had time to become after her father's death, and she wanted to knock Gabe silly with his first sight of her. She didn't care if the whole world knew.

She smoothed her dress, delighting in the feel of the silk against her skin. She couldn't wait to see Gabe's reaction.

The chords of an organ drifted up the stairs. "Time to go." Cara's voice wavered. "I love you two so much."

"You look beautiful, Mom. I mean, really, really." Sophy's grin threatened to swallow her young face. "I heard Uncle Tate tell his brother if there were any more delays, he was going to kidnap you and make you elope with him.

He said he was in major perpetual pain, whatever that meant."

Audra swallowed a giggle, and Sophy's smile faltered. "If you eloped, could we go, too?"

Cara held her daughter tightly. "You bet. We'd all sneak away together. We'd make it a big adventure."

But Audra just sighed. "Come on, Mom, you and Uncle Tate don't need us hanging around. You've got better things to do on your honeymoon than babysit."

Sophy's head tilted. "A honeymoon—that's like phone sex only better. Right?"

Half-giggling, half-sniffing back tears, Cara hugged both her daughters. "Close enough, honey. Someday you'll understand, believe me. Just don't be in too big of a rush, okay? I don't want you leaving for a long, long time." Her voice broke. "I'm so sorry if things have been rocky these last few years. I'm sorry you lost your dad and I'm sorry about the way he . . . changed. Most of all, I'm sorry about my job, my crazy hours, about not being with you all the time."

"Don't worry about that stuff," Audra said calmly. "We turned out fine. Besides, you do really important work. Sophy and I are cool with that, aren't we, Sophy?"

"Sure. We're completely cool at that."

Audra looked at her sister. "*With,* not *at.*"

"With what?"

Audra shook her head. "Never mind. I'll explain later."

"You're both growing up too fast. One day I'll turn around and it will be you two getting married and I won't be able to bear it."

"You'll never lose us, Mom," Sophy said. "We'll come back to eat and do our laundry and—well, probably to borrow money and ask for legal advice and job references. All kinds of stuff."

"Promise?"

"Promise." Sophy wrinkled her nose. "Besides, there's no way I'm ever getting married. No boy is going to stick his nasty tongue down my throat, and Tiffany Hammersmith says that boys always want to do that when you go steady. Does Uncle Tate want to do that to *you*?"

Reproduction 101, Cara thought. She shared a glance with Audra, who couldn't resist a smile.

"Ummm—we'll talk about that soon, honey, I promise."

Organ music rose in a crescendo, echoing up the grand timber staircase. Clearly it was time Cara had a long discussion with her younger daughter. But first she had a wedding to attend.

One that had been delayed far too long.

"How about we go see how handsome Uncle Tate looks? Ready, Summer?"

"My service revolver is loaded, and my handcuffs are ready. Let's go track down some poor, unsuspecting males and knock them dead with our brains and stunning good looks." She rolled her eyes. "But let's do it fast. These shoes are killing me already."

As Sophy giggled, Audra straightened her shoulders. "I think brains are more important than beauty, don't you, Mother?"

"Definitely. The body will sag, but if you start with brains, you end with brains. No need for a lift or a tuck or toxic bacterial injections." Cara linked her arm through Audra's.

"I always wanted to get married during a snowstorm," she said softly.

"Not me. I'm going to get married on a beach in Tahiti." Audra sniffed. "But he has to know how to cook and do dishes and give back rubs, too."

"Excellent idea," Summer muttered.

"Does Gabe cook well?" Cara's eyes twinkled. "And give good . . . back rubs?"

"He has a number of endearing traits."

"So it wasn't just his superior landscaping skills that caught your eye?" Cara teased.

"No comment. I'm saying nothing that could be used against me in a court of law."

Audra sniggered, and Sophy giggled, their laughter spilling together in a rich cadence of age and youth, innocence and experience. For now, the shadow of Amanda Winslow and her madness was finally lifted.

Tate paced the foyer impatiently. The snow was picking up again, and any guests who hadn't made it to the ranch by now were flat out of luck.

That suited him just fine. The junior senator from California wanted to get this ceremony over pronto, so he could go make love to his wife for five or six days. He had wanted that since the first moment he'd set eyes on Cara back in law school, but a career and heavy family expectations had made him miss the chance. But Cara wasn't getting away again. They were going to be a family, damn it.

Unaware of his scowl, Tate strode through the living room, passing two old neighbors, his brother, and a lobbyist friend from Washington. Nearby were Cara's sister, her husband, and their children. He managed to summon up a smile before nodding at the organist, who broke into the opening bars of the wedding march.

It was time to get this show on the road.

Tate headed for the downstairs study, where Gabe was slipping his last cuff link into place. The SEAL looked unusually pleased with himself, and Tate was certain it had to do with Summer. If his instincts were right, their night in the SUV had resolved most of the questions between them.

At least, Tate hoped so. There wasn't a woman better suited to this tough, seasoned soldier than Summer. Maybe Gabe's bitter memories would finally be laid to rest, Tate thought.

On the far side of the room, he saw Izzy Teague speaking quietly on a high-tech cell phone and looking very elegant in an Armani suit. He also looked fully alert and ready for a guerrilla raid at any second.

With operatives like Summer, Izzy, and Gabe present, the wedding would be safe from any and all intruders, Tate thought wryly. Now if only the bride would deign to put in an appearance.

He was about to send Gabe up to reconnoiter when he heard Sophy's laughter from the top of the stairs, followed by Cara's husky questions. Suddenly he was caught on a wave of panic. What if Cara got bored with him? What if the girls thought he made a bad father? What if he was too busy, too old, too cynical?

Tate Winslow, the most popular senator in America, a man who made four-star generals quake and Beltway journalists squirm, felt sweat beading his brow.

What if he was a failure at the things that really mattered, like love and commitment and family?

He turned to face the doorway, dimly aware of Gabe moving to stand on one side of him and his brother on the other. Izzy waited nearby, his handsome face set in an easy grin. "A very beautiful lady is waiting for you out there." Izzy glanced outside. "Correction, Senator. Make that three beautiful ladies."

Organ music filled the room, but Tate couldn't seem to move. He wanted to give Cara the sun, moon, and stars, but what if he failed her? What if his murderous eighteen-hour days and nonstop meetings made her—

Gabe touched his shoulder. "Senator, I believe that organ music was your cue."

Tate took a deep breath. He loved Cara, had loved her for years. He'd make damned sure they had another thirty or so more years of arguing and laughing and driving each other crazy. Only a fool would ruin a future like that because of *maybe*s or *what if*s.

And Tate Winslow had never been a fool.

He smoothed his lapels and looked at his three best men. "Thank you all for being here, for helping Cara and me through these last difficult months. Even if the rest of the world won't ever know the truth, you three will, and your support means everything to us." He cleared his throat. "Now it's time for me to go marry the woman I've loved forever."

And he walked outside.

The first thing he saw was Audra, looking very grown-up in a long dress of pink satin. Beside her, Sophy's face was full of light as she carried a small basket of roses and baby's breath. Finally there was Cara, tall and radiant and nervous as he was.

Tate saw nothing else in the room after that, only Cara's smile.

They were a family, he thought, struck dumb with awe. At times this moment had seemed like an impossible hope, but now it was as real as the snow leaving white tracks against the windows.

Summer appeared, absolutely stunning in a dress of fiery red. Izzy muttered something that made Gabe lean forward tensely. The SEAL said something under his breath, but Tate couldn't make out what.

He didn't try too hard, because Cara was finally framed

in the doorway, smiling at him, and suddenly all the air was sucked out of the room, out of his chest, and there was no past, no future, only Cara's radiant face and the wild beating of his heart.

He couldn't wait to say "I do."

chapter 44

"Can we sneak away yet?"

Tate smiled at his wife. "I thought that was supposed to be my question."

"You're thinking it. I'm just the one who's stupid enough to ask."

"Brave," Tate corrected, brushing a swift kiss across her lips. "What about the garter? I seem to recall some sort of ceremony is required."

"To heck with the garter," Cara muttered. "Except Audra will kill me, because she wants everything done just so." She breathed deeply, as if savoring all the happiness in the room. "Actually, I can't wait to tear your clothes off, Senator Winslow."

"Actually, I can't wait to let you, Mrs. Winslow."

The look they shared stretched out in heated understanding. Both had waited too long to deny the passion they were feeling. With any luck they would be ready to leave in—

"The wedding was lovely." Cara's sister and husband cut into the silence, beaming. Their sons looked stiff in their suits, but pleased with the general company in spite of that. "When are you two leaving?"

"As soon as we can manage it." Tate smiled at Cara's sister. "But the party should go on for hours, so please make yourselves at home. The rooms we prepared for you are comfortable, I hope?"

"Beyond comfortable. We just got back from a rafting trip in Texas, so these accommodations are pure luxury. Audra's been watching over us like a regular mother hen, too." Melody straightened her eldest son's tie. "Jordan's home from college, did you know? Hard to believe he's so grown-up."

"*Mom.*" With the universal cry of youth, the handsome, dark-haired boy rolled his eyes.

Cara patted Jordan's arm. "In time she'll realize you're an adult and loosen up, honey. We all do, sooner or later."

"I doubt it."

Melody gripped her son's arm, brushing away a tear. "You really are beautiful, Cara. It's a great wedding, but you two ought to sneak away now, and we're going to help you start by getting out of your hair."

Cara and her sister shared a tight hug, then the bride and groom were finally alone. They were just about to make their escape when they were cut off by Tate's brother.

"Sorry to bother you, Tate." Greg Winslow shifted a champagne glass from hand to hand, looking uncomfortable. "The ceremony was perfect, but there's something I have to tell Cara. It's a long-overdue apology."

"Greg, you don't have to—"

"Just listen, please. I was wrong about you, Cara. I was certain you wouldn't stay the course. You were busy, you had a demanding career, and you already had a family." Greg Winslow frowned down at his empty glass. "I told Tate he was making a big mistake, that you'd hurt him, professionally and personally. I was a damned fool for that."

Cara took Greg's arm gently. "That's very nice of you to say."

"I'm afraid there's more." Greg looked warily at Tate. "About a year ago Mother came to talk to me, Tate. She said she was worried about Cara distracting you from your career. I—I'm afraid I gave her a little encouragement in that view."

Tate's mouth flattened. "You did what?"

"I . . . told her you were working too hard, passing up crucial meetings so that you could fit in time with Cara and the girls. I wanted her support if it ever came down to a family discussion."

"You mean a showdown," Tate snapped.

"I didn't know she had been medicating herself in Mexico." Greg looked pale. "The guilt has been killing me, Tate, ever since I heard about what she did. I want to make amends."

The senator didn't speak, his eyes dark with anger, and it was Cara who finally broke the tense silence. "I love you both. I loved Amanda, too, strange as that may seem now. I think it's because you're all so intense, committed two hundred percent to the things you think are right. You did what you thought was right, Greg, and Amanda . . . well, Amanda was not in her right mind."

After a long time Tate shrugged. "Hell, Greg, if Cara can forgive you, I can, too. So how about you handle the pleasantries here so Cara and I can leave? Bud fixed up the guesthouse. There's champagne on ice and a fire going . . ."

"Get lost." Greg grinned. "If anyone asks, I'll say you had an urgent call from Washington."

Cara stared anxiously around the crowded room. "But the girls—"

"Between your Mr. Morgan and your ex-nanny, the girls are in excellent shape. Bud and Ellie have promised them a Monopoly marathon later. I believe I'll sit in, too."

Tate crossed his arms. "Excellent planning. Now I know why I hired you as my chief policy advisor."

"You hired me because I came dirt cheap," Greg said wryly. "Now get moving before someone else decides to offer their congratulations. Here comes Audra, and I intend to ask her to dance. She looks a little wistful."

"She's missing her friends, I expect. Tate, maybe we should stay a while longer."

"Hit the trail, Counselor. The bases are covered here." Greg Winslow straightened his tie. "If I can handle the devious, underhanded power brokers of Capitol Hill, I guess I can handle two young girls."

"You might be surprised," Cara murmured as Greg wandered off. She looked up at Tate. "What are you looking so cat's-got-the-canary about?"

"You and your sister." Tate waited, studying Cara's face. "You've kept the secret very well."

"What do you mean?"

Tate spoke very quietly. "I figured it out while you were in the hospital and Melody came to stay with you. You didn't have an abortion that day in Mexico. Jordan is a very handsome young man, and he happens to have your eyes."

Cara took a sharp breath. "Tate, you haven't told—"

"Nothing to no one, and I never will. The secret is yours and Melody's alone, honey. And if I didn't love you already more than I can bear, I'd definitely be a goner now." Tate took her hand. "You're lucky to have Melody—and Jordan's lucky to have you both."

Cara stared at the child she'd given up years before to a sister who had despaired of ever being able to conceive.

"He's wonderful, isn't he?" Cara whispered. "Mel's going to tell him next summer. We agreed on that, and I had to keep my promise. I'm sorry I couldn't tell you, Tate."

"You are one thickheaded, stubborn woman. Fortunately, stubborn women are a major turn-on for me." Tate's eyes narrowed. "Your room or mine?" he whispered.

"We're staying down in the cabin, remember?"

"Right. Then your bed or mine?"

"There's only one bed."

"Better and better."

Cara pulled him down for a hungry kiss that involved a healthy amount of tongue. "But first we try out the floor in front of that roaring fire."

Tate was dragging her toward the door before she finished the sentence.

Wind whispered over the windowpanes and snow dusted the meadow. Music from a string quartet filled the magnificent log house, mingled with the sound of noisy toasts to the bride and groom, who were largely oblivious to everything but each other.

It was nice to know that life could still dole out happy endings, Summer thought. As she sipped her second glass of champagne, she realized that the sight of this newly formed family filled some deep part of her heart that she hadn't known was empty.

Her own memories of home and family were far from inspiring. But her marriages didn't always crumble into resentment and pain. The living, breathing proof was in front of Summer now.

She felt a grin slip across her face. She wasn't seriously considering marriage. Neither was her stubborn, gorgeous SEAL.

Were they?

From force of habit, she scanned the crowd for threats, but all she saw were beaming relatives, laughing ranchers, local dignitaries, and several famous politicians who had flown in from Washington.

Except that Sophy was missing.

Summer turned sharply, checking for her service revolver. She frowned when she realized she'd left the weapon upstairs when she had changed for the wedding. What would she do if—

"Relax." Callused fingers settled on her shoulder. "Sophy's out in the greenhouse with Izzy, shooting hoops. He just called me on my cell phone."

Gabe looked ruggedly handsome in his tuxedo and formal white shirt. With his dark hair and the sexy little scar at his jaw, the man could have scored big money in an ad for fast, expensive cars.

Or fast, expensive women.

Looking down, Summer noticed something on his wrist. "What's this?"

His face filled with a tinge of color. "Something."

"What? It looks like a rubber band."

Gabe sighed. "It's yours, okay? The one you had in your hair that night you took on the cactus back in Carmel. I . . . kept it."

She felt her heart take a slow tumble. "You did? A cheap little rubber band?"

"Yeah, so sue me."

She ignored an urge to kiss him senseless. "Why are you grinning at me?"

"No reason in particular." He stared at the crowd. "Can we leave yet?"

"Morgan, we've only been here an hour. You can't be that bored already."

"Not bored, restless. I have better ways to spend my time than drinking toasts with strangers." He fingered Summer's long, dangly earrings. "Most of them involve the backseat of a Jeep."

"Don't remind me."

"Which part, where you made those sharp, squeaky sounds when you came, or when those lace panties of yours fell in your face and you threw them out the window."

Summer closed her eyes. "Neither."

"Hell, yes, I'll remind you. They're some of my finest memories. When I'm an old man in a walker with three teeth left, I'm going to be living off memories of you like that." He smiled crookedly. "Damn, I don't think I've ever seen a woman so crazed."

"You'd be crazed, too, if you kept slipping on your own underwear. Good thing I'm not wearing any now."

Gabe's eyes narrowed. "Any what?"

"Anything at all," Summer said sweetly.

"Now I *definitely* want to leave."

"I forgot. I'm wearing stockings and a garter belt. The kind with the little snap things that take forever to undo. My sister sent it to me and she said—" Summer cleared her throat. "Never mind what she said."

Hell. She was killing him. Cutting him up into tiny, painful little strips. Gabe's zipper strained, tighter than it had ever been. It would only take a minute to sneak out and unlock their rental car.

And offend people he knew as good friends.

"Since the Jeep seems to be out, let's dance," he said hoarsely.

Summer stiffened. "No way. With these heels, I'll probably trample small children and mutilate innocent animals."

"Just let me hold you. You don't have to do anything more." He drew her into his arms against the smooth beat of vintage Frank Sinatra.

Blue Skies.

"See, you're doing just fine."

"No, I—" Summer bumped a potted orange tree near the door, catching it seconds before it toppled. "See? I told you something bad would happen." Her voice was tight as she stared down. "I just managed to dump a plate of chicken salad from that table onto my dress. I have to go clean up."

Red-faced, headed for the powder room just off the kitchen. Dozens of candles burned in silver holders as she tried to blot the stain on her dress. So much for playing Cinderella, she thought miserably.

"Move over," Gabe said gruffly.

"Why?"

"Has anyone ever told you that you talk too much?"

"Sure, but—"

He nudged her aside, closing the door with his foot.

Locking it, while their eyes held. "You aren't wearing a weapon, are you?"

"N-no."

"Good. I don't want to get shot."

Summer felt excitement bubble through her. "Gabe?"

"So will it be there on the vanity or down on the rug?" He pulled off his jacket. "I've always had a great fantasy going about sex in a public place."

She made a low, strangled sound as he slid down the tiny straps of her dress. "We can't just—"

"It's been six hours, eighteen minutes, and twelve seconds, honey. Damned if I'm stopping."

Cool air brushed Summer's skin, followed by Gabe's hands. Outside Frank Sinatra moved smoothly into "Summer

Wind" while her zipper came free. "Right here," she said huskily, then turned, one hand against the timber wall.

"Good call." Her dress fell a few more inches.

"The FBI . . . always aims to please, Lieutenant."

"I'm delighted to hear it. So does the Navy."

Her dress hit the soft rug. Gabe gave a long, slow whistle as he saw the white stockings and the white lace garter belt with pink silk snaps. "The wall it is," he said hoarsely. "Hold on, honey. This could get rough."

Summer licked dry lips. Maybe there was something to this fantasy stuff.

"I had something important I was going to ask you." His pants were gone, his shirt kicked aside. "Something about rings and families." He pressed her up against the wall, fingers circling her wrists as he traced damp, impatient skin. She reached for him, but he pushed her hands back against the wall. "My turn to lead, honey." His fingers eased inside her. "God, I love touching you."

"Hurry up," she rasped.

"Not too loud. Someone might hear us," he whispered in her ear. "They're right outside, remember? Probably sixty people eating chocolate cake and canapés. We don't want them to hear us in here having great, noisy sex."

He got no answer except for a sexy moan.

His fingers moved. Summer gasped as he impaled her with slow, deadly accuracy. "I'll ask my question later," he said raggedly, holding her steady as he pinned her against the wall with deep, hammering strokes.

She moaned again, biting his shoulder, her body twisting.

This was going to get noisy, he thought as she arched, slapping the wall. A glass figurine toppled, and Gabe barely managed to catch it.

"*Hu-rry,*" she gasped.

"Yes, ma'am." He closed his eyes as she shuddered, her body closing around him, climaxing hard.

Yeah, this particular fantasy was going right into the keeper file, Gabe thought. After this, he'd try out a few more variations before they went back.

Right after he asked her to marry him.

And if she said no, he had a whole lot more ammunition where this came from.

She took a long, shuddering breath, staring into his eyes. "Hurry up, Navy. The FBI is about to come again and you don't want to miss the ship." She bit his jaw, smiling wickedly as he complied with fierce intensity. "And just for the record . . . I love you. Deliriously, as it happens."

She smiled as he pinned her, groaning a release.

"And my answer is yes. . . ."

author's note

Thanks for spending some quality time with Summer and Gabe, Cara and Tate, and those two terrific girls! Summer's cool strength and Cara's fierce love of family won my heart from the first moment they came to me, fully formed and unforgettable. Like many women, Summer has struggled hard with her past, fighting bias and closed minds to become strong and confident.

I'm delighted that she and Gabe make an unstoppable pair.

Will they be back? You bet.

If you want to read more about surveillance procedures and training methods inside the FBI, look for *Cold Zero,* by Christopher Whitcomb (New York: Little, Brown and Company, 2001), a fast-paced true story of one man's training for the FBI's elite Hostage Rescue Team. For a different insider's look at the FBI, check out *Special Agent,* by Candice DeLong (New York: Hyperion, 2001). This 20-year agent faced down serial killers as well as brutal harassment from her own colleagues, going on to a distinguished career that included work on a string of key cases, including the Unabomber manhunt.

If you've ever been to Monterey and Carmel, you know the rugged beauty of these coastal towns. For more details, check out the wonderfully informative *Monterey Bay Shoreline Guide,* by Jerry Emory (Berkeley and Los Angeles: University of California Press, 1999). Even if you can't visit, make an Internet stop at the Monterey Bay Aquarium, where live web cams track the bay scenery and the antics of the resident otters. As of publication, the otter cam was up and running at the following link: http://www.mbayaq.org/vi/vi aquarium/vi monterey cam.asp.

Drop by. The otters are guaranteed to make you smile!

For those who want to get some sand on their feet and sun in their hair, plan ahead by reading *California Coastal Access Guide* (Berkeley: University of California Press, 2003). An excellent resource for campers, swimmers, and hikers alike, the book includes invaluable maps of trails and beach access points.

Do Sheriff McCall and his wife seem familiar? You may remember them from *2000 Kisses,* set in a sleepy Arizona town in the high desert where sunsets are unforgettable and people treat one another like family. Tess and T.J. McCall faced terrible danger together once, and the process bound them forever.

For more juicy details, read *2000 Kisses!*

Now to Izzy.

What am I going to do with this tough, cool operator? The man has charmed his way into five of my books so far, starting with *The Perfect Gift* (A Draycott Abbey novel), followed by *Going Overboard, My Spy, Hot Pursuit*, and now *Code Name: Nanny.*

Will Izzy be back?

Count on it.

Will he and Sara duke it out and end up in bed?

I still can't say. He's a hard man to pin down. Stay tuned

to my website (www.christinaskye.com) for breaking news on the Izzy front! All your letters keep telling me that you love this cool operator just as much as I do.

But before Izzy finds his match, I hope you'll enjoy spending time with Summer's sister. Like Summer, Jess Mulcahey has a closet full of personal demons that she's struggled hard to slay. Jess is smart but not terribly worldly, and now her life is about to carry her into strange and uncharted waters.

To find out how, watch for *Code Name: Princess,* coming this fall.

I've included the first chapter just to get you in the mood.

A *very* hot and sultry mood, that is.

Happy reading!
Christina

About the Author

Award-winning author Christina Skye lives on the western slope of the McDowell Mountains in Arizona. *CODE NAME: NANNY* is her eighteenth novel. She holds a doctorate in classical Chinese literature and has traveled ten times to the Orient. Her favorite things are desert wildflowers after a spring storm, lightning in the high country, and a good ghost story. Be sure to visit her online at www.christinaskye.com.

Watch for

CHRISTINA SKYE'S
Code Name: Princess

Read on for a preview. . . .

Code Name: Princess

The wind hit him like an ice pick from hell.

It was a nasty night in a week of nasty nights, but Hawk Mackenzie barely noticed because nasty nights happened to be his specialty.

He studied the rugged cliff terrain around him. Layered tracks led up the steep hill, then turned, looping back to the road.

That answered his first question.

As he maneuvered his powerful motorcycle through the mud, his encrypted cell phone beeped. "Yeah."

"Teague here. What have you got for me?"

"Motorcycle tracks. Probably a dozen or so here, but only three sets look fresh. Hold on." Hawk smiled when he found what he'd been looking for. "Someone's been through here recently. It's raining, so most of the detail is gone, but I'd say we're talking four men and three dirt bikes." Hawk ran a small flashlight over the wet, freshly gouged earth. "The tracks heading back to the road are noticeably deeper, too." His voice was grim.

Since the man on the other end of the line was one of the government's finest security operatives, Hawk knew that every word between them was being recorded.

"You're sure they had more weight when they left than when they arrived?"

"No doubt about it." Hawk pulled out a digital camera and powered up the flash. "I'm running some shots for you now. Maybe you can pull something out of these tracks. Looks like three or four sets of footprints, too."

Ishmael Teague was silent for long moments. "What's your gut instinct? Are they moving south, or are they headed for Canada?"

"Impossible to say without more tracks. Given this rain, finding anything more here is damned unlikely." The Navy SEAL squinted into the icy rain sheeting over the cliff face. "They know the terrain, Izzy. If I hadn't been right on top of these tracks, I never would have found them. The obvious answer is Canada, but my guess is they're expecting that." Hawk studied the ground, frowning. "I think they'll stay local, go for cover, and try to wait us out."

As he listened to keys tap swiftly at a computer, Hawk was keenly aware of the brilliant mind at work on the other end of the line. On several other occasions he had worked with Izzy Teague, always in dangerous covert ops in towns unnamed on any map, and Hawk knew he could trust the man without reservation.

And trust was something Hawk didn't treat lightly.

"So we scratch our surveillance in Portland?"

The SEAL hunched his shoulders against the driving rain, feeling the stab of old instincts. "Put a skeleton force there for insurance. Meanwhile, I'll stay put. Call it a bad ache in my bones, but I think something's out here."

Ignoring the rain, he left his bike and walked in a careful circle, trying to piece together what exactly had happened here twenty-four hours before.

Three dirt bikes, traveling fast.

Men with heavy boots. Men who stayed close to the granite ridge so they'd leave no prints.

As his flashlight swept the ground more carefully, he frowned. There were no dropped cigarette butts, no water bottles, no candy wrappers. Nothing left a trace of their identity beyond some scattered prints and a few partial tire tracks.

The SEAL stared up at the forbidding cliff face above him. "They're pros, Izzy. Everything here is clean as a nun's conscience. If they go to ground and try to wait us out, the weather is on their side."

"Afraid it's going to get worse, too. I just pulled up a weather satellite map, and tonight's winds are expected to top forty miles per hour."

Hawk said a few choice words under his breath. More dank clouds were already shouldering their way toward the coast.

"It's your call." Izzy Teague sounded irritated. Hawk knew that any other man would be screaming in frustration, faced with the same set of problems. "If you think they'll stay local, maintain your cover on the coast. Check in every six hours. Record any and all information you turn up. I don't need to remind you that heads are going to roll if we don't recover our package within forty-eight hours."

"No need for reminders." Hawk's C/O had already drilled him on exactly what this mission entailed and why the stakes were so high. As a SEAL, he was used to hearing mantras about national security, but warning of *scientific debacle* and *cataclysmic medical consequences* meant a whole new threat level. "I'll hang around here for another twenty minutes and see if I can find anything else before the rain washes everything away."

"Copy." Izzy cleared his throat. "How's your rib holding up?"

Hawk scowled. The pain was constant and growing, despite the top-secret experimental meds the Navy was testing on him. "No worse than it was yesterday."

Which wasn't saying a hell of a lot.

But Hawk Mackenzie had a reputation for success in the face of any odds, and he didn't cave in to pain.

Ever.

He walked back to his mud-spattered bike, scowling. "Gotta go, Izzy."

"Okay, we'll play it your way. Keep your search short, and upload those images as soon as you get back to the hotel. If there's any evidence left, I'll dig it out."

Hawk knew this was no idle boast. Izzy could geek one pixel out of millions and then tell you exactly what it meant—who, what, when, where, and why. The man's electronic and surveillance skills were legendary in a field in which legends were commonplace. "Roger that. Signing off now."

"Keep your powder dry, Navy."

Hawk stared into the sheeting rain and muttered another choice set of phrases. Tonight staying dry would be about as likely as getting laid.

Thirty minutes later the rain had struck in angry force. All trace of prints had been washed away.

Cold and disgusted, Hawk packed up his flashlight and waterproof camera and kick-started his bike, finally noticing the stabbing cold. The pain at his side was insistent, like a crowbar going in slowly under the bone, and the sooner he got inside, out of the storm, the better.

Izzy had arranged a room for him at a swank hotel

along the coast, where Hawk could power up his laptop, dry off, and upload his high-resolution images.

But first he had a treacherous ride ahead of him.

A section of the cliff crumbled away in a brown slide of mud as he toed his bike into gear, all the while struck by the sense that he was being watched.

By the time he made his way down the mountain, he was drenched to the skin and covered in mud, his rib throbbing angrily.

His carefully manufactured identity as a nature photographer on assignment for a respected travel magazine ensured no questions about his odd hours and bedraggled appearance. Hawk tried to hide his exhaustion as he shouldered his backpack and strode through the lobby toward his room. The night manager nodded as he passed, and Hawk noticed that the waitress in the lounge off the lobby gave him a glance full of intimate possibilities.

But the SEAL wouldn't have time to explore those possibilities until the government's missing "package" was recovered.

His boots squished softly as he left the elevator. When he was certain no one was too close or too interested, he inserted his room key and waited impatiently for the green light to flash on the entrance pad.

All he got was red.

Damned electronics.

He swiped his key card again, controlling his impatience as icy water trickled down his neck. When the red light continued to flash, Hawk pulled out the small silver box that could trace the security code of every room in the hotel. A gift from Izzy, the device could have been used for some serious B&E.

Hawk gave a little hiss of satisfaction as the box clicked once, and the red flashing light changed to solid green.

Mission accomplished.

He pocketed his priceless and highly illicit technology, then stepped inside. He was immediately hit by a wave of steam and the faint scent of perfume. A suitcase stood on the floor next to the closet, and a robe lay neatly folded across the end of the bed, next to a woman's bright silk scarf.

Hawk stood intent, every nerve focused as off-key singing drifted down the hall from the shower. Only two people knew that he was here and both of them had security clearance at the highest levels. It was impossible that either would have betrayed his location.

Palming his field knife under the sleeve of his leather jacket, he moved silently down the narrow hall. Rings of steam drifted past as he put down his knapsack and inched closer. When Hawk glanced around the corner, he came to a complete stop.

There was a naked woman in his shower. She had damn amazing legs, and her ass was pretty spectacular, too. He waited for her to turn around, feeling a sudden jab of desire, which he repressed ruthlessly.

As he stood in the shadows, she lathered shampoo into her hair, cranking out an off-key Rolling Stones classic while hot water pounded over her shoulders. When she turned, Hawk's eyes narrowed, and he took time for a careful view of the rest of her body, chin to toe, which proved just as interesting as what he had seen so far.

When she started into a new song, he moved back toward the front door and fingered his cell phone.

Izzy picked up on the second ring. "Joe's Pizza."

"There's a woman in my shower," Hawk whispered. "She looks to be five eight/one forty/Caucasian. Black hair. No distinguishing scars." Bending down, he studied her suitcase. "Initials are J. M. Check the hotel database and see what you find."

As he waited, Hawk glanced through the closet.

A worn denim jean jacket. A pair of black jeans. A gray University of California sweatshirt. A pink satin suit with puffy sleeves.

Hawk frowned at the incongruity. He was about to go for her purse when Izzy came back on the line.

"Hotel has a new person registered in your room. Her name is Elena Grimaldi. There's no one with the initials J. M."

"If she's *here*, where am I supposed to be registered?"

"You appear to have been moved to a different wing. It could be a computer error."

"Yeah, and I could be *Time* magazine's Man of the Year." Hawk cradled the phone, watching the hall to the shower. "What do you have on this Grimaldi woman? Is she a foreign national?"

Keys clicked rapidly on a keyboard. "No sign of any passport registered in that name entering the U.S. in the last six months." The keys clicked again. "The U.S. Embassy has nothing available on any Elena Grimaldi."

"So she's an illegal?"

"Maybe. She's definitely not your normal, garden-variety consumer. She's got no driver's license, no car or health insurance, and only one credit card listed under that name. The credit limit is five hundred dollars."

A fake identity, Hawk thought grimly. Someone was baiting a nice mousetrap for him with a wet, willing, and very attractive female body.

The singing halted. A towel slid over the shower door and vanished. "Gotta go, Izzy. Keep digging."

"Will do. Watch your back, pal."

Silently Hawk broke the connection. The field knife

was still hidden in his sleeve when he sat down in the shadows, his exhaustion forgotten as he waited for his intruder to emerge. He'd give her five seconds to start explaining who she was and why she was in his room. If he didn't like what he heard, he'd start eliciting answers. Naked or not, gorgeous or not, the woman was a simple military objective as far as Hawk was concerned.

Down the corridor the shower door opened. Steam billowed into the airy bathroom, and Hawk watched her toss a towel around her head. As she attacked her hair, she switched to an old Beach Boys tune, and with every movement her towel hitched up, offering him an excellent view of long legs and gleaming skin.

Water ran in the sink, and bottles slid across the vanity. Hawk stood up, his back to the wall, as fabric rustled in the room next door.

When she finally appeared in the doorway, a towel was wrapped around her damp body and her hair lay thick and dark on her shoulders. Big balls of white cotton were stuck between her toes and she walked carefully, rubbing some kind of cream on her bare arms.

He spun her hard, his hands around her shoulders a second later. He felt her body tense.

She didn't make a sound. She didn't waste time or energy on protests or screams. As far as Hawk was concerned, this was proof enough that she was a professional, not an innocent stranger.

Except for one brief moment when her eyes went blank.

Almost as if she were about to faint.

And that was the oldest dodge in the book, he thought grimly.

"Who are you?" she rasped. When he didn't answer, she swallowed hard. "Are you from Kelleher's office?"

"Never heard of him."

Her face was sheet white. "Did Isaacson send you?"

Hawk filed the names away in his memory, on the slim chance she had revealed her contacts. But he doubted she would be so stupid. So far her responses had been well trained and flawless.

He decided the greed angle would work best, and he was about to offer her triple what the others were paying her when he noticed a mesh container leaning against the wall on the floor. It was reinforced black nylon, like the carrier used for a small dog.

Or for a priceless government lab animal.

Hawk checked the floor, but saw no movement. Outside lightning cracked and the wind hurled itself against the windows.

She dug her nails into his shoulders and began to scream.

Hawk cut her off with a hand clamped across her mouth. After ten hours outside, he was cold, wet, and exhausted. His rib hurt and his disposition was getting nastier by the second.

He checked the floor with every movement, turning her at the same time so he could make a careful sweep. If the animal was here, it had to be guarded at all cost. Hawk was fully prepared to give his life to guarantee its safety.

Something stabbed him hard in his side, just below his rib. He grunted at the sudden wave of agony, and in a second she shot past him.

She was struggling with the front door when he caught up with her, gripping her mouth and shoving her against the wall. "Where?" he growled.

She didn't answer, fighting him furiously.

"Where is the *animal,* damn it?"

Somehow she had managed to wedge one bare foot in

the open door. Down the hall Hawk saw two men approaching. The damned female was going to create a scene, and that was the last thing the government needed.

"Move your foot out of the door," he said quietly. "Otherwise, I start breaking small bones."

His arm circled her throat as he pinned her to the wall. The towel fell as she continued to fight wildly, slamming him in the rib with her elbow.

So she'd been briefed on his weak points.

His arm tightened, cutting off her air. Hawk spun her back against the wall, holding her in place with his body while she made angry, muffled threats.

But her foot was still wedged in the door, and the two men were getting closer.

She was bordering on hysteria now, thrashing wildly, and Hawk saw his options dwindling fast.

That left him only one choice.

His fingers feathered along her collarbone, moving fast and expertly. Then they tightened. Three seconds later she stopped fighting him.

Five seconds later she was sliding down the wall, out cold.